THE PRESCOTT JOURNALS

By Reva Leah Stern

THE PRESCOTT JOURNALS is published by:
Deer Hawk Publications
www.deerhawkpublications.com

Copyright © 2023 by Reva Leah Stern
http://www.revaleahstern.com

All rights reserved. Without limiting copyrights listed above, no part of this publication may be reproduced, stored in a retrieval system or transmitted in any form or by any means: electronic, mechanical, photocopying, recording or otherwise without prior written permission of the copyright owner and/or the publisher, except for excerpts quoted in the context of reviews.

The author has tried to recreate events, locales and conversations from memories of them. In order to maintain their anonymity in some instances the names of some individuals and places have been changed as well as some identifying characteristics and details such as physical properties, occupations and places of residence.

Cover design by:
Tami Boyce
https://tamiboyce.com/

Layout by:
Aurelia Sands

"A writer writes in solitude but lives in fellowship."

As the days dwindled toward the reality of the publication of "The Prescott Journals," I began to recall with humility how I got here; and it wasn't on my own.

I had close family, friends, neighbours, and colleagues who were all unknowingly my collective muse. Among them were those anxious to see the novel published, eager to read it, and ready to spread the word. I'm grateful to them all. But in the interest of "fellowship" I have to mention a few by name:

My brother Sandor, an accomplished screenwriter/director, and novelist in his own right. When I pitched an idea for him to write a screenplay, he pressed me instead to write it myself, as a novel... this novel. I've been published many times over the years, but this particular novel was my first written and last to be launched. He's been my ardent supporter both when I was a theatre director and then as a writer. This novel is dedicated to him for his support and belief in me.

Two amazing people in my life have passed on: my brother Steven H, a film producer/director, who was my protector and confidant, always looking out for me. And Sybil Cowitz, my wise and generous friend and neighbour. Both of these wonderful people encouraged me and wanted so much to see this book published. I sense they are here in spirit spurring me on.

My supportive, classy, and confidence-instilling sister, Ruth; and Andrea Bricks my life-long friend and sometimes adviser, both of whom were always there for me, whenever I needed them to listen to some pages over the phone or hear me if I was having a bad day.

My "Writers' Bloc" fellow authors, Larry Rodness, Marsha Nicols, Herb Ware and Deedee Edelstein *endured* many drafts of this novel over many years. Their honesty and sharp minds were instrumental in keeping my keyboard active.

And finally, Deerhawk Publishing, and my editor, Aurelia Sands, who, over the process of launching this novel, was struggling with more insurmountable obstacles than any individual...besides perhaps, "Job" of biblical renown. But she worked through her pain, distress, and many arduous challenges to get it launched. As an editor myself, I can say that in spite of her burdens, she was still able to zero in on any tiny little mistake I made...and called me on it. ☺ And I'm grateful.

SPECIAL THANKS

In the name of fellowship, there are others to thank. Crown Attorney, Elizabeth Smythe who, beginning with the early drafts of this novel, patiently waded through my legalise to make sure I was on track.

My PR Rep, Mary Ellen Koroscil who exhausts herself reaching out to TV, radio, print media, bookstores, libraries, and just about anyone she casts an eye upon who, with friendly persuasion, might be willing, to promote the novel.

My cover designer Tami Boyce for creating the amazing image that initiates interest, intrigue, and conversation. The cover scene conjures both chills and empathy.

The amazing authors who so readily and respectfully endorsed this novel, Andrew Neiderman, Diane Jermyn, and Jeff Bailey.

My creative photographer, Karen Belne who nudged me into taking the customary photo for the book when I wasn't dressed up or made up for the occasion. She caught me by surprise on that day, and it turned out to be a brilliant idea resulting in a great shot.

Zohra Zoberi poet, memoirist, and friend with whom I shared the difficult trek around seemingly impossible publishing detours through her books and mine.

My focus/readers group, Shiny Baine, Stacey Balakofsky, Steven Bricks, Franci Williams, and Andrea Bricks, all of whom gave such honest and essential feedback, early on in this journey.

My children, friends and neighbours who came out to help with the launch of the book, doing all they could to make the event memorable.

Shari Bricks Young, Anthony Nijmeh, Michael Young, and Impact AV Solutions for setting up the launch event on zoom so that people could join in from anywhere in the world.

CHAPTER ONE

TORONTO SUN-TIMES
Saturday, September 19, 1992
Child Prostitution Ring in Prescott, Circles Around Again...

August 1988, Prescott, Ontario. Seven men were convicted of multiple sexual violations. Those prisoners have now come forward to accuse Earl White, a successful businessman in the Prescott area, of being the ringleader of those child pornography and sexual abuse crimes.

A real-estate law firm in Prescott has on behalf of Mr. White, engaged the services of a Toronto criminal defence lawyer.

* * *

As the train chugged out of Union Station, Sarah settled into her coach seat, cracked open her briefcase, and withdrew a slightly wrinkled section of the *Toronto Sun-Times*.

A week had passed since the paper was dropped at her door.

At the time of the trial, around 1987-1988, Sarah was embroiled in her own personal universe. If she had taken notice of the news reports back then, she might have known that those repulsive crimes were committed in her old hometown; a place her memory had long-since abandoned. Prescott was where she had spent an often-isolated, and uncomfortable childhood.

Back then, horrific crimes like those reported during the late 1980s pedophile trial, were unheard of.

Rereading the caption, she wondered, *Why would the Sun-Times offer so little copy on the story, after such a provocative headline?*

She lowered the newspaper onto her lap and squeezed her eyes shut as freakish images darkened her thoughts.

* * *

At eighteen, Sarah had dodged a dismal future in Prescott when the University of Toronto accepted her application. Her plan was to either graduate law school or find a husband. Thirty years later, she was without a law degree, and soon to be without the husband she had chosen instead.

Dreams shattered, she found herself demoralized and alone in a cheap bachelor apartment. Although at forty-eight, she was a natural brunette with sparkling blue eyes and a trim body, that still turned heads, she was convinced that her recent separation made her undesirable.

Her friends urged her to find a diversion. She answered an ad for a ten week, eighty-nine-dollar journalism course. After completion, she was eager to get started. First job was writing classifieds for a buy-and-sell circular, then as a gossip columnist for a bridge club bulletin, which led to writing puff pieces for a community paper. Soon she was getting investigative assignments for *The North York Sentinel*, a small regional newspaper. Although the articles offered little in financial reward, they were effective in boosting her confidence.

The *Sun-Times*'s headline clung to her like toilet paper to a damp sneaker. She couldn't shake the images monopolizing her mind, so she handed in her latest *Sentinel* column about the scourge of dog poop on Toronto streets, then hopped a train for Prescott.

* * *

As the train hummed along, Sarah put down the newspaper and immersed herself in the more tasteful fantasy of the Harlequin paperback she bought at the newsstand. Her reverie was interrupted when she glanced up to find a young, perky nun cloaked in a pale grey habit that revealed only her rosy oval face and twinkling green eyes. Seated next to the novice was a mature, bitter-faced nun.

Both women appeared to be intently studying their seatmate. Sarah's cheeks burned with embarrassment as she realized that these two sisters had slipped into the seat across from her unnoticed and were now privy to her dirty little paperback secret. She shut the book and slipped it under her thigh.

"Do you mind sharing?" The novice politely asked while extending her hand.

Sarah slyly slid the book out from its hiding place. "Uh, sure. Uh, I don't usually read this kind of stuff, but, uh, you know, it was all they had at the train station," Sarah flushed as she awkwardly offered it to the nun. "I'll never finish it before I get to Prescott anyway."

"If you don't, I can tell you how it ends," the perky nun replied with a naughty grin as she lowered her hand.

Sarah gulped back a gasp. "Oh, wow, you actually read this stuff?"

"We vacation at summer cottages like the rest of the world," the novice snickered. "Ah, sorry, I'm just kidding. I don't read them...well, not anymore." She shifted a quick glance toward her sober-faced superior before continuing. "At least, I haven't since high school. Reading a trashy romance while wearing this habit would definitely send a mixed message, don't you think? But then, I did read that one, and as I recall, I found it quite thrilling," she teased. "Perhaps that's why they've reprinted it!"

The irony of the moment elicited a giggle from Sarah as she thought of a headline for this scene: *Neurotic Jewish House-Frau Shares Harlequin Adventure Ride with Formerly Frisky Nun*.

Sarah reluctantly held out the prurient novel.

"Thank you, Miss, but I was actually asking if you would share your newspaper with Sister Mary Margaret here."

A smile of relief crossed Sarah's lips. "Oh, I see. Well, you wouldn't want this one. It's a week old," Sarah casually suggested as she pushed the paper aside.

"I'm well aware," The older nun curtly replied. Sarah felt strangely intimidated by the stoic nun who had, until that moment, been silent.

Aware of Sarah's discomfort, the elder nun smiled softly, "The paper was lying there and I couldn't help but notice the headline you've circled in red. So, Sister Catherine and I are curious to know if there's some new developments in that terrible child abuse case."

Sarah gasped. "You're familiar with it?"

"We are," they replied in unison.

The novice presented her business card: *Sister Catherine Grace of Holy Trinity.*

"May I have yours in return?"

"Of course." Sarah fumbled through her briefcase and handed over her quick-print card that offered the barest of essentials: name, Sarah Berman, her phone number, and a quill graphic at the top that humbly indicated her budding profession.

The novice looked quizzically from card to Sarah, then hesitantly asked: "Are you related to one of the prisoners?"

"Oh, heavens, no! Sorry, Miss, Sister, Ma'am, is it sacrilegious to say heavens?"

"Never," the elder nun insisted, shaking her head. "Heaven is always welcome."

Sarah exhaled a sigh of relief as the nun smiled kindly at Sarah and asked. "Are you from Prescott, my dear?"

Sarah felt herself melting slightly by the warmth the stately woman had begun to exude, and curious to see where this unusual conversation might lead. She smiled warmly and responded. "Actually, yes I am, or at least I was. I left there about thirty years ago as a starry-eyed teenager heading for university. I met my husband in my first year and that was that."

"So, is this a sentimental journey then?" The novice asked with a wink.

Sarah paused to consider just how much she was prepared to reveal to strangers on a train. She leaned forward and whispered: "No. To be honest, I couldn't get that horrid headline out of my brain." She clenched her jaw as she continued. "To deal with it, I needed to do something out of character, maybe even daring; so here I am, bound for Prescott." She announced with a shrug.

Bewildered and curious, the novice asked, "I don't get it. What could your trip to Prescott do to erase that awful headline? And how is it daring?"

Sarah inhaled a gulp of courage then spoke quietly but with resolve. "I arranged to meet with the suspect's lawyer and hope to get the real story. It's a move that's out of character and pretty daring, for me. I'm not a very courageous type."

"Well, if you could up and follow your journalistic sense just like that, it seems pretty courageous to me." The elder nun offered with a reassuring smile.

"Ah...well, I actually write for a very small local newspaper. You know, missing dogs, loud neighbours, who is and who isn't recycling properly. That kind of stuff." She didn't mention her fantasy of producing a freelance article for the *Toronto Sun-Times,* and that she hoped this article would get her stilettos through their door.

As the conversation continued, Sarah discovered that the nuns lived less than twenty miles from Prescott and met regularly with the seven convicted pedophiles at the Kingston Penitentiary.

"I don't want to be crass, but they don't seem like the kind of people that would typically be part of your prayer circle. Were they members of your Holy Trinity church at one time?"

"Holy Trinity isn't a church, my dear. It's a Catholic seniors' home," the elder nun clarified.

Sarah nervously whispered. "But, surely there isn't, um, a connection between seniors and those convicts."

The elderly nun squinted over her wire-rimmed glasses, then leaned in and patted Sarah's hand: "All God's children are connected. It happens that one of our residents is married to a prisoner in the Kingston Penitentiary."

As Sarah's eyes grew wide, the nun nimbly added. "Oh, no, no, not to one of those seven, dear. Just to a man unfortunately in the wrong place at the wrong time."

Sarah offered a sympathetic "Ah, I see." The nun nodded, smiled politely, and continued. "Another resident used to be our police chief, but now his son is the chief. I believe he was actually involved with the arrest of the seven. So, that's our connection, my dear."

The younger nun's eyes twinkled playfully. "Sister Mary Margaret, you have to admit, we do have some interesting dinner conversations."

Sarah smirked. "Now I'm picturing a bevy of nuns discussing the evils of pornography over cucumber soup."

The younger nun giggled as she shared another brow-raising gem, "Not over soup, Miss, but sometimes over tea and brandy, we hear things from the patients. I mean, they are talkers..."

The elder nun barked. "That'll be enough of that, Sister Catherine." Then she offered Sarah a glimmer of a smile and continued in a gentler voice. "To answer your question, my dear, it became obvious to us that there were many remorseful souls languishing in that prison who could use some spiritual assistance. We worked it out with the warden to let us visit and pray with them. And we've continued to do that for several years." With a satisfied sigh, the nun sat back content with her answer.

The novice, anxious to appease her superior, added. "It's our duty and privilege to pray with them...and for them,"

Sarah's skepticism was evidenced by her pinched brow and pursed lips. She cleared her throat several times, took a breath of courage, and whispered. "I mean no disrespect, but wouldn't praying for convicted pedophiles require an invocation of biblical proportions?"

The senior nun sat erect, placed her hands in her lap and replied. "Miss Berman, I believe it would do you some good to understand that even though it's the prisoner who's incarcerated, their loved ones also suffer a terrible and enduring punishment. They all deserve our prayers and God's grace."

Feeling duly chastised, Sarah lowered her head.

"Miss, may we have a look now?" The nun nodded toward the newspaper. Sarah timidly placed it in her hand.

The elder nun scanned the paper while Sarah uneasily returned to her Harlequin. In minutes, Sarah nodded off, Sister Mary Margaret unobtrusively returned the paper, and both nuns picked up their rosaries and closed their eyes in prayer.

* * *

Two hours quickly and quietly slipped away, as did the two nuns. A fact Sarah only noticed when she was jostled out of her sleep by the conductor's announcement: "Per-escott...all off for Per-escott."

As the train slowed to a halt, Sarah felt anxiety creep up her spine. Was it an omen? A warning to turn back? A meaningless panic to be ignored? She gathered her things and scurried down the aisle to avoid the rush...she was the only one to disembark.

She stepped off the train and onto a dark and isolated platform. There were no cabs waiting for passengers.

Shivering in the dimly-lit railway yard, Sarah felt the October chill slide up her thighs. She pulled up her collar and stamped her feet to warm up.

After an eternity, of five minutes, Sarah spotted a lone cab edging toward her. She remained cemented to the spot, unsure if it was real or if she was hallucinating.

The driver stopped, opened the car door, and smiled. "Hey! Hey there young lady! Hope ya weren't waitin' too long. I was droppin' off some piss-drunk hockey fans and got a bit sidetracked." He jumped out and headed toward her. "Hop in now, the car's all warmed up for ya."

Sarah felt a wave of relief rush over her as the mirage became a reality. "That's great. Thank you so much."

The cabbie ushered the frosty visitor around to the front seat, then placed her bags in the back. "I'm guessin' you're staying at the O'Brien?" He snickered. "Well, not much of a guess since it's the only place in town, huh?"

Sarah offered a grateful smile and a weary, "Hmm, I guess."

The quiet drive through the barren streets of town gave her the chance to warm her numbed body and silence her noisy thoughts.

* * *

The O'Brien Hotel lobby had been fairly well-preserved with its original faux-regal style, except for some selective modernizing, like the television that dangled above the art deco bar, and a large hump-backed computer perched on the gnarly old reception desk. Most important to Sarah was that, in spite of the fact that the décor clearly showed its age, the lobby was impeccably clean.

Mr. Reynolds, the short, stocky built, and sullen hotel manager, grudgingly stepped away from his baseball telecast to show her to her suite.

* * *

Dread instantly set in as she peered around the room in search of a television set. To a television addict like Sarah, who was lulled to sleep each night by the sonorous voice of Ted Koppel, not finding one was unthinkable.

"Where's the TV?"

The irritated manager looked anywhere but at her while he fumbled for words to extricate himself and get back to his baseball game. "Uh, it's out for repair. Be back by morning," he mumbled as he dropped the key on the table.

"Well, I can't sleep without it." She grumbled as he headed out the door. "Morning huh? Damn. You're sure?" she called out after him as he scurried along the corridor.

"You betcha, Ma'am," he burbled as he headed down the stairs.

She turned and faced the dismal décor of the room, the spot where a TV should have been, the draughty frost covered windows and tiny kitchenette area. She turned down the bed and thoroughly checked the linens for bedbugs, then the towels and glasses for makeup or lip prints. Everything was surprisingly clean and up to her standards. But she was still without a TV to soothe her to sleep. As she unpacked her things and placed them in the drawers and closet, she kept hoping to uncover a concealed radio or Walkman, anything that could bring a joyful sound into the depressing silence. Finally, spent from the trauma of it all, she could only hope that sheer exhaustion would help her through one night without Koppel. She washed up and slipped into bed.

She twisted and turned throughout the night as visions of nuns commingling with perpetrators, and images of horrific crimes, kept her awake until after midnight when somnolence finally acquiesced to sleep.

* * *

The morning sun streamed through a slim opening in the curtains as if pledging an oath to a glorious day.

Through half-mast lids, Sarah stretched, yawned, and stumbled into the shower before choking down an in-room granola bar. After realizing that the coffeemaker only brewed hot water, she decided to forego it.

Her confusion of thoughts congealed while she brushed her teeth, put on her makeup, and got dressed. Rifling through her briefcase for her address book, she paused to reread the newspaper headline that had prompted the journey to her hometown. Having decided on the places she needed to see. Her mission was about to begin.

Like a domesticated tiger returning to the jungle, Sarah burst through the hotel doors and onto Main Street with a sudden and overwhelming desire to sniff out old, familiar watering holes.

A few doors from the hotel, was the shop her parents had opened after they moved from Toronto to Prescott.

Her father, David Klein, bought a greasy auto-repair shop and turned it into a dry-goods store with two floors of apartments above it. He rented all of the apartments out, except for the one at the back of the building that Sarah's family lived in. From the rear exit, a rebellious teenager could escape onto a black-tar shingled roof, down a flight of rickety wooden stairs, onto a gravel road that meandered along the shoreline of the St. Lawrence River. On warm, summer nights, the Klein family would sit out on the roof and gaze across the river to the U.S. side, mesmerized by the spectacle of lights that reflected off the crystal-clear water.

Two bevelled glass doors stood like sentinels at the front of her father's old shop, but the three display windows that used to be dressed in colourful fashions of the season were now stocked with chainsaws and shovels. Klein's Department Store had morphed into Kerr's Hardware Emporium.

As she wandered about inside, her mind was filled with images of her father designing, painting, and glittering decorative stars for his signature signs that adorned everything from ladies' fashions, underwear, and men's suits to baby bibs and jock straps. But the shop's most popular commodity was her dad's free advice. Klein's was as much a community drop-in centre as it was a retail store.

A hollow emptiness crept over Sarah, and the pain of loss struck deep as she realized there was no hint that her parents' shop had ever existed. The only staff present, ignored the potential customer. That fact both perplexed and relieved Sarah. She had no interest in communing with the interlopers that turned her dad's welcoming soft goods boutique into a stark, cold, hardware store.

In less than 4 minutes, she was out the door and around the block, stopping behind the building at the foot of the old wooden staircase. She looked up at the back door remembering the squeak-free hinges that had provided her a covert escape on many a summer's night.

Her gaze shifted and abruptly halted on a rusty sign still attached to the back wall. It proudly proclaimed the existence of *Klein's Department Store, established in 1949*. Tears flowed as she stared at the old sign, her dad's cenotaph...a Klein monument.

* * *

Still misty-eyed, she continued along the river road, prickling at the sight of the decomposed fish carcasses and putrefied garbage that had washed up onto the shore. She frowned at the gigantic freighters that lumbered by, carrying toxic cargoes through the once-pristine waters of the St. Lawrence River.

* * *

Sarah fidgeted with her briefcase as the lawyer's plucky assistant, Joannie, led her into Richard McCall's cozy office. He greeted Sarah with a stiff handshake and an obligatory smile.

"Please, have a seat." He politely offered, gesturing at the chair across from him as he settled in his own seat.

"Thank you."

She sank into a buttery leather chair and discreetly scanned the room. Two walls of walnut bookcases, an artfully etched and opaque glass wall separated his office from Joannie's reception area, and a large bay window behind the lawyer's desk framed him in silhouette as the sun streamed in.

"I'm impressed with your office, Mr. McCall. This is definitely the civilized way to practise law."

"Well thank you." He leaned back and gazed at his collection of old books, and framed awards, all meticulously dusted. "I'm happy with it."

"Of course, it's in a lovely house," Sarah noted the lack of family pictures and scanned the book titles. "Is this your residence as well?"

"Would the warden live in the prison?" he retorted with a grin. "Joannie said your phone call was vague, Mrs. Berman, but you did mention that you're a journalist. I don't have a lot of time, so how about you tell me why you're here?"

She placed her briefcase on her lap, clicked open the snaps, and withdrew the *Sun-Times* article. "Mr. McCall..."

"...Richard will do."

She nodded her agreement "Richard, the headline on this brief article in the *Toronto Sun-Times*, sparked some interest..."

He dismissed the newspaper with a gesture and watched her close her briefcase. "Yes, I understand you were assigned to this case by the *Sun-Times*."

She shook her head. "I actually write for the *North York Sentinel*. It's a regional Toronto paper." Sarah shifted in her seat while he remained stoic. "Look, uh, Richard, I was disturbed by that headline in reference to this town, so I'm hoping to look into it and..."

He shifted in his seat. "And maybe exploit it?" he suggested with a sharp edge to his voice.

"Uh..." she fumbled for words, "Well, uh, not exactly. I admit, it sounds bad when you say it like that...but the truth is, I feel like I kind of have a stake in this case."

"A stake? Why? Are you related, or know someone involved?"

It wasn't a question she had planned to answer so early in the interview, but after confessing she wasn't with the *Sun-Times*, she would have to admit her connection to Prescott or lose all credibility. "No, I don't know any of them. It's just the idea that these horrific events could have happened in the town where I grew up..."

"...Seriously? You're telling me you're from here? I've been here my whole life and I don't remember any Bermans in Prescott, ever," he snapped.

"No, not Berman." She insisted. "My parents were Hanna and David Klein."

He paused a moment and studied her closely. "Klein's Department Store?"

She nodded. "Yes, that was us."

"Everyone in this town knew your family. Which one are you?"

"I'm the third kid. I have a younger sister and two older..."

"...brothers. Sure...Allan and Lewis; I went to school with them." His icy attitude defrosted in that moment. "How are they doing?"

She perked up, "Oh, they're terrific. They're..."

16

Joannie popped her head in the doorway. "Sorry to interrupt, Richard. Laurie Cowan is here. Well, not here exactly, but in the washroom, I presume freshening up from the drive."

"Okay, thanks." Richard replied. Joannie nodded and exited.

Richard shrugged and opened his hands in a gesture of helplessness. "So sorry, Sarah. I'm a real-estate and tax lawyer, but the colleague Joannie just mentioned, is a criminal lawyer from Toronto. I admit, I was curious to meet you, but I don't think I can help you. If by chance I can, I'll let you know."

She nodded and smiled politely, "Great. I'd appreciate that."

His voice suddenly took on a softer tone. "Listen, Sarah, just so you know, I've been handling Earl White's legal matters from day one. He's a self-made man who's built a very lucrative construction and real estate business. And honestly, the police haven't got a shred of evidence to back up any of the terrible accusations against him. Clearly, Earl's being set up."

Sarah felt a weird pang of disappointment at the lawyer's sincere defence. "Really? I see. Well, that might be the perfect place for me to start, then." Sarah closed her briefcase and stood.

Richard offered a sympathetic smile. "Listen, if Laurie says it's okay, I'll do what I can to help you get the story out there. My guess is, I can reach you at the O'Brien, right?" He extended his hand.

"Sure. Where else?" She grinned and firmly shook his hand.

* * *

Sarah stepped onto the street and inhaled the crisp, northern breeze before she began her brisk walk. She slowed as she passed a quaint little Cape Cod house with yellow shutters that faced Kelly's Beach. In the corner pane of a lace-curtained window, a cardboard sign quietly informed passersby that there was a "DRESSMAKER WITHIN." She had a silly impulse to peer through the curtains, but an urgent shiver prompted her to move on.

Sarah's stomach rumbled like a bowling ball down the gutter. She stepped into Tim Horton's, picked up three large coffees in a paper tray and a handful of creamers and sugar packets.

She detoured to Kelly's Beach where she discovered a tempestuous cold grey river in place of the sapphire blue calm of her childhood memories.

Kelly's Beach was never much more than an empty sand lot at the river's edge, but decades ago, it had been *the* summer meeting place for all the local youth.

It was a time of Elvis magic, summer crushes, and girls in two-piece bathing suits on a mission to attract the golden lifeguard. Every pre-nubile sand sprite fluffed and strutted in his presence. Mothers knew that from June through August, they could find their daughters where the boys were...at Kelly's Beach.

In preparation for Mother Nature's winter blanket, the chilly autumn rains had flattened the hills and valleys of sand so that Sarah's sneakers barely left a footprint as she padded along the rigid shore, draining her first caffeine fix of the day.

With a shake of the head and a wistful grin, Sarah set aside her stroll down memory lane, deposited her empty cup in the trash, and headed nimbly to the Prescott Journal office.

The engraved brass door handle was an emotionally tactile reminder of the many years that had slipped by since she had been a regular visitor to that establishment.

"Hello-o. Hello?" Sarah called out to an empty room.

A scruffy-looking young man in his twenties appeared from a back entrance. "Yeah. Can I help you?" He asked officiously.

Sarah gave a tight smile, "I sure hope so. I'm looking for someone who can give me some information on that pedophilia scandal." In the uncomfortable silence that followed, Sarah chewed on her bottom lip, as she considered how grossly insensitive her request must have sounded. "Look, I brought a couple of Tim's coffees to warm two potential somebodies. Please, take one." She offered the java with a warm, tentative smile. "Oh, and here's some cream and sugar." She added as she pulled the packets out of her pocket.

The young man took a coffee, sniffed the bouquet, then set the cup resolutely on the desk and asked. "Coffee bribe aside...and assuming we have any info, why would we want to share it with you? I mean, who are you?"

Disappointed that her ploy wasn't working, Sarah charged ahead, chattering like an excited hyena over its prey. "Well, I'm a fellow journalist from Toronto who used to live in Prescott. I even used to write for this paper. '*Up to Date with PHS*'. That was my column. Of course, I was only a kid at the time; but nevertheless..."

The young man sat down, took a swig of black coffee, and rested his feet on the desk, leading Sarah to conclude that he was neither curious nor interested.

"Ah, come on, give a desperate old Prescott girl a break." She entreated.

"Look, I appreciate the coffee, but this decision's not mine to make. Wait here. I'll ask the boss." He stood up and started toward the back but stopped abruptly as he reached the archway and shouted. "Oh, forgot to ask, what's the name?"

"Sarah." She shouted back.

"Okay, Sarah, I'm Braydon, do you have a last name?" He sighed impatiently.

An Oz-like voice from the back shouted, "Klein. Bring her through."

"Sure thing, Boss," Braydon instantly replied with a quizzical glance to the visitor.

"Did I just hear my name?" She asked as she spun around, her mouth agape.

"If you're Sarah, uh, Klein, you did." Braydon replied as he led a stupefied Sarah into a toxic-smelling and cramped back room. They passed a variety of silent monster-machines, typical of an archaic small-town print shop. From behind a giant piece of equipment stepped a balding, bowed-at-the-knees, and ink-stained, old man. Sarah's eyes widened as she gasped.

"Speechless are ya, Sarah?" the gentleman mused as he shuffled closer. "Did I ever tell you that a good journalist should die only after he's written his own obituary? Well, I'm still blocked on that, so I'm still here."

"Oh my God, Mr. Jackson, I'm sorry to stare like this, but..." She remained fixed to the spot.

"I should be dead 'cause I was ancient even when you were a kid. Is that what you're trying to say, Sarah?" He punctuated his quip with a chuckle.

Sarah finally inhaled. "Well, Mr. Jackson, I wouldn't have put it that way. It's just that I really didn't expect to find you here after all these years." She shook her head in confused wonderment. "I mean, maybe on a beach in Florida, or on a golf course in Palm Springs...but not still running the *Prescott Journal*."

"I started here when I was seventeen-years-old, my dear. That was sixty-nine years ago. And I'll be here for another seventeen years unless I drop dead first."

"I'd put my money on at least seventeen more years," Sarah mumbled. "Now, can I have a hug?"

"I don't know, my hands are kind of inky." He snickered.

"I'm wearing black," Sarah giggled as she stepped forward and embraced him for a few awkward seconds. Mr. Jackson then stepped back and smiled proudly at his old protégé before turning to his new one. "Braydon, at the age of say...twelve, thirteen...Sarah here won an essay contest we ran."

"You remember that? Oh my God." She squealed and clapped her hands.

"Yup, I do. The prize was a weekly column for the *Journal* called '*Up to Date with PHS...*'"

"And I wanted it so desperately..." She purred.

"And you got it, and you deserved it." He crinkled his brow and paused for a few seconds. "Ah, as I recall, you had a good amount of free rein over the articles, too. In fact, you demanded it." He wagged his finger at her to punctuate his assertion.

Sarah flushed with embarrassment. "I did. Sorry. I was a bit of a brat back then, but nevertheless, you still coached me like a champ. I loved it. Unfortunately, I didn't get around to writing again for decades."

He shook his head in bewilderment. "Why? You were bloody good at it, and yeah, you sure did love it."

"Uh-huh, but I also loved my husband, kids, dog...all that other good stuff. Now, they've all moved on for one reason or another and I'm doing what I can to make use of what's left behind."

Mr. Jackson led Sarah back to the reception area. "Okay now, let's relax." He motioned for Sarah to take a seat across from him while he settled into the swivel chair behind his desk. With an impish grin, she placed the coffee, sugar, and cream on the desk and nudged it toward him. He smiled, stirred a packet of sugar into the cup, folded his hands over his sizable belly, took a sip, and listened as she confessed her plan to eke out a great story in order to try to get her toe in the door of a major daily.

"Now, can you understand why this story means so much to me, Mr. Jackson?"

"Yup, I can. But please stop making me feel so damn ancient, 'Mr. Jackson, Mr. Jackson'. To politicians and lawyers, my name is Wesley, to friends, it's 'Wes'."

"Sorry. I seem to be addressing everyone in Prescott as if we're in a Dickens novel. You're right...Wes." She giggled.

"Okay, that's done. Now, what do you want to know?"

Sarah inhaled a hefty supply of courage. "Well, I just came from Richard McCall's office where he allowed me five minutes of his time. I wouldn't say he's an objective or cooperative player..."

"In fairness, Sarah, Earl's been his client for decades, so Richard's in a tough spot." Wes, interjected. "I mean, this clearly isn't about real estate or taxes, so it's a dicey situation for him."

"I guess. Holy crap, the fact that this could happen in Prescott makes me feel like barfing." She professed, adding a theatrical shiver.

"Well, I don't know how much help I can be on your article," Wesley confessed, "but I can maybe settle your acid reflux by clarifying that, in spite of the media reports, none of the seven were from Prescott, including Earl White. They actually lived miles north of town. Richard told me that, as far as he knew, the worst Earl ever did was get rounded up by the cops when he was a kid...for pranks, you know, like pushing over outhouses, soaping windows..."

"Cow tipping," Sarah mused. "I gotta wonder if Richard and Earl hung out together when they were kids."

Wesley guffawed. "Sorry, Sarah, but it'd be hard to imagine those two hanging out together at any age. Richard's the quintessential nerd, and Earl is...uh..." Wes grimaced at the thought. "I take it you haven't met the guy yet?"

Sarah looked askance. "Nope, I haven't had the pleasure. But, by your reaction, I'm guessing it won't be a pleasure, huh?" Wes winced and nodded as she continued. "Anyway, I just got here. I've barely had time to see the entire town yet. I'll need at least another ten minutes to complete the tour." She quipped.

He shook his head and smirked. "Well, after you meet him, we'll talk. But I'm curious as to why a journalist would contact Earl White's lawyer instead of us journalists?" He peered over his glasses, waiting for an answer. Sarah squirmed in her seat as she tried to think of a compelling reply, but humility was her only option.

She smiled ruefully, "I can see it was a huge mistake not to come to you first; and thanks for the *journalist* title which I obviously have yet to earn, but I'm here now, so will you help me?"

Wesley remained silent while studying the coffee cup. He took another sip of coffee, placed the cup on his desk, and squinted over his glasses. "Sarah, my dear, I don't know if we have anything of value to offer, but if it turns out that we do, I promise to make it available to you."

"Oh, thank you, thank you, Mr. Jackson! I owe you," she vowed as she prepared to make her exit.

"It's Wes, remember? Boy, you sure have a short memory." He teased. "So, my dear, are you ready to start?" He asked as he rose from his chair.

"You mean now?"

"Now's good." Wes assured her.

She responded with childlike glee. "Wow!" Then she paused, reclaimed her dignity, and entreated. "Yes, okay, Wes, but before we begin, do you think we could grab some lunch first? And maybe, in the meantime, someone could pull out the microfiche files for me?"

"Microfiche? Really?" Braydon's scoff was louder than he'd intended it to be.

"Yes, really. Why? Is microfiche a problem, Braydon?" Sarah asked as she looked at him in bewilderment.

He shook his head in despair. "Is that some kind of cruel joke? Microfiche? I would've been happy just to see our old paper copies catalogued, but change isn't the boss's strong suit. He's still upset that we finally evolved from his nineteenth-century printing press to a new offset printer." Braydon sniffed. "Trust me, there's no microfiche here. Our paper's morgue is just a dusty basement downstairs, and a warehouse in Brockville filled with another pile of old, yellowed newspapers."

Wesley stared down the young apprentice who understood the wordless message.

"Okay, Boss, I'm going." With that, Braydon brushed his thick mop of blonde hair out of his eyes and slunk to the basement.

Sarah was puzzled but nodded politely to Braydon as he exited. She then turned back to her mentor and asked. "Wes, can you start by telling me how they caught those degenerates?"

"Sure. The police received an anonymous tip that there were some strange goings-on at an old farmhouse way north of town. The cops showed up, and those seven bastards were caught with their pants down; and that's not figuratively speaking."

"And right there on Mayberry's doorstep," she interjected with a sneer.

"Yup! And that's how Operation S&G got its start." Wesley added as he buttoned his waistcoat.

"S&G?" Sarah repeated with a raised eyebrow.

He nodded. "Uh-huh. Sodom and Gomorrah," He chuckled.

"Hmm, Sodom and Gomorrah. Now, I'm not only intrigued, I'm impressed. Good for you, Wes." Sarah chirped.

"I'd like to take credit for the creative ingenuity, but it was the police that coined it."

Sarah chuckled at the thought, "Poetic police? Now there's a novelty. Okay, let's go and eat and you can tell me all about what really happened out there in the sticks."

"Are you sure you're up for this?" Wesley asked as he moved toward the coat rack.

"I didn't come here expecting *Alice in Wonderland*." She affirmed.

"Okay. This might ruin your lunch but let me give you a quick overview on those seven sick bastards, and the fact that we don't know yet if there's any basis for the allegations against Earl." Wes removed his woollen scarf from the hook. "First of all, you know that the victims were all kids, right?"

"Well, yeah, the crimes were referred to as a 'child porn ring'."

"They were mostly little girls, but there were a few little boys as well. And to get them to perform, they were 'rewarded' with treasures like Trash Can Trolls, G.I. Joes, Barbies, and Smarties. The cops confiscated a few videotapes that would make your worst nightmare look like a Disney flick. I, unfortunately, ended up at the trial on the day they showed them to the jury. I saw a little boy who could have been as young as six. I'll be kind and spare you the details." Wesley draped the homespun scarf around his neck and held on tightly to the fringy ends. "There was a sad little girl who couldn't have been more than nine, standing naked in front of a group of howling, drunken, pissing slobs…I better stop there, or you'll want to pass on lunch." He paused to take a breath. "I don't have to tell you what it would do to your head to have to sit in court and witness something like that." He slowly criss-crossed the scarf ends over his chest and pulled on his overcoat. "My God, what those poor children endured." He shook his head, as a haunted look came over him, "And what makes it worse, Sarah, is that they were being pimped out by their own fathers."

As Wesley continued to share, Sarah's revulsion continued to rise. She began to contemplate whether she really wanted to make this story her entry into the big time. "You've been a fount of stomach-churning information, Wes," she replied as she robotically zipped up her jacket and pulled on her gloves.

"Yup, and now that you've had a meagre glimpse of it, if you still have an appetite, we can continue talking over lunch." Wesley muttered as he popped his fedora on his head.

"Sure, but no gory details for now, please. So, where do we eat?"

"The Best Service Diner of course." He replied.

"Mmm. They're still in business?" She asked, with a smack of her lips.

"Yup, and still in the same spot up the street," Wesley confirmed. "Listen, you go on ahead and save me a seat. I'll be along in a couple o' minutes. I wanna wash this ink off my hands and let Braydon know which piles to drag up here for you."

CHAPTER TWO

The Best Service Diner was just as Sarah remembered it: rows of faded red vinyl booths, gray Formica tables with shiny chrome trim, mini-coin-jukeboxes at every cubicle, and brightly-painted walls filled with framed photos and posters of rock and roll heroes of the fifties and sixties. It was still noisy and friendly and smelled of delicious promises.

She waited impatiently in her chosen booth while visions of hot turkey, mountains of mashed potatoes, soft green peas, and lakes of gravy beckoned her.

Five minutes later, Wesley slid into the booth across from her.

"We're ready," he shouted to no one in particular.

An attractive middle-aged waitress sauntered over with pad in hand. "Okay, let's have it," was all she said.

Wesley politely insisted that Sarah go first. "Okay, thank you, I will. I'll have a hot turkey sandwich with gravy. I mean smothered in gravy. Mashed potatoes also smothered in gravy. Canned peas not frozen, and a diet coke with just one ice cube and a large wedge of lemon on the side, but no seeds."

"Yeah, okay, is that all?" The waitress grunted as she flicked her mane of curly auburn hair.

"Yes, thank you." Sarah wanted to tell the waitress to 'hold the attitude' but she was restrained by visions of hair or spit in her much-anticipated meal.

The waitress sucked air through her teeth before responding. "Ma'am, we don't have turkey. I can give ya hamburg meat. We don't have mashed. I can give ya fries. We don't..."

"That's fine," Sarah interrupted. "As long as it's drowning in gravy, you can give me whatever animal and vegetable you've got back there."

The waitress sassed back in her small-town twang, "Well, Wes, seems we got ourselves a little radical, here, ain't we? Like she was just born to live on the edge, eh?"

Wes looked over at Sarah. "Just ignore this smartass, Sarah." He then turned and faced the waitress. "You like to give visitors a hard time, don't ya, Shiny?"

The waitress stood there, impatiently tapping her pen against the order pad.

"Okay, I'll make my order real easy on you, Shiny Penny," Wesley promised with a wink. "Just bring me the same artery-busting crap you're bringin' her."

"Wait a minute, Wes. I don't want the blame if the meal kills you." Sarah jibed.

"Impossible. I've been eatin' like that every Thursday of my life." he confessed. "All week, while I'm gettin' the Journal out, I live on all that godawful healthy grass-grazer stuff my daughter-in-law brings me for lunch. So, on the day it's done, I celebrate. That day's today. Let me tell you somethin', Sarah, a relationship with a newspaper's like a relationship with a hooker: you work all week to pay for her; on Wednesday night, you get her to bed; by Thursday mornin', she's back out on the street and you're lookin' to satisfy another itch..." he smiled as he tapped on the menu, "and this here is mine."

* * *

Lunch was a great bonding experience, during which Wesley gave Sarah an avid historian's overview of the Prescott she had absented decades earlier. By the time they returned to the Journal office, Braydon had transported a stack of back copies from the morgue to a designated folding table in the reception area.

"I hope these'll work for ya, because this is pretty much all we've got down there."

He shook his head in sympathy and muttered "Good luck." He quickly bundled up and headed out for his lunch break.

* * *

By five o'clock, the office was ready to shut down, and Sarah was too. As she gathered her notes, Wesley stopped by to ask if she would like to join him the next evening at his son's home for a fundraising dinner. They were collecting money to buy new instruments for the high school band.

"Let me sleep on it, 'cause tomorrow's my last day here unless I find some compelling reason to stay." She pulled on her jacket and began to feel inside her pockets for her hotel key. "The truth is, right now, my head's full of images I really need to purge before I can think of glockenspiels and trombones."

Wesley sat on the corner of the desk and flippantly asked. "Tell me something, Sarah, when you planned your trip here, did you figure you could investigate this mess, write a Pulitzer Prize-winning article, and become an overnight sensation, all in the two whole days you allotted for the trip?"

She smirked, placed her hands on Wesley's shoulders and then offered a sincere confession. "Wes, the truth is, if I'd actually planned this trip properly and not just acted on an itch, I would've done my homework like a good journalist, and that would've brought me directly to you in the first place. I didn't even tell my boss at the *Sentinel* that I was going to be away for a couple of days. I dropped off my article for the week just before the train pulled out. Since he's always late with his assignments, I figured I'd be back before he even noticed I'm missing. That's the joy of being a freelancer."

She dug into her handbag and exclaimed: "Ah, found it! The key to the kingdom of O'Brien." She proudly dangled the rescued key as she moved to the exit.

Wesley smiled as he opened the door for her.

"Listen, Kiddo, if you decide not to join us for dinner tomorrow, at least drop by to say so long, okay?"

"I will, I promise."

* * *

The prior sleepless night and her disturbing homecoming ended in a tiring day for Sarah whose eyelids began to close with the last bite of her room-service dinner.

But slipping into bed exhausted didn't mean sleep was inevitable. Instead, she tossed and turned as if she was wrestling a pride of lions. Insomnia was a strange new affliction for a woman who, her husband often joked, fell asleep after whispering "good" and before she got to "night."

* * *

The clock face glared 4:10 a.m. at Sarah, and she scowled back. She slipped out of bed and wandered toward her hopeless in-room coffeemaker. She stared at it, as if willing it to brew her a cup. Sleep was evading her, but sleepiness was haunting her. She filled the tiny pot with water and waited for it to boil. Sleep drifted over her several times as she stood by the pot, weaving and waiting. She poured hot water into a cup, took a few sips, and returned to bed. She strained and kicked, but just couldn't relax. Her heart was racing as fast as her thoughts, and she finally concluded that sleep wasn't returning that night.

By 7:00 a.m. showered, made up, and dressed, she dragged her glassy-eyed self into the Best Service for breakfast.

Shiny, looking crisp and fresh for the day, didn't ask for her order this time, she simply handed her a pen and notepad and walked away.

* * *

As Sarah finished her bacon, eggs, and hash browns, Shiny slid into the booth across from her. "So, whatcha doin' in town, anyway?" she impertinently asked.

Since Sarah seemed startled by the question, Shiny repeated it in a manner generally reserved for, and known to irritate, the mentally challenged or hearing impaired. She slowly and loudly enunciated her words, "WHAT ARE YOU DOING IN PRESCOTT?"

Sarah looked baffled, unsure whether to be offended or amused. "Well, since you're obviously eager to know, I happen to be interested in that child abuse case." She replied with an air of annoyance. She stiffened, sipped the remains of her coffee, then curtly asked. "Why do you want to know, anyway?"

Shiny smiled unapologetically, "I'm a curious person who you obviously don't remember. We were in band together. Well, not together, exactly. You were the snazzy majorette, and I played the tuba."

Sarah cocked her head and shrugged. "So, you graduated from tuba player to waitress?" Sarah thought she had struck a righteous blow, but she wasn't done. "Sorry, but high school band was a lifetime ago. I have a hard time remembering back that far, but I think I'd remember a name like Shiny."

The waitress laughed and shook her head. "Oh that. Well, that needs a bit of explaining. When I started working here after high school, Wes insisted on calling me Shiny Penny. Everyone liked the name, including me, so it stuck; but back in school when we knew each other, I was Shari Copper."

Sarah gasped and laughed simultaneously. "Oh hell, I remember you, Shari. Of course, I do."

"Shiny suits me better." The waitress confirmed as she struck a playful pose.

"Okay, Shiny it is." Sarah proclaimed with a salute.

"Thanks Sarah. And to complicate things further, I'm Shiny Dumas now; that's my married name."

"Pleased to meet you, Shiny Dumas. Kids, no kids?" Sarah was now enthusiastic about making this connection with her past.

"Lots o' kids. Five, to be exact. Most are married and moved away. Others just moved away. I've got a son and a couple o' grandkids still in town, though."

"Grandkids? Amazing. Who would have thought that could happen? You're way ahead of me. I have two kids and they're not even close to step one. Shari...sorry, I mean Shiny, I'm so glad you remember me."

"That was easy. But I'm a little worried that you remember me," Shiny mused.

"Come on, don't be modest, Shiny. You were the tallest and best basketball player on the girls' team. No one can forget that."

"Oh, that." She smiled and nodded. "I thought maybe you remembered me 'cause I was the schoolyard comedian...or maybe, bully. Unfortunately for some, I used any student in my eye-line as the butt of my jokes."

Sarah nodded. "Yeah, I can vouch for that," Sarah concurred with a grin. "As I recall, you had more than a few good laughs at my expense. But hey, if you can keep the cook feeding me meals like this, I can find it easier to forgive you."

Shiny inhaled a slow, comforting breath. "I'll tell my husband you're a fan. He's the cook. We own the place. We have for over twenty-five years."

"Really? So how come you're not three hundred pounds?" Sarah offered glibly.

Shiny snickered. "'Cause runnin' back and forth from table to kitchen all day just burns it off. O' course, I should gain it all back sittin' in front of the TV every night when there's nothin' goin' on in town, which is most of the time now. So, back to the question. Why would you be interested in that disgusting sex scandal? I thought that was all done and buried two or three years ago. But if you've got questions for me, go ahead, ask." Shiny looked around a moment, "Oh, damn. Hold on while I give old man Sanders another refill of his java. It'll be his third freebie." She slid off the seat, performed the service, and returned within seconds. "I'm back. Go ahead, ask away."

Sarah sized up Shiny, then determined to change her modus operandi from timid to daring, she forged ahead. "All right. What do you think about Earl White? And do you think the alleged charges fit with what you know about him?"

"Hell, everyone in this town would be fine seein' that a-hole locked up just 'cause he's so damn obnoxious. It may end pretty quick though, 'cause no one really seems to think Earl's involved. Why would he be? The man is richer than God. I doubt he'd need to lower himself to becoming a kiddie porn king."

For an uncomfortable moment, a thick silence inhabited the space. before Sarah pierced through it. "I'm leaving tomorrow morning, Shiny, but if this all works out, I hope to be back for the trial, if there is one. That means I could be here for a while. Then maybe we can get together for a real visit when you don't have to be a coffee-filling-jack-in-the-box." Sarah smiled, pulled on her jacket, and headed to the counter to pay.

"Well, sure," Shiny agreed, following Sarah to the register, "and I'll even let ya tell me what kind of a shit you remember me to be, if ya really do remember me."

"Are you kidding? I remember the deafening sound of about a zillion screaming teenagers when you led our team to that basketball championship against Ottawa."

Sarah left her old friend blushing and rehashing every glorious play of that championship game.

* * *

The walk from the Best Service back to the Journal office took barely two minutes, but it was enough time to chill Sarah from toes to teeth.

As she entered, Braydon was coming up from the basement carrying more back copies.

"I took down the ones ya already looked through and brought ya up some more," he proudly declared.

Sarah didn't have the heart to tell him that she found no references to Earl White in any of the back copies he'd already dragged up from the morgue. Out of respect for Braydon's efforts, however, she would go through the motion of scanning every page.

The seconds ticked by sluggishly while Sarah leafed through issue after issue. The enormous office clock edged toward 9:15, and Wesley hadn't arrived yet. Sarah had cut her breakfast conversation short in order to be in by eight, assuming that Wesley would be there well ahead of her. Perhaps, it was part of his day-after ritual, but his lateness was beginning to worry her. She didn't want to be a busybody, but she needed to know.

"Hey, Braydon. What time does Wesley usually get here?"

"Eight-thirty at the latest."

Sarah continued going through the motions of scanning the brittle pages, and finding nothing. At 9:32 a.m., she was considering giving up, when Wesley swept through the door, looking quite cheerful.

"I'm glad you're here, Sarah." He theatrically doffed his hat before hanging it on a hook.

"I'm really glad to see you, Wes. I came in at eight thinking you'd be here."

"Well, I was comin' in to phone you just now, 'cause I have a little tip for you."

"Great! Do tell." Sarah stopped turning the yellowed pages and sat back to listen.

"If you want to meet Earl White in the flesh, head across to Richard's office right now, 'cause he's there."

"Really?" She replied, as she waited for a punch line.

"Yeah, really." He countered with a bit of an edge to his voice. Sarah was bewildered. She still wasn't sure if it was real or a joke because Wesley was known for his wry sense of humour.

She sighed and decided to play the game, "Okay, Wes, I'll play. How come he's there?"

"Well, Richard *is* his lawyer, but what's more important is he's got a meeting with the city lawyer they hired who, I have it on good authority, will be late."

"And how would you know that?"

He chuckled and replied. "Well, it seems their big-city lawyer can't get up in the morning without a wake-up call, which the O'Brien failed to make this morning, so Richard got word the meeting was delayed a half-hour. Fortunately for you, Earl was right on schedule."

"Oh my God! You think it's okay?" Sarah stood motionless, as she waited for Wes to answer.

"Go! Get your coat on and get movin'! Clock's tickin'. I told Richard I'd try to get hold of you so you could meet Earl. He said, okay, but your time would be limited. So, go!"

"I owe you," Sarah confessed as she pulled on her coat and rushed toward the exit.

Wes raised his eyebrows and smiled: "Yeah, so I guess that means I'll see you at the fundraising dinner tonight then, eh?" he announced.

"You betcha," she winked as she raced out the door.

In less than a minute, Sarah was cordially greeted by Joannie, who immediately buzzed her boss.

Richard stepped into the foyer, remaining at a distance; and rather than extend his hand, he simply nodded his hello. He appeared more red-faced and anxious than at their previous meeting. "Wes told me he was going to try and get a hold of you, but he didn't say you'd parachute in seconds later. But that's good, because he probably mentioned, our visiting lawyer will be here any minute, and it's best you're gone by then."

He silently paced in a small arc, as if trying to gather his thoughts. "Mrs. Berman, I hope you realize we don't have a hearing date yet."

Sarah nodded.

"Well, I talked to Mr. White, and he's happy to chat with you, off the record, of course, as long as there's a lawyer present; and it seems, I'll do for now. Please, go in." He pointed the way with an open palm, and followed her inside.

All Sarah could see was the back of the two deep, buttery, leather wing chairs.

"Mrs. Berman, this is Earl White."

The client slowly rose and turned toward her. The man had a short, apish build, purplish translucent skin, pink-rimmed eyes, and oily wisps of orange-dyed hair. She was fascinated by his resemblance to an orangutan.

As he lunged forward and grasped her hand, the overwhelming reek of stale tobacco and perspiration prompted goosebumps to march down Sarah's back. He leered and smirked at her conspicuous discomfort. He released his tight, clammy grip, and returned to his seat while Sarah did her best to overcome her urge to leave. She reminded herself why she was there, and she focussed: *inhale slowly...hold...exhale slowly...*

"Mrs. Berman, grab the seat next to Mr. White." He declared, as he moved behind his desk and settled into his chair. She took the long way around and sat uncomfortably in the same leather chair she had found both comfortable and luxurious on her previous visit.

"I suggest you get started, Mrs. Berman. You likely have less than twenty minutes." The lawyer brusquely noted.

"Thank you, Richard." She politely replied. She took an energizing breath and proceeded. "First off, Mr. White, can you clarify, what crime you've been charged with?"

He sneered then chuckled as he looked over at Richard, waiting for him to join in. The lawyer offered a nod and a benign smile that seemed to satisfy the client.

"That's an easy one, Missy. None. And I won't be either, 'cause I didn't do nothin', so they got no case." He offered himself a snappy applause along with another obnoxious chuckle.

Sarah ignored the actions, took another life-affirming breath, and continued.

"If that's the case, then can I ask why you imported an expensive lawyer all the way from Toronto?"

A wolfish grin inched across his face. "I can assure you, Honey, expense is no problem for me."

"Honey? Really? Come on, Earl, a little respect here...okay? Richard awkwardly suggested.

"It's okay, Richard. 'Honey', isn't the worst thing I've been called. Tell me, Mr. White, how's your family handling this situation?"

Sarah noticed that Earl squirmed before answering. "They're handlin' it jest fine. They know it's a bunch o' bullshit."

Sarah sat straighter and turned directly toward him. "Then why do you think you've been implicated?"

Earl shuffled his ample bottom toward the edge of his chair. "You wanna know what I think? Here's the story, plain and simple, eh? Ya got seven perverts who'd say or do anythin' to cut a couple o' years off their prison time."

She rebounded with another question. "But why pick you? Why not someone with a record?"

Earl's hue changed from red to purple; and his attitude, from snide, to irritated. "Why? 'Cause it's me the bastard wants. He always resented my success, and now, he thinks he's got his chance to bring me down. He's just plain out ta get me, that's fuckin' why!"

Sarah remained calm and pressed on. "Who's the 'he' you're talking about?"

Earl sat back and took a few seconds of his own to regroup. "'Sorry about that little outburst there, Missy, but it's very upsetting."

"No problem Mr. White, we all have those moments." She civilly replied as she calmly waited for an answer.

"So, to answer your question, 'he,' is Zane Fergusson. He's my wife's cousin. A bunch o' years ago, he had his whole family livin' out by the dump in an old canvas tent, so my wife nagged the shit outta me until I finally gave him the key to an empty farmhouse I own, so the poor lot of 'em would have a roof over their heads. I charged him hardly nothin' fer it neither, but he ain't happy with almost nothin'. He wanted it for not one penny more than nothin'. He brought a shitload of his relatives into that place without payin' extra, and then he gets caught doin' all that crazy shit with them kids, in my house?" He sat back with his head in his hands, seemingly in pain.

Sarah's voice softened as she proceeded. "What about the children, Mr. White? Who do they belong to?"

He rubbed his eyes and shook his head. "Most o' them kids is his."

Horrified, Sarah tried but failed to stifle an audible gasp.

Earl heard it and stiffened. In the callous silence that followed, he drummed his fingers on the arm of the leather chair. While failing to tender sympathy or concern for his nieces and nephews, he managed to excel in expressing his moral certitude, "Personally, I'd never be caught dead foolin' around with any of them kids. Hey, if Zane wanted to stick it to 'em, that's his business...but when that asshole gets caught doin' it on my property, then it's my business."

Sarah gulped back a tinge of nausea, but forged ahead. She gently prodded. "So, what action did you take, Mr. White?"

He curled his upper lip and snarled. "What'd I do? Me? Soon's I heard 'bout it, I told 'em all to get the hell off my property. But by then, Zane was in jail and my wife was beggin' me to let his family stay on. An' I got this big ole soft heart, so I say his wife and kids can stay, rent free, for now. But I didn't mean forever. That was like three years ago for Christ's sake, right? So, some weeks back, I hated ta do it, but I told them they gotta get out 'cause I'm plannin' on sellin' the place. And that's when Zane started throwin' around all these wild claims. Now, who in hell wouldn't be upset after openin' your heart and then bein' screwed over like this?"

As beads of sweat began to bubble on Richard's forehead, he rose from his chair and nodded toward Sarah. "I think that's about all the time we have for now, Miss Berman." Sarah took the hint, stood up, and turned her attention to Earl. "Thank you for your time, Richard. Mr. White, may I call on you again, if need be?" she asked in a most guileless way.

"I'll be happy to fill you in whenever and wherever ya want," he winked and cackled.

Richard seethed with exasperation. "Earl, really? I'm sorry, Mrs. Berman, he's just a bit rattled by this whole scandalous situation."

Sarah shrugged and moved on. "It's okay Richard. It's stressful. I get it.

"Mr. White, when, or if, the time comes, I'll need you to sign a consent form, and might eventually need a picture of you. But if I do, the paper will send their professional photographer around to snap it. Will those conditions be okay with you?"

"Yeah, I'll sign the form; and if ya promise to make me look handsome like Perry Mason, ya can snap away, Baby," His uproarious laughter turned into a full-blown wheeze.

Sarah gritted her teeth and headed for the door.

Sarah's impulse was to rush from Richard McCall's office and jump into the frigid St. Lawrence River to rid herself of Earl White's stench; but she wisely decided that a warm, cleansing bath, a good lunch, and later on, the national news with Peter Mansbridge, trumped diving into the ominous waters of Kelly's Beach.

* * *

The fundraising event was set for seven o'clock that evening, which left Sarah plenty of time to wander around the town before heading back to the hotel. She stopped to pick up a large bottle of Remy Martin for her hosts, and, despite the fact that she wasn't a drinker, she couldn't resist buying a cute miniature Remy as a keepsake.

She entered her suite, and in a flash, rushed back down the stairs in search of the manager. "Where is Reynolds! Where's my damn TV?" Sarah demanded. The unfamiliar desk clerk twitched and sputtered "Uh, the boss is gone for the day...and uh, I don't know nothin' about any TV."

Sarah muttered under her breath, turned on her heel, and headed back up to her room to face the fact that she would be without her favourite voice to lull her to sleep when she returned from the fundraiser.

She ordered a wholesome lunch, wolfed down a cup of creamy cauliflower soup and a grilled cheese sandwich, then sat on her bed, opened her Harlequin, and picked up where she left off on the train. After a couple of short chapters, she was fast asleep. She awoke suddenly to find the room bathed in semi-darkness. It was almost five-thirty.

She took a quick shower, spun her hair into a chic French roll, freshened her makeup, and changed into a frilly blouse and navy pin-striped business suit. Other than jeans and sweats, it was all she had packed.

* * *

The Jacksons' home was a majestic and elegant estate that could have been as easily situated in Beverley Hills or Rosedale, as at the east end of Prescott. It was surely a heritage home. It was decorated in rich woods with crafted stone and plaster relief flourishes on ceilings and walls. Although the colonial house was of another age, the décor was current, colourful, and replete with soft and silky textures on draperies, sofas, and chairs.

After the introductions, she was escorted into the great room with its reflective marble floors and glistening crystal chandeliers. There, a crowd of at least forty guests were enjoying the sounds of a local jazz trio, an abundance of tasty hors d'ouvres, and an impressive array of wines.

With a glass of white pinot noir in hand, she now possessed the elixir that she hoped would transform her from retiring wallflower into fascinating guest. Since strange social environments had always been her Achilles' heel, she searched for a lone corner to stake her claim for the evening. She spotted an isolated cove and proceeded toward it until she was halted by a firm hand on her shoulder. She froze on the spot and held her breath as she slowly turned toward the interloper.

"I thought I might see ya here," Shiny offered with a wink. Sarah exhaled a laugh of relief.

"Hell, I didn't think I was that funny, Girl." Shiny jibed. Sarah smiled, shook her head, and held out a submissive palm in a gesture to proceed. Shiny didn't need a formal request. She shrugged and continued. "I knew you'd be here. Since Wes and Hartley always hit Ronnie and me up for a donation when they run one of these things, it didn't take a journalist or lawyer to figure out you wouldn't get off scot-free. So, ya got to meet Earl White this mornin', huh?"

Sarah stood stock still, mouth agape. "How did you know about that?"

"I have my wily ways." Shiny jovially replied, then noticed that Sarah's demeanor and tone were not frivolous. "Okay, kidding aside, every Friday, I deliver breakfast over to Richard's office for him and Wes. They've been doin' that for as long as I can remember. Richard gets to let off steam about the crazy justice system, and Wes gets to hear the latest courthouse gossip. That's when we all found out about that fancy lawyer sleepin' in. So, he's really somethin', that Earl, huh?" Shiny queried with a cynical grunt.

Sarah offered up a contrived shiver before agreeing. "Oh, yeah, he's something all right..."

"Well, ya know what they say, Sarah: you can't judge a book by its cover and all that crap...but if you could, then Earl's would be *Tales from the Crypt*."

The two old friends giggled like schoolgirls. Shiny proposed a toast: "May stronger stomachs prevail." Just as they raised their glasses, Richard appeared.

"Whatever the toast, I agree. Cheers, Ladies."

With that, he continued on his way, leaving the two women giggling once more like teenagers.

They remained by the wine bar where they could follow the action. Dozens of vaguely-familiar people passed by throughout the evening, but after so many years, it was impossible for Sarah to place the faces or the names. Shiny tried to remain within earshot to help fill in the blanks, but at some point during the evening, she was compelled to drift away with some potential donors.

Sarah claimed a corner where she could sit quietly and watch as she sipped her second glass of wine. Suddenly, she spotted Richard staggering toward her with a half-filled wine glass in hand. Clearly, he'd had too much to drink. As they stood almost toe to toe, Sarah observed that, in spite of his slight build, he carried a sizeable pot belly; and judging by his lack of taste in clothing, it was evident that someone else had designed his well-appointed office space.

"Listen, Sarah, I wanna talk to you about this crazy quest you're on. I know you've probably been fed all kinds of wild stories about Earl White, but I hope you're gonna write a good story about the guy, 'cause you don't wanna see him mad. It's not a pretty sight. I saw it once a long time ago, and I'll never forget it." He chuckled half-heartedly, then looked fervently at his glass and downed the remainder. The last few ounces seemed to put him over the edge. He leaned against the wall and stared at his empty glass. "S-somebody polished off my w-wine, so if you'll 'scuse me, I need ta f-fill up. But m-member, don't poke a s-sleeping dragon, 'kay?"

Sarah snickered at the idea. "No worries, Richard. I doubt I'll be poking that sleeping dragon 'cause, so far, there doesn't seem to be a viable case."

"G-good girl." And with that, he staggered back to the bar, leaving Sarah torn between the comedy and tragedy of the encounter.

After finishing off her glass, Sarah felt relatively blitzed and was relieved to see that event had begun to thin out. Guests who hadn't done so already, were offering their contributions or excuses as they exited. However, each time Sarah attempted to leave, Wes would find a reason for her to hang back with him. She began to get the feeling that Wes was either every bit as uncomfortable as she was in social situations, or he was waiting for her to make her meagre donation. To assuage any guilt, Sarah dropped a twenty-dollar bill into the gigantic brandy snifter by the front entrance even though Wes assured her that her contribution was unnecessary because several new brass instruments were guaranteed without it.

Just before midnight, Sarah returned to the hotel by cab and crawled into bed.

* * *

At 3:00 a.m., the alcohol and fatty food had amalgamated in a tumultuous, head-pounding, stomach-exploding battlefield. Throughout the night, Sarah carefully bivouacked between the bed and the bathroom during several precarious manoeuvres. She floated on torrential waves of nausea and vomit without a moment of calm until morning.

By 9:00 a.m., after downing a glass of seltzer and two aspirins, Sarah was marginally stable and ready to head down to the hotel's dining room where Wesley was waiting to share their final breakfast.

"You should eat something before you board the train," Wesley insisted.

"Not a chance, Wes," she moaned. "I don't know if it's the wine or a bout of flu, but the very thought of food makes me want to heave. I'll just have a cup of black tea, thank you."

* * *

Wesley had consumed several glasses of wine to Sarah's one, but he still managed to eat a full plate of bacon and eggs while Sarah struggled to get past the odor.

"Your people just aren't genetically crafted to tolerate alcohol like our people," Wesley quipped.

For once, thought Sarah, *I'm being singled out as a Jew with a deficiency I can live with.*

As they drove along Main Street toward the edge of town, she thought about how good it would be to finally have a full and restful night's sleep, in her own bed, under her favourite down duvet.

As the car drifted by the little Cape Cod house with the yellow shutters, it once again caught her eye.

"Wes, I meant to ask you about that little house with the dressmaker sign in the window."

"That's the Miller place. Years back, Mrs. Miller was the best dressmaker in town. She probably did alterations for your dad's store. Maybe you knew her daughter, Eleanor. She took over the shop when her mom passed away."

"Hmm, I don't remember," she replied.

* * *

The few minutes that remained before Sarah boarded the train were spent in pensive silence, until Wes broke in: "Listen to me, Sarah Klein, don't ever stop writing. Ya hear me? You gave it up for whatever your reasons, but I know you've got the gift. So, case or no case, you keep on writing. Now, before I get all maudlin, give an old mentor a hug and get the hell aboard that train." She smiled and embraced him.

As they separated, she spotted tears in his eyes that matched those she had been trying and failing to keep in check.

A lingering dose of cottonmouth and nausea accompanied Sarah as she shakily weaved down the aisle hoping to find a lone seat where she could stretch out, maybe joy down some notes and then sleep the rest of the way.

She finally weaved her way to an empty row and plopped down in the seat. Her nasty hangover made her think about what she had missed on Saturday nights as a teenager in Prescott, when her dad insisted she had to stay home and watch TV, while the rest of her underage friends were racing across the US border to drink in bars that couldn't care less about ID. While most teens would return home safe but barfing drunk; too many were injured or killed in car accidents after those Saturday night blitzes.

She leaned her woozy head against the window and thought *Father really does know best.*

She struggled to stay awake in order to record some events in her notebook while she could still remember them.

The train chugged along, and she nodded off with pen and notebook in hand.

CHAPTER THREE

It had been several months since Sarah moved from her stately Forest Hill home and into her tiny, dark box of an apartment. As she entered the lobby of her low-rise building, a familiar emptiness began to gnaw at her like a desperate hunger. The putty-coloured walls seemed more insipid, and the nicotine yellowed ceiling, more oppressive. This was the kind of existence she had pitied when one of her friends had become the victim of a bad divorce.

Sarah had never contemplated the thought that one day, when her children grew up and left home, she'd become disposable to her soon-to-be, ex-husband.

The day after her son, Jordie, left for Dalhousie University, her husband announced that he was done. For some time, Sarah suspected that something was seriously amiss, but she chose to hide from the truth. There were many nights he claimed to be on-call at the hospital, but if she tried to reach him, Dr. Berman was nowhere to be found.

Another clue happened accidentally. Sarah had never opened, seen, or paid a bill during her marriage. Taking care of their finances was her husband's domain. One day, however, there was an overdue Visa statement lying open on his desk. Her eyes zeroed in on the *Birks Jewellers* entry...a $4,500 purchase. She hadn't received a piece of jewellery from Saul in a few years and had no birthday or other celebration coming up. She called the credit company to report the mistake and discovered that there had been no mistake, at least, not on Visa's end.

Saul had suddenly remortgaged their home which they'd paid off years before, and, just as suddenly, claimed it was being held hostage by the bank. Grave debt appeared in an avalanche of maxed-out credit cards and unpaid bills.

With the help of an elite group of lawyers, Dr. Berman pled poverty at their separation hearing, and Sarah was bled dry of any settlement funds. She walked away with only enough furniture to fill her cage-sized apartment, and an assurance of sufficient support to cover her rent. Since the actual divorce was still in the offing, a murky cloud hovered over her as she wondered each day, what else he could take from her.

Her stomach grumbled and she realized she hadn't eaten all day. She stopped recounting her misery and heeded the call. She stared into the refrigerator and found it still as empty as it was when she'd left, two days earlier. She gathered her wits and dialled for pizza delivery.

Ever since she moved into the tiny apartment, she struggled with how to begin life again, when all she'd known until then, was home and family.

That Saturday night felt like a bleak Monday, until a crude reminder came from the pizza delivery man. Maybe it was the steep, three-flight climb that had him contemplating his gloomy life, or perhaps, it was the tip she robotically offered.

"Oh man, I can think of so many better ways to spend my Saturday night," he grumbled as he closed his hand around the ten-dollar bill which contained his forty-one-cent tip.

Sarah's expedition had emptied her wallet and filled her brain with disappointment. As she devoured half the pizza and a diet Pepsi, she contemplated the cruel reality that no news editor at the *Toronto Sun-Times* would send a virtual amateur miles away to follow such a crazy lead.

* * *

On Monday morning, after two superb nights of uninterrupted sleep, Sarah headed to the *Sentinel* office to pick up her next assignment. *Would it be the nail-biting excitement of a kite-flying contest, or perhaps the poignant thrill of a new litter of kittens at the local pet shop?*

As her editor relayed her next brain-numbing assignment, it was obvious to her that he had no idea she'd been away. "Yeah, so, we've been getting complaints from readers about price-fixing in supermarkets, so take this shopping list to these four different venues, make the purchases, write up your findings. And, uh, you can keep the groceries, as a perk."

* * *

For the third time that afternoon, Sarah veered her shopping cart up and down a variety of supermarket aisles, tossing the listed items into her cart.

There was only one store left to visit, and, if that investigation went like the others, then Sarah would have to report that on average, all the prices were fair and competitive. That would likely mean that the article could be cut, as would her two-hundred-dollar fee.

Sarah returned home without a compelling case against the price of canned tuna or baked beans; therefore, she'd need to try to write something spicy enough to keep the readers and more importantly, the editor, interested.

As she was putting away the last of her grocery perks, she got a call from her best friend, Madeline, who at "hello" unleashed a barrage of unflattering epithets.

"You're an idiot, Sarah. You just disappear without telling anyone? Are you out of your mind? I even sunk so low as to call Saul, hoping that he hadn't carved you into pieces and dropped you into Lake Ontario. I'm not even going to ask where in Hell you've been and why you haven't called or picked up your messages, but I'll assume until I hear differently, that you have a really good answer. And I hope you remembered that you're supposed to be here for Rosh Hashanah dinner tomorrow, and don't you dare disappoint us."

It had completely escaped Sarah that tomorrow was the beginning of Rosh Hashanah, her new second-least favourite holiday now that her hearth and home was a splintered memory. It had always represented a time of family togetherness and the traditional five-pound weight gain, followed by Yom Kippur's competitive fast, and the five-pound weight loss. It was an annual win-lose situation. Now, in spite of the tongue-lashing, the prospect of dinner at Maddie's was manna from heaven.

"Where in Hell have you been anyway?" Madeline demanded.

Sarah sighed deeply, closed her eyes, and surrendered one word: "Prescott."

"Prescott? As in, 'I have absolutely no desire to visit my hometown, ...that Prescott?" Maddie seethed.

"Uh-huh." She awkwardly replied.

"What is happening to you?" Maddie ranted as Sarah squirmed in her chair. "Everyone's worried sick about you for God's sake, and all you can do is grunt?"

"I'm sorry, Maddie, I didn't tell anyone, because if it all worked out, I'd be a success and you'd all be proud of me. And if it didn't work out, no one would know, and I wouldn't have to be embarrassed."

"Embarrassed about what?" Maddie shouted into the receiver.

"About failing again, damn it."

"Shit, Sarah. Saul failed, not you." Maddie's voice softened as her empathy deepened. "Jeez, Kiddo, we all know you honoured your part of the deal." An awkward silence ensued, until Maddy offered a hopeful thought. "And hey, you took that journalism course and you got yourself a real job at a newspaper! That's something to be proud of!"

"Yeah, I'm the next Diane Sawyer, except I cover the dog poop beat." Sarah scoffed as she stood and dumped her pizza crusts into the garbage.

"I can't stand that self-pity shit, so if you're not going to tell me why you went and what you did, then I may as well..."

"Okay, okay," she surrendered, sat back, and took a breath. "I saw Prescott mentioned briefly in the *Sun-Times* the other day, so I went there on a whim, hoping it might be a huge story that could get me in the door of a major daily."

"Wow. That's amazing! You were obviously inspired. So, tell me, tell me!"

Sarah interrupted "There's nothing to tell. Really, I mean it. It turned out to be a nothing story."

"Oh. Then I'm sorry." Maddie offered.

"Yeah, me too." Sarah mumbled as she raised her Pepsi can in a mock toast.

"Do you want to talk about it?"

"Nope, I'm done. I'll see you tomorrow."

* * *

The glow of laughter and camaraderie from the holiday dinner dissipated as Sarah was en route back to the eerie silence of her apartment.

She entered her flat and solemnly closed and locked the door behind her. As she turned toward the sofa, her eyes were drawn to the flashing message light that brought a rush of faint hope that her children might be returning her holiday wishes. Sarah thought about how distance allowed a person to avoid harsh reality. A stranger delayed in an airport would tell another stranger their deepest secrets. Vacationers would eagerly participate in edgy activities that they would never dream of doing at home. Twenty-something-aged-children, studying far away, didn't want to think about their parents' pending divorce, so they simply stop communicating. Phone messages and letters remain unanswered.

Sarah steeled herself and pressed play. There was only one message:

"I'm sorry to bother you, Ms. Berman. We met on the train from Toronto last week and we exchanged cards. My name is Sister Catherine Grace and I'm hoping you will call me back..."

Sarah's curiosity was keenly awakened and her heart raced with anticipation. She paced nervously, trying to decide if 9:45 pm was too late to call a House of God.

By the second ring, Sarah's anxiety had climbed from one to an eleven. She gasped as she heard the ringing stop and Sister Catherine Grace's voice drifted over the line.

"Thank you for calling back Ms. Berman, I hope I'm not bothering you."

"What? No, of course not. Please, go ahead." At that moment, Sarah had no patience for even the slightest interruption.

"Thank you. I was pretty sure you'd want me to share this message with you. I visited a couple of the inmates we'd briefly talked about on the train. Now, other than listening to their prayers, I usually don't pay much attention to what they have to say, but when I mentioned there was a journalist from Toronto interested in the Earl White case, one of the prisoners said he'd like to meet with you, if you're interested."

Sarah could feel her delicious holiday meal decomposing in her stomach as she imagined meeting face to face with one of the perpetrators. She swallowed hard before responding. "I'm so honoured that you even thought of me...uh, do I call you Sister or Miss? I'm not sure about the protocol here."

"Sister Catherine...or Sister. Either is fine, Ms. Berman."

"Okay, thank you, and please call me Sarah. Sister Catherine, could you give me a second?"

"Of course." With that, Sister Catherine remained patiently silent.

Sarah paced the room with the phone pressed tightly against her ear. "Uh, Sister, I'm not sure I can afford the time away right now, but can I think on it for a few days?"

The nun was bewildered by the reply, but she graciously agreed. "Of course, you can."

Sarah lowered herself into the armchair and stared at the nun's business card. "Sister Catherine, as soon as I figure it out, I'll call you, if that's okay."

"I'll leave it in your capable hands. And Sarah, I pray you have a happy and healthy New Year."

"Oh, yes, uh, thank you so much." Sarah hung up the phone, rose from her chair in a boisterous leap, clapped her hands, and squealed into the empty room, "Oh my God! After a wonderful Rosh Hashanah dinner with friends, I get invited to interview someone at the centre of a big story...and then a nun prays for me on a Jewish holiday...Holy crap! Who says weird and wonderful miracles don't happen?"

Reva Leah Stern

* * *

It was mid-afternoon when Sarah stepped off the train and onto the familiar platform. Colourful October hadn't yet yielded to glacial November, but its bitter wind still claimed victory over the midday sun. As she walked toward the O'Brien, Sarah took comfort in the thought that she'd be gone before the chafing onslaught of a Prescott winter began.

With suitcases in tow, Sarah and Mr. Reynolds struggled up the staircase to her room. For the same price as a regular room, Wesley had booked her into the O'Brien's "Royal Suite" with its plastic, cushioned loveseat and faux marble arborite coffee table. She peeked around the needlepoint folding screen that separated the sitting area from the bedroom. The TV was there, as promised.

Sarah unpacked her cleaning supplies and waged mortal combat against any germ or insect that dared to invade her bathroom or the microwave/mini-fridge area that Mr. Reynolds referred to as her kitchen.

Before she headed out to shop, to make the place bearable, she made a list of items she'd need from the local market and the five and dime.

For twenty-nine dollars, she was able to place a small fruit bowl on the coffee table, adorn the sofa with a bright, velvety throw, and set a yellow mum plant on the counter. She topped the bed off with her own brought-from-home colourful duvet and, when she was all done, she thought, "This place looks pretty damn good for the O'Brien."

Having completed her domestic chores by four-thirty, she headed to the Journal office to meet Braydon who'd offered to drive her to a car rental agency on the outskirts of town.

She lingered for a moment in front of the dressmaker's house, fascinated by the contrast between the lifeless garden plots on either side of the rickety steps, and the hand-hewn window boxes with their array of vibrant, autumn flowers. Acting on a puerile impulse, Sarah leaned in to admire the asters and cyclamen. Her eye was suddenly drawn to a fluttering lace curtain at the front window. She immediately backed away, feeling foolish for having invaded the dressmaker's space. She continued on her way to the Journal office. When she arrived, Braydon welcomed her with the aggravating news that there would be no rental car available until Wednesday.

After an enthusiastic embrace from Wesley, Sarah shared the details of her initial meeting with Sister Catherine Grace on the train, and their several follow-up phone exchanges.

"Now, for the piece de resistance...I have an appointment on Thursday to meet Sister Catherine at the Kingston Penitentiary." She announced with an impish chortle that drew no reaction from either man.

"I mean, to be honest, it creeps me out a little. Have either of you ever been inside?" She nervously asked.

"Nah," Braydon confessed. "The worst crime I ever committed was stealing a chocolate bar from

Perkins Candy Store when I was seven. But they didn't put you in the pen for that back then."

Sarah offered a patronizing smile. "Come on, seriously?"

"Seriously." Braydon puffed out his chest and answered somewhat defensively, "I've interviewed my share of inmates over the years, ya know."

"Braydon, you're about twelve now, so over how many years was that?" She chuckled.

"Hey, I'm twenty-seven, alright?"

Sarah playfully peered at him over mimed spectacles. "Okay fine, I've never been inside the actual prison walls." He admitted. "But I interviewed a couple of burglars at the police lockup last year."

The gripping tension of entering a prison to interview a convicted child predator had given Sarah an actual pain in the neck. She was certain that if Wesley or Braydon were to accompany her, it might ease the tension and, therefore, the pain. She was reluctant to ask but hopeful they would offer. Silence prevailed and the pain persisted.

As she headed out the door, Wesley handed Sarah a weathered, manila envelope and the latest October 1992 issue of the Prescott Journal.

She returned to her suite, tossed the envelope and newspaper on the sofa, and ordered up soup and a sandwich. She snapped on the TV, only to find black snow vibrating against a white backdrop.

She found Mr. Reynolds laughing it up at the bar with a couple of loud, obnoxious lumberjack types. Before she could give him an all-out tongue-lashing,

Reynolds was ready with a feeble attempt at reassurance. "Miss, I know all about it, but I assure ya, the TV repairman was called, and he's promised to have it up and runnin' real soon."

Exasperated, Sarah returned to her room, resigned to facing another long night without Brokaw or Koppel. She sat for a moment and browsed through the Journal but found nothing that sparked her interest. She rose and paced, carefully maneuvering around the obstacles, while quietly chanting; "I can do this. I can do this..."

Her mantra was interrupted by a brisk knock at the door. A young man entered carrying her dinner tray covered in a crisp, white cloth. Sarah signed for it and handed the bill back to the smiling waiter, who nodded and exited. She started across the room to lock up after him, but he reappeared from the corridor holding a large, portable radio.

"Here, this is a loaner, Mrs. Berman. Mr. Reynolds feels bad about the whole television thing."

"Uh-huh. Well, thank Mr. Reynolds for his outstanding generosity, but please take it back." She clenched her teeth in indignation and folded her arms. "I'd be afraid his radio might accidentally fall and end up smashed." She sarcastically suggested.

The waiter smiled but choked back a desire to laugh., "Oh no, Ma'am. This isn't his radio. It's mine."

Sarah's patience had reached its limit. "I don't want to get you in trouble, young man, but did Reynolds coerce you into this?" she seethed.

Reva Leah Stern

The young man shook his head and offered another shy smile. "No, Ma'am, it's not like that. It was my idea. When I heard about your television problem, I called my mom, and she brought the radio over. By the way, my name's Mitch Martin. My mother's name is Bev, and she's really excited that you're here."

Sarah scrunched her brow in bewilderment.

"Actually, the truth is, my mom told me not to bother you. But I was just wondering if you might remember her. Bev Martin?"

Sarah repeated the name. "Bev Martin?" But there was no recognition.

"I think you may have known her as Ket Hall?" Mitch added.

As the name registered, Sarah's smile was Mitch's guarantee that she did remember. "Mitch, you tell your mother that I could never forget Ket Hall."

"Jeez. She'll be really glad to hear that." He assured her as he gently placed the radio on the coffee table.

"Wow, Ket Hall. Oh my God. How is she?" She clasped her hands together in delight.

"She's real good, Ma'am."

"That's great to hear."

"Anyway, I better get back to work."

"Okay, Mitch. Well, it's really good to meet you." She reached out to shake his hand and he obliged. "Thanks for the radio and please send your mom my warmest regards."

"I will, Mrs. Berman." He turned to go but paused and pointed to the radio. He added; "The dial's set for *Golden Oldies*; you know the fifties and sixties stuff my mom listens to, but you can change it to whatever you want. Personally, I'd rather listen to Nirvana, Eric Clapton, or U2, but suit yourself."

Sarah smiled and pondered her good fortune.

"Golden Oldies sounds perfect, Mitch."

"Good. If you need anything just call the desk and ask for me. Good night."

As she closed the door behind him, Sarah's mind was cheerily flooded with images of Beverly Hall, Ket, the quirkiest girl in the school. Ket was given the nickname because she slathered ketchup over everything from peanut butter sandwiches to pretzels.

Sarah flopped on the bed, giggling like a schoolgirl while "Don't Be Cruel" floated over the radio waves. Cocooned in a wonderful time warp, she dined on a tuna sandwich and mushroom soup.

Her musical journey ended abruptly at eight-thirty when all the radio stations began their local hockey coverage. No matter which way she turned the dial, she was doomed to listen to the nasally drone of the sportscaster.

Utter boredom propelled her to plop herself on the settee and have a look at the manila envelope. One by one, she slid the contents out of the envelope and placed them in an orderly fashion on the coffee table. There were several photos of Earl White and family. One that particularly caught her eye and funny bone, was an old wedding portrait. The couple resembled *American Gothic* with a shotgun where the pitchfork should be. There were a few faded black-and-white landscape shots that were of no interest. But amusing and intriguing, were several group shots featuring Earl, the devoted husband, Earl, the head-petting dad, and Earl, the benevolent boss. There was something curious about the fact that, in every photo, the subjects appeared in front of the same background. The expressions on their faces ranged from sad to bitter with the exception of Earl White, who was always situated centre stage, wearing a wide, frozen grin. Sarah saw something woefully absurd in the images. She needed to talk to Wesley about why he thought this bizarre photo gallery would be useful to her.

By 9:45, Sarah had grown restless, and she was losing her battle against a sugar craving. She stood and stretched, and tried to think of something that would distract her, but ultimately, she gave in to the urge. On impulse, she heading out to Perkins Candy and Smoke Shop which, in the good old days, was always stocked with an array of homemade candies and a variety of ways to imbibe tobacco.

As she was crossing the street, the biting wind offered a chill reminder that she had just ventured into it without a jacket, scarf, or gloves.

The familiar jingle of the overhead bell announced her entrance. The sweet aroma that hung in the air reminded Sarah of the cinnamon jawbreakers that old Mrs. Perkins used to create in the back room. After carefully choosing a few selected sweets from the familiar rows of apothecary jars, Sarah browsed through the colourful rack of magazines.

"We're about to close up, so-o, if there's somethin' else you want, ya better make it quick." The attitude and expressionless face belonged to the sombre teenaged girl seated behind the counter, cracking her gum, and blowing lime green bubbles.

"Actually, there is." Sarah didn't like the attitude and wasn't about to take commands from a testy, pimple-faced teenager. "Do you have any cinnamon jawbreakers?"

Sarah received an abrupt, "Nope."

Annoyed by the inimical clerk, she added a "Variety" magazine and a Pepsi to her order, then waited for the ancient cash register to ring up her purchases.

Outside, sleet had begun to relentlessly buzz-bomb the frosty windows.

Sarah picked up her loot bag and headed for the door. She pulled and pushed to no avail. "Excuse me, young lady, but I think I'm locked in. Can you open the door please?"

The clerk burst her bubble and grunted her annoyance. Sarah was close to the end of her tether. "You're upset because I'm shopping? You don't close until ten o'clock, so what's the problem?"

"It was ten o'clock ten minutes ago and you were still browsin' around, Ma'am. It's my job to lock up at ten. Just wait there." She snivelled, as she disappeared behind the saloon doors and reappeared seconds later, zipping up her ski jacket and brandishing a key. She unlocked the front door and they both stepped outside. The clerk grunted again before running past Sarah, seemingly without locking up. Sarah scowled at the rude, irresponsible, and rapidly-disappearing young woman. Then she quickly turned her thoughts to her warm suite where she'd blissfully satisfy her sugar craving.

She was about to step off the curb when a set of blazing headlights from the lane across the street startled her. Sleet obliterated her vision, her legs felt like rubbery liquorice lace. She shambled backward and lowered herself onto the shop's wet stoop. As she sat, rocking with her head on her knees, she failed to notice that the car had casually turned onto Main Street and continued on its way.

A gentle tap on the shoulder and a quiet, comforting female voice urged Sarah to slowly rise and follow her into the shop. "You sit right here, Dear, and tell me what happened." The woman guided Sarah onto a chair near the front of the shop and placed a dry tea towel in her hand.

Sarah was still dazed and her eyes were wet with icy tears, but she struggled to respond. "The lights were blinding...and I thought the car was...out of control."

The kindly old woman replied, "Well, thank goodness you're okay!"

"I overreacted," Sarah volunteered. As she dabbed the frost from her lashes, the face of her rescuer came into focus: "I'm so sorry. I don't mean to stare, but...you're Mrs. Perkins, right?" The woman nodded. "Mrs. Perkins, I used to live in Prescott many years ago. Do you still run this shop?"

Mrs. Perkins chuckled. "Oh, my heavens no! My granddaughter, Terri, does, and my great-granddaughter, Cindy, helps out. I just come here sometimes to keep them company. Cindy usually walks me home, but tonight, it got to be too cold and wet to walk, so she ran home to get the car. And speaking of the weather, young lady, why are you out on a night like this without a coat?"

"I'm staying right over there at the O'Brien. I figured it was safe to run across in ten seconds without dressing for the North Pole." She replied as she brushed strands of wet hair from her cheek. "Mrs. Perkins, I remember a hundred delicious things covered in chocolate you used to make. But my all-time favourite treat was your secret..."

"Cinnamon jawbreakers," The old lady interjected.

"Mm, yes exactly. When I walked in here tonight, I swear I could smell them."

"Sorry, Sarah, dear."

There was an audible intake of breath as Sarah tried to grasp what she had just heard. "Mrs. Perkins? You said my name? You remember me?"

Mrs. Perkins chuckled. "Of course, I remember you my dear. You were always curious about everything...and you were a handful, I must say. Now would you excuse me for a minute? I just have to grab my coat before Cindy starts honking her horn. I'm sure you figured out, she's not Miss Patience." Sarah nodded and smiled. With that, Mrs. Perkins disappeared behind the saloon doors, still keeping up the chatter from the back room. "Anyway, my dear, I know why you're in town and I'll bet you'd love to know how I know, wouldn't you?" She shouted.

"Absolutely," Sarah shouted back.

"Well, I play canasta every week with Richard McCall's mother, Estelle, who, I might add, has not lost one whit of her ability to gossip like a dirty tabloid." She giggled at her own joke. "And since she knows you're in town and why, she's been only too happy to share the news."

"Really? His mother is still around? She must be a hundred by now." Sarah mused as she patted her face and hands with the towel.

"Well, she's older than me by three years, but I'd say we're both pretty well preserved and feisty for pushing or pulling ninety. I suspect it's our card games and my stimulating jawbreakers that keeps us perpendicular."

Mrs. Perkins reappeared wearing her coat, hat, and scarf, and carrying a small paper bag which she placed in Sarah's lap. "It's a gift to warm you, Dear."

A quick peek left Sarah overwhelmed by the familiar sweet, spicy scent of the crimson jewels within. "This is amazing. But your granddaughter said there weren't any?"

"Well, Cindy tends to be a bit impatient at times. As fate would have it, I just finished making a batch for my family for Halloween."

The sound of a bleating horn disrupted Sarah's reverie.

"That'll be Cindy. Come, you jump in the car, and we'll go 'round and drop you off right in front of the hotel so you won't have to cross the street." Sarah rose and warmly hugged her rescuer.

"Thank you so much for everything, Mrs. Perkins, but a ride isn't necessary. In fact, I'd feel really pathetic ever having to admit I needed a lift to get across the street." Sarah laughed, and the shopkeeper joined in.

"Please go ahead, Mrs. Perkins. I'll be just fine."

The old lady smiled warmly, "Okay then, Dear. I don't see any runaway cars in the lane, but I'm gonna watch until you're safely across anyway."

Sarah patted her arm and cautiously walked out the door, waiting a few seconds until the proprietor locked up. She then stepped to the curb and looked both ways before dashing to the other side. Once safely across, Sarah turned and waved to her protector who waved back while the 'now, not so impatient, Cindy' held the passenger door open until her great-grandmother was safely settled in her seat.

Inside her room, Sarah launched an all-out attack on the nagging chill that clung to her like a parasite. She placed one of the precious ruby crystals between her lips and eased her frigid body into a steamy bath.

When the last drop of the crimson elixir disappeared from her tongue, she slipped into bed and drifted off to sleep.

Reva Leah Stern

As the night matured, aberrant images crept into her dreams: *A battalion of demonic creatures chasing her...A small, frail body encased in a frozen waterfall...A shadowy figure illuminated by the blinding glare of a klieg light...*

The unconscious assaults continued until 2:29 a.m., when she awakened in a frosty mist of perspiration. Unsettling fragments of her nightmare flickered through her mind, but no clear picture emerged.

To get any sleep at all would require unusual measures. Remembering Wesley's endorsement that a single shot of Remy Martin could melt an iceberg, Sarah rescued the miniature keepsake from her suitcase, uncapped it, and took a few tiny swallows of the burning sedative.

She had barely sipped half an ounce before the warm, comforting ether anaesthetized her into a deep slumber.

CHAPTER FOUR

Through the lacy curtain, Sarah could see a silhouette moving about. A moment later, the door eased open to reveal a slender woman with salt-and-pepper hair and a beautiful, although pale and delicate, face. The two women stood silent for a moment. "Uh, I'm sorry to bother you, but I, uh, noticed your dressmaker sign as I passed by earlier, and I have a few things that need alteration," She stammered. "Uh, may I bring them to you?"

The dressmaker lowered her head for a second, in what Sarah assumed to be a nod.

"Okay, then, I'll bring them by tomorrow, if that's all right?"

This time the enigmatic woman offered a more definitive nod.

"Good. Um...thank you." Sarah awkwardly replied. As she turned to walk away, she added, "Oh, in case you need it, my name is Sarah Berman."

The dressmaker offered a strained half-smile and lowered her gaze as she gently closed the door.

* * *

A greeting, a booth, and a menu awaited Sarah as she entered the warmth of the Best Service Diner. Remembering that this was the traditional gossip den from whence all spicy stories emanated, Sarah had made a deal with Shiny: "If you'll have breakfast with me, I'll agree to go with you to that bloody open house thing at our old high school. And Shiny, it's a one-sided deal that leans toward you, 'cause you're obviously a fan of eating in your own restaurant; while I'm not a fan of school reunions, of any kind."

Before breakfast was served, Sarah got right to her brief encounter with the seamstress behind the lacy curtain, and, without wasting a second, Shiny cleared the window on a foggy history, where memories of Sarah's past connection to the dressmaker began to surface. As a teenager, Sarah sometimes hung out with a group of friends that her best friend, Anna, described as 'mind-blind.'

Anna and Sarah loved to sit together under a huge shade tree at Kelly's Beach, discussing books and dreaming about what new worlds they might discover one day.

From that perch, on many afternoons, they would watch girls in bikinis scream with glee, while being chased by hormone-driven boys determined to capture a bra as their flag.

Of course, there was usually at least one free-spirited girl in town, whose erratic hormones were as accelerated as the boys'. Inevitably, she would be willingly caught in the bushes, and soon after, her reputation would get burned in the brush fire. Once the boys were called to the hunt, they were impossible to control. That left vulnerable girls and a few fragile boys at risk of getting tossed into the river, buried up to their ears in sand, or having to rescue their shoes from a nearby rooftop.

One sweltering August day, as Sarah and Anna emerged from the limpid, cool river, word spread of an impending raid. The two were scurrying away when they spotted a girl with silky black hair and an enviably endowed body ambling toward the beach. Anna bellowed out a warning; "Hey. You better go back. There are a bunch of jerks planning to chase..."

The girl shot back, "Not planning." With that, she pivoted and ran off with her emissaries.

The girls turned to see the wild stampede of boys closing in on them. Wet and barefoot, they raced up the hill. As they reached the corner, the new girl whispered, "Follow me!" All three dashed across the street to a little Cape Cod house with yellow shutters.

Once inside, the girls introduced themselves properly to Eleanor and her mother, who enthusiastically welcomed the visitors. "I'm delighted to meet you. And so happy Eleanor decided to bring her friends to visit. I always encourage her to do that, but she tends to be a bit shy. Please stay as long as you like."

The girls chatted away the afternoon while Mrs. Miller indulged them with home-baked cookies and cherry Kool-Aid.

After they'd had their fill of refreshments, Eleanor offered the irresistible suggestion that they all head to her room. The visitors oohed and aahed at the loveliness of it. The bedroom was decorated with beautiful home-made adornments: a lilac silk comforter, a variety of delicate pastel throw cushions, and a petit-point portrait of a ballerina that graced a bench by a Victorian vanity table.

"Your room is so pretty," Anna sighed. "Did your mom do all this?"

"She did it when I was about five years old and I don't know how to tell her, I've outgrown it." With that, she released a shy giggle, and the girls joined in.

"Well, at least you've got some colour." Anna muttered. "My room is beige from the floor to the ceiling and everything in between. So, a little girly colour would suit me just fine. How about your dad? Does he go for pastels?" Anna cheekily teased.

"My dad was an air force pilot. His plane was shot down over Europe just a few weeks after the war was supposed to be over. So, I never knew him; but I have pictures of him. Do you want to see them?"

The girls stared at Eleanor, wide-eyed and silent.

"It's okay if you don't want to. I just thought you might like to see what he looked like."

"Yes, of course we do! We're just a bit shocked," Sarah explained.

"She's right, Eleanor, I shouldn't have made a joke like that. My big mouth gets me into trouble more times than I can count. Sarah can vouch for that." Anna admitted.

"I can, and she's right: more times than I can count too." Sarah offered with a snicker which seemed to loosen up all three girls.

Eleanor hesitated for a moment, then lifted a jewelry box from the vanity and placed it beside her on the bench. She began to share the contents with her visitors. There were photos, letters, and air force war medals belonging to her deceased father. All, emotional tributes that she deeply treasured.

In spite of the excitement that the young women shared on that beautiful mid-summer day, the friendship metaphor they sowed blossomed for a few summer days, but somehow wilted as autumn set in.

* * *

"Shiny, other than the few days we spent together that summer, she's a blank. I know she went to our high school, but I really don't remember her."

"No, 'cause that was probably the year she quit midterm."

"But she was just a kid. Why would she quit?"

"There was a lot of whisperin' about it, but the rumour was Eleanor had been attacked."

"How? I mean, what kind of attack?"

Shiny rolled her eyes. "Jeez-Louise. What kind of attack do you think? I'm talkin' about rape, Sarah."

"Oh my God! That's horrible." After a moment of contemplation, Sarah pressed on, "Come on, if a kid in our school was raped, no matter how many years ago it happened, wouldn't you think I'd remember that?"

"She was probably around fourteen at the time, so you must have been maybe twelve. I hardly think, in those days, your parents would have been discussing rape while passin' the pot roast. Hell, I was like, uh, fifteen and I didn't know about it 'til much later myself. But ya know what I think? I think our town harbours years of unresolved shit around that poor girl. The adults yapped behind closed doors, and speculation grew; but nevertheless, it seemed that no one really doubted that the rape happened.

"At work, Eleanor's mother couldn't take the ugly whisperin', so she left the factory. When she put out her dressmaker sign, people in town were more than eager to use her services. She was a great seamstress, but she knew it was plain old curiosity that brought the customers in. She's been gone for years now. But hey, on the plus side, I think Eleanor makes a decent livin' from that business her mom started."

"How does she manage to keep her sanity without talking to anyone?" Sarah asked with a slight hint of indignation.

Shiny looked at her quizzically. "What do you mean? She talks."

"Not to me she doesn't...other than, uh...goodbye," Sarah snorted.

"Really? Well, maybe she's just shy with weird strangers from the big city." She teased. "I know she reads a lot, 'cause I often bump into her at the library. We've talked, ya know, weather, books, TV shows, and stuff like that, but to be honest, I don't get the idea that she's ever had a circle of friends." Shiny began to fiddle with her napkin.

"That's so sad." Sarah added. A hint of melancholy hung over the booth as they quietly sipped their coffees.

* * *

Sarah strode to the Journal office to ask Wesley where the odd collection of photos came from.

"Earl's wife dropped them off a few days after you went back to Toronto. I guess she thought you might like to see a fine pictorial history of Earl White and his family," Wesley jibed. "Somehow, Earl got the notion that you're writing a big front-page story about the great injustice he's suffering and thought you could use a few noble images to bolster the article." He grunted.

"Damn. I may have unintentionally had something to do with that, Wes." She sheepishly lamented. "When I met him, I did mention; if the article was accepted, I'd need a good picture of him. But I was very clear it would have to be taken by the newspaper's professional photographer."

"Yeah, well that's Earl. He makes his own rules and expects all minions to follow them." He shook his head in disdain and handed the envelope back. Sarah returned it to her briefcase.

"Okay, on a different topic: how come when I asked you about the dressmaker, you didn't say a word about an alleged rape?"

Wes lowered his eyes and hesitated for a moment before answering. "Come on, Sarah, I was dropping you off at the train station and thinking it was likely that I'd never see you again. So why would I suddenly mention an ugly old rumour like that? What kind of a send-off would that have been?"

"I guess you're right. It probably would have been in poor taste." She admitted with a timid shrug.

* * *

Seven chimes from the old Journal office clock reminded Sarah that she lost track of time again. She had been perusing the remaining archives but had to meet Shiny at the high school in less than an hour. She hadn't yet dressed for the occasion or figured out how she would get there. She rushed back to the hotel, freshened up, then changed out of her jeans and into a little black suit.

After standing outside for five minutes hoping for a cab to pull up, she had no alternative but to go back inside and ask Mr. Reynolds to call one for her.

"Can't," he smugly replied. "All our cabs are droppin' their loads off in Brockville for the big hockey game tonight. They need the ride so they can get piss drunk after the game and not have to worry about the cops. The drivers oughta be back in about a half-hour, and since you city-folk won't walk nowhere anyhow, I figure you'll be waitin' right here."

"You couldn't be more wrong!"

She turned on her heel and stomped out the door. The upside to her anger was the heat it engendered in her. It was the fuel she needed to set out on the long walk on a chilly night.

She hurried past the landmarks of her childhood, but the closer she got to the school, the further removed she was from the welcoming streets and cozy houses. The comforting clamour of barking dogs and playful children had disappeared. A bleak darkness enveloped her as hungry, black clouds slowly consumed the trillions of stars that flickered in the night sky.

The biting cold of autumn challenged every breath, forcing her to slowly lumber to a halt. Suddenly, like a St. Bernard in a blizzard, a taxi light appeared in the distance. With an outstretched arm, Sarah stepped into the lane, forcing the car to come to an abrupt stop. As she folded herself inside, she caught a whiff of the stale smoke that seemed woven into the upholstery. The croaky voice of the smoking cabdriver quickly identified the source of the fusty odor.

"Where in hell do ya think ya're, lady? This ain't New York City. Do ya see anybody fightin' ya for this cab? I saw ya wave. I wanted to pick ya up, not kill ya."

"I'm sorry, but I'm in a hurry to get to the high school."

"Ya almost killed yourself to get to Prescott High? I heard o' people dyin' to get outta that school, but you're the first one willin' to die to get in."

He spotted the five-dollar bill waving at him in the rear-view mirror.

"Five bucks for six blocks?" he shook his head and laughed, "Ma'am, you must be crazy."

Any doubt of his willingness to drive her was eliminated by the centrifugal force of his U-turn that pinned her against the back seat. Her discomfort ended three minutes later, when she arrived safe and warm at her old alma mater.

A sudden self-consciousness brought a crimson blush to Sarah's cheeks as she entered the school gym. People were scattered over the area, laughing, and talking, but in the myriad of faces, no one seemed familiar. Had the town changed so much, or had the years simply stolen their identities?

She exhaled a sigh of relief when she spotted Shiny and her husband standing by the buffet. After a hasty hello, Sarah filled her plate, and just as quickly, her stomach.

Shiny was giddy with excitement. "If you're done feedin' your face, come with me. I wanna show you somethin' amazing!" She led Sarah through the crowd toward a bank of showcases proudly displaying a variety of high school artefacts.

"Okay, ya gotta see this," Shiny enthused. It was Sarah's old drum majorette baton. It had been through many incarnations of band leaders. The brass crown and tip were dented and oxidized, but still intact. The two women marvelled at the relic and reminisced over their discordant experiences in the school band.

In another showcase, Sarah spotted several copies of their old school newspaper. Across the front page of one, in old English typeface, was the banner *The Tattletale* and along the bottom of the cover, *Editor, Sarah Klein, Spring Edition.*

"Isn't it amazing how even small reminders can bring back such a huge rush of memories?" Shiny mused.

Sarah felt the crowded room suddenly grow oppressively hot. The air felt stale and milky. Beads of sweat crawled from her hairline toward her brow. In a moment of onset dread, she excused herself, pushed through the throng, and exited through a fire door into the dimly-lit student's corridor. Using the exit light in the distance as her compass, she reached the emergency door. She thrust it open and stumbled onto the back stoop.

She breathed the cool night air deeply into her lungs and stared soulfully into the dark night, surrendering to the fresh air that embraced her. By the time Shiny caught up to her, Sarah was sure she'd managed to overcome all signs of whatever initiated that strange episode.

"Do ya think it's somethin' you ate?"

Sarah shrugged. "You ate the same thing as me, so I doubt it."

"Any chance you're preggers?" Shiny mockingly whispered.

"Are you looking for another virgin birth from my people?" Sarah meekly chuckled.

"No? Then, it's definitely hot flashes kiddo. I get 'em all the time." She asserted as she folded her arms and leaned against the railing.

"Now, you've cut me to the quick!" Sarah teased. "I'd prefer to admit insanity over menopause. Besides, I thought I was done with all that stuff already."

"Well, right now, you're sweatin' like Mohammad Ali and you're whiter than Casper. Did ya drive yourself here?"

She shook her head, "Uh-uh. There were no rental cars available."

"Well then, I'm drivin' you straight back to the hotel...unless you prefer that I call an ambulance?"

"Very funny. What about Ronnie?"

"I'll come back for him. He won't even notice I'm gone." She chortled, "When the boys are talkin' football, time stands still. So, it's me, or an ambulance. You choose."

"I'm not big on social events, so if I have an excuse to leave, and in style, I consider it a bonus." She quipped.

"Okay then, let's go." Shiny pulled her car keys out of her purse, took Sarah by the elbow, and led her to the car.

As they pulled up in front of the hotel, Sarah turned to her rescuer. "Shiny, you were right. I did need the ride and I'm really grateful. I owe you."

Shiny smiled a little too confidently. "Well, my friend, since you put it that way. If you really want to pay the debt, I have an idea. I know you're planning to go to the prison with Wes. So, what do ya think if I join the adventure.? I mean, ya don't have ta decide this minute, but will ya think about it?"

Sarah smiled softly and replied. "I will, I promise. I'll think about it and let you know."

"Great. That's all I ask."

Shiny didn't realize that Sarah, who was having some anxiety over the proposed visit, would have gladly paid her to join the expedition.

Sarah eased herself out of the car, waved goodbye, rushed inside, and dragged herself up to her suite.

Subdued by exhaustion, she forfeited her nightly skin care ritual, barely managing to brush her teeth and change into pyjamas before climbing into bed.

She drifted into an abstract limbo that gnawed at her consciousness. She thrashed and whimpered in her sleep. Her heart thumped like a bass drum. She awoke and squinted at the hands on the clock. They taunted her as they imperiously pointed to 3:20 a.m.

After licking the last drop of Remy Martin from the lip of the miniature bottle, she pressed the sleep button on the radio and released an hour of therapeutic symphony.

Remy and Mozart, the perfect cure for insomnia, successfully lulled her back to sleep...and to dream:

She is in a classroom filled with neat piles of paper stacked high on short glass desks. A dozen dwarf-sized journalists scurry around the room, chattering incessantly as they collate and staple. A neon sign announces that Good Friday is on its way.

There is a dark silence. Everyone disappears.

She hurries down the hallway toward her locker. Every classroom is vacant. A giant clock face at the end of the hall shouts, "You're too late!"

She ignores an urgent need to relieve her bladder. Her locker pops open. She pulls on her coat, jams her books into her bag, hoists it onto her back, and shuffles toward the flashing red exit sign. As she approaches the endless hallway, the exit light dims. She sees the door. She barely touches it. It flies open.

She stumbles onto the landing and into the biting cold. A blue haze of smoke hovers above, while under the stairs, a gang of Neanderthals stand huddled together, puffing on Export A's.

With leaden feet, Sarah plods down the steps and past the smoking, cursing pack.

"Why the hell did ya let the fuckin' Jew git past ya?" one yells.

She quickens her step.

A cacophony of croaking voices shout:

"Hey kike!"

"Let's see how you like hangin' from a cross."

"Yer gonna pay for killin' Jesus!"

She ducks under an arch of faded evergreens that form a prickly portal to the overpass. She hangs on to her gaping school bag as she rolls down an embankment. There is nothing at the bottom but a giant cement pipe. She watches as the frigid water rushes through the pipe, dragging with it chunks of ice and all manner of trash. She crawls inside the bleak, frozen refuge.

Sarah awoke abruptly. Her hair and bedclothes were drenched with perspiration, yet she was chilled to the bone. She wanted desperately to go back to her dream and find out where it would take her, but sleep eluded her. With a drumming heart and a dry mouth, she snapped on the light, picked up her notebook, and with pen in shaky hands, she clenched her teeth and did her best to write down every detail of the dream she could recall.

* * *

Showered and dressed, Sarah reached into her closet for a jacket, a skirt, and a pair of slacks. She anxiously snipped off buttons and ripped out hems before folding the items and placing them in a shopping bag. She took one sip of the dreadful in-room instant coffee she'd prepared, then, with briefcase in one hand and shopping bag in the other, she headed purposefully up Main Street.

From the moment she entered the seamstress's home, Sarah felt obliged to fill the silence with an interminable monologue. The dressmaker quietly measured and pinned while Sarah's curiosity mushroomed.

"You have a lovely home. Have you always lived here? I'm so glad you had time for me. I can't sew a stitch. Neither could my mother. Did yours sew? Oh, I imagine that's where you learned your trade?"

Some mundane questions, Eleanor answered with a nod, a shake of the head, or a deferential smile, and some, she ignored.

"So, when shall I pick everything up?"

"Uh, tomorrow." Was the slow and timid reply.

It was brief but Sarah welcomed the sound of her voice.

The seamstress walked her client to the door, opened it, and handed over a business card imprinted with a phone number and the words *Eleanor Miller, Seamstress*.

Sarah smiled. "Thank you, Eleanor." She placed the card in her purse. "I'll see you tomorrow." Sarah stepped out, turned, and waved. "Bye for now."

"Yes...bye for now." Eleanor waved as she slowly closed the door.

* * *

Sarah stepped up to the reception desk. "Hi Joannie, it's nice to see you again. Do you think Richard might have a minute for me?"

"Hi there, I heard you were back. Have a seat and I'll check."

After a brief, muffled exchange on the phone, Richard stepped out of his office looking every bit the polished lawyer.

"Well, hello again." Richard said as he bent over and offered his hand, which Sarah graciously shook.

"I was beginning to think you'd given up, but it's good that you haven't." He seemed in very good spirits.

"I just have one question for you." She stated as she rose from her seat with her briefcase in hand, and walked toward the reception desk.

"Okay, ask away. I'm sure I can handle even two questions." He punctuated his assertion with a patronizing half-smile.

Sarah opened her briefcase, took out the manila envelope, and spread the photos across the desk. Richard briefly scanned them, gathered them up and handed them back.

"I think Earl got the feeling he didn't leave you with a very good impression, so I'm guessing he wanted you to see a different side of him." Richard's demeanor seemed far more confident and relaxed than at their previous meeting.

"But Mrs. Berman, as luck would have it, Earl's in my office, so you can ask him yourself. Please come in."

With some reluctance, Sarah followed Richard inside. Seated in the comfy chair she had chosen at her last meeting, sat the lawyer's client who offered a hand in greeting. Sarah obliged while holding back a full-body shudder.

"Please Mrs. Berman, have a seat." Richard offered.

"I'm good standing, thank you. May I lay out the photos on your desk?"

"Sure." He turned to his client, "Earl, Mrs. Berman has some photos she'd like to show you and wants to know why you felt they were important."

Earl seemed more laid back as well. "No problem. Lay 'em down so I can see 'em and remember."

As Richard settled in his office chair, Sarah methodically placed the photos on the desk as Earl White peered over her shoulder, too close for her comfort.

"Oh yeah, sure. I had them pictures taken right after I got accused," Earl crowed with a smug twisted grin. "I wanted to show, I'm a respected member of the community. Perry Mason said on TV, one picture's better than a hundred eyewitnesses."

With that, he strutted back to the comfy chair, and plopped down. Sarah remained standing. She had learned in her journalism course that stature could be a useful power play when interviewing someone who was perhaps 5'6" but believed he was 6'5".

She conducted the interview as she gathered up the photos and returned them to the manila envelope. "Mr. White, the word is that you're an astute businessman, but I've been wondering: if your cousin Zane is of less than average intelligence, how could he outsmart you? I mean, crimes were being committed on your property and you really had no idea?"

Earl White's heavy, acrid breath wafted through the room. His grey pallor turned purplish, and his hands clenched the arms of the chair as he lunged forward in the seat. "I did ya a favour, gettin' them copies to ya and now yer questionin' my smarts? Who in hell do ya think yer talkin' to? I'm a big fuckin' deal. I'm not just named Earl. Around these parts, they see me like an Earl or a Duke or somethin'! And you? You're just some half-assed wannabe writer that ain't good enough for a city job, so they sent you off to the boonies ta get rid o' ya." While Sarah was immobilized into stunned silence, Richard burst from his chair like a bottle rocket. He steadied himself and leaned across the desk panting. "Earl...you owe...Mrs. Berman...an apology!"

"N-no apology necessary." She stammered, relieved to hear the sound of her own voice.

"No. He's right. Ma'am. I apologize. I shouldn'ta let myself get outta control like that. It's just been real hard bein' accused...an' it's been real tough on my wife. I'll be as quiet as a pussycat now. You go ahead and ask any questions ya need ta, Mrs. Berman."

Richard sat down and nervously fiddled with a paper clip.

Sarah stifled her contempt and forged ahead as if the encounter had never happened. "Okay then, Mr. White. Thank you. At our last meeting, Mr. McCall said he'd asked you to bring him your gas receipt, restaurant charge slip, and bowling score cards from the night they arrested the others, but you hadn't done so. He said they were needed to show that you couldn't have been where the witnesses said you were. I was wondering if you'd gathered that information for him yet."

"Jes-sus Char-ist!" The shake of his head and the elongated hissing sound as he articulated those two words, was evidence that Sarah had once again hit a nerve. "What the hell am I paying Dick and his fancy-ass city lawyer for, if I'm supposed to do all the work?"

Richard tossed the paper clip on the desk, sat forward, and through gritted teeth, suggested a cynical option. "Earl, I can hire you a private detective from the city, at a hundred and fifty bucks an hour, to get the info. Just give me your signed approval and I'll make the call."

The wall of tension thickened with each silent second that ticked by. Sarah finally cut through it. "Well, I have to get going. But to be honest, Mr. White, if I might suggest; it seems worth it to get Richard the stuff he's asked for, especially if it'll only take a couple of phone calls?"

"It would be helpful, Earl," Richard skittishly added as nubbins of sweat beaded on his upper lip.

The client growled. "Ya want the receipts? I'll get ya the fuckin' receipts."

Sarah picked up her briefcase, lifted the envelope from the desk and headed for the exit. Richard quickly followed, they shook hands in his doorway and smiled feebly at each other.

Sarah offered a nod of goodbye, toward Earl White as she exited the office. Richard walked with her to the front door.

"Let me know how it works out, Mr. McCall."

"He's not usually like this, Sarah. I'm sure you can imagine. It's the terrible stress of these unfounded accusations. I hope you'll be fair to him in the *Sun-Times*."

Sarah didn't dare mention that she still had no assignment from the *Sun-Times* or even the *Sentinel*.

CHAPTER FIVE

The inky outline of the looming structure ahead, framed by an ominous grey sky, resembled an Etch-a-Sketch drawing. As the car inched closer, the chain links and barbed wire surrounding the monstrous cement vault disproved any similarities to kitsch art.

The humour that had accompanied Sarah, Shiny, and Wesley on their road trip to the Kingston Penitentiary darkened as the glutinous shadows of the towering edifice sucked all light from the environment. A sober silence fell on the visiting trio as they drove through the prison's sentry points. Once the car reached the other side of the gate, a harsh twang reverberated through Sarah's limbs as a gigantic iron door slammed and bolted behind them. Panic grew like a bacterial culture, but Sarah concentrated on appearing calm while they parked and entered the prison's reception area.

That morning on the phone, Sister Catherine Grace had warned her: "Prisoners can smell fear, Sarah, and they use it to unnerve you for their own warped entertainment. Don't let it get to you. They got to me on my first visit, but I persevered, and now, it's okay. So, good luck, and I'll meet you inside."

The three visitors were led into a cold, concrete waiting area. The space echoed with the droning voices of abject characters whose lives had been inevitably altered by the prisoner that each came to see. At one end of the room, a sullen-faced little boy gnawed at his fingernails while his mother stared vacuously at the crimson exit sign. The deluge of sadness that engulfed the waiting room caused Sarah to recall the senior sister's message to her on the train: "Keep in mind that, even though it's the prisoner who's incarcerated, their loved ones also suffer a severe and enduring punishment." Her reflection was jarred by a shrill, discomfiting clang as a guard entered. Sarah's heart raced as she nervously anticipated his instructions. Dispassionately, the guard called out the name Boyd, and Sarah's anxiety was temporarily neutralized. She scanned the myriad of waiting faces and identified Boyd's visitors by the energy that spontaneously transformed the sullen little nail-biter and his despondent mother, who jumped to their feet and eagerly fell in line behind the guard.

There was no such euphoria the next time the guard appeared. "Fergusson," he growled.

The trio rose as Sister Catherine Grace stepped out from behind the guard to greet them. As the four visitors stood in line ready to be led forward, the jailer snorted and barked, "Only two allowed."

"Please choose Wes," Shiny urged. "Believe me when I say that this is as close as I wanna be."

"You two go ahead. I'll stay here and wait with your friend," the sister proposed.

"I'm really good with that idea," Shiny agreed.

"Are you sure you shouldn't be there with us, Sister?" Sarah anxiously queried, hoping to change the nun's mind.

"I think you'll be able to speak more openly without a cross hanging over your head," Sister Catherine mused. "Go on. I'll be right here." The nun waved her on, then closed her eyes for a moment, in what Sarah hoped was a prayer of good luck.

"Okay. Well, uh...thanks then, Sister Catherine."

Sarah and Wesley followed the guard along the hollow corridor.

In spite of Sarah's desperation to tread softly, the click of her high heels echoed with every step. She looked down in envy at the silent rubber soles that Wesley wisely sported, and yearned for her sneakers.

They were led into a room with a long counter separated by partitions at six-foot intervals, creating cubicles for the visitors. Also separating visitors from prisoners were Plexiglass dividers with chrome microphones set into them, resembling old-fashioned bank tellers' cages.

"Ya got fifteen minutes." The guard growled.

Sarah and Wes stood stark still, fearful that any move could be the wrong move.

"Hey, you two? Sit down! Right there, on them orange chairs." The guard barked. The visitors turned away from the partition and cringed as their eyes settled on the cold, rigid plastic chairs. The guard added with a wry smirk: "Get comfy, I'll be back to get ya in fifteen minutes." With that, he stalked away.

Sarah sat stiffly, opened her notepad, and showed Wes her list of questions. She waited anxiously for suggestions, but with his pat of her hand, he offered the approval she needed.

"Sarah, this is your interview. If you need me, I'll step in. Otherwise, I'm a bystander, okay?" He punctuated his assurance with a comforting smile.

She took a deep, affirming breath, then replied. "Okay."

The two visitors looked up as an eerie shadow appeared on the other side of the cage, A light suddenly clicked on above the partition. As the prisoner became visible, Sarah sensed that the limits of her fortitude were about to be severely tested.

Zane Fergusson's barren head sported tufts of yellowish fibre and his heavily- scabbed and pock-marked skin radiated a mealy taint. As he spoke, his thin, crusty lips revealed a cavern of slime and rot reminiscent of the maggot-infested carcasses she'd recently witnessed on the shores of the St. Lawrence.

Sarah surreptitiously reached out and touched the plexiglass wall to confirm it was a reliable barrier. Within seconds of their meeting, Zane Fergusson burped, hacked, and passed gas with abandon.

Sarah ignored the "gestures" by concentrating on her notepad and formally beginning the interview. She spoke loudly and toward the microphone. "Mr. Fergusson, why did you ask for this interview?"

"That nun says you was interested in Earl's story an' I figured I could help ya out. We can start by ya callin' me Zane."

"All right, Zane," she agreed. With her eyes still downcast, she turned to her notes. "What light can you shed on Mr. White's case?"

"M-mi-st-er White?" he spat out the words like tainted food. "Just goes to show, if ya got money, any piece o' shit can cover hisself in gold, and no matter how bad he stinks, they'll tell themselves it's perfume and call 'im *mister*. That motherfucker should be in here instead of me."

Sarah clenched her teeth trying hard to heed the nun's warning about not letting Zane get to her.

"But, Zane, he wasn't caught with his pants down, was he? I know you're the one locked up in here, but who did those terrible things to your kids?"

"They was my fuckin' kids. And if I'm feedin' 'em and dressin' 'em and givin' 'em a roof over their heads, the government should stay the hell outta my private business. They wasn't doin' nothin' they didn't wanna do. They got lots o' attention, and they was treated damn good, too. They weren't bein' beat or nothin', and they was happy makin' a whole bunch o' other people happy."

Sarah struggled to unlock her jaw to articulate a word...any word. Her head was spinning, and nausea began to overtake her. Wes spotted the signs and broke the silence.

"Was your wife happy?"

"As a pig in shit...and if she says different, then she's a lyin' bitch." He shouted as he threw a fake punch toward the barrier.

"While we could sit here all day listening to your heartwarming story about your close-knit family, our time's limited, so please just answer Mrs. Berman's questions."

Sarah nodded a thank you toward Wes, cleared her throat and continued.

"Mr. Fergusson...Zane...you asked for this meeting, and I'm just trying to understand why?"

"Hah. Simple. Me an my buddies in here are upset that ya don't wanna write about us. We got all the time in the world to give ya a real good story, but ya wanna go an' write about Earl. That really pisses us off, 'cause he's nothin' but a rich con man who'll convince ya that he's a fuckin' saint."

"Okay. Then let me ask you this, Mr. Fergusson. Do you have any proof that Earl White was involved in your, um, enterprise?"

"Yup." The convict replied with an irritating smirk.

"The clock's ticking," Wes muttered as he tapped the face of his watch.

Sarah continued. "Is his attorney aware of this evidence?"

"You mean that asshole, McCall? Hah!" Zane guffawed like an ass. "We wrote that turd and told 'im we was gonna testify that Earl should be right here with us, and he says to us that it's bullshit and no jury's ever gonna take our word over an upstandin' citizen like Earl. What the prick meant was Earl's his big cash cow and he don't wanna see him goin' to prison." Zane hacked and spit into his hand. "Then we told the crown lawyer, another big prick, and he says, 'I'm a busy man. I can't waste time drivin' out there so you assholes can dick me around. Besides,' he says, 'who's gonna believe a bunch o' dumb perverts anyway?'" With that, he wiped his spit on his shirt.

Sarah snapped the notebook shut with a huff. "I'm wasting my time here, Mr. Fergusson. Either tell me something that makes this trip worth my while, or I'm out of here." She rose and opened her briefcase. Zane seemed clearly taken aback.

"Wait. Wait a minute. I'll give ya somethin'." He suddenly sounded desperate. Again, Sarah's power play of standing while questioning seemed to be working. "I'm waiting."

"Okay, ask Earl how much I paid 'im every month for the rent on that shithole he called a farm. Ask 'im and see what he says."

"How is that relevant?"

"Huh," he smiled evilly, "well if I ain't got a job and I'm payin' him big bucks for rent, then where did he think I got the money he didn't mind takin'?"

"That hardly makes him complicit."

"What the fuck does coplitsit mean?"

"Complicit. It means, a partner in crime."

"Earl's no fuckin' partner. He's the big boss. I'm tellin' ya, I ain't got no contracts to show ya, but I'm tellin' ya, he was encouragin' us to run this business with his blessin'. That makes him complitsit."

"So the bottom line here is that you have no hard evidence." She sneered, then turned toward Wes. "Let's go, Wes." He heard her, but remained seated.

"Hold on a minute, Lady. We ain't got no pictures o' Earl diddlin' the kids, if that's what yer lookin' fer. And we ain't got a condom full o' Earl's spunk or nothin' like that, but there's stuff to be found and a smart reporter'd find it."

Sarah spoke clearly and directly into the microphone: "I came all the way from Toronto because you claimed you had something useful to tell me. I've heard nothing useful. You've just wasted my time."

He slammed his fist down. "You wasted my time, goddammit! We told Sister Catherine to bring ya out here 'cause we thought we was doin' ya a favour, but yer too fuckin' green for the job."

"You've been jerking Sister Catherine Grace around for your entertainment, but you're damn well not gonna jerk me around."

He burst into a lascivious cackle. "Hey, no call for that kind o' language, Ma'am. Sister Catherine's gonna be so disappointed in you. Listen, I don't get a lot o' pretty women droppin' by, so I'm happy to have ya come and visit, but if ya want the story, go listen to what my wife says in court and then come back."

"Mr. Fergusson, I won't be coming back."

A sardonic grimace slowly loosened his clenched mouth. "Oh, look how you're gettin' yerself all worked up. The thing is, we gotta do this when we're all ready."

"Well, when you're ready, I'll be gone."

The prisoner leaned into the partition and whispered; "Hey, Mrs. Berman...do ya think the sister would say a prayer fer me?"

"Why don't you ask her?" she snarled.

"Well, I'm a bit shy with the nuns, ya know, so how's about I tell you the prayer and you ask her to say it?"

Curiosity got the better of her and she acquiesced. "Go ahead."

"Okay. I'd ask us all ta join hands, but as ya can see, that's impossible. So here it is: Dear Jesus, it ain't nothin' personal, we just wanna see our mother-fuckin' cousin in here so's we can show him how we feel about him. And we'd really appreciate if ya can get Earl's dumb-assed lawyers run over by a Mack truck. Amen."

"Is this a damned game to you?" She roared.

"It ain't no game, but if yer gonna write about him bein' an innocent victim and bein' set up and all that kind o' shit, yer just gonna be influencin' the fuckin' jury so they end up lettin' him go."

"So far, he hasn't even been indicted, and as far as I'm concerned, if he's innocent, then he should be free; and I have no control over that no matter what I write."

The prisoner pushed himself to a standing position and screeched into the microphone: "The other guys said you'd be nothin' but a newspaper whore that any asshole can buy, but I said I'd give ya the chance 'cause o' the nun. I asked her to bring ya here, but now I see yer nothin' but the whore they said you was!"

"We're done! Guard!" Wesley hollered as he rose from his seat. The guard quickly appeared.

"Come back when ya change yer mind, Babe." He grabbed his crotch. "If you get horny, ya know where ta find me." The prisoner's odious cackle merged with Wes's huffing and the clacking of Sarah's heels along the endless hallway.

* * *

The duo returned to the waiting area, clearly showing signs of distress. They did their best to offer Shiny and the nun a sanitized version of the meeting; but both listeners were still shocked.

Sister Catherine was devastated. "Sarah, when I told Zane that a journalist was interested in Earl's story, he said he wanted to share some important information that wasn't getting out there. He assured me that it would serve both parties' interests. I would never have set this up if I'd known he only wanted to play cat and mouse with you. I'm so sorry."

Sarah shook her head. "Not at all. I assure you, Sister Catherine, it won't scar me for life. It was my first visit to a prison, and my first prison lesson is that I have to toughen up. I had about six questions ready to ask him, and I barely got to ask two...but I did get answers to questions I never would've thought to ask. I also learned that if I'm going to succeed, I'm gonna have to get used to dealing with others like him, no matter how reprehensible they might be."

"Why would you want to get used to it?" Shiny queried. "Forget the prisoners. I was a nervous wreck sitting here just looking at the visitors."

"Oh, no, no, no!" The nun interjected. "Some of the inmates are very dear, but I admit, some are truly a challenge. And with that, I must go and finish my rounds. One thing I've learned is that you don't keep prisoners waiting or they can get very testy. I've had to avoid being hit by flying paperbacks, and I've wiped spittle off my habit more than a few times."

"It takes a strong constitution and commitment to do what you do, Sister Catherine. I wouldn't last a week, but I really appreciate you for setting this up for me. Who knows what might come of it?" Sarah extended her hand, and the nun accepted graciously.

"That's true. We never know what God has planned for us, do we? Please stay in touch, Sarah."

"I will for sure."

The nun shook hands with Wes and Shiny, then smiled and strutted off with the guard.

* * *

Wesley was uncharacteristically silent as the trio strode toward Shiny's car. They all piled in, Wes in the front with the driver, and Sarah opting for the back seat.

The hush continued as they passed through the final gate that marked their re-entry into a better world.

"Hey Wes, you've been awfully quiet," Sarah noted. "What's up?"

"Small town people are gossip junkies, am I right, Shiny?" Wesley asked.

"Absolutely," she confirmed. "Most Prescott folks would prefer a juicy coffee klatch to a TV soap opera."

He tightened his lips and scrunched up his face. "Exactly! And that's the point that's causing me concern. The facts and scope of this crime unnerved this entire town for two years, and the fallout radiated for miles. During all that time, these town folks, with their strong sense of family values and morality were being choked by this disgusting crime; and until today, I'd never heard the actual voice of that perversity."

He stared out the window in sad silence. After a few minutes, he turned to face Sarah in the back seat. It was clear that something was deeply affecting him, yet he struggled to say what was on his mind.

"Wes, what's going on? Come on, you can't look like a dejected puppy and then not fess up." Sarah gently prodded.

He nodded. "You're right, Sarah. Look, I never covered the original trial. It was nine miles away, and I was too old, too disgusted, or maybe just too lazy to drive there every day, so I assigned it to an old freelancer buddy who lives near the Brockville courthouse; and across from a local bar where he spends way too much of his time. Now, after meeting Zane, I really wish I'd covered it myself."

"Great! Perfect even," Sarah's response became animated. "If you need redemption, then you can come and help me dig deeper."

He offered a wry smile that turned into a chuckle. "You think that dragging an octogenarian around for the next few days will make your investigation easier?" Wesley asked.

"Absolutely! Much easier," Sarah insisted.

* * *

Shiny stopped her car in front of the Journal office. Sarah jumped out and held the door open for Wesley. He ambled out of the car, offered a glib two-finger salute, and headed into the Journal office. Sarah leaned toward the open door. "Thanks for driving, Shiny. I sure hope our little visit doesn't give you nightmares, although I hold out no such hope for myself. I'm sure I won't get a wink of sleep tonight."

Shiny smiled, shook her head, and offered a playful grimace. "Yeah, well, if I don't get any sleep and end up pouring coffee on your eggs tomorrow, you'll know why." With that, Sarah snickered, waved, and shut the car door.

* * *

On the walk back to the hotel, Sarah stopped by the dressmaker's shop. She rapped tentatively on the door, which was quickly opened by the seamstress who offered a polite, "Hello."

"I didn't mean to rush you, Eleanor. I was just passing by and thought, 'if my things were ready, I might as well pick them up on my way home.' But I can come back." Sarah proposed.

Eleanor smiled warmly and invited her in. "Please have a seat."

Sarah obliged and sat on the antique settee by the front window. "They're all ready for you. Please check them over to make sure you're satisfied." With that Eleanor lifted the items out of the shopping bag and placed each one on the seat beside her client.

"Oh, okay. Thank you." Sarah obediently held up each piece and gratuitously oohed and aahed over it. As Sarah finished fawning over each item, Eleanor took the article, folded it, and carefully returned it to the shopping bag. "You did a great job, Eleanor. Everything looks perfect."

"Thank you," the dressmaker replied as she blushed and lowered her eyes.

In a moment of uncomfortable silence, Sarah began digging through her purse to retrieve her wallet. "Now, to business; how much do I owe you?"

"Is twelve dollars all right?" Eleanor asked.

Sarah handed her a ten and a five-dollar bill. "Eleanor, in Toronto, they'd charge twelve dollars to sew on a button."

The seamstress countered with a grin. "Then aren't you glad you brought your repairs with you?" She reached into her apron pocket and retrieved the three dollars difference, which she handed to Sarah.

Sarah thought about not accepting the change; but then, figuring that it might be an insult to offer a 'tip,' she accepted it with a smile.

"You know, Eleanor, I used to live in this town? I think we went to school together...different grades, but..."

"Yes, it would be different grades, because I'm certain you're younger than me."

"Maybe a year or two at best. It's strange how important it is when you're a teenager and how little it matters after you pass forty, huh?"

"That's true enough...or even after fifty," Eleanor added with a twinkle in her eye.

"You know, I was having breakfast and reminiscing with Shiny Dumas the other day, and I had this awesome memory of the summer you rescued

Anna Daniels and me from utter disaster when a bunch of boys were trying to swarm us. You brought us back to your place and your mom gave us cookies and Kool-Aid. God, that was such a great day."

Eleanor smiled. "Of course, I remember that day. Do you also remember another day, you were here, and my mother was having trouble fitting a wedding gown on a mannequin, so she insisted I put it on?" She paused for a second. "Of course, you wouldn't remember, but I remember, because when I refused to do it, you volunteered." Eleanor snickered, masking her mouth with her hand.

"Well, that was darn nice of me." Sarah replied with a grin and a toss of her hair.

"It might have been, except no one wanted to tell you that you were about five sizes too small." Eleanor snickered again, but this time with no attempt to hide it.

"Too small? Uh-uh, with an ironing-board chest is what you mean," Sarah laughingly proclaimed.

"Yeah, it's true. That was the part no one wanted to mention. But since Anna was the perfect size, my mother suggested she put the dress on and you could offer your opinion, like a fashion critic."

"See! You could buy me with a compliment. I haven't changed much, Eleanor." Sarah grinned and wiggled into a more comfortable sitting position. It appeared to Sarah that the solid dividing wall she'd encountered on first meeting Eleanor was now crumbling. She leaned forward and surprised herself at what she unexpectedly proposed. "Hey Eleanor, I don't know how long I'll be in town, but I'd love to have dinner with you sometime...if you're up for it, I mean. The food's pretty good at the O'Brien. What do you think?"

After a brief lull, Eleanor replied, "That's kind of you. Thank you, I'll think about it." Eleanor stood up and handed the shopping bag to Sarah, who wasn't quite ready to give up.

"How about tonight?" She asked as she confidently rose from her seat.

The dressmaker turned toward her front door. "Oh, I couldn't tonight; I have a lot of work to finish up."

Sarah tried to hide her disappointment. "Okay then, maybe tomorrow or whenever you feel you're free."

"Sure...maybe, sometime." Eleanor offered.

Sarah thanked her and left.

* * *

Wandering along the edge of Kelly's Beach, Sarah was drawn to The Old Willow landmark. Over many decades, the story of that old stump had grown more mythical with each telling until it took root as a town legend.

The tale began: *One autumn night in the fifties, a group of teens was partying around a huge bonfire at the shore when the sky exploded in a cacophony of thunder and flares of lightning. The revellers panicked and hightailed it for home, abandoning the bonfire. Its blazing sparks tripped swiftly across the sand while compounding raindrops raced them to their* destination. But the torrential rain came too late. The rabid flames were already biting at the supporting posts of the gazebo, threatening its collapse.

Next door, inside the wooden house, a young mother rushed into her baby's room to comfort the frightened infant. She froze in place as she witnessed the blaze cannibalizing the gazebo just inches from her window. Then, in a mystical instant, a blade of jagged lightning pierced the heart of the old willow, felling the venerable giant with its millions of rain-drenched leaves, onto the burning gazebo, and suffocating the flames like a thick, wet blanket.

The remaining stump was wide enough to seat three sumo wrestlers. Instead of destroying it, the town council had it sanded and lacquered, and then mounted a brass plaque on it to honour the old willow tree that saved the mother and child.

"In Honour of the Heroic Old Willow--1953."

As Sarah scanned the plaque, she noticed at the bottom, was an additional narrow, brass plate with the phrase: *Remembering DAP*. She couldn't remember seeing those words before.

* * *

Stopping by Mr. Reynolds' desk each day to ask, "Is my television fixed yet?" was becoming a sadistic ritual for Sarah. Today, she chose to forego the aggravation, and trudged up the stairs to face another remoteless evening. She turned on the radio, removed her papers from her briefcase, and tried to focus on her notes.

As darkness set in, Sarah spotted the flashing red message light.

There were two phone messages. The first was from Mitch, letting her know that there was an envelope at the desk from Earl White. The second was from Earl White with the same message.

Sarah called to the front desk, and within minutes, the envelope was slipped under her door. It contained credit slips from Earl White's account, a receipt from the Brockville bowling alley, and a handwritten note that simply stated: *Now you seen the stuff and you can take it to McCall yourself.*

E. O. White

"What the hell? Why would he send this information to me, instead of his lawyer?" She muttered aloud. However, she wasn't about to ignore the gift. She carefully inspected the information before leaving a message for Wesley, telling him about the delivery from Earl White, and asking permission to use his photocopier the next day.

* * *

Through a blast of steam, a wet naked Sarah emerged from the bathroom, snapped off the rock and roll, and grabbed up the ringing phone.

"Good mornin', Sarah," Wesley cheerily began. "Yeah, you can photocopy that Earl White stuff here, but there's a cost."

"No problem, I can pay for the copies."

"The copies are free. The price is, you have to come to dinner on Sunday."

"You cook?" she chuckled.

"Not me, but my daughter-in-law's pretty good, if you like all that healthy tofu and seeds crap." There was silence. "I'm kidding. She's a great cook and Hartley feels they didn't get to really talk to you at their fundraiser. They think you'd be an interesting dinner guest, so say yes and I'll be a hero, and you'll have your photocopies."

"If I say yes, then it's only fair that I take you to lunch today. Agreed?"

"Sure, but can we make it fish and chips and a root beer float?"

"Okay, fish Friday a la mode it is."

* * *

Passing Kelly's Beach after their lunch, Sarah paused at the stump. "Wes, what does '*Remembering DAP*' mean? I don't recall ever seeing it before."

"It was engraved in memory of a terrific young swimmer who drowned trying to cross the St. Lawrence, back in the fifties." He pensively replied.

"He couldn't have been that terrific if he drowned." She sassed.

"'He' was a 'she', and I had no idea you were such a cynic. But now I know why I like you so much." He joshed as he shook his head.

Sarah gave Wes a friendly shoulder punch in playful retaliation before they veered off in separate directions.

After dropping the originals at Richard's office, Sarah took her photocopies back to the hotel, resigned to the probability that she'd be holed up for a bleak weekend.

A note under her door caught her interest:
Good news, Mrs. Berman. Your TV is working. Check it out.

Have a good weekend.
Mitch

Sarah was bubbling with anticipation and hope that Mitch wouldn't be added to her growing list of disappointments. She pressed the remote, and there it was: a full colour screen of glorious companionship. When she was done reviewing her notes and musing over her strange week, she could just hunker down and watch TV to her heart's delight.

* * *

By the time she had washed up and changed into her sweats, her dinner was being rolled in on a nicely decked-out dinner cart. With flair, Mitch poured her a glass of ice water and uncovered her salad. Before exiting, he placed a card and a chocolate mint by the phone.

Sarah was delighted by the special attention. "Thank you again Mitch for the TV, the lovely dinner service, and your thoughtfulness. By the way, did you give your mom my regards?" She inquired.

He blushed and stammered a bit before finally delivering his message. "You're very welcome. And um...yes, I did give her the message. And she would really love to get together with you, if you have any time, that is. Enjoy your meal and let me know when you're done, and I'll come and get the cart." He nodded politely.

"Great, Thanks again, Mitch."

He began to head for the door but stopped mid-step. "Oh also, I left my mom's number by the phone for you just in case."

She smiled and nodded.

* * *

Sarah tuned into *Jeopardy* while she dined.

As the show ended, Sarah muted the sound, picked up the phone, and made a call.

"Hi, Eleanor, this is Sarah, I know you're pretty busy, but I was wondering if you would do me a huge favour and have lunch with me tomorrow..."

An ominous silence prevailed for a few uncomfortable seconds.

"You will? That's great!" Sarah's face was aglow over her success at winning the standoff. "Oh thanks, Eleanor, I'd love to come to you for lunch another time, but believe it or not, tomorrow's going to be a warmish, sunny day, so if you don't object, this time I'd like to arrange a picnic lunch for us..." She shook her head. "No, we'll stay close to your house, I promise. How about at one? Noon is better? Okay, good...Yes, if you could bring two chairs and a tablecloth that'd be great. I didn't happen to bring any from Toronto," Sarah joked. "Oh sure, you absolutely can bring the dessert! Thanks so much! I'll see you tomorrow at noon."

CHAPTER SIX

"Hi Eleanor." Sarah warmly greeted her picnic guest and stepped jauntily into her vestibule. "Are we all set? Chairs, tablecloth, and that dessert you kindly offered?"

"I have the cloth and the chairs, but I thought it would be easier to have dessert here...after...if that's all right with you?"

"Is that pie I smell?" Sarah inhaled deeply with her hand over her heart in feigned ecstasy.

"Uh-huh, apple. I just took it out of the oven," Eleanor coyly confessed. "So, it's too hot to bring along."

"Yum. Apple pie, here? That'll be perfect. Thanks."

Eleanor smiled with relief. "I guess we have everything, then."

With that, they each picked up a chair, grabbed a handle of the picnic basket, and strutted across the street to Kelly's Beach.

Eleanor threw the chequered cloth over the old wooden stump and Sarah laid out the BBQ chicken, corn on the cob, and potato salad prepared by the O'Brien's chef.

While they ate, Sarah plied her guest with her scanty recollections of Prescott. Her hope was that Eleanor might share hers and satisfy some of Sarah's curiosity about her, but Eleanor seemed content to remain an audience for Sarah's exuberant storytelling. However, as time ticked by, her tightly-wound demeanour slowly unraveled like a loose thread on a woollen muffler.

The chit-chat sashayed from best authors and musicians to favourite TV shows. Hearing that *Murphy Brown* was Eleanor's favourite television show was Prozac to Sarah's angst. As the women recalled snippets of Murphy's cosmopolitan comedy, Sarah giddily revealed a secret lust. "I'll bet you wouldn't know to look at me now in my sweats and jeans, but next to delicious food, my favourite vice is fashion. I would star in a TV show like that just for the wardrobe. They wouldn't even have to pay me."

"Me either," Eleanor agreed. "But I don't want to wear the clothes, I want to design them. My fantasy would be to have a celebrity wear one of *my* designs on TV."

"Really? Well, the first step to fulfilling a fantasy is believing you can." Sarah punctuated her aphorism with a nod.

"Yes, well, that's where the fantasy ends then." Eleanor shrugged. "Some things are best left to the imagination, so you don't have to face the reality of failure."

"That's silly. since you're a dressmaker, that's already a great beginning. I mean, I couldn't have that dream because, as you noticed, I can't even sew on a button. So, that fantasy is all yours."

A momentary silence was broken with a sudden rush of words. "Sarah, would you ever want to see my stuff? I mean if you're interested." Eleanor blurted.

"Your stuff?" Sarah cocked her head in bewilderment. "Sorry, Eleanor, maybe I'm a bit slow, but I'm not sure what 'stuff' you're talking about?"

"Oh. Uh, my design collection."

"You mean design, as in fashion design?" Sarah's question was met with excited nodding. "When you say collection...do you mean a dress or two?"

"No. I've actually finished twenty-nine pieces, so far." By now, Eleanor was bubbling with excitement while Sarah was left awed and confused.

"Holy crap, that's amazing! Who are they for?"

She shrugged. "I don't know...myself, I guess. I've been designing clothes on paper for years. I love to read, and I collect books on design and cooking. That's how I learned; in case you were wondering. I've figured out how to do a lot of things from books, and from television, too. I videotape my favourite shows so I can study the fashions. But last winter, I started to build actual samples using the best fabrics I could find. I can show them to you when we go back if you want?"

"Really? If I want?" Without pause, Sarah stuffed the picnic remains into the basket, folded the chairs, and all but jogged back to the little Cape Cod house with Eleanor by her side.

The chairs and basket were hastily abandoned inside the entrance and jackets were tossed on the settee by the front window. Eleanor motioned Sarah to follow as she led her down the hallway to a dark panelled door.

"Look Sarah, before we do this, I want you to know, I've never shown my stuff to anyone, so if I'm putting you on the spot, please say so and we'll just forget it."

"Are you kidding? I can't wait!" Sarah clapped her hands in delight and jumped an inch or two off the floor.

Peering through the opening, Sarah could see only blackness.

"Stay here a minute. I have to go and turn on the light," She started down the groaning staircase into a dark cavern while her guest waited on the landing. A brisk snap cued a dim glow that skulked its way up the stairs.

At Eleanor's urging, Sarah cautiously felt her way down the creaky basement steps, holding tightly to the spindly wooden rail. Suddenly, a terrifying gasp surged from her throat as an unidentified beast swooped toward her head.

"Oh my God, it's a bat!"

Eleanor casually pointed to the shadow that followed the swaying light bulb on a chain and chuckled at the image of the lady journalist glued to the step. Sarah was duly embarrassed, but still shaken. After all, wasn't climbing down into a dark, creepy cellar, of a quasi-stranger's home, the way most horror films began? Eleanor kindly encouraged her to continue down the stairs, while at the same time, muffling giggles.

Sarah began to thaw. As she reached the bottom step, she was aglow in a rosy sweat of humiliation.

"Honestly, I can't believe I actually thought I was being attacked by a bat the size of a dog!"

Eleanor was eager to change the mood. "Actually, Sarah, I think you're brave. If I thought giant bats were flying at me, I'd have been on my way to Alaska."

She led her guest to a long, shrouded rolling rack, where, with the magical finesse of David Copperfield, she swept away the cover and illuminated her exhibit with a strategically-placed floodlight.

There, lined-up like a corps de ballet, was a spectacle of couture creations in an exquisite array of textures, styles, and colours.

Gowns, cocktail dresses, and business outfits were all beautifully designed, cut and stitched in the same sumptuous way as her fashion idols: Donna Karan, Giorgio Armani or Ralph Lauren would have created in their luxury design-houses with a staff of hundreds of couture seamstresses.

The fabrics were luscious, cool silks and satins, fine woven Italian merino and worsted wool, and soft, velvety cashmeres. Sarah had never felt such exquisite cloth, or seen such delicate craftsmanship; all the samples were elegant and timeless. The attention to detail was flawless, right down to the inside hand-embroidered labels sewn slightly above the hemline: *E. Miller Couture Designs*.

Sarah remained silent, but her face radiated awe and respect. Since Eleanor understood the silence, she blushed at the unspoken praise being heaped upon her.

"Now, shall we go upstairs for a cup of tea and some apple pie?"

"Sure. Will the pie be as amazing as this collection??" Sarah quipped.

"I'll let you be the judge. But you'd best head up the stairs before I turn off the light and another monster stalks you." Eleanor watched and listened as Sarah headed up the stairs still complimenting the seamstress. "Eleanor, I'm honestly blown away by your collection! You're truly a remarkable talent."

Eleanor couldn't stop glowing like a red lantern and return to her usual alabaster shade. But Sarah wasn't done yet. "Could you ever consider duplicating one of them for me? Of course, it would have to wait until I sell my first big story so I could afford an E. Miller Couture design."

"Then you'd best get me while I'm still cheap." She punctuated the quip with a sassy wink.

"No, Madame Designer, you might be *affordable*, but never cheap." Sarah returned the wink.

"Truthfully, it'd be a privilege to have you wear one of my designs at some fancy gala." Eleanor dreamily contemplated.

"Oh wow, sorry to shatter your dream, but that's not me, at least not anymore." A chord was struck, and Sarah became detached for a few moments before rallying. "Truthfully, Eleanor, there was a time when I routinely went to those glittering soirees and might even have been able to influence some wealthy clients, but unfortunately, no longer. Divorce will do that to you." A sullen hush again enveloped the space.

"I'm sorry, Sarah. I didn't know. I'd heard you were married and had kids, but it seems I didn't get the whole story."

"Hey, that's pretty much the whole story."

In truth, it wasn't, and Sarah's moist eyes were evidence of that fact.

"I understand. But there's always much more to a person than what people think they know." The shy seamstress seemed struck with melancholy.

Their brief philosophical exchange strengthened Sarah's hope that one day, she might get to hear the rest of Eleanor's story. But for those hours, on that sunny, cool Saturday, Prescott was a warm, serene oasis, at the ironic edge of a depraved wasteland of pedophiles, sketchy memories, and a wannabe-journalist's desire to learn about it all and make a name for herself.

Sarah returned to the hotel, her mind buzzing with thoughts about the young girl she had barely known, who was now the woman she was determined to discover.

* * *

Even though his house was only a few blocks away, Wesley's son, Hartley, insisted on picking Sarah up for their Sunday dinner.

Hartley shared his immense home with his wife, Carole, two dogs, one iguana, and, to Sarah's surprise, his father.

Fresh out of college, Hartley had tried unsuccessfully to dabble in journalism, a concept that offended his father. Wesley could never accept that a writer could give less than twelve hours a day and still call himself a journalist. Hartley, now in his late fifties, had acquired the bulk of his wealth by dabbling in real estate instead.

Dinner was delayed while Hartley and his wife, Carole, squabbled over how best to cajole their three visiting grandkids into bed. Sarah considered that Wesley's fear of retiring and spending his golden years at home with "The Bickersons" might well be the driving incentive for him to show up for work every morning.

"So, my dear, I meant to ask how you like the facelift they gave your dad's store?" Hartley asked.

Hartley took note of Sarah's look of derision. "I can see, you're not impressed. But that's progress today, Sarah. They take the heart and soul out of history and replace them with new, mechanical parts. We all miss that store, and moreover, we miss your mom and dad."

"Yup, that's for sure. Your dad was quite a fellow," Wesley added as he poured his guest a glass of wine. "Did you know that a group of us used to visit his store every election season to try and persuade him to run for mayor?"

"I remember. He would have made a great mayor too. I never understood why he didn't do it." Sarah shook her head in bewilderment.

"Many people speculated about that," Wesley intimated. "It's true, they wondered why he wouldn't step forward, but I had a theory. I think that after what Hitler did to your people in Europe, Jews living here in small communities were still fearful and preferred to keep a low profile. I know he wasn't a Holocaust survivor, but he was proudly Jewish. I think he was flattered that we kept trying to convince him to run, but he just didn't want to be in the public eye; and I couldn't blame him."

Throughout the meal, Wesley captivated Sarah with unfamiliar but intriguing stories about her family. With each anecdote, she gave off a glow so warm it could melt a glacier. "More Wes, come on! The night is young." She urged, and he eagerly continued to entertain and inform even "The Bickersons."

"I remember one year, when a group of religious Jewish folks from the area gathered to pray on your High Holy Days. They were using the old Orange Hall over the dry cleaner shop for a make-do synagogue. Well, one night a bunch of vandals broke in and trashed the prayer books, graffitied the walls, and tried to smash open a locked cabinet to get at those religious scrolls. The dry cleaner ran up the stairs to investigate the noise, but the damn cowards heard him coming and disappeared down the fire escape.

"The next morning, the worshippers were pretty shook-up, but your dad talked them into going on with the service as if nothing had happened. Afterward, he went straight to the police station and lodged a formal complaint.

"Before the week was out, they'd caught two of 'em and, believe it or not, your father convinced everyone those hoodlum buggers shouldn't be sent to reformatory. Instead, he saw to it that they apologized to the Jewish community, paid for replacing the books, repaired every chair they broke, and repainted every wall."

"Really?" Sarah sighed happily.

"The funny thing is, when they were done, the Orangemen admitted that the hall had never looked so good."

Hartley chuckled as he applauded his dad's storytelling skills.

Wes continued. "You probably wouldn't remember 'cause you were a wee wisp of a kid, but one of those young lads they caught got sent to Calgary to live with his grandparents who straightened out the criminal bent in him. Believe it or not, the other one went to work in your father's store on weekends and summers. It turned out, the kid was a good worker, too. He stayed there part-time for three or four years while he finished high school. Your dad mentored him well. Eventually, he moved to Ottawa to go to university. Folks tell me he's a high school teacher there now with a wife, kids, and a couple o' grandkids too."

"Wow. I never heard about any of that." Sarah's face was lit with pride.

"It doesn't surprise me. Your dad was a humble guy." Wesley declared as he softly patted her shoulder.

"Do you think Braydon could search out that incident in the archives? I'd love to read about it."

Wes shook his head. "I can't say we'd ever have made it public."

"Why in hell not?" Sarah's question was charged with inuendo. "I mean, it was vandalism and antisemitism at the very least." She indignantly pushed her chair away from the table. "My God, Wesley, it was news. Surely, you weren't censored?"

The old editor exhaled a long, mournful sigh. "Like I said before, Sarah, unlike your parents, most of the Jewish people who lived in or around Prescott were Holocaust refugees. They shied away from being in the public eye. They didn't want to draw attention to themselves or their families, so we respected their right to privacy. Today, maybe they'd call it censorship, but in the fifties, we considered it a 'show of respect'."

Sarah fiddled with her napkin, endlessly folding and unfolding it, as she contemplated his words. "Respect, really? How?"

Wesley scratched the back of his neck, "Well, back then, if we were to write about a case like this kiddie porn one; not that there was anything like that to write about, but if there had been, we would've been very discreet about it...maybe like...*The police are presently questioning several townsfolk for purported unseemly behaviour*. Something like that, maybe." He concluded with an impish snicker.

Sarah played along, flippantly suggesting: "Uh, Wes, I'm guessing you might be only slightly exaggerating."

As the snickering subsided, Carole rose from the table and offered a suggestion: "You two keep goin'. Hartley and I are gonna check on the grandkids, clear up some dishes, and get dessert started."

Sarah jumped up from her chair. "Oh, please, let me help. I can clear the dishes while you tend to the grandkids."

"Thanks for the offer, but the truth is, if you just keep Dad busy out here, that's all the help we need. Honestly, when he's in the kitchen, something scary always happens. Hartley's mom always said Wes should never be allowed in a kitchen or a woodworking shop, 'cause in either place, he's sure to commit an unintended crime."

Wes grinned and shrugged. Sarah obeyed her host and sat down. "Let me ask you, Wes, back then, would the paper hear about an incident if the police were keeping it under the radar?"

"Well, the truth is, I've always had insiders who'd call me day or night if they saw anything suspicious, so I'd often hear about an incident before the police even arrived on the scene. Hell, my intel was so fast, the chief of police often came to me for information."

Sarah squirmed in her seat before mustering the pluck to ask some crucial questions. "What about the attack on Eleanor Miller?"

"Like I told you before, Sarah, there were rumours." Wesley's voice sounded strained, but Sarah was undeterred.

"Okay, was there ever a rumour that they arrested the animal that raped her?"

"Nope," was an unusually clipped answer from Wesley.

"You can't be serious, Wes? In a town of four thousand persistent gossips, no one saw or knew anything? Damn. In Toronto, a city of a million apathetic citizens, police usually manage to find the rapist, so why in hell not here?" Sarah's frustration was beginning to show as the volume was rising.

"Simple. If she never filed a complaint and if no one was ever charged, there would be no crime on the books, which would mean no investigation, no trial, and no news to report. There would be nothing the police could do. Even if they had an alleged rapist on their radar, they had no rape victim on record." His response sounded frustrated and despondent.

"And they say there's no such thing as a perfect crime." Sarah muttered.

After an uncomfortable pause, Wes ventured to ask, "I'm curious, have you broached this subject with Eleanor?"

Sarah scoffed and sniffed indignantly. "'My God, Wes, I had lunch with Eleanor yesterday, but I didn't ask while wolfing down her amazing apple pie, 'When you were a kid, were you raped?' What kind of person would ask that?" Catching a glimpse of disappointment in Wes's eyes, she changed her tone. "Sorry Wes, I didn't mean to get so worked up." He reached out, squeezed her hand and offered a conciliatory smile.

She released a mollifying sigh and changed the subject. "Something fabulous happened at my lunch with Eleanor! She showed me a design collection she's been working on. Did you know she was a fashion designer?"

Wesley stitched his brow and peered at Sarah while waiting for a punch line.

"Honestly, Wes. I couldn't be more serious. She's a real artist. Her stuff is incredible!" Sarah vowed with her hand over her heart. "Shiny said this town has always believed the rape rumours, so maybe after all these years, it's time to find out the truth?"

"I can see it's gonna drive you nuts, so let me tell you how we zig-zagged our words around serious rumour mills back then. We wrote 'fictionalized' articles about 'anonymous' victims. If you drop by tomorrow afternoon, I'll have Braydon dig into our archives and see if there's anything to find there."

"Oh, Wes, thank you so much! You're a saint." She jumped up and air-kissed his cheek, which was, by then, a radiant shade of red.

Doing his best to recover his curmudgeonly status, he boldly asked: "Does this mean you're giving up on the Earl White story?"

"Hell, no! Let's just say, I'm covering all my options."

"Okay then, I'll do my part by getting Braydon to do his part." Wesley offered a wry smile to end the conversation just as a three-layer chocolate cake made its entrance.

* * *

First thing Monday morning, Wesley exiled Braydon to the Journal's morgue to search for back copies from the fifties.

The first challenge was to determine when the alleged attack on Eleanor Miller would have taken place. They estimated it between 1957 and 1958. So, to be on the safe side, he had Brayden start at 1956 and go to 1959.

Most of the archives stored below the Journal office were recent, which meant that Braydon had to travel twelve miles to the Brockville warehouse and spend the entire day looking through dusty, yellowed piles of newsprint in search of four years of brittle copy.

* * *

After hours of scanning crusty, broken pages, Sarah was exhausted.

"Holy cow, Wes, couldn't you have modernized to microfiche at least? It's been around for at least thirty years."

He ignored her jibe and went about his business.

There was some comfort in the fact that the Prescott Journal wasn't a daily newspaper. Nevertheless, as she continued to carefully turn the fragile pages of old *Prescott Journal*s, her blackened fingers became a testament to the gallons of toxic ink, spread across tons of paper, over the decades. Words flew by as she flipped the pages, but a couple of headlines caught her attention. The first was from a 1956 issue entitled:

Who Sparked the Fleischman Fire?
by Wesley Jackson.
Did someone intentionally set fire to the wooden stands in front of the Fleischman's market? Or was it an accident?

Thanks to the quick response of our volunteer fire department, they managed to get the fire under control before more serious physical damage could be done.

But what happens to the owner's sense of security and safety if their property was intentionally attacked? Will that leave a lasting scar?

The Fleischman family had moved away when Sarah was quite young and, although she did remember them, she was unaware of the incident.

Wesley filled in the gaps.

"They mostly kept to themselves like the other Holocaust survivors who'd settled in the area after the war. The Fleischmans focused their attention on their family business and their three kids. People loved their little grocery shop, displaying their wares in barrels and baskets, like in the markets you see in European movies." He smiled wistfully as sentimental memories crowded his mind. "They would often throw a treat in the bag for our kids, and they'd say, *'Nem fer de kinder,'* or something like that. We figured it meant, 'be kind to kids.'"

"What a sweet gesture." Sarah wistfully replied. "But I think it literally means 'take some for the children,' which I guess, is pretty close to what you just said, Wes."

"Close enough, huh?" He agreed with a chuckle. "Now, what's the other headline you were wondering about?"

"It's not a headline." She pointed to the page, "See here, it's a picture and obituary of Daisy Panasar, a fifteen-year-old girl who drowned in the summer of '58. Is that the D.A.P. you were talking about the other day?"

Wesley nodded and stroked his chin, "Yeah, that's her. She was training to swim across the St. Lawrence to the U.S. side. She'd already won the first-place junior swim medal that summer, and she was the favourite to win the big race too. We were all rootin' for her to beat the American who was competing from the other direction."

Sarah looked up, confused. "But if she was such a great swimmer, how did she drown?"

"She was warned not to swim without a spotter, but she didn't listen." He shook his head and furrowed his brow. "She went out to practice alone before the big event, and the next morning, they found her body washed up near Kelly's Beach. She would have made it too, if she'd had the chance, 'cause she was a strong swimmer. Just not strong enough that night."

Wes shook his head, "God, just thinking about it makes me shudder. It was a really sad situation. Her parents had moved here from India, hoping to give their only child the opportunities they didn't have."

"Jeez, that's so awful." Sarah closed the pages she'd been scanning and slouched in her chair. "It seems Prescott's a real hub of tragedy, huh?"

"You think, one accident in '58 and a scandal thirty-five years later constitute a 'hub of tragedy?'" His tone was indignant, and it sharpened as he continued. "If you want to compare notes on mayhem and mischief, let's look at what happens in one day in a city like Toronto." His voice had grown louder and edgier. Sarah was taken aback by his sudden mood shift. She calmly stood up and stretched before continuing.

"Anyway, Wes, as much as I like a good debate, I better stop, 'cause I have to get ready for a Halloween party tonight." She smiled at him wryly. "And as much as you may feel I am one, no, I'm not going as a witch!"

He grinned and lightheartedly asked. "Then it begs the question: What are you going as?"

"I thought maybe a journalist, if I can pull it off," she mused.

CHAPTER SEVEN

Halloween was a big deal in Prescott where eerily decorated storefronts paid homage to the toothy sardonic squash that grimaced at spectators as they passed by. Witches, skeletons, and monsters beckoned onlookers to come in and buy their Halloween goodies for the tiny neighbourhood goblins, who would descend on them as evening fell.

On this wickedly-delicious night of little monster raids, Sarah had been invited to join Shiny at a kids' costume competition in their old high school. She had nudged Sarah to accept, in the hopes it would tilt the vote in favour of her grandchildren.

At 6:45, Shiny called to say "Ron's gonna drop me off at your hotel, and then he's drivin' over to the school with the grandkids; but I've decided we should walk over and take in the sights, so dress warm and meet me downstairs at seven."

"A promise is a promise," Sarah muttered as she hung up the phone. She would've preferred to stay inside and watch *Seinfeld* or *Murphy Brown*, but again, she repeated her mantra: "A promise is a promise". She wasn't about to abandon Shiny who had, thankfully, not insisted she go in costume. She pulled on her Uggs and layered on the rest of her outerwear.

* * *

The lobby was quiet and empty, but an echo of raucous sounds drew Sarah, toward the bar to wait for her friend.

A parade of unholy sights strutted by as Sarah stood at the crossroads of the bar entrance and the washrooms. Dracula ambled toward the men's room, while a hulking werewolf salivated after a curvaceous Miss Piggy, who playfully ducked into the ladies' room. But Shiny was nowhere to be seen.

As a Chiquita Banana squeezed past her, Sarah chuckled at the thought of a six-foot banana perched on a toilet. Chiquita stopped and turned abruptly. "Hey, Sarahchita! Let's vamos, eh?"

It took Sarah a second to realize who was lurking inside the banana peel, but once reality hit, she quaked with laughter.

"Okay, okay, it's maybe chuckle-worthy, but it's not that hysterically funny, I'm just tryin' to be a cool grandmother is all." Shiny insisted. "But then, hmm," she added as she looked Sarah up and down, "I admit, it's funnier than your costume."

"I'm just your run-of-the-mill Toronto tourist taking in the sights, and oh, what a sight you are." Sarah giggled. Shiny slipped her yellow fleece-covered arm through Sarah's and shouted: "We're off to see the Wonderful Wizards of Odd."

With that, the two women scurried out the door and along Main Street to the tune of the Chiquita Banana jingle hummed by almost everyone they passed.

The streets were like storybooks, and each home, another book cover. The decorations were even more elaborate than those Sarah remembered from her childhood. Robotic bats swooped through the

Halloween sky like phantom dive-bombers. A ragged broom-riding, wart-covered witch cackled in rhythm to the eerie sounds wafting from her rooftop perch. On a massive cobweb-veiled veranda, two life-sized puppets rocked on a porch-swing to the pulsating blast of Michael Jackson's zombie anthem, "Thriller."

As the women continued their tour of the town, Sarah realized that, although many of the houses looked familiar, she couldn't recall who lived in them. Within the walls of every home was a story, and Shiny had lived there long enough to have collected a library of them.

As they approached a large, brick house on Henry Street, Sarah stopped abruptly while Shiny continued on. Sarah cocked her head in thought as a memory emerged. She called out to Shiny. "Hold on. Come here for a sec, please."

Shiny managed to twist in her banana skin and shuffle back.

"Shiny, there used to be a small, wooden cottage right here on a huge lot that belonged to the Gormans. Them, I remember clearly. What happened to their house?"

"The new owners tore it down and built this place, years ago."

"Then what happened to the Gormans?" Sarah seemed more agitated than curious.

"What do ya mean, 'what happened'? Nothin' happened. They just up and sold their house one day and moved to Montreal the next. No one had a clue they were goin' until they were gone." With that, Shiny started to move on but Sarah grabbed onto her arm.

"Wait a minute, please. Why would they just leave like that?" She asked while still gripping the banana.

"I have no idea why." She confirmed as she gently freed herself. "Come on, let's go. One thing I can tell you is that they were the kind of people that wanted, or maybe I should say really needed, their privacy. It was a known fact that they had trust issues."

"Wow. Wes was just talking about trust back then being a huge issue for Holocaust survivors in Prescott." Sarah mumbled.

"Yeah, well, they were definitely a different breed of folk." Shiny scoffed. "The truth is, they never really tried to blend in, if you know what I mean."

There was a tone to Shiny's comments that made Sarah uncomfortable. A murky silence hung in the air but Sarah decided for the sake of diplomacy, to change the subject. "Isn't that the old high school?" She asked as she pointed to a large, brown brick building in the next block.

"It was, before they built the new one you went to. After that, the town council turned this old brick shithouse into a community centre for seniors. Imagine the old and the handicapped trying to get up four flights of stairs? Then they turned it into a nursery-slash-daycare which it still is, and now an army of toddlers have to navigate those lofty heights."

It somehow comforted Sarah to discover that small town politics were just as senseless as the big city kind.

The two women stood for a moment in front of the old schoolhouse, admiring the spooky decorations. Yards of black and orange streamers floated randomly in space while moaning and cackling sounds seeped from the walls, and plastic creepy critters peeked out from the corners of blacked-out windows.

Sarah headed inside to claim seats in the auditorium, while Shiny lagged behind, struggling to manoeuvre her unwieldy second skin. Many of the adults in the audience were as fully costumed as the little competitors. Sarah took comfort in the fact that some townsfolk were camouflaged, which meant that she wouldn't have to remember the unfamiliar faces of people who might readily recognize hers.

In the next row, the back of Richard McCall's head caught Sarah's eye. When he turned in response to her tap on his shoulder, she was stunned to see him decked out in a bowtie and blackface. Richard grinned toothily and extended a white-gloved hand.

Sarah thought: *This is Prescott, Canada, not Korowai, Indonesia. Have they not yet heard about political correctness?* But instead of offering a lesson in race relations, she shook his gloved hand and managed a tense smile.

"Do you have grandkids in the competition too?" She innocently asked.

"I do and they really want to win, so can I count on your vote?"

Shiny caught up just in time to offer a playful punch to his shoulder. "Hey! You lawyers never give up, do you? You're always lobbyin'. Well, buddy boy, I saw her first; and anyway, I saw your mother out in the hall rounding up all the votes you'll need."

"I sure did," croaked a craggy voice from behind Shiny.

"Hi, Estelle," Shiny muttered while still facing forward.

"Well, aren't you being a bit rude, Shari Copper? Turn around and tell your friend who I am." Shiny heaved a weary sigh and prepared to do as asked, but it proved unnecessary. "Oh, never you mind. Hi, I'm Estelle, Richard's mother, and I know who you are." Before Sarah could react, Estelle prattled on. "You're that nice Jewish Klein girl. My son told me you were here to get the story about how they were framing Earl White. Good for you."

Richard sunk lower in his seat as his mother continued unabated.

"It's a terrible thing what those animals did to those poor, innocent children, and they shoulda castrated; the whole damn bunch o' them. If that goddamn Crown Attorney wasn't asleep at the table, they woulda locked 'em all away forever, and not just for a few years. As for Earl, he's an upstanding businessman that gives lots o' jobs to lots o' people around here, and those jealous lowlifes in prison are tryin' to kill the golden goose. Listen, young lady, if you ever need to talk to somebody who knows every inch o' this town and every person in it, I could be very helpful. So, feel free ta call me up...but make it soon, 'cause I'm not gettin' any younger." She cackled.

Sarah squirmed as she tried to think of the kindest way to remain non-committal. "Well, it's good to meet you, Mrs. McCall, and thanks for the offer."

"I could be even more helpful if you were to vote for my Richard's grandkids." Estelle cackled again.

Sarah playfully whispered to the crone. "Mrs. McCall, since it's a blind ballot, I want to assure you that I will make a fair and honourable decision."

Estelle McCall offered up a Cheshire grin before shuffling into her seat beside her son.

Shiny bent toward Sarah and quietly grumbled, "Don't underestimate that old gossip. She can get anyone to do anything by just threatening to blab their secrets. We've all got 'em, you know...and if you don't have 'em, she'll spread ugly rumours about you anyway."

"Oh great. Just what I need, ugly rumours to add to the misery of the case I'm dealing with." Sarah lowered her head in feigned defeat.

"So now, Miss Sarah," Shiny leaned in conspiratorially. "You should be thinkin' about who you're gonna vote for. And while you're thinkin', I'm gonna sit down, if I can get this damned getup to bend."

Sarah snickered as she watched her costumed-friend struggle to sit. Before Shiny's bottom could make contact with the seat, her banana ripped down the back, leaving her open to an inevitable bunch of banana-split jokes. Thankfully, underneath, she was dressed in a yellow fleece jumpsuit from neck to ankle. By the time the curtain rose, Shiny had wisely peeled off her costume and was sitting comfortably in her sweats.

Shiny's grandchildren proudly strutted across the stage in their grandma-made Robin Hood and Friar Tuck costumes to the exaggerated oohs and aahs of the crowd.

The audience reaction was impressive, but not fulsome enough to win. Shiny took some cynical joy in the fact that none of Richard's grandkids' portrayals of *Dracula*, *Frankenstein*, *Morticia* and *The Joker* made the final cut either.

The first prize winner, who was decked out as a mini, bowler-hat-wearing, Mayor of Prescott, received a blue ribbon for her unique imitation of her father. Estelle's opinion on the choice was clear when she declared, "Well, of course the mayor's kid would win 'cause everyone wants to see those new beachfront renovations he's been promising us. That lousy, cheap, blue ribbon was probably made in China anyway." She struggled to rise abruptly in a huff, but it was more of a slow-motion grunt that finally got her to her feet.

As the festivities came to an end, *Robin* and the *Friar* pleaded with their grandmother to walk them home rather than drive with their parents or Ron.

"And please, Grandma, can we take a shortcut through the forest, 'cause it's so-o dark and scary and we love it! Pl-e-ease?"

"Forest?" Sarah snickered, "in the middle of town?" She offered a cynical snort.

"Oh, yes, indeedy," Shiny nodded.

"Since when?" Sarah asked.

Shiny smirked and waved her forward, "You'll see."

They marched on in unison, led by the delighted grandchildren, who were doing their best to frighten each other with quiet eerie utterings and subtle pranks.

As they drew closer to the corner, Sarah could see the weathervane on the roof of a house barely visible behind the tall trees and wild bushes. She stopped and gaped, seemingly confused.

"That's the Daniels' house, right? Jeez, Shiny, I barely recognize the place. It's bloody creepy."

Shiny put her finger to her lips to shut Sarah up.

"It's just friendly Sherwood Forest to these merry men. Right kids?"

The two adventurers answered with a unanimous "Yes!"

Sarah shook her head and smiled.

As they drew nearer, Sarah thought about the many summers she spent in Anna's well-groomed yard; roasting under the sun basted in a concoction of baby oil and iodine; devouring books by Tolkien, Salinger, or Steinbeck; and fantasizing about how the two of them would change the world when they grew up.

A tinge of anxiety came over her as she asked: "Do you know anything about the Danielses?"

"No, they're long gone from here. It's been years since I've even heard that name." Shiny explained, then abruptly shouted: "Hold on, you little rascals! Listen to me, you'll never get through there! The bushes are way too thick."

Her grandchildren remained undeterred.

"Grandma, we can do it. We're Robin Hood and Friar Tuck, and we live in a thick forest, remember?"

The children offered up some additional, "Aw, come on, please," whining, and then bolstered their 'cause with the quiet imploring eyes of two cocker spaniels."

"Yeah, Shiny, where's your sense of adventure?" Sarah taunted. Shiny flickered a scowl toward Sarah, then gave a resigned sigh and led the brigade through the foreboding thicket, with no casualties, other than some messy hair.

* * *

The next day, Sarah headed to the Journal office. With a pair of surgical gloves tucked in her purse, she was ready to search every toxic page, in her quest to find some clue to Eleanor's alleged attack.

* * *

It was well after closing time when Braydon rose, stretched, and bailed. "I've had it, you guys. I don't know how you can keep going. I've missed most of the hockey game already, so I'm goin' home to at least catch the sports roundup."

Sarah retorted without raising her head. "Okay, but don't be jealous if you get here in the morning to find that we broke the story, or cracked the case, or whatever those TV crime fighters call it now," Sarah teased.

* * *

After scanning every newspaper from December 1956 to February 1958 without turning up a hint of the incident, Sarah was beginning to join the doubters.

She leaned back with hands clasped behind her head and rested her feet on the desk. "Wes, this creepy Sodom & Gomorrah case has me suspicious of everything in this town. If the Millers never admitted it, and the Journal never mentioned it, am I crazy to assume it's anything but an urban myth?"

Wes looked up, removed his glasses, and slowly rolled his chair away. "This may sound crazy, Sarah, but I remember in the fifties, I knew this guy, Chris, who was an orderly at St. Gabriel's Hospital in Brockville. He told me that some kid had shown up there looking like she'd been run over by a cement truck. She was gushing blood, covered in bruises and cuts, but there had been no car accident or crime reported that night. Word quickly spread through the hospital that a young girl had been brutally raped.

"By the time Chris called me the next morning, the mystery girl had left the hospital. He knew which doctor had attended to her, so he tried to sneak into the files to have a look, but he never got to see the medical report. In fact, he got caught. Luckily, he managed to talk his way out of losing his job. Of course, once word leaked out that there was a rapist on the loose, and because there was never an official denial from police or the hospital, he was petrified it could be true. After that, he saw the police silence as a threat to every daughter in town, including his. He felt there was nothing he could do but call and tell me about it, off the record.

"Sorry I didn't make the connection before, but there really could've been a rape. I just don't recall when that was; and I have no idea if it was Eleanor."

"What matters is that there's something to all this. It needs to be dealt with, Wes. Let's call this Chris guy and tell him we want to come over to talk."

"Sorry, but Chris died about twenty years ago. Anyway, he was never able to give me a name, and since what he told me was off the record, I promised to keep what little I knew, confidential." Wes turned and stared pensively out the window. Within seconds, he stiffened in his chair and cleared his throat to speak. "Sarah, oath aside, in some carefully veiled way, I know I must've written about it, mentioned it somehow...I just can't remember how or when."

Sarah perked up, set her feet on the floor and announced. "Okay. Then it's here somewhere. So, Wes, can we just keep going?"

Wes offered an upward nod and slid a pile of copies onto his desk.

They continued to scrutinize every page until Sarah came across an editorial dated, March 28, 1958.

Where's the Justice?

Two weeks ago, a child was discreetly hustled into St. Gabriel's Hospital. Her frail body had been battered, torn, and violated.

Since the incident, no police report has been filed, no criminal charges have been laid, and the medical records have been sealed.

Reva Leah Stern

The parents can do nothing for their daughter because they know that to encourage her to face our present judicial system is to commit her to be assaulted again and again by the very law that is meant to protect her. Yet, without a trial, this youngster will be sentenced to a lifetime of personal torment.

How will this child ever find justice?

Is there no one who could spark a flicker of light on this cold blackness? How can we allow the monster that perpetrated this savage act to remain free to violate another innocent victim?

If you saw or heard anything that could help shed some light on this crime, do the right thing and call the police immediately.

* * *

"Holy crap, Wes! This has to be it." Every muscle in Sarah's body became galvanised like steel cables.

Wesley closed the paper he was scanning and slowly stood up. "I think we've had enough for one night, Sarah." Wesley concluded as he reached out and switched off the desk lamp. "Since you've found a clue, I suggest you leave it at that for tonight. It's time to head home."

Head home wasn't the response she'd hoped for. Where was his old journalistic curiosity? Now her initial shock was beginning to subside; but the article had ripened her imagination and left her dreading the walk back to her hotel alone.

"Yeah, I guess you're right, Wes. It's awfully late and, um, pretty dark out there," she hinted. "I guess

I'd better get going." She lingered, waiting for Wes to offer to escort her home.

Wesley looked up over his glasses. "Okeydokey." He picked up some papers and headed into the back area.

That was it? Okeydokey? Sarah thought to herself. *So, either I sleep beside the printing press and gamble the toxic fumes don't kill me, or I head out and try to outrun the boogieman?*

The boogieman solution meant if she made it to the hotel, she could at least end up in a comfy bed, alive.

Peering through a clear spot in the etched-glass window, she could see that streetlights were still a scarcity in Prescott. Main Street had always appeared eerily dark after the shops closed and their lights went out.

Sarah slipped on her coat and offered a wistful goodnight to the empty room. Cautiously, she stepped onto the sidewalk and proceeded gingerly toward her hotel. As the darkness engulfed her, every innocuous sound grew suspicious. Was that mournful wail a desperate cry for help, or the nightly marauding of a horny tomcat? Was that sudden hollow thumping, the laborious footfall of a grotesque serial killer or the wild pounding of her heart?

She quickened her step, but the sound kept pace. Again, she moved faster, and again, the sound shadowed her. The steady, rhythmic drumming of heavy footsteps drew closer, gaining on her. She broke into a run.

A forceful voice bellowed through the gloom initiating a heart stopping dread in Sarah.

The concept of reality finally reached her frontal lobe. "Oh my God, Wes, I didn't know it was you."

"Did you honestly think I was gonna let you walk home alone after midnight and our discussion?" He asked as he gasped for breath.

"Sorry, I was just anxious to get to sleep. I didn't mean to make you chase me. Are you all right?" She asked as she placed a comforting hand on his shoulder.

"Yeah, yeah, I'm good. Just not used to running marathons these days." He joked as he patted her hand.

He accompanied her into the desolate hotel lobby. It was obvious as she looked around, that Prescott was closed for the night.

As Wes bid her goodnight, he quipped, "Listen, when an old geezer like me can still attempt to run a block for a damsel thinking she's in distress, don't ever say gallantry is dead, young lady."

With her giggle still resounding in his ears, he headed for home, leaving Sarah to think about how grateful she was that her childhood mentor was now also her protector.

* * *

Most of her bedtime rituals were cast aside as Sarah, changed into her nightgown, brushed her teeth, and slid into bed exhausted from the adventures of the day.

Sleep was a challenge. It took "The Best of Johnny Mathis" to finally calm the flurry of ink-filled pages that swirled through her thoughts. But finally, she succumbed.

With every breath, Sarah sank deeper and deeper into the grip of her serial nightmare. She kicked, squirmed, shouted, and punched the air and pillows as the night wore on and the dream became more vivid:

"Come out, come out, wherever you are, Jew girl, 'cause we're gonna find ya, nail ya to a tree, 'n ram a crucifix up your ass."

Hideous laughter crescendoed as a lone voice edged closer to the embankment, "Don't you fuckers know ya have to look under a rock if ya wanna find a Jew?"

Paralyzed with fear, Sarah's feet slipped slowly down the concrete wall and into the icy cascade below. The frigid marsh filled her boots. A thunderous noise, a blaze of blinding light and her knees buckled...

Sarah lay rigid in her bed, moaning and whimpering through chattering teeth.

* * *

Wesley had barely slipped into the booth before Sarah pushed the latest issue of *The Prescott Journal* across the table.

"I'm flattered you bought one," Wesley noted, "but I would've gladly comped you."

"Thanks, but I wanted to look through it before our breakfast."

Shiny stopped by their table to say good morning, pour their coffee, and take their order. "Let me guess, you both want your usual bacon and eggs, right?"

They nodded in unison without looking up. Shiny sensed some tension, and scurried off to the kitchen.

"And you know what I found interesting, Wes?"

"I hope the whole paper was interesting." He smirked and sipped his coffee.

"I'm sure it is. But there wasn't even one mention of vandalism on Halloween night. Hell, when I was a kid, we were always up to some mischief. Do you remember that big old, deserted house on the hill near Wexford?"

He cocked his head. "Sure, it burned down years ago. So?"

"Uh-huh. But before that, Wes, it was the perfect place to end up on Halloween night. I remember we set squeaky toys on the basement steps so kids would crap themselves when they crept down the stairs in the dark and stepped on one."[i] Sarah mused nostalgically Oh, speaking of crap, I remember once, some lunkhead taped butcher paper over the toilet hole in farmer Hanes's outhouse. But Donny Birch engineered the worst gross-out caper of all. He took the milk from a nasty neighbour's stoop, drank some, and filled it back up with urine."

"Okay, yeah, there were disgusting pranks." Wes shrugged.

Sarah's frustration levels were rising. "Yes, exactly, Wes, there were pranks and then there were the destructive idiots who torched the old, haunted house."

"Are you trying to make a point, Sarah?" he shoved the paper back toward her.

"I don't know if I have a point, Wes. It's just that I don't get it."

The conversation took a pause as Shiny placed their sumptuous breakfast in front of them. "Thanks, Shiny. I'm starving and it looks great." Sarah remarked.

"Thanks, you two, enjoy." With that, she hurried away.

Sarah folded the newspaper and waved it at Wes.

"If those terrible things happened in the time of 'Donna Reed' and 'Father Knows Best,' how is it that today, with rampant drug abuse and drive-by shootings, there's not one incident of vandalism?" She slapped the paper down on the table and began to eat.

Wesley shifted in his seat. "Maybe we should just be grateful that this Halloween, no haunted houses were torched."

"Yeah, well, the old Wesley Jackson would've found some malicious offense and written about it." She slumped forward and focussed on her meal.

"You know, my dear, for over three years, this town has taken a hell of a beating over this goddamned child porn case that just won't die. We've seen smarmy tabloid newspapers and invasive TV cameras come here to twist any little piece of nothing into some repugnant revelation they can use to bolster sales or ratings. For example, do you remember Brian Gerrod, the optometrist?"

She offered a shrug and a curt shake of her head as she bit off a hunk of crispy bacon.

"You must. His office was just up the street from Perkins Candy Shop."

Sarah nodded. "Uh-huh, yeah, I kinda remember," she concurred as she spread jam on her toast.

"Well, he and his wife, Heather, retired some years back, but two summers ago, their son and daughter-in-law came up from Ottawa and left their three-year-old daughter, Tracy, with them while they slipped away for a weekend." He took a few bites of breakfast before returning to his story.

"So, at the time, that group of seven degenerates had just been indicted and every lousy motel and cabin within thirty miles of here was filled with media people just itching to put their face or by-line on that disgusting story."

"Isn't that what they're paid to do?" Her indignation wasn't subtle.

"Do you remember when you were working on your column here as a kid, the 'Wesley Rule' I taught you?" he continued eating.

"I think so," she dutifully replied.

"Then, let's hear it." He gestured for her to oblige.

"Umm...okay. You invent novels, you report news, and...you must never confuse the two." She offered a heavy sigh of satisfaction that earned her a long sip of coffee.

"Right," he confirmed, "but today, with the invasion of technology and the scarceness of integrity, that journalistic rule is being flushed down the damn toilet."

"Flushed and toilet are not topics that go well with bacon and eggs." Shiny giggled as she refilled their coffee and sped away. Silence sucked the antagonism from the space as Wesley paused to contemplate whether or not to continue. Finally, he seemed to make a decision.

"You eat and I'll tell you a story, Sarah. It's not *Cinderella*, but I think you'll agree, it's a classic." He took a reassuring breath, popped a forkful of egg into his mouth, chewed and swallowed before proceeding.

"One miserably-hot summer day, the Gerrods were looking after little three-year-old Tracy, who wanted to go to Perkins Candy Shop for ice cream.

"Brian didn't melt in the heat, but he always melted over the pleas of his precious grandchild. 'Please, Grandpa, please can we go for ice cream?' She begged. So, Heather put her granddaughter's hair up in a ponytail, dressed her in a pinafore and sandals, and off she scampered with her grandpa." Wes paused and looked at Sarah.

"Seven blocks, in oppressive heat, was a virtual marathon for a toddler."

Sarah nodded but said nothing for fear he might stop.

"Inside the candy shop, the child chose a cherry ice-cream cone and a bag of treats. Then, as they once again hit the veil of heat outside, she whimpered that she was too tired to walk, so, Brian scooped her up and carried her.

"Just as they got to the corner gas station, Tracy whispered that she really had to go to the bathroom! Brian grabbed the gas station key and rushed her inside. As they left the bathroom, Brian tossed the soggy remains of the melted ice-cream cone into the trash which initiated a major tantrum. Brian picked her up, bucking and screaming, and hurried home.

"After dinner, Heather and Brian were watching the Kinston evening news, that went something like this: *The story that surfaced in the little eastern Ontario town of Prescott last week only gets more bizarre each day. The public must be made aware of the horrific fact that adult men from around this town have been sexually entrapping and abusing little children for their own warped gratification and financial gain. There are many good men in this town to be sure, but this scandalous situation has cast suspicion over everyone.*

"The TV newsman continued to broadcast, while behind him, Brian's innocent trip to the washroom with his granddaughter was played over and over again."

"Oh my God, Wes, that's horrible." Sarah felt a wave of revulsion sweep over her. "But this town knew him; surely they ignored it?"

"For the first few days, everyone reassured Brian that no one thought anything of it and he should forget the whole thing; it was merely a coincidence and everyone in town knew what a fine person he was. Then, one of the Ottawa papers somehow got a hold of his name and 'inadvertently' printed it. After that, Brian received dozens of vile anonymous calls and hate mail. A few weeks later, he suffered a massive heart attack and almost died."

Sarah winced. "Oh, Wes, I'm so sorry..."

"So, you see, Sarah, on Halloween, if a bunch of smart-assed kids set a bag of dog shit on fire on someone's porch, it's not worth reporting some insignificant nothing that could have any media scumbag come rushing back, looking for something."

"But then, aren't they holding your town hostage, for Christ's sake?" She groused.

"Two years ago, we thought this was finally over and we could get back to normal. And now, there may be another trial and the nightmare will start all over again unless Earl White goes directly to jail without a trial."

"What do you mean 'without a trial'? How in hell does that work?" She snapped.

"Easy. He can plead guilty and get locked up immediately. If that happens, the TV cameras will quickly move on to some other town's misery." Wes paused for a sip of coffee.

"As far as we know, there isn't any evidence that these accusations are anything but prisoner's revenge. I mean, come on, Zane Fergusson as a credible source? Really? Hey, I have as much trouble looking at Earl White as I do his creepy cousin, but you can't convict someone of a crime because you don't like their looks." She paused and took a bite of egg. "Besides, Earl didn't bring an expensive hotshot lady lawyer all the way from Toronto to stand by and watch him plead guilty."

Wesley's frustration was telegraphed by the throbbing vein in his temple. "So, you're resigned to the fact that he could walk away a free man?"

"I just accept his right to a fair hearing." She defiantly replied.

"You know what, Sarah? Our conversation has gone way off topic. You were asking me about Halloween."

"Yeah, right. On Halloween night, we passed by the old Daniels' house, and I asked Shiny if she knew anything about them, but she kind of drew a blank. I lost all contact with Anna and her family years ago, but since I've been here, I've been thinking about her a lot. We were such close friends."

Memory suddenly brought Sarah to a rush of joyous images. She smiled wistfully. "What a pair we were. Anna, the tall, curvy, smart immigrant kid, and me, the short, flat-chested, book-nerd. It even makes sense that we befriended Eleanor that summer, 'cause all three of us were geeky outsiders."

"So, why did you stop communicating with Anna?" Wes asked in a unexpectedly judgmental tone.

She frowned. "I didn't. She did."

"Isn't that what the other party always thinks? It wasn't me; it was him or her?"

She shook her head. "No, honestly, it really was her. And it was a strange situation. Anna had moved to Montreal and married a good-looking French-Canadian guy named Luc. Eventually, she realized that what she'd thought were Luc's strong, attractive assets had quickly turned into abusive liabilities. She called up late one night in a panic to tell me that she and Luc had separated. She sounded distraught but wouldn't talk about the details. She just gave me a new, unlisted phone number and told me not to give it to anyone...especially Luc. She had planned to come and stay with me and Saul in Toronto for a few days, but she never showed up. She never called, and the number she gave us wasn't in service. Naturally, I was worried sick, so I contacted her father who was still living in Prescott at the time, and he assured me that she was fine, and she'd call soon. I waited, but 'soon' never happened.

"Several weeks later, she called to tell us that she and Luc had worked everything out. She talked non-stop, as if she was a record being played on high-speed. I couldn't get a word in. I was dumbstruck. She was clearly not her normal self."

Sarah began to tear up. Wes handed her a napkin. "Sarah, if it's too painful for you, you don't have to tell me."

"No, I want to. What really hurt was when she railed at us about us sitting in judgement of her husband's drinking during their last visit. We're not drinkers, a fact that Luc ridiculed, but we happily provided as much beer and wine as he wanted without comment. She also accused Saul of inferring that the black and blue mark on her forehead wasn't there by accident.

"I was really shocked. She seemed so much in love with Luc, and he seemed so attentive to her; we hadn't considered, until she said it, that the bruise on her face could have been caused by Luc. But then, the breakup, the hiding, his drinking, the bruising...it all made perfect sense." She blew her nose and shook her head.

"Ah-ha, so let me guess, Sarah: you shared your opinion with Anna?"

"I did and I never heard from her again. I tried, but it was hopeless."

"Sorry about that, my dear." They both poked at their leftovers and sipped their coffee. After a few moments, Wes, put down his mug and reached for Sarah's hand.

"Listen here, my dear. I can tell you what I do recall. I remember that Anna's parents separated, and her father moved to Montreal. Sophie ran the restaurant on her own for a time, but she was insulting the customers and screaming at the help. She was so completely out of control that Anna and her dad were forced to close up the business and sell the house. They got Sophie into an institution in Montreal where she died several years ago. I think the old man may have died a year or two before her."

Silence hung in the air like a bad odor as Sarah tried to absorb the flood of sad history she'd missed.

Another thought struck Wes. "I remember, a few months after Sophie's death, I wrote a memorial piece on her and sent a copy to Anna."

She squeezed the hand holding hers., "So you have Anna's address?"

"Well, the one I have is pretty old, but I'll bet it'll be easy enough to find her current address. Do you want to write her?"

"Yeah, I think I do. This is crazy, you know, but Prescott feels even stranger without her. All those years, I figured I could never find her and maybe it was always just this simple." She offered the best smile she could muster as thanks.

Wesley returned her wistful smile. "Maybe you didn't have a need to find her before, my dear."

"But I should have, Wes. We were so close. I should have. I just hope it's not too late." Sarah wiped away another tear and looked on as Shiny poured another cup of coffee with one hand, and affectionately tousled Sarah's hair with the other. The aura of something deeply emotional was clearly hovering over that booth.

CHAPTER EIGHT

Sarah hadn't yet been introduced to Laurie Cowan, and she understood that Richard's reluctance was likely due to his ethical commitment to protect their client. She didn't question it, but she did keep an eye out for a sophisticated, well-dressed woman who would look out of place amid the local sweatsuit and polyester-wearing rural population. She thought she might bump into her in the O'Brien's lounge or even the Best Service, but their paths hadn't crossed.

This was the first day of hearings and Sarah arrived at the courthouse, anxious to catch a glimpse of the dedicated (or desperate) lawyer who came all the way from Toronto to defend the foulmouthed Earl White.

* * *

Sarah was trying her best to convince the officer guarding the entryway to let her take her coffee cup into the courtroom when she spotted Richard in close conversation with the well-dressed, well-coiffed lady lawyer and a distinguished-looking gentleman. She waved and called out Richard's name, trying to get his attention, but he didn't notice. The gentleman did notice, however, and pointed Sarah out to Richard, who scurried over to her. "I'm about to head into the courtroom, Sarah, what is it you need?" He impatiently barked.

"Jeez, I'm sorry to be a bother, Richard, but I see some people taking their coffees into the courtroom and I need to do the same, but the guard is giving me a hard time."

Richard bristled but concluded it was better to resolve the problem than create a scene, which he worried could be Sarah's next move. He gently pulled the officer aside, whispered a few words, and Sarah was soon ushered inside with her coffee in hand. She nodded her thanks to Richard.

All were seated and waiting for the judge's arrival. After a few restless minutes, the court clerk entered and declared, "All present and officially involved with the Earl Otto White matter, please stand and state your names for the record."

The distinguished gentleman stood. "Laurie Cowan, representing Mr. Earl Otto White in the matter before this court."

Sarah's misplaced assumption that Laurie Cowan was a female came as a surprise and an embarrassment causing her to sink a bit lower in her seat.

After the Crown Attorney's introduction, the court clerk continued. "Thank you. You may be seated," He paused, took a nostril-wheezing inhale, and continued. "I've been advised to inform you that Judge MacMillan is otherwise engaged, and therefore, this matter is postponed until Friday morning. The court is dismissed." With that, he turned on his heel and exited through the judge's door.

A collective moan which included Sarah's voice, surged through the courthouse.

* * *

"Goddamn it! I hate when they do that," Richard sputtered as he gathered up the files he'd removed from his briefcase. "I'm really sorry, Laurie. I know you wanted to get this first step over with and get back to Toronto."

"It's no problem, Richard. The food's pretty good at the O'Brien, and I have other briefs to work on while I wait." He lifted his briefcase, turned, and then stopped mid-swivel to ask, "By the way, who was the woman with the coffee issue?"

"Oh, she's that journalist I told you about who wants to do a story on Earl for the *Toronto Sun-Times*. It's probably a good idea to be helpful to the media. Anyway, she comes from good people, and she's really enthusiastic. Listen, if you want to talk to her, she's also staying at the O'Brien."

"Hmm. Let's wait and see what happens after we get before the judge." Laurie Cowan replied with measured consideration.

* * *

Sarah hurried back to the Journal office to update Wesley. After she finished, she sat patiently waiting for his sage advice, which emerged in a flash.

"Well, Sarah, that city lawyer is stuck here for a while. So, now's your chance to convince him to give you an in-depth interview with Earl."

She became pensive for a moment. "Hmm, okay, and how do you propose I do that?"

"Well, since you asked...I suggest just you put on a sexy little black dress, and no doubt, you'll have better luck convincing *Mr.* Laurie Cowan than you would have had if he'd been *Mrs.* Laurie Cowan." He punctuated his cheeky scheme with a mischievous grin.

"Wow, Wes, getting a little sexist in your old age, huh?" She taunted.

"Mail delivery, Sarah," Braydon chanted. "It's our address, but your name."

"Oh my God, this is *ba'shert*," Sarah shrieked as she studied the return address. She held the envelope to her heart. Braydon scratched his head and dared to ask. "What does bah-shit mean?"

"It's not 'bah-shit', it's 'ba'shert'," she giggled. "It's Jewish for fate, kismet, providence, all rolled up into one tidy word, *ba'shert*." With that, her attention returned to the envelope clutched in her hand. She quietly migrated toward a private corner where she hastily opened and read the letter from Anna Daniels:

Dear Sarah,

When I received your Fed Ex, I was spooked, because for some strange reason, you've been on my mind a lot lately. I'm going to keep this short, because I'm hoping that by sending you my phone number, we'll speak soon. I think we probably have a lot to talk about, don't you? Please call me ASAP.

Anna

Sarah wistfully steered herself back to her chair. No one in the room dared to intrude on such a clearly contemplative and poignant moment.

* * *

Reva Leah Stern

It was a clear, glorious day and Sarah was driving along the highway in her rented turquoise Chevelle en route to a Montreal adventure. As the car radio trumpeted Helen Reddy's declaration of independence; Sarah added her less-than-dulcet voice in harmony with Helen's manifesto.

Although she handled the wheel with the confidence of Mario Andretti, navigating gave her palpitations. Travelling strange territory on her own was a terrifying new experience for a woman whose previous journeys had been confined to a five-mile radius of her home. Driving and navigating had always been Saul's job, but she was now determined to overcome her fear and find her way on her own. She would use this desolate stretch of highway to vent some of the anger she'd stored away since Saul's painful exit.

As Sarah cruised along, her jumbled thoughts gave way to youthful memories of her last contact with Anna; the willowy, raven-haired beauty with an outrageous sense of humour.

She began to feel anxious about her pending divorce; a humiliating fact she wasn't prepared to share with her old friend just yet. She wasn't ready to admit the failure of her "perfect little life," as Anna had once bitterly described it. She considered, if their reunion turned out well, she'd share the whole sordid story and look forward to hearing Anna's humorously cynical view of Saul.

The sudden switch to foreign road signs was becoming a growing obstacle between her and her destination. Sarah had hoped that her high school

French would kick in when she crossed the Quebec border, but the best she could do was recognize the gas pump image on a sign. She pulled into the service centre to ask for assistance. The unilingual, French-speaking, gas station attendant seemed to have difficulty with, "How do I get to the Queen Elizabeth Hotel?" but he clearly understood, "Fill it up," and "How much do I owe you?"

After due consideration, she purchased a five-dollar English map of Montreal from the French speaking attendant, who clearly understood that request as well.

* * *

Sarah arrived safely at the hotel. The valet handed her a parking stub, then jumped into the front seat and tore away like a bandit on the lam, leaving her standing there wondering if Hertz would ever see its car again. As she watched her rental car burn rubber, she thought:

It's a strange ritual that valets perform: They take your vehicle into custody for safe-keeping. But in those few moments between the time you step out of your car, and they step in, your seat has been adjusted, your mirror shifted, your radio is on some foreign station, and there are cigarette ashes on the floor.

She shrugged, picked up her overnight bag, and headed inside the hotel.

An ambitious porter had convinced Sarah that transporting her single bag up nineteen floors on the elevator would be his pleasure and his duty.

Once inside the beautifully-designed suite, he turned up the heat, turned down the bed, and opened the blinds. All that, it seemed to Sarah, warranted a larger tip than she had planned to offer. She had booked a high-end hotel to maintain the image of her successful life, but she still needed to be frugal where possible; and that was evident in the meagre tip she handed the overly-eager porter.

After admiring the attributes of the luxurious room, Sarah settled into a cushy comfy chair, dialled Anna's number, and left a message confirming their nine o'clock breakfast date.

* * *

It's only 9:20, Sarah rationalized. *Maybe Anna missed the message.*

Sarah had downed a cup-and-a-half of morning coffee while she patiently waited in the designated café. After another fifteen minutes, she bristled at the idea that she could have come so far just to be snubbed once again by the same old friend.

A sure indication her resolve was evaporating was how aggressively she was doodling on her paper placemat with only black and purple crayons. She tried to concentrate on her *Montreal Gazette,* but the caffeine was working against her. She tapped her fingers on the fake wood table, keeping time with her angry heart palpitations.

Her edginess increased when she spotted her waitress engaged in animated conversation with a matronly woman dressed in management attire. They appeared disgruntled as they glanced toward Sarah. She deduced that they were unhappy that she was taking up a booth during rush hour without ordering. Sarah raised the *Gazette* in front of her face and feigned deep concentration as the stocky woman with steely hair and red-framed glasses moved aggressively toward her. The intruder stood steadfast and silent by Sarah's table.

Sarah finally set the paper aside and glanced up at the formidable woman who Sarah was then able to identify, by the bright eyes and impish smile, as her childhood friend.

"I'm still late and you're still baffled by it." That was hello in Anna-speak.

Sarah exhaled her name and rose to her feet, "Anna?"

Without a word, Anna bent over, and bear hugged Sarah. "Yup, it's me in here under all this blubber," she confirmed as she let go and sat across from her friend.

The two sat in silence eyeing each other like a gazelle and a rhino in the Serengeti.

"What really pisses me off, Sarah, is that you've barely changed since I saw you last. Do you sleep in a cryogenic chamber or is that what a wealthy, privileged life does for you?"

Anna saw the glint of disappointment in her friend's eyes, so she leaned forward, offered a humble smile, and a mea culpa. "I'm sorry, Sarah. That was meant to be funny, but it only took a second before I realized it wasn't."

"Forget it. I wouldn't recognize you if you didn't start this reunion with your foot in your mouth." The friends shared a relieved giggle.

The two women, having discarded their defences, began the process of reminiscing over the lost years.

Anna was keenly interested to hear about the children, but to Sarah's relief, when it came to Saul, she merely asked if he was well and still practising.

The waitress took their order, poured coffee, and silently sashayed away.

Sarah took a sip of coffee and replied, "Saul is doing very well. And yes, he's still practising, thanks for asking, Anna." That was all she said, and Anna did not pursue. She seemed thrilled by Sarah's unusual evolution to budding journalist.

"You were always a serious bookworm, and I remember you had that weekly column in the town paper. It was great."

"You remember that? Wow, I'm flattered. I always wondered how many of my peers actually read the column back then. You might be the only one." She grinned.

"Nah, kids are narcissistic. They would have read it, if only to see if you mentioned their names." She smirked.

The waitress placed two warm bagels in front of the women and asked; "Will that be all?"

They replied in unison, "Peanut butter please." Another throw-back connection that made them shake their heads and laugh. The waitress pulled two packets from her apron, plunked them down, and left.

"So, Sarah, come on, what's the story? What took you back to that godforsaken town...and what could be keeping you there, as you shockingly told me on the phone, for weeks or possibly even months?"

"Hey, Prescott's not so bad. We had some really great times there. Don't be such a cynic. There are still a lot of nice people left in town." At Anna's look, she acquiesced, "But yes, truthfully, sometimes I do wonder what's keeping me there."

"Maybe it's Mrs. Perkins's cinnamon jawbreakers," Anna winked. "Come on, just give me a quick synopsis of why?" She urged as she lifted her coffee in a mock toast.

With that, Sarah nodded, spread peanut butter on her bagel and proceeded to explain how she came to her mission.

"Okay, that's my story. Anna, now it's your turn. Tell all, puh-le-ease while I eat."

She found no urging necessary: Anna was ready and willing to update her.

Only two years after her falling out with Anna, Luc had beaten her so badly she lost the only pregnancy she'd ever have. "There had been a warrant issued for his arrest, but he was never found, or more likely, they never bothered to search. In spite of that awful experience, I spent twenty-three years living happily in sin. I met my guy, Marty, through Bayla and Asher Fleischman. Do you remember them?"

Sarah nodded vigorously. "Of course, I do." She assured as she popped the last bite of bagel into her mouth.

"Whew, that's good, 'cause I told them you were coming in and they're gonna call you to come for a visit."

Sarah stopped chewing as a look of reticence slowly surfaced.

"Come on. Don't look so worried. They're great people and I couldn't help myself." Anna waved, dismissing the subject, "Anyway, back to my story. When my dad told Bayla that I was single again, she played matchmaker and chose her nephew, Marty, a high school history teacher. It was a perfect match. Luc had disappeared, so I couldn't get a divorce, so we couldn't get married. But it didn't matter much to either of us 'cause I could never have kids anyway.

"Ya know, before Marty passed away, I was a raving beauty; but since then, I stopped colouring my hair and wearing makeup. I eat everything in sight, and I'm not even depressed."

"Do you ever think about meeting someone else?" Sarah asked.

"I had the best, until five years ago, so I have no interest in meeting second best. Besides, I'm too busy to deal with all that shit. After my parents split, I opened a little restaurant here with my dad. And I've got all my community activities, and Marty's wonderful family; and at this moment, sitting here with my old friend, I feel like my life's pretty complete."

Sarah smiled warmly at her friend while considering whether to pursue her next line of questions. But the inquisitor in her won out. She leaned forward and softly asked; "Anna, it's so hard for me to believe that your parents split up. They were so devoted to each other. Do you mind me asking about it?"

Anna shook her head, "I expected you to ask. It was all so sad. My mother had fallen into a wildly-deep depression, and my dad did everything humanly possible to help. But she'd scare away the customers, spouting crazy, irrational gibberish about them stealing from her...or...threatening that she was going to poison them. One time, she headed out the restaurant door with a customer's baby in her arms, screaming that she was going to protect her from them."

As Anna spoke, Sarah's eye filled with tears. "Oh my God, Anna, I had no idea. It must have been hell for your dad."

"He couldn't leave her at home alone because she'd leave the stove on all day or forget where she was and mistake her armchair for a toilet. My father would come home exhausted after an eighteen-hour day and have to clean up her mess.

"Sometimes, when my father tried to help her, she'd fly into a rage. Since she couldn't...or wouldn't take her medication properly, she overdosed twice." Anna wiped away a tear.

"Finally, he found someone willing to help. It was a retired auto worker from Germany who, oddly enough, ended up in Prescott after the war. And no, he wasn't a Jew. His name was Hans Gertner. Maybe it was restitution he wanted to give, or absolution he wanted to get, but for eleven years, he fed, cleaned, and comforted my mother."

"That must have given your dad some relief?" She smiled wanly.

"Yeah, well, just months after Hans began caring for her, she chased my father out of the house. He came here to Montreal and started a new life.

"For a while, my mother really seemed to improve. She and Hans were even able to continue running the restaurant. But her illness returned with a vengeance, and she became more debilitated than ever. Hans couldn't handle her any longer, so Dad and I brought her here and got her into a nursing home. Then, Dad sold our house and restaurant in Prescott."

"Did she improve in the home?"

Anna took a deep, reviving breath and continued. "When I'd visit, I'd find her sitting in a corner, rocking, and babbling under her breath in Yiddish. She always had a pile of scrap paper bits in her lap that she'd stuff between the pages of a book." Sarah cocked her head and listened as if she was hearing some discordant melody.

"Every night, the caregivers would shake the bits loose and dump them. The next day, my mother would repeat the exercise."

Sarah was perplexed. "That's so bizarre, Anna. Why do you think she did it?"

Anna shook her head slowly and shrugged. "Oh God! There have been so many things in my life that have been way too difficult for me to understand, much less explain to others. I'm a child of Holocaust survivors. Hah! Survivor is such a misleading term, because it implies that you live on. For my father, living on was a possibility, but for my mother, it was a condemnation."

Sarah's jaw dropped and her eyes widened. "But Anna, I remember her laughter. I remember her teaching us Yiddish songs. I remember us lying on the lawn roasting in baby oil and iodine concoctions, and your mother waving at us from her upstairs window. I remember the three of us learning the Hora from that *Barry Sisters* album. It must give you some comfort to know you made her happy?"

Anna smiled. "You're such a Pollyanna. You buy into the idea that anyone who laughs or smiles is happy. For a lucky few, maybe. But most survivors are hiding their misery behind a paralytic smile that masks their pain. My mother hid until the day she died."

A contemplative silence filled the moment as Anna buttoned her jacket, gathered up her handbag, and began to slide out of her seat. "So, you're free for dinner tonight, yes?" She confirmed as she rose.

"You bet," Sarah eagerly replied.

The waitress approached with the check and Anna grabbed it. Sarah clasped on to the edge of the bill and pulled. "You can pull all you want, but I'm not letting go. My city, my treat."

Sarah finally let go and sat back. "Fine, I won't argue. But then dinner is on me, tonight."

"You mean I'm inviting you to dine with me in my restaurant and you're planning to pay?"

Sarah flushed a little and twisted in her seat. "I didn't know we'd be eating in your restaurant."

"My God, woman, you really haven't changed. You're so worried: 'Ooh, what'll I say if the food tastes like shit? What if the place is a godawful dump?' Well, am I right?" She ended her playful taunt with a broad smile.

Sarah had unwittingly lowered her eyes as Anna's observations accurately described her apprehension. She looked up, grinned, and cheekily asked, "Well, what if?"

Anna smiled, scribbled down the address and hurried out the door.

Sarah took a moment to sit and calmly collect her thoughts before returning to the hotel.

When she got back to her room, she was relieved to discover that the telephone message light wasn't a warning of some dreaded crisis, but was instead, an invitation to join the Fleischmans' for lunch at 1 p.m. at their home. It came complete with precise directions.

CHAPTER NINE

Self-congratulations were on Sarah's mind as she arrived at the entrance of a beautiful condo building without getting lost. A uniformed valet rushed over to take the car, but declined the tip she dutifully offered. She was grateful again for a good start to the day.

As she rode the elevator to the top floor, she was awestruck by the vast difference between the Fleischmans' tiny, rustic flat in Prescott and this exquisite, luxury high rise.

Stepping inside the marble foyer and being greeted by their maid, prompted Sarah to muse, that like TV's, "The Jefferson's," the Fleischmans had definitely moved on up.

Both Fleischmans looked well-preserved and stylish. They warmly welcomed Sarah with hugs and flattery.

The sumptuous lunch was served in their sunroom which was a domed glassed-in dining space. The food was prepared by Bayla but served by the crisply-uniformed maid.

As the social graces of reunion subsided, the conversation progressed. Sarah was hopeful she'd hear about details that had been lacking on Halloween.

They offered a narrowly-focussed view of their arrival and permanent stay in this lovely building...but not of the journey to get there. It was obvious that Asher and Bayla Fleischman had found security in the cosmopolitan lifestyle of Montreal. Their three children had impressive careers, successful marriages, and provided an abundance of grandchildren. It seemed that was all there was to tell.

Of course, in return, Sarah updated them on the life and passing of her parents. After a couple of pots of tea, and hours of vibrant conversation, the wily journalist in Sarah finally emerged. "Mr. and Mrs. Fleischman, what motivated your family to leave Prescott?"

Asher lowered his gaze. Bayla patted his hand and smiled wanly at their visitor. "I can answer that, my dear, if you have the time?"

An enthusiastic nod was all that was needed from Sarah. Once Bayla recalled the disturbing incident, she continued with determination. Although her telling of their plight was detailed and animated, she seemed able to keep her emotions in check.

She described the vandalism pretty much as Wesley's article had, except that he failed to mention what prompted their rush to leave. "Who knows what kind of crazies it takes to commit such acts?" Asher interjected. "But it wasn't the vandalism, or the theft, or even the fire...it was the swastikas and hateful words they left in bright red paint on our front door: 'THE ONLY GOOD JEW IS A DEAD JEW.'" He shrunk down in his chair shaking his head.

Bayla continued. "They left hateful messages on our outside walls...and the sidewalk..." She grimaced, "words I can't even say. We've never been back to Prescott, but we've been told that there are still traces of that paint on the stone walls."

"For us, this was an echo of Hitler's voice," Asher asserted. "Just in time, we escaped that hell in Europe by taking our children to England. The rest of our family wouldn't leave Poland. They didn't believe the signs. When the war was over, every one of them was dead."

Tears glistened in Bayla's eyes as Asher explained their dauntless belief; "After the Holocaust, we each tried to find purpose in continuing to live. But we were blessed. We had found each other, had our children, and that gave us purpose. Hitler incinerated six million of us, and we needed to find a way to emerge from those ashes. We needed to find hope and purpose in family, friendship, charity...in all things that require human compassion. Eventually, we realized that the best memorial tribute we could offer to our loved ones, and to strangers alike, was to succeed at life...for their memory, for our children, and for our People."

A light rapping at the door prompted Asher to make a hasty exit. After a moment, he returned, accompanied by a frail old woman. She smiled at Sarah and, in a childlike voice, exclaimed, "Sarah, my darling, you still look like a young girl."

In spite of the ravages of life and age, Sarah was able to recognize Esther Gorman, the lady whose house and whereabouts had been of concern to Sarah on Halloween night.

A sudden montage of pictures fluttered through Sarah's mind. Images of Mrs. Gorman's auburn hair in a neat French twist, and always dressed in a crisp, clean cotton frock. Now, Sarah was standing before the weathered incarnation of the beautiful woman who had always welcomed her and her little sister into her home. and regaled them both with stories of fairy-tale princesses and evil kings.

Again, the distance gap quickly closed, and through the course of the afternoon, Sarah learned that the Gormans with their two daughters, followed the Fleischmans to Montreal. After Esther's husband, Albert, passed away, she moved into an apartment in the same building as the Fleischmans.

"Sarah, darling, I loved your parents. They were always so kind. Oy, your daddy was such a hero. We remember when a bunch of hoodlums ruined our Shul at Rosh Hashana. Graffiti, torn prayer books, ach, you name it, right, Asher?"

He nodded and continued. "It's true, Esther. We thought, *that's it, there won't be services this year*. Even in the camps, we managed to hold services in complete secret, so the Nazis wouldn't find out and beat us to death." A cold stillness filled the room.

Esther kept the story going. "Yes, but in this time, in this place, your father took care of everything. He made sure we could pray at Rosh Hashanah and Yom Kippur without fear. Such a mensch, he was."

Esther's childlike voice conjured colourful memories for Sarah of her unique tales of good and evil. The fact that Esther remembered Sarah's family in such a respectful and affectionate way, brought shared pleasure to both of them.

After sitting for hours and downing an entire pot of tea, Sarah was rocking in her seat, desperate to use the washroom, but not wanting to pause the conversation. It was getting late however, and she needed to leave to meet Anna. So finally, she ceded. "Mrs. Fleischman, before I go, could I use your bathroom? I wouldn't want to have an accident on my way."

Esther chuckled. "No, my dear, you certainly don't want to do that again."

Sarah cocked her head in bewilderment, but accepted that Esther's peculiar utterance was an unfortunate factor of aging.

* * *

At 4:57 p.m., the turquoise Chevelle rolled to a stop at 763 Rue de Marcelle. Sarah looked at the note once again and confirmed that the address was correct, but nowhere on the paper did it mention the name of the restaurant. She studied the neon sign in front: BENANNA BISTRO. She smiled wryly at the amalgamation of the names; Anna, and her father, Ben.

Sarah looked up to see a red-jacketed valet waiting to harass her car. This time, without hesitation, she relinquished the keys, but offered a warning. "I don't expect to find a scratch, or even a drop of pigeon poop on this beauty when I get her back." She declared with a wink and a smile.

Anna was waiting at the entrance, her eyes twinkling.

"Your mouth's open again, my dear." She teased.

"Of course, it is! And that's exactly what you expected. This place is absolutely gorgeous." Sarah exclaimed as her friend took her by the arm and led her inside.

"This is my baby, and it inherited my good looks." Anna hardly took a breath before adding, "We don't officially open 'til six, but by seven, you can't get in the front door. That's why I wanted you here early, so we can talk and talk until we need tongue-splints. Come on, I'll give you the Pope's tour."

As they glided through the dining room and bar area, Anna proudly pointed out the design and decorative choices that were her own, explaining symbolism and significance.

"You see over the bar, those big palm tree chandeliers with beaded crystal bulbs and brass palm fronds dripping tear drop crystals? I designed those and had them made for my dad, who never got to see California but always dreamed of going. When he passed away and I was able to redecorate this place, I thought of him and my mom in almost every choice I made. Check out the dividing wall between the bar and dining room. There see; two large, black marble silhouettes dancing toward each other, inset into the white marble wall. It represents their liberation from the camp."

"It's beautiful...but where are you in that memory?"

"I'm the one committing that image to memory, Maybe I was smart enough at eighteen months to know

I'd use it like this one day." She replied with a winsome smile.

  The rest of the tour included viewing lush fabrics, rich textures, and subtle colour choices that gave the bistro a cozy and elegant ambiance; navy blue leather seats, taupe granite tables, soft grey textured walls resting above Wedgewood blue wainscotting. Every private booth had its own crystal palm, table lamp, as well as a crystal pineapple candle holder.

  "Anna, this is spectacular! No wonder the crowds are lining up."

  "It's true, but initially, they came for my dad's incredible cuisine. He truly was a chef extraordinaire. He taught our chefs, who still teach their chefs, and so on. This is all because of his culinary expertise. He was the inside genius, and I the outside, if you get my meaning."

  Sarah shook her head and chuckled. "You're still the same amazing freak of nature, Anna, and I couldn't be happier about that."

* * *

  Tucked away in a private corner, the two friends enjoyed a quiet cocktail and an outstanding dinner. Sarah was sure she had won a gastronomic lottery with two restaurateur friends who provided her with the best of the highest and lowest-style cuisine in the country, from crunchy, almond-crusted duck breasts, with Chanterelle salad, at Benanna Bistro, to hot beef sandwiches with gravy and creamy mashed potatoes at the Best Service Diner. Life was improving deliciously.

* * *

The two women laughed and reminisced all evening, "Remember that sickly-hot summer night we had a pyjama party at your apartment?" Anna prodded. "It was one of the few parties I ever attended with a bunch of your air-headed friends, and you know what? It wasn't worth it." She smirked and sat back with folded arms, awaiting Sarah's reaction.

Sarah tilted her head in amused bewilderment.

"Come on, Sarah...that was the night those dumb-assed girls sneaked onto your roof to flirt with a bunch of loud-mouthed motorcycle bums on the street below."

Sarah, caught mid-sip, suddenly swallowed and squealed "Oh, my God, I remember that! They were so obnoxious. The yelling and swearing were disgusting, right?"

"Yup, and your neighbours called the police, who threatened to throw us in the 'hoosegow.' Then one of the idiot girls asked, 'What's a hoosegow? Is it a fun place?'" Anna rolled her eyes, "God, they were dumb."

Sarah shook her head. "Not all of them. Do you remember the summer we met Eleanor Miller?"

Anna squinted. "Eleanor Miller? I'm not sure."

"She lived in that little cottage across from the beach."

Anna knitted her brow in thought. "Oh, yeah, of course! She's the one who saved our asses on the beach one day, right?"

"Yup. That's how we met her."

"Sure, I remember. We spent a few days with her that summer and I remember seeing her at school in the fall, but she seemed to distance herself from everyone. Then, she kinda faded from the picture altogether. Hm, do you know why?"

"I'm trying to find out. What I do know is, she had a really rough time as a teen."

"Ah, yeah...yeah, I remember. Customers in our restaurant would blather salacious gossip about her, but I never believed it."

Sarah gasped and sat poker straight. "You knew about her being raped?"

"Raped? What are you talking about? Raped?" Anna grimaced as she repeated the word. "No. For God's sake, Sarah. The talk was, she got pregnant by some teacher or minister and her mother sent her away to a home for unwed mothers."

Sarah's face flushed at Anna's casual declaration. "Jesus, Anna, she wasn't pregnant! I haven't found even a suggestion of that, but I'm becoming more and more convinced she was raped."

"Shit," Anna slumped back in her seat and mumbled; "I'm not sure which is worse."

"Well, I do!"

"Jeez, you're really touchy about this, Sarah. I barely remember her, but you seem pretty invested."

"I've been intrigued by it since I arrived back in Prescott. She's an amazing person, Anna. This thing hangs over her head like Damocles' sword, and I want to help her." Sarah's eyed welled with tears. "Maybe it's *B'ashert*. I mean, I started out thinking I was gonna make my big entrée into journalism writing about this kiddie porn crap, but maybe I need to be changing my focus. I'm sorry, Anna. I didn't mean to get all maudlin on you. It's your turn. Give me a memory that's not going to make me wanna shoot myself." She sat back and tried her best to offer a smile.

Anna thought a moment. "Okay, I've got one. Do you remember a special birthday gift you got from your Aunt Bracha?"

Sarah perked up. "Do I? Are you kidding me? It was a wonderful book of Jewish bible stories. I took it with me everywhere. I figured if I learned everything in it, all my dreams would come true, like in Esther Gorman's fairy tales." She paused and took a breath, "I also recall that you decided that now that I had read one book on Jewish history, I should have a *Bat Mitzvah*..."

Anna laughed, "It didn't take too much convincing to sell the idea to your mom, but she was baffled by my insisting that it was to be a 'surprise' *Bat Mitzvah*."

"Yeah, my mom, the Jewish secularist who was raised Orthodox. Christmas trees and Easter eggs, she understood, but a *Bat Mitzvah* wasn't really on her radar, or more specifically a '*surprise' Bat Mitzvah*.'"

"Between your pinko father and your assimilated mother, I'm amazed that you grew up giving a shit about being Jewish at all."

"Well, they definitely preached what they didn't practise; and I guess I listened more than they ever thought I did, 'cause they always seemed happy when I was trudging along a Jewish path, and oddly enough, so was I." She punctuated her claim with a sassy nod.

"That's why I was so anxious to do that *Bat Mitzvah* thing for you, Sarah. I never had one. My parents didn't even want me to acknowledge the fact that we were Jews." Anna lowered her head and shook it vigorously as if to shake away a bad dream. "Like it was even possible to deny that fact. I mean, the whole town knew the long, blue number engraved on their arms was no Hells Angels' tattoo! Besides, what other restaurant in Prescott listed gefilte fish, boiled flanken, and matzo ball soup on its menu, along with Irish stew, bacon burgers, and Hungarian goulash?" She laughed with abandon.

Sarah let the weight of the moment settle before she returned to the *Bat Mitzvah* topic. "Food is like a secret informant. All that week before the surprise event, I remember smelling cinnamon, vanilla, and maple when I got home from school, but I could never find a trace of the goodies anywhere. Mom claimed to be baking for some fundraising bazaar." Sarah smirked, "She was a lousy liar."

"Hey," Anna protested, "your mom lied expertly plenty of times to get you out of trouble with your dad, so why not for a surprise *Bat Mitzvah*?"

"Anyway, of course I remember that day, 'cause it was one of the worst of my life!" She pouted.

"Then you lied to me, and I'm appalled, 'cause you told me it was the best day ever." Anna countered with a cheeky grin.

Reva Leah Stern

"It's debatable. It was a cold, crappy day in March, and I spent most of it sulking because I had to help out in my parents' store the entire day.

"By noon, Resa showed up in her parka, taunting me, '*na-na-na-na-na*'. She waved a two-dollar bill in my face and sniped, '*Mommy says, you have to take me to the Best Service for lunch.*' So, I had no choice. I schlepped through muddy, brown snow while Resa jumped in every filthy puddle she could find. Oh yeah, it was a hell of a birthday all right. Oh, and at the end of the day, Mom came down to the store, wished me a happy birthday and proudly announced that the whole family was going to the O'Brien Hotel for dinner. Like I was supposed to be grateful for that? Really? From dawn 'til dusk, it was like I'd never been born and then, a simple 'happy birthday' and fish and chips served on a white tablecloth was supposed to make it all better? I refused to speak through the entire meal...but believe me, I still ate. Then, I laid eyes on the gorgeous birthday cake the chef had made for me. But Mom insisted we had to have it at home because it was too late for Resa. Well, I let loose. I didn't care if Resa fell asleep in her plate. I wanted my birthday to last as long as possible, since I'd been denied the first eight hours of it. But, of course, we left 'cause of Resa, Resa, Resa!

"Allan opened the door first and snapped on the lights and I almost lost my dinner when everyone yelled 'surprise'. I had no idea what was happening. Then I spotted you, behind a garden of colourful balloons and a huge bouquet of flowers, and you were. grinning like a cartoon character." Sarah's eyes twinkled as the memory came alive. Anna caught her drift, and she picked up the story.

"I was very proud of myself, Sarah. I decorated the table with a lace cloth borrowed from Mrs. Gorman, and I placed your prized book next to the Manischewitz wine. I added that big flower arrangement I co-opted from Locke's funeral home."

Sarah retracted in feigned horror. "I was sniffing some dead man's bouquet? Really?" She groaned.

Anna shrugged. "Hey, the guy or woman was dead, they didn't need it. Okay, maybe it was kind of tasteless. Oh shit, do you remember the ceremony?"

Sarah giggled and nodded. Anna proceeded to recall the ritual.

"Sarah Klein, you have met the requirements of Jewish law, as far as we know, since we don't know what Jewish law really requires, other than the Ten Commandments blah, blah, blah. We have all gathered together to witness your transition from young girl to young woman, blah, blah, blah. Your careful responses to the 'Rabbi's' challenging questions are crucial...or something like that."

"I think it was exactly like that Anna!" Sarah responded breathlessly with a strange fusion of laughter and awe. "Oh, oh, remember? My dufus brother, Lewis the 'Rabbi' walked in, decked out in a *Yarmulke* and *Tallis*. He asked me a couple of questions like 'what makes kosher pickles, kosher?' I think he *did* manage to ask a few pertinent questions, although I can't for the life of me remember even one."

Anna shook her head and waved dismissively, "I can't help you. I wasn't in charge of the brainy stuff."

"At the conclusion of the ceremony, he informed me that I had officially passed from girlhood to womanhood, so I should now take over his duties, which would have been a cinch, because he never did anything.

"I hope I thanked you that night, Anna, because it was a really sweet thing you did, and I would have been a real shit if I didn't." She reached across and squeezed Anna's hand.

"Ah, you're a shit anyhow, but if you even think about getting all mushy and nostalgic on me, I'm taking your lousy glass of pinot away 'cause you obviously can't handle booze." With that, Anna pulled her hand away and slid Sarah's wine glass aside.

"Come on, Anna, underneath all that tough bravado, you're just a sentimental sissy and I'll bet you think about the good old days just as much as I do. I only wish I could find them again."

Anna slid Sarah's glass back to its spot and continued in a more contemplative mood. "I'll demonstrate my continuing thoughtfulness by sending you to Prescott tomorrow with the rest of this fine bottle of wine, your own box of ultra soft Kleenex, and a gourmet doggie bag of the chef's best...but not before you tell me about your visit with the Fleischmans."

CHAPTER TEN

As Sarah was relating the revelations of the Fleischman visit, she grew inspired to ask Anna whether she had ever felt the misery of anti-Semitism when she lived in Prescott.

Anna gave it a moment of thought. "I do remember Fleischman's grocery store being vandalized, and how the Jewish families in the area panicked when they heard about it. I know it was described as a random attack, but to them, it was anything but. As far as my family goes, I don't remember a particular incident, but the hate was always there, simmering under the surface. But I'd bet if anything of consequence did happen in our family, it'd be in one of my mother's journals."

"Journals!" The word resounded in Sarah's head like the warning toll of a bell. She leaned in.

Anna nodded, "Yeah, do you ever remember my mom walking around the house mumbling and clutching a notebook to her chest?"

Sarah nodded. "Yeah, yes, I do. Go on."

"Well, those were her journals. Oh man, how I wanted to get rid of them."

"Why? You and I kept diaries and I recall some pretty interesting entries...like the time you stole a lipstick and shoved it into _my_ pocket so _you_ wouldn't get caught."

Anna brightened, "Oh crap, yeah! Remember when that fat, acne-faced stock boy grabbed us both and told us we were going to rot in jail?"

"Oh, I thanked God he called your parents instead of mine, 'cause my dad would've tarred and feathered me," Sarah snickered as she offered an exaggerated shiver.

"Sure, joke if you want...it worked out fine for you, but my mother almost had a coronary when she heard the guy was threatening to imprison me, for life."

Sarah scoffed and rolled her eyes, "Oh, come on, she knew he was bluffing."

Anna's expression turned deadly serious. "My mother could never conceive of a bluff. The very idea of imprisonment was a lifelong fear of hers."

"But she'd been living free in Canada for over a decade by then." Sarah protested.

Anna's face paled and her body tightened, "Shit, you're naïve. A goddamn decade? Is that supposed to mean it's all over; forget it and go have a devil-may-care future?

"For shit's sake, Sarah, get real! The fact is, on the day Auschwitz was liberated, my mother became a prisoner for life. When the allies found her, she was crouched in a corner of a camp kitchen with one arm around emaciated me and the other around a small, bloated flour sack."

"A bloated flour sack in Auschwitz?" Sarah gasped. "Sorry to seem astonished, but isn't there some painful irony in the idea of a bag full of flour at the end of a war that was intended to starve those they didn't outright massacre?"

Anna offered a wry smile. "Yeah, it would seem so; but this bag was stuffed with paper and fabric marked with smudges of coal and blood. Those ragged remnants held the secret to my mother's destiny."

"What?" She gulped. "You never told me about any secret flour sack?" She emphasised.

"There were things that I couldn't or wouldn't talk about when we were kids. And then there were things that I didn't even know about until many years after our friendship had gone silent." In the pause that followed, Anna stared into her wine glass, as if looking for an answer to float to the top. She suddenly raised her head and looked directly at Sarah and continued. "Here's the thing. Your parents were born in this country. You're a real Canadian, Sarah. But I was a survivor, an immigrant, a Greenie, a misfit. I didn't feel comfortable anywhere, except in your home. Your family was accepting of me, and you were smart enough, or scared enough, not to ask about my former life." She took a sustaining gulp of wine before continuing. "Sarah, did you know that the word 'Holocaust' wasn't even in the dictionary at that time. Now, it's become synonymous with the word 'survivor', and most people still have no concept of what Holocaust survivors actually had to endure in order to be labelled with that title."

Sarah drew in a long, desperate breath. "Then start with me, Anna. Educate me. Tell me what Holocaust meant to a survivor like your mom."

There was a prolonged silence before Anna began to speak in a hoarse thrum.

"In 1943, my mother was five months pregnant when her family was rounded up and shipped to Auschwitz in a cattle car."

"I knew about that. We talked about it when we were kids."

"What did you know?" She sharply retorted.

"I knew they were transported by train to a concentration camp and that you were born there, and, you all survived."

"So, that's it? It's all just that fucking simple?" She sputtered in anger.

"No, of course, it was anything but simple! I just meant that I knew those basic facts." Sarah shook her head in remorse. "I'm sorry, Anna, if you'll forgive my blunder, I'm ready to listen."

After a bit of fidgeting and a few more sips of wine, she attempted a warmup joke. "Okay, but if you end up with indigestion after this, don't blame my chef." She began twisting and unfolding her napkin. Finally, she set it down and sat back, looking dispirited. "Honestly Sarah, this is so bloody hard; I don't know where to begin."

"Maybe start at the railway station. I've certainly read about how those Nazi bastards forced Jews into crammed cattle cars with no regard for human life."

"Human life? To the Nazis, Jews were never human." She seethed.

Short of breath and trans-like, Anna began to recall the story of her parents' survival. The painful images her parents shared with her had been burned into her history from birth; and now, they flashed through her memory like a Chaplin film on Benzedrine.

She told of the hoards who suffocated on the journey from lack of air in the cattle cars.

"For those who made it to the destination alive, they emerged from the overwhelming stink of feces, urine and vomit-filled boxcars, with a first breath of fresh air that felt like a critical and welcome reprieve.

"Then, everyone, no matter how old, feeble, sick, or infirm, was ordered at gunpoint to march the seemingly endless distance from the train stop to the camp. Hoping not to anger the guards, my parents and grandparents trudged along, doing their best to keep up while concealing their weakened bodies.

"After finally arriving inside the camp gate, my mother was forced to watch as her parents were humiliated, beaten, and then shot dead. Their slaughters were used as confirmation that all who were about to enter the gates had no power over their lives.

"My grandparents were among the 'chosen people' who didn't have the privilege of politely refusing to be chosen. My mother, always believed that those who died at the gates were the lucky ones.

"My mom, five months pregnant with me, was also selected. While others might argue that she ultimately survived, they would be hard-pressed to get her to agree.

Reva Leah Stern

"My father remained in line, frozen with fear and evidently immune to the repeated demand of a German guard, that he step out of the line. An SS officer marched up to him, yanked him out of the queue, and dragged him before the camp's commandant. My mother never forgot the wide sardonic grin that flashed across the Nazi leader's face as delighted in watching my dad being dragged like roadkill over blood-stained gravel.

"Before the war, my dad, Benjamin Daniels had been the executive chef in one of the best hotel restaurants in Warsaw. The commandant had recognized him in the line and called over a nearby guard, ordering him to 'bring the ugly little Jew to him...alive.'

"As the guard forced the chef to his knees, the commandant paced back and forth, eyeing the chef all the while. Finally, he spoke.

"'You! Juden, get up. You're a lucky Jew. We can use a cook with some imagination besides sauerkraut, boiled potato, and sausage every night. I'm a generous man, you have a choice, cooking in the officers' kitchen or digging shit out of the officers' latrine. For this minute, it's up to you.'

"Thinking that he might be in a bargaining position and with little to lose, Benjamin Daniels told the commandant that he'd cook for the officers, but only if his wife remained with him and her safety was guaranteed.

"The commandant was incensed. He shoved him back onto his knees. "Do you think you're applying again for a position at the King's Hotel? You are Jewish vermin, and this is not a request, it's an order. If you refuse, your Jew wife will be shot, immediately." With that the commandant kicked the chef in the chest, knocking the wind out of him.

Ben Daniels rose to his feet and proclaimed that if they killed his wife, they could kill him as well, or he would do it himself because his life was worthless without her. The commandant was livid. He ordered them both to be taken away and shot. But before the guard laid a hand on him, Chef Daniels offered one last persuasive argument. "Commandant, do you remember the wonderful meals served at the King's Hotel? All those revered recipes were created by me and stored in my memory. They're not in books, they're nowhere but here." The chef pointed slowly at his temple. "If you shoot me, all those gastronomic miracles will be gone. But on the other hand, even with what I assume are limited food rations, I can create meals, fit for a king. But I can't do that if I'm dead; and without my wife, I'm dead."

So, Benjamin Daniels became the officers' chef, and to keep him from attempting any *heroic* gestures, they made Sophie the official taster. That way, if he entertained any thought of adding some lethal seasoning to the officers' dinner, he'd have a serious deterrent.

The Danielses were given living quarters behind the kitchen in a five-by-six-foot storeroom with concrete walls and no window. It served as Anna's birthing room, living room, and playground. In fact, it represented the boundaries of her entire world.

Her mother's "career" as "poisoned food tester" kept her moderately healthy, so that she had milk to feed her baby for as long as possible. But Anna still spent almost all of the first two years of her life in that tiny cell, surviving on her mother's milk and the soul-nurturing songs and stories her parents shared with her in the middle of the cold, dark nights.

Other than her parents, she never saw another human being until she was over a year old. Then suddenly, for no apparent reason, the commandant began to insist that Anna be brought to his table where he offered her the odd piece of dried apple or a slice of bread with honey. He also brought her hand-me-down stockings, blankets, sweaters, bonnets, and a warm bunting among other clothing items.

"Poppa rationalized that somewhere inside that Nazi uniform was a father who missed his own child. But imagine the hypocrisy of this top-ranking Nazi who, with equal delight, could order the murder of my mother's parents, and my parents, and then play hide-and-seek with their toddler. The commandant taught me German songs. Perhaps, for a moment, he allowed himself to forget that I was a Jew. My dad observed that with every conciliatory gesture, my mother became more and more withdrawn." Anna exhaled a heavy sigh, then paused to finish off her wine.

Sarah was morbidly spellbound. She didn't want the story left unfinished. "After ordering the murder of her parents and then seeing that Nazi bastard interacting with her baby, that must have been the trigger to your mother's serious illness. I mean, that kind of trauma would break anyone."

"Perhaps. But I don't think that's what broke her." Anna whispered as she slumped in her seat. "After the war ended, my father finally learned what my mother had done in Auschwitz that caused her to retreat into her solitary world." Anna shook her head and raised her hand like a stop sign.

"No Anna, you can't just stop there. What do you mean, what she did? What the hell did she do?" The words came out far more conspiratorially than she had intended.

Anna pretended to ignore the questions. She motioned to the bartender, and in an instant, he placed two glasses of Grand Marnier in front of the emotionally-exhausted diners. They silently toasted then drifted into their own silent escape.

Finally, Anna broke the tension with a lightly tinged suggestion. "Believe me, Sarah, you don't want to spend all night hearing about this morbid shit."

"Yeah, weird as it sounds, I do. Yes, I do. For God's sake, Anna, it's early!" There was no response. In the aching void, Sarah felt obligated to break the silence. "Please, Anna, you were about to tell me something monumental about what your mother did in Auschwitz."

Anna sighed and waved her hand as if swatting at a fly. "Let it go, Sarah. I shouldn't have brought it up."

Reva Leah Stern

Sarah cocked her head and stared at her friend with pleading eyes. "Anna, come on, don't make me beg. You know I'm not good at it," She chafed. "Fine, I'm begging now. Please?"

"Shit. You're not going to let go of that bone. I get it. Okay, you asked for it. Don't call me when you can't sleep tonight."

Anna drew a deep breath and continued. "When food supplies were delivered to the officers' kitchen at Auschwitz, every package had to be accounted for, making it impossible to steal a crumb. But my mother managed to save leftovers from the officers' plates. It was hardly sustenance, but any morsel offered hope..."

Slowly and systematically, Anna described how Sophie would cut a tiny strip of fabric from f a flour sack and write a coded message on it with wet coal dust or animal blood drawn from the meat that Ben was preparing. And if the meat was too dry, she would nick herself and use her own blood. Twice a day, she walked through the children's compound to distribute meals to the officers on watch. She would cautiously search for the designated prisoner to whom she would slip a message, letting him know what time and which way she would pass that day on her return from her deliveries. Then, the response would be discreetly handed back to her as deftly as it had been received. She would surreptitiously study the reply, which contained the name and cellblock of the child to whom she would give the precious rations, hidden under her shirt. For the sake of secrecy, there was only one recipient at a time. The food was given only to children who had a chance at survival; the stronger children who were beginning to show signs of weakening were the priority. Once children were already too deathly ill or too weak to recuperate, they were no longer candidates. When Sophie would return to her room, she would shove the shred of message-bearing fabric into a hole in her rotting mattress."

"Wasn't your father terrified of the risk?"

Anna's shoulders sagged as she quietly replied. "My father didn't know."

Sarah's slack-jaw gape demonstrated her astonishment. "Holy crap! Why did she do it? Why did she take such a chance?"

"My mother hated and loved my father for stepping forward to save us all by providing his services to the Nazis. She loved that we had some food and shelter but hated that our people were suffering and dying all around us from starvation, torture, and the elements. She suffered from survivor's guilt, but desperately wanted someone to make it through the nightmare to tell the civilized world what happened there.

"On the day that the liberators marched in, my mother grabbed an empty flour sack from the kitchen, ran to her mattress, ripped open the rotted cover, removed all of the hidden bits of fabric, and stuffed them into the sack. I was barely more than two years old, but I feel as if I remember her desperately begging me to keep the secret."

A notable change in Anna's demeanour followed a brief pause. She returned to the divulgence with a tone of hostility. "In spite of my mother's wish that someone should survive the war and tell the world about the horrors, she made it perfectly clear it wasn't going to be her. My mother rejected the world. The only person, other than my father, she ever told the story to, was me; and frankly, I didn't need to hear it. But I didn't have a choice, and every time I looked at those bits of fabric, I was doomed to remember. So that's it, Sarah. Pardon my verbal diarrhoea."

Sarah was riveted. She took a sip of water and a deep breath before urging her friend to continue.

"So, your mother brought that flour sack all the way to Canada?"

"Not only did she bring it with her, it became her life's work. You know, I have trouble remembering my phone number, but my mother spent years on those albums, gluing in every piece of fabric, recording the date and name or initials of every child, and mounting a tiny, dried flower or leaf beside each one. Even when no trace of a message remained, the remnant was still included like a tribute to an unknown soldier. I think my mother fantasized, that by keeping all the fragments together, she could somehow make the children whole again.

"There were many times I'd actually find her smiling and humming while gazing at a ragged scrap like she was comforting an orphaned baby. I had no idea what it all meant back then. But I called those albums 'her Auschwitz logs.' My dad found them in a steamer trunk when we were moving her to Montreal." Anna shuddered as she collected her resolve to continue. "My father came to believe it was after she completed the last of those albums that she spiralled completely out of control."

"And those were the books she used to walk around with clutched to her chest?"

Anna held up her palm in a stop gesture. "No. No, those books you're talking about were journals she started keeping on the advice of an old therapist Dad found in Brockville, Dr. Goderich who had treated a lot of WW2 veterans who suffered from PTSD. He suggested an exercise he thought might help. He encouraged her to record her traumatic experiences in the hopes that she'd eventually purge herself of all horrific memories. She remembered and recorded dates and incidents from her childhood in Poland, right through Hitler's rise, and then Auschwitz." A heavy sigh was expunged before Anna proceeded.

"How her memory worked was even stranger. On the same day, in Prescott, she couldn't remember to turn off the stove or flush the toilet, she could recall that in 1931, her Polish neighbour's dog was hit by a car.

"It was bitter irony to discover that, by chronicling her experiences, her mind became so trapped in the horrors of her past, that she couldn't escape." Anna's wine glass pinged as it slammed down on the marble table. "As far as I'm concerned, complete denial of her past would have been a damn better option.

"I've often thought about searching through those journals to see if I can find out who my *real* mother was..."

A gasp escaped Sarah's lips as she lunged forward in her seat. "If you can find out? You mean you still have them?"

Anna tilted her head and stared quizzically at her friend.

"The journals, Anna...you still have them?"

"Yeah, I stored them away when we moved my mom into the home. I never told my dad, 'cause he would have burned them if he'd found out. I have the journals and her Auschwitz logs as well, but...I've never looked at them."

An expression of utter confusion came over Sarah as she tried to digest the revelations. "My God Anna, never? What happened to that hyper-curiosity you had as a kid?"

"Deflated like my tits." The quip, elicited a shared snicker that slightly eased their tension.

Anna continued with a more mellow tone. "The truth is, Kiddo, I've contemplated destroying those journals dozens of times over the years, but for some insane or maybe sadistic reason, I've always talked myself out of it."

"Well, I'm glad you did 'cause those books are a link to your past, not to mention how important they could be to historians. I'm no scholar, but I'm damn curious."

"Listen, I haven't touched them in years, but maybe someday we'll head down to the basement and look through them."

Sarah's eyes widened and her head swivelled. "Here? You mean they're here?"

"Well, yeah. Where should they be? In my bedroom? Or on my coffee table? I couldn't bring myself to throw them out, but I certainly didn't want them playing with my emotions every day of my life."

"My journalistic radar is on fire. Anna, please, I don't mean to be a pain in the ass but I really do want to see them."

"Well, actually you are a pain in the ass...but okay. One day, you'll come back to Montreal and stay with me for a while, and we'll have a look."

"No, I mean tonight. I want to see them tonight, Anna. Please."

The idea caused an instant spit-take as Anna's swig of wine sprayed across the table. "Are you kidding me, Sarah? We haven't seen each other in decades, and you think I want to spend our one evening in a dusty basement looking through boxes of Holocaust shit? No way!"

"Please, Anna...I really want to understand; and I know in my bones this'll help."

"Not tonight, Sarah. How about you come back next weekend?"

The contrived sad face she affected from across the table was a clear reminder to Anna that her friend had not lost her persuasive charms.

"Okay, you win. Fine, we'll go to the cellar." She grumbled. "But I wanna warn you before we do, restaurants have been known to share basement space with rats the size of pit bulls."

"Really Anna, are you actually trying to psyche me out? Haven't you learned yet, it can't be done?

Listen, if we run into one of those rats, I'll invite it to the Kingston Pen for a reunion with its Fergusson cousins."

Anna chuckled and then nodded to her friend to rise and follow.

* * *

A cold silence joined them as they headed down the unsteady staircase. There was a dull thud of sawdust beneath their feet as they reached the basement floor. The space was an assault on Sarah's senses. The single fluorescent bulb shed a grey cast on the weathered stone walls; and the dank, musty air weighed heavily on her lungs. She was beginning to feel that Anna's story about the cellar being populated by crawly creatures the size of pit bulls was plausible.

"Holy shit, this place is eerie. How can it smell so good up there and so awful down here? It's like an occupied civil war bunker."

"Yeah, well, it's a presidential palace compared to the crapper my family inhabited in Auschwitz."

"Jesus, Anna, that's a chilling thought."

In a dark corner, the sound of jazz from overhead, oozed through the dust-filled cracks.

As their eyes became accustomed to the dimness, they spotted a jungle of cobwebs inhabited by troops of arachnids and their imprisoned prey. The two women stood mesmerized by the performance of an overly-confident spider trying to annihilate a large, blue fly. The captor repeated his attacks without mercy until the fly capitulated. As the fearless spider turned away, the fly rallied and began a frantic struggle to free itself.

Slowly and erratically, he flew away while the patient spider waited. Seconds after its escape, the disoriented fly found itself tangled in another web, and the spider resumed its approach toward dinner.

Sarah reached up and deftly released the tasty prisoner. In a flash, Anna squashed the fly with a rolled-up magazine. Spotting the shocked look on her friend's face, Anna, defended her action, "Sarah, just so you know, that was a pretty useless rescue. It would've headed upstairs where someone else would have swatted the filthy thing dead," She paused and then added with a sheepish grin, "but likely not before it shit on your crème caramel."

Sarah winced and chuckled. "Ugh. Well, I'm glad I've already had dessert. I get your point, but it was being held hostage, for God's sake. At least it was free to make its own fatal mistake...and on the plus side, it died quickly. I honestly felt disgusted watching the thing being trapped and tortured."

"Will you feel that way if they send the accused, you're hoping to write about, to prison?"

She had no quick or clever retort for the question, and aware that Anna was about to turn this scenario into a political allegory, Sarah chimed in. "Anna, listen, I really don't want to stay down here searching through these musty storage boxes; and I'm pretty sure you don't relish the idea either; so, let's take them back to my hotel. We can look through them in a clean, dry, well-lit, and sweet-smelling environment. What do you say?"

Anna paused, and then faintly nodded. It wasn't exactly the enthusiastic response Sarah would've preferred, but it would suffice, for now.

Before leaving the restaurant, Sarah thanked Anna for getting the bus boys to fumigate the cartons. "It crossed my mind that I might have ended up with some rather unwelcome guests in my bed, But I wasn't going to ask you, in case it might have been a deal breaker. So, I'm grateful that you insisted on it being done."

* * *

Once settled inside the hotel suite, the two old friends sprawled on the floor scrutinizing the Auschwitz logs. Sarah listened while Anna painstakingly translated into English the messages that her mother had inscribed in Yiddish below each remnant.

"In my mother's peculiar fantasy, it was as if each child who received a portion of food had been given some kind of spiritual communion. Potato peels, crust of bread, or a morsel of cheese was, in my mother's eyes, a sign from God that this was the child who would survive to testify; but instead, the albums are filled with epitaphs."

Tears settled in the corners of Sarah's eyes but dared not escape. "These are precious memoirs, Anna. Maybe your mother was subconsciously motivated to bring these 'children' with her to this country to provide an historical account. You could do that for her. Donate the albums to the Holocaust Museum in Toronto, and they'll see to it that these children will never be forgotten; and maybe that would help your mother fulfill her mission."

Anna's eyes glistened as she quietly contemplated the proposal.

As Sarah perused the first of the two journals, she noted that on some pages, the items were dated, whereas some only contained a couple of scribbled lines. While some entries were fluidly written in Yiddish, others were scratched out in disjointed English.

Yiddish was culturally familiar to Sarah, but she didn't read, write, or speak it, so while she leafed through the diaries, Anna continued to translate.

The secrets hidden within those pages ranged from the disturbing to the insightful. Sophie's frustration with her husband's mystifying ability to rebuild his life and her inability to tolerate her own was clearly and painfully defined. But, as dark as the majority of entries were, the light consistently broke through whenever Anna's name appeared on a page.

Even Anna's first menstrual cycle was logged into the journal, partly in Yiddish but mostly in garbled English. Sophie both praised and lamented the fact that after Anna was born, her own menses had been halted forever. *I protect my Anna to my life so Nazi hazzerim, murdered momma and poppa, stole my life, no ever her life. I glad my blood end after Anna. I no bring more child into this Gehenna. But now my shaina Anna is a woman with blood every month. She can choose to bring children or no.*

Anna set the journal aside and leaned back on her elbow. "It's eerily ironic that I never got to make that choice either," Anna quietly reflected. "God really has a ludicrous sense of justice." She mused.

Another entry caught Sarah's attention. It was written in Yiddish, but the letters were uneven and sloppy, and sometimes the words ran right off the page as if Anna's mother had written it while blindfolded.

"Look at this strange one, Anna."

Anna slid the book onto her lap and read the page silently several times before she began to translate.

I hear uh, whimpering...like wounded dog. I must to stay silent. No moonlight, but I see arms glowing in black.

Dear God, they sound like rabid hyenas. I must not to cry out. I must not to cry out. I must to be invisible. Forgive me.

In a cautious, whisper, Anna asked, "So what do you think, Sarah: Raving lunacy or rational prose?"

Sarah shook her head. "Look, I'm not a psychologist, but it's pretty obvious that your mother was suffering from PTSD. Seriously Anna, maybe your mother's demons can be exorcised by sharing these albums with the Holocaust Museum. Maybe it's exactly what she might have chosen to do herself had she been given the opportunity. What have you got to lose?"

Anna began to aimlessly stack and unstack the journals. Finally, she stopped and shrugged. "I don't know what to do, Sarah. Maybe my mother would have felt it was like abandoning or dumping those children's ashes."

"No, you're wrong. It's just the opposite. You'd be finding a permanent resting place for all those little souls to be remembered and honoured by every visitor to the museum. And your mother would rest more peacefully."

Again, she held up her palm like a traffic cop. "Don't over-sell it, Sarah, it's okay."

"Okay?" Sarah's optimism was palpable.

"Uh-huh. But curb your excitement, it just means I'll think about it."

"If you say yes, then you can deliver the artifacts when you come to Toronto to visit me."

"Artifacts." Anna scoffed at hearing such an elitist word used to describe the ragged remnants of her mother's living nightmare. "Artifacts huh? Well, '*A rose by any other name*'...which in this case, is just a garden of rotting weeds."

"Maybe to you, Anna, but to the world, it's a history that must never be forgotten. So, please consider it?"

She looked up and offered a wan smile. "Yeah, I'll think about it. But if I decide to come, you'd better warn Saul that trouble is on its way."

"You better believe I will." Sarah replied with bitter irony. "But I don't intend to leave Prescott for a while yet, so in the meantime, why don't you come and hang out with me there for a couple of days. It'd be fun..."

Anna grimaced as if caught by a gas pain. "Have you lost your mind? Prescott with all that awful crap going on there? Fun?"

"Listen, all those criminals came from miles outside of town, but unfortunately, it's Prescott that's getting the bad rap," Sarah replied defensively. Anna scowled, but Sarah forged ahead. "Oh, come on, Anna, where's that feisty spirit? You know we'd have a good time. At least tell me you'll seriously think about it?"

Anna pursed her lips, hemmed, and hawed, and finally offered an ambivalent assurance, "I promise, I'll seriously think about it."

* * *

Later that night, the two friends said their goodbyes, vowing that this time, they'd see each other again, very soon.

CHAPTER ELEVEN

By midday, Sarah had navigated safely back to Prescott and the O'Brien Hotel, accompanied by graphic thoughts of her encounters in Montreal.

On the night table, she spotted a short stack of phone messages. The first was from Anna checking on her safe return, a reassuring warranty on their renewed friendship. The second was a message from a Toronto real estate lawyer, a call she wasn't anxious to return. The third was a two-day-old note from Laurie Cowan.

Hi, Ms. Berman,

We haven't officially met yet, but I'm representing Earl White for Richard McCall, and I understand that you're working on a story about our client.

Richard informed me that the judge has postponed again. We won't be heard now until Monday at 11 a.m. I wanted to save you a wasted trip to Brockville. I'm going home for the weekend, but I'm staying in town for the next two days...so if you want to grab a bite and talk, please call.

"That bloody judge!" Sarah grumbled to herself. "I could have stayed over in Montreal." As for having missed the lawyer's invitation to meet, she wasn't quite ready to bring him into her cabal just yet.

A file folder by her coffeemaker caught Sarah's attention. She approached it cautiously, as if it was a foreign interloper. On the folder was an attached sticky note with her name and suite number, hand printed; but there was no indication of the sender. She nervously lifted the cover of the folder with the point of a paring knife to reveal a sealed and weathered envelope. She cautiously sliced open the envelope and retrieved two strips of black and white negatives.

A quick call to the front desk confirmed that the folder had been left at the front desk with her name on it, but no one had seen the messenger.

Handling her celluloid discoveries with great care, she scrutinized them under the sixty watts of her bedside lamp, but all she could see was varying shades of black.

Thoughts dashed around her brain, imagining the most outrageous scenarios. Was someone trying to threaten her, warn her, or offer her some useful information? But who would do that? And to what end?

She placed the negatives in a fresh envelope and headed to the pharmacy.

The nametag on the crisp, white, lab coat of the man behind the counter identified him as, Tom Cook, pharmacist. He was well-mannered and middle-aged, with a friendly voice that remained calm, even as a hawkish old woman was trying to squeeze some juicy gossip out of him.

"Now, Mrs. M., if it were your pregnancy test, would you want me to go telling your neighbours the results?"

"Well, Tom, if it were mine, at my age, I'd not only be tellin' my neighbours, I'd be tellin' Wes at the Journal office that he'd better be writin' about it before all those big city papers come runnin' for an exclusive." She guffawed.

"You're a joker Mrs. M., but I'm still not tellin' ya." He grinned as he handed over her purchase.

Sarah recognized the woman as the geriatric busybody Shiny had sparred with on Halloween, and the same gossipmonger Mrs. Perkins had mentioned during that first bizarre encounter in the candy shop. Sarah remained out of view, choosing not to reintroduce herself to Richard McCall's mother. Having clearly received the pharmacist's message, the disgruntled old woman scurried to the exit.

Mr. Cook squinted as he held Sarah's negatives up to the light, punctuating his doubts with a groan.

"Hmm, I don't know a whole lot about photography," he offered, "but I've looked at a slew of old negatives in my day, and I gotta say, these are in pretty bad condition. I can barely make out any image at all." He set the negative down carefully, "But if you're really intent on knowing whether there's anything there, I mean if it's real important, we can send them out to the lab in Ottawa to see what the experts have to say."

Sarah's curiosity was piqued, and there was no turning back.

"Sure, go right ahead, thank you. I'd appreciate that. And, Mr. Cook, let me know, but pretend it's a pregnancy test and don't tell the neighbours. Okay?"

He chuckled and nodded.

* * *

She returned to her suite, still unsettled by the appearance of the mysterious negatives. She decided that rather than struggle to navigate the stormy seas of rational thought for the rest of the evening, what she really needed was a diversion and she wasted no time in finding one.

* * *

Eleanor agreed to warm up the TV and put on some coffee while Sarah volunteered to pick up a pizza.

Their conversations had become more candid and comfortable over the past weeks, which emboldened Sarah to probe a bit. "Eleanor, I hope you don't mind me asking but...how come you've never shown any curiosity about the article I'm working on?"

There was no hesitation in Eleanor's response. "Remember the night you thought there were bats in my basement and I said if there were, I'd be the first one out the door?"

"Uh-huh."

"I told you I thought since you believed there were bats down there, you were brave to continue on down the stairs. You laughed at the idea that anyone could think of you as brave; and to prove the point, you described one of your childhood phobias. You said that each time you came across pictures of snakes in the encyclopaedia, you'd hold the book at arm's length and turn the pages with your mother's eyebrow tweezers. Well, that's how I feel about the news topic you're researching. I don't read about it, I don't listen, and I don't watch anything that has to do with it. I'm well aware it exists. I know if children have intentionally been hurt, someone's guilty. But I also know they'll never be punished. So, I just choose to flip past it without letting it touch me. I enjoy your company, Sarah, but the last thing I want to talk about, or think about, is what brought you to town."

Sarah took a long, slow breath. "I get it, but there's this thing that's been gnawing at me since I arrived back in Prescott. It happened a long time ago..."

Eleanor's animated enthusiasm slowly devolved into a frozen silence. Receiving no verbal resistance, Sarah pressed on. "I started to recall rumours from decades ago about a terrible incident...an attack. I think you know what I'm referring to and you don't have to give me any details if it makes you uncomfortable. I just want to know, if it did happen, did your mother ever file a complaint? I mean, she...and you...would want the truth...the facts to come out, right?"

Eleanor gasped for a breath of air before responding. "It's ironic that you'd ask that question, Sarah. Isn't it part of your job to ignore the facts and write whatever makes for a good story?"

It was an invisible stinging slap to Sarah. Now she had to try to respond while keeping her pain in check.

"No Eleanor, a journalist's job is the same as the court's...to pay close attention to the facts, in search of the truth." She knew she was getting into dangerous territory, but she felt a need to defend herself.

"You think the courts give a damn about truth?" Eleanor sputtered as she rose, picked up a couple of dishes from the table, and placed them in the sink.

Sarah remained fixed for a few seconds before trying a different approach. "I'm so sorry, Eleanor. I honestly don't mean to upset you. I'm here as a friend. I won't push you, but I really wish you could trust me. I mean, maybe talking about it would help?"

Her host quietly returned to her seat at the table. "Let me sum it up for you, Sarah. If it did happen, then I'll feel that pain 'til the day I die; and talking about it won't change a thing for me. As for you, I'm sure that this is a diversion from what you feel as the boredom of Prescott, but my bet is, you'll forget about it as soon as you return to Toronto."

A shake of the head was all Sarah could summon over the dressing down she was getting. "Come on, Eleanor, we still know very little about each other, but I asked only because I care. And to tell you the truth, I've never been bored in my life, not even when I lived here." Sarah slowly pushed her chair away from the table and stood. "Listen, Eleanor, I know this is a difficult conversation to have and if I've been insensitive, I'm really sorry. But here's something you should know about me: I'm obsessively loyal and even worse...I'm mercilessly persistent!" Sarah offered a humble smile, hoping Eleanor might be persuaded to supply one in return, but she didn't flinch.

After an uncomfortable pause, Sarah whispered goodnight to her host and after a brief pause, she turned and left the room. Eleanor remained stoically in place as her guest slipped out the front door.

* * *

The next morning, Wesley's welcome back phone call gave Sarah the opportunity to share the saga of her trip to Montreal, and to mention the appearance of the mysterious negatives.

"So, Wes, that's my life to date, now what do you have to contribute?" She giggled.

"Jeez, I don't know, Sarah. Nothing extraordinary ever happens to me, but your life seems to be one incredible miniseries. I could follow you around, take notes, write a bestseller, and live out my remaining years a very rich man."

"Speaking of retiring, Wes, what's with the judge? This is the second delay, and they haven't even started yet. Does he have a gambling problem, or drugs, or maybe some bimbo on the side?"

"I think not." he answered in a mildly-amused tone. "Judge MacMillan is a seventy-eight-year-old curmudgeon with a bad temper, a wife of fifty years, a bunch of kids, umpteen grandkids, and who knows how many great-grandkids. He's also got an impeccable record for service and moral fortitude, both on and off the bench."

Sarah winced. "Oh crap."

"Wait, wait, I'm not done yet," Wesley declared. "You're gonna feel even worse when you hear that the delay was because he was taken to the hospital with a medical emergency."

Sarah sighed, "Okay, you win. I feel guilty. Does anyone know what's wrong?"

"It's unlikely that anyone would ask; but since I know something about old age, it's more than likely, heart related. If the story doesn't leak out by Monday, and if he shows up, you can bet that the entire courtroom will be breathlessly waiting to see if the old coot drops dead right there."

* * *

Thanks to the court delay, Sarah was stuck in town for the weekend. It was a cold, miserable Prescott evening, and in spite of her recent declaration to Eleanor, she now feared that boredom might be introducing itself.

She thought of calling Eleanor to apologize for unlocking bad memories, but she knew it wouldn't be a genuine *mea culpa* because she had intended to unbolt that prison door.

* * *

As evening wore on, even the hotel room-service irritated Sarah. The salad was too limp, the chicken too dry, the pie too runny, and the coffee too weak. To make it even more disappointing, the meal was delivered by a shy, pimple-faced newcomer instead of her favourite bellhop, Mitch.

She missed Mitch's sprightly conversation, smart-assed rhetoric, and his private revelations about the hotel's kitchen calamities. It had been at least an hour since she called down to the kitchen to have the dinner cart removed.

"It's almost nine o'clock. No damn tip this time," Sarah mumbled when she heard the knock on the door. "Who is it?" she barked.

"It's Eleanor." Came the tentative voice from the other side.

Sarah tried to hide her astonishment as she opened the door and let Eleanor into the room. Without glancing up, the surprise visitor placed two large cups of Tim's coffee on the table.

"Wow, thanks. I was just thinking about running out to pick up a real coffee. Please, have a seat." Sarah pushed a chair forward, and the visitor eased into it. For several minutes, all that could be heard was Eleanor's anxious breathing. Sarah moved about the area, setting out a plate of cookies while keeping her eye on her guest and biting back an impulse to shake the words out of her.

Eleanor took off her jacket and folded it over the arm of the chair. Finally, in a soft monotone whisper, she struggled to begin.

"I'm sure you want to ask me, why I'm here." Fearful of breaking the spell, Sarah nodded, but said nothing.

"Our last conversation has been playing over and over in my head, and I realized that before you, no one had ever actually come straight out and asked me. And all I've wanted to do ever since you asked...was to tell. When I think about what happened, I want to force time backwards to the second before it stopped for me."

Sarah sat down across from Eleanor, and leaned in. "Eleanor, only you can decide when to reset that clock."

Eleanor squirmed. "I know. That's why I came here tonight. I think I want to talk about it. I just don't know where to begin."

"Well, it's frigid and sleeting outside...and the coffee's hot, so...take your time and start whenever you feel ready."

Sarah sat quietly, sipping and waiting.

"It was miserably cold that night. My mother was in the kitchen cleaning up after dinner. She didn't see me leave the house, but I heard her calling out to me: 'Eleanor, dress warm. Don't forget your hat and mittens. And don't go without your ski pants 'cause your legs'll freeze solid.' But I was a teenager. I knew better.

"I was halfway to my 4H Club meeting when I admitted to myself that my mother was right. It was bitterly cold, and I was just wearing a knitted scarf and winter jacket over my uniform. No hat, no mitts, no ski pants...just a blouse and skirt. In spite of the fact that my fingers and toes were numb, I arrived at my meeting on time and was grateful for the warmth of the radiator." She placed her hands in her lap and stared fixedly at them as she continued.

"It was a wonderful meeting that night. Weeks before, we'd collected a bunch of those empty papier-mâché egg cartons and filled each section with soil and dropped in a seed. Three times a week, one 4H member was assigned to go to the club and water the seedlings.

It had been a while since it was my turn, so you can imagine how excited I was to see how they were growing. It was late winter, and we knew we'd soon be transplanting our little egg-pot sprouts into our own home gardens.

"The meeting was over around nine. I was thinking about how I'd soon be able to plant a beautiful flower garden for my mom. It was dark when I walked out the door. When I felt that bite of frigid wind, I was really sorry I hadn't listened to my m..."

For a moment it appeared that Eleanor was having a lapse of memory. Sarah remained riveted not daring to make a sound.

"I took a shortcut." Her fingers were now firmly interlaced, and her brow tightly stitched. "I heard a rustling sound. I felt a hard tug at the back of my head. I could hear this sort of wet breathing from behind me..." She spoke in hushed tones through clenched teeth. She released a low, guttural whimper before she continued. "He forced a large, revolting, leather glove into my mouth. It tasted rancid and smelled like rotten meat. I began to heave, but nothing came up. I tried to scream, but the only sound I could make was this horrible rasping gagging noise..." An unexpected sob escaped and shut her down once again. Sarah remained silent.

"A rough burlap sack was pulled over my head. It felt like thousands of glass fibres piercing my face. I was thrown onto the frozen ground...I felt jagged bits of ice stabbing my back...my legs...everywhere...One of them was holding me down by my wrists, another by my ankles."

She unlaced her fingers and pressed her palms forcefully together in an effort to relieve her tension.

"I heard one of them whisper, 'they were going too far, and he was going home if they didn't stop.' I tried to figure out how many there were...three, four...maybe more, but I couldn't focus. I couldn't think. They were shouting profanities at the one who wanted to leave. I remember the hopeless sound of crunching ice as he raced away. I prayed that the others would follow, that they'd end this evil game and let me go. For a few seconds I heard nothing, but I was still trapped. Not a footstep, not a voice; only the horrid sounds of my own gagging on the disgusting thing that filled my mouth and blocked my throat. Then came the paralyzing fear that I might never catch my breath again.

"I heard them hovering above me, uttering vicious threats...I could hear at least three different gruesome voices. I thought for a moment, this was, at worst a diabolical prank, but that thought was instantly erased when they knelt on my arms and legs, completely pinning me to the frozen earth. They tore open my jacket. I felt the buttons pop.

"Then...I heard the hissing of a zipper opening. I wanted to kick...scratch...bite...scream...cry...but...it was impossible. I couldn't understand what was happening. It was as if I was captive in someone else's nightmare. I could hear my voice screaming inside my head, praying over and over again they would stop..."

Eleanor closed her eyes, crossed her hands over her throat, and rocked repetitively in her seat. Sarah waited and listened as Eleanor's erratic breathing escalated into frantic gasps for air.

"They...laughed...like lunatics, as one pounced on top of me. I heard a click...I felt a knife pressing against my thigh. I heard a ripping sound. My panties were torn away..." Her voice ebbed to a stop.

Suddenly, she leaned back in her seat and stated resolutely; "My brain couldn't handle any more. I lost consciousness."

"Eleanor, it's okay, you don't have go on, if it's too..."

"No! I have to. I need to!" Eleanor took a shaky breath.

"I came around to the smell and taste of vomit and blood. I felt numb and disoriented. I tried to remember what happened, but somehow everything had short-circuited. I tried to lift my head. I felt the wet, sticky glove oozing against my cheek, my back felt sliced to ribbons, I pulled the sack from my head, but all I could see was darkness. I couldn't seem to focus my mind or my eyes. I couldn't wrap my mind around the fact that the battered body lying on the icy ground was mine. I wasn't sure where I was or why I was feeling such ungodly pain over my entire body."

Another curtain of silence filled the room. "But then, I began to remember...and I knew I had to get away. What if they came back?

"I felt around in the dark. Every movement was excruciatingly painful. I don't know what possessed me, but I frantically gathered up everything I could find and shoved it all inside my torn jacket. I managed to make it home. I dragged myself into the parlour. My mother looked up from her sewing machine, and I saw the light fade from her eyes. She said nothing, but it was the loudest sound I'd ever heard. All at once, she seemed to float out of her chair and drift toward me in a daze. She guided me toward the bathroom and peeled off my clothes. She helped me into the tub. I stood there shivering while my mother trickled warm water over me again and again and again. She was desperate to rinse away the filth. She shushed me and comforted me as you would a small child who had simply grazed a knee. She asked no questions and expected no answers. While I dried myself, she threw my things into a bag and carried it away. She returned with a folded towel that she placed between my legs in an effort to soak up the relentless flow of blood. I put on the fresh pyjamas she handed me. She wrapped a quilt around me, and we left by taxi for St. Gabriel's Hospital." A shudder rippled through her body as she revisited that ride. "I could see a slight sense of relief in my mother's face when we arrived. She was gratified that I was in good hands. She had unwavering faith that the doctor could fix everything, including my psyche.

"Just before they took me into the operating room, the doctor asked if I knew how many attackers were involved. I told him that I thought one had run away when they first grabbed me, but I still heard three voices. I recall the doctor whispering to the nurse, 'Three? It looks like an army.'

"Shortly after I was out of surgery, the doctor came into the recovery room. He told my mother that with all the blood I'd lost, it was a miracle I'd survived. He didn't ask me how it happened, if I knew who did it, or what he could do to help.

"My mother, with alarming restraint, asked, 'What do we do now, Doctor?' He looked at her kind of quizzically and abruptly replied; 'Nothing.'

"My mother clenched her teeth and squeezed her eyes shut. 'Doctor, I don't understand what you mean! Are you saying, the police will take care of it? Or you're going to handle it for us; is that what you mean? Please look at my daughter and me, and tell us please, what do we do?'"

Tears gathered in Eleanor's eyes, threatening to expose her vulnerability in spite of her determination to remain stoic while she bared her soul. The images racing through Eleanor's mind were now so vivid she could almost hear her mother's voice in her head regurgitating her anguish as she begged the doctor for help. She could remember the pathetic sight of the doctor sitting there fisting his hands tightly as if trying to flex his courage.

"Finally, he dryly explained: 'In the majority of rape cases that are reported, the rapists are almost never found; and if the police do make an arrest, the accused is almost never convicted.' He warned of the pain and public humiliation a rape victim can face in the courtroom under scrutiny by an unmerciful lawyer, who would ask; 'What was the alleged victim wearing?' If it's deemed inappropriate attire, he'll brand her as a slut who was asking for it! He'll ask or say anything to get his client off. He'll have no regard for her feelings.'" A single tear escaped and rolled down her cheek, but Eleanor swiftly wiped it away and continued. "The doctor capped off his illuminating advice with, 'On the slimmest of chances that they could ever find and convict the culprits who did this, the rapists may be sentenced to as little as a year and would probably never serve a day. Then they're out and free. Do you understand what can happen then? So yes, I'm suggesting that you do nothing. Over time, forget about this terrible incident so that your daughter can heal as best she can, and her life can go on as she'd planned.'

"In the taxi, on our way back from the hospital, my mother, who had barely said a word to me during the entire ordeal, turned to me and whispered in my ear, 'Eleanor, the way you were dressed, uh...I mean, maybe the doctor's?'" Now an avalanche of tears cascaded like a waterfall.

"I put my hand over her mouth. I wouldn't let her finish...and we never spoke about it again.

"I never planted the seedlings in her garden. In fact, I never planted a garden at all, until after my mother passed away." Eleanor rose and walked across the room to grab some tissues.

"The doctor was so wrong, Sarah. My life didn't go on as I'd planned, and I'll never forget!" She returned, sat down, wiped her tears, and took a few seconds to regain her composure. "As for our public humiliation and the pain he was so concerned about, people in this town still speculated, and I was still branded and ostracized."

Sarah slumped in her seat, exhausted from the horrific revelation, and feeling guilty over initiating it. "My God, Eleanor, I had no idea what kind of nightmare I was actually asking you to recall."

"I know." Eleanor simply uttered. "Sarah, until tonight, the only person I ever wanted to talk about it with, was my mother, and she's the one who sealed it up inside me. After you left last night, all I could think about was the possibility of unsealing this trauma and what might happen if I did. But then I realized that you were the first person with the guts to ask me, so maybe this was my opportunity to find out." Eleanor affirmed.

"Eleanor, have you ever talked this out with a therapist, or a social worker, any expert?"

Eleanor glowered and curtly shook her head. "That night, while my mother tried to wash away all traces of the attack, I tried repeatedly to recount the details to her, but she didn't want to hear it. I told you the doctor suggested it was best for me to stay silent. I did as I was told by the experts in my life at the time. So now that you've heard the story, what do you think will really change, huh? Will my pain disappear? Of course not. I'm living with a chronic disease. There's no cure, no treatment...no hope."

Eleanor fretfully picked up her cup of cold coffee, took a gulp and winced.

"At least you've said it out loud, Eleanor. Maybe that's the first step." With that, Sarah gently took the cup from Eleanor's hand, picked up her own, popped them both into the microwave and waited.

"Talking doesn't change a thing, Sarah. A rape victim remains a victim forever. And if you're worried that you forced open a Pandora's Box, have no fear. Even though I haven't talked about it, I've thought about that night over and over again for thirty-five years, and I'm still functioning."

"You need to tell this to the police, Eleanor. They may be able to help you, even after all this time, 'cause what you really need is justice." She handed back the heated coffee.

"Thanks. You couldn't be more right on that point, Sarah. I do need justice, but the only place I can still hope it exists is in heaven, unless the church has been lying too. So, on that profound note, I'm going home to another in my continuing series of sleepless nights." She stood up and pulled on her jacket.

Sarah put down her cup and picked up her coat from the rack.

Seeming bewildered, Eleanor asked, "What're you doing?"

"I'm gonna walk you home." Sarah confidently replied.

Eleanor smiled. "And who will walk you home?"

"The point is Eleanor, even for me, walking alone at night can be pretty nerve-wracking."

A cynical chuckle escaped Eleanor's lips. "'Even for me?' The truth is, Sarah, this incident didn't leave me frightened of the night. I often go out for a walk in the dark and feel safe. The worst has already happened to me. Anyway, most people think I'm strange, so I just look their way and they head off in another direction. I'm afraid of a lot of things, but, not of the night. More of life happens in the day, and life is what frightens me now. So, I insist, you stay right here." Eleanor eased the coat from Sarah's hands and placed it on the chair. "Anyway, I have this hot cup of coffee to warm me; and renewed energy to motivate me. So, good night, Sarah...and thank you. Truly, thank you." Eleanor smiled tenderly and gently closed the door.

Overwhelmed by the traumatic revelations, Sarah sunk into her chair and began to mull over all that she'd learned. She raised the cup to her lips and took a sip of coffee that comingled with her salty tears.

CHAPTER TWELVE

The bedside clock glowered 1:23 a.m. and Eleanor's agonizing disclosure was still echoing in Sarah's head. She was unnerved and awake amidst a mess of scribbled notes recalling the details of Eleanor's assault. Exhaustion increased as night crawled toward dawn, but each time Sarah nodded off, nightmares returned.

By 8:00 a.m., with renewed tenacity, Sarah was rapping on Eleanor's door. She answered with a kindly smile. "Good morning, Sarah, I hope I didn't upset you too much last night. Were you able to sleep?"

Sarah smiled back. "I assure you, Eleanor, I managed to get enough sleep to still be creative; and I have ideas. Will you hear me out?"

She smiled and shook her head. "Do I get a choice? Come on in."

"Oh, thanks, but I can't stay right now, I have an appointment. For now, I just want to ask one question. If the monsters that did this to you are still around, wouldn't you get satisfaction in seeing them tried and convicted?"

"Only if I had a guarantee they'd be lined up in front of a firing squad and I was the one who got to yell *fire*." She sardonically jibed.

"Well, who knows? Maybe it can be arranged." Sarah chuckled. "Anyway, that's it. thanks. Gotta go.

We'll talk later." She rushed off leaving Eleanor standing in the doorway, bewildered and slightly amused, by her friend's quirky yet unexpected cameo appearance.

Sarah's next stop was to meet up with Shiny for breakfast at the Best Service and discuss plans for their 9:30 meeting at the Journal office.

* * *

Once both women were comfortably seated by Braydon's desk, Sarah initiated the conversation. "Listen Braydon; Shiny and I have an idea about an investigation, and we're hoping you'd consider helping us ...not during your work hours, of course."

Always suspicious, Braydon asked. "And just what would we be investigating?"

"The Eleanor Miller attack," Shiny bluntly stated.

"And why would he want to do that?" Wesley queried as he entered the room.

"Because now we have every reason to believe Eleanor's been an innocent prisoner for thirty-five years, and it's time she was liberated," Sarah declared.

"I've already offered to do what I can to help," Shiny added. "I can do pickups or deliveries or look up phone numbers and addresses or whatever."

Sarah cocked her head and pleaded. "Come on, Braydon? You can use a little excitement. And you don't get off the hook either, Wes."

The old editor smirked and raised his hands in surrender, and Braydon followed suit.

* * *

Early Monday morning, Sarah was dressing for court when the call came in:

"Hi Sarah, this is Joannie. Sorry to tell you but the clerk just called to say that the Crown's prior case wasn't completed last week because of the delay, so the Earl White case is bumped again. Richard thought you'd want to know."

Sarah's fury spiralled like a tornado in a trailer park. Her face glowed crimson and the hairs on her arms stood at attention. She wanted to spew a litany of obscenities, but instead, she politely thanked Joannie for letting her know.

By midday, Sarah was on a train heading for Toronto.

Shiny would make sure the detective work continued in her absence, and Reynolds even agreed to leave her room locked up rent-free, until her return, providing it was by Friday.

* * *

Stepping from the train at Union Station, Sarah felt a prickly rush of sadness spread over her like a case of shingles.

The perennial romantic in her had imagined a homecoming as be a Hollywood event; a collage of all those wonderful movies in which memorable stars like Ingrid Bergman and Humphrey Bogart said their weepy goodbyes, or breathless hellos at famous railway stations around the world, while in the background, violin music soared to erotic heights.

She emerged from the train station and stepped onto the sleeting, bustling main street of Toronto where her renewed sense of loneliness was instantaneously amplified. She dragged herself along the taxi line with her bag in tow, starkly aware that this homecoming was a cold reality away from a Hollywood production.

She had decided not to let anyone in Toronto know that she was home, since there were things she needed to take care of without any distraction or interference.

She spent the next day hibernating in her cave-like apartment; but by noon on Wednesday, she'd organized her first task which was to stop by her old house en route to the *Sentinel* office.

* * *

Although a few dried leaves still clung to the tall birch trees that lined her street, they looked sadly anorexic.

An urgent and intimidating message from a real estate lawyer coerced Sarah into making the trip. He had officiously notified her that her home was up for sale, as per the separation agreement, and she must immediately remove any remaining personal items before the first open house.

As she pulled up in front of the majestic colonial-style house, she was numbed by the estrangement she felt. The once-familiar key felt alien in her hand; and the *For Sale* sign on the lawn was a crass reminder of her loss.

Anxiety overwhelmed her as she crossed the threshold into the foyer of the only home she'd known for decades. The door seemed heavier than she remembered. A familiar sounding foot-shuffle signalled the approach of her dedicated housekeeper, Cora.

All the way there, Sarah had steeled herself against the possibility of suffering a meltdown when she entered. She feared that the sweet, elderly woman who helped raise her children through the colourful evolution of their lives, could abolish Sarah's resolve with one simple embrace. She swallowed the lump in her throat and managed to conjure a faint smile.

"I was so happy to get your call," Cora bubbled as she reached out and welcomed Sarah with a determined and fateful embrace. "I've missed you so much, Mrs. B!"

"I've missed you too, Cora." She murmured as she gulped back tears. As the hug unfolded, Sarah looked around as if she were a first-time visitor. "The place feels so strange to me. I know it's only been months, but it seems like years."

As she scanned the familiar spaces, she became angry with herself for so meekly submitting to the lawyer's demands. Try as she might, Sarah couldn't remember what she'd left behind and if any of it was worth the pain of re-entry. She only hoped that whatever she'd find would fit into one duffel bag, because that was about all she could squeeze into her apartment.

"Mrs. Berman, when you called, I was so excited you were coming, I baked fresh cranberry muffins for you. Please come and have a cup of tea."

"Oh, Cora, I just came to pick up a few things." Sarah demurred as she moved toward the staircase. She paused and offered a gracious smile as she politely declined. "I can't stay but thank you so much."

The maid looked devastated. "But Mrs. B, they're your favourites."

Sarah backed up, placed her hands firmly on Cora's shoulders, and looked her in the eye. "Oh, what the hell? I'd love a cup of tea, Cora, and I could certainly use a treat right about now. Please, bring on those fabulous muffins of yours!"

"Wonderful! Because I already boiled the kettle and warmed the muffins when I saw you pulling up."

Sarah chuckled and said: "Okay, then, lead the way. I'm not sure I remember where the kitchen is," she teased.

The two women sat in the kitchen, enjoying their break while pretending to ignore the impenetrable iceberg that had risen at 25 Oceanic Drive.

A half hour had raced by before Sarah realized, she needed to get to her reason for being there, and then get out so she wouldn't bump into her ex.

She climbed the stairs and tentatively entered the master bedroom. She began to squirm as if she was surveying a crime scene. She stuffed anything of hers that had meaning into her duffle bag; but all the time she was gathering her things together, she had a nagging feeling that someone else had already rifled through them. She chose only the personal mementoes that her children had made and given to her over the years. Perhaps, one day, her kids would appreciate seeing those keepsakes that their mother had salvaged and protected from the scourge of the divorce.

To quell a rapidly growing tension headache, Sarah headed into the bathroom to grab a pain reliever.

As she removed the Advil bottle from the shelf, something caught her eye. She quickly closed the cabinet, grabbed her duffel bag, and headed back down the stairs where Cora stood waiting.

"Mrs. Berman, are you all right? How about another cup of tea?"

"Sorry, Cora, but I really have to go. It's getting late and I definitely don't want to bump into Saul."

"I was praying that you'd both be able to work things out."

"Oh Cora, that's im..."

"I know. I know what's going on with the doctor, Mrs. B., and I'm so sorry. I've been with you for well over twenty years, and I never suspected that such a thing could happen here. I really did hope it could be mended."

For an instant, Sarah felt chagrined. "Mended? Cora, the fabric is frayed beyond repair." She started for the door.

"That's what I'm trying to tell you. I know about the uh...woman."

Sarah stopped abruptly and turned to ask. "How? I mean, how did you find out?"

"I figured it out when Dr. Berman brought that woman he called 'his colleague' home for dinner one a Friday afternoon. I went for my weekend off and when I returned on Monday morning, she was still here...and she looked a lot more worn out than when she arrived."

She saw a flash of pain cross Sarah's face. "I'm sorry, Mrs. Berman. That was really insensitive of me."

Sarah reached out and gently squeezed Cora's arm. "Not at all, Cora, I'm sure this isn't easy for you, either. Will you move with them?"

Cora recoiled. "God forbid! No, Ma'am. I'd already decided when you left that I'd be leaving too. I'm planning to tell Dr. Berman very soon. With the children and you gone, it's time for me to retire." She retrieved a tissue from her apron pocket and wiped away a tear. "Not to worry, I've got family back in England who'd love a taste of my home cooking before I'm too old and crotchety to bend over the oven. And, frankly, I just don't want to be anywhere near that bleedin' woman." She waved a hand in front of her face as if to wave away the foul essence of *that bleedin' woman*.

Sarah cracked a wry smile, dropped her bag, embraced Cora, then quietly picked up the bag and exited.

* * *

The reception Sarah received at the *Sentinel* came as a bewildering surprise. The editor, Stanley, seemed conciliatory, even enthusiastic, over her return. He knew she'd been out-of-town but didn't seem the least bit curious or miffed by it.

Given such a friendly signal, Sarah made use of the opportunity. "Listen Stan, I need to be out of town for a while, but if you can give me a variety of topics you want me to cover, I can still write my commentary pieces and fax them to you."

"Absolutely, my dear." He placed a patronizing hand on her arm and continued. "Listen, you pick the topics, write them up, and send them to me, and I'll tell you what. I'll even raise you to twelve hundred words and increase the fee per article by fifty dollars...how's that?"

"That's um, good, Stan, I appreciate it."

As she headed out of his office feeling completely bewildered, a female colleague pulled her aside and whispered, "Stan heard that the *Sun-Times* offered you a free-lance job covering that funky shit going on down east, and now he figures you're more valuable than he thought. So, he's going to do his best to keep you here."

In response to the colleague's wink, Sarah mouthed a silent "thank you," and flashed a secret victory sign that set both women to giggling.

Sarah had managed to cross the "to do" items off her short list and concluded it was time to return to Prescott for the twice-rescheduled hearing to begin.

* * *

Mr. Reynolds seemed truly pleased to see his feisty tenant return.

"So, Mr. Reynolds, I'm trusting you kept my room under lock and key as agreed and my TV is still there and working?"

He nodded.

"And there'll be no charge for the three days, correct?" Reynolds brusquely cleared his throat, fiddled in his pocket, intent on inventing whatever distractions he could devise so he didn't have to answer Sarah's question. But Sarah was becoming bolder by every tick of the clock.

"Now, Mr. Reynolds, you wouldn't want me to move to the Holiday Inn in Brockville, would you? Spacious rooms, TV, VCR. Just blocks from the courthouse." She picked up her travel bag, stepped away from the desk and added. "Oh, wow, come to think of it, I wouldn't even have to rent a car. That would save me money. Damn, that's a good idea. Maybe that's what I should do." She took a few more slow and deliberate steps away. He rushed around the desk and cut her off.

"Ya know, Mrs. Berman, I'm thinkin', we weren't full up this week and you deserve a break, so let's say we forget the entire week and just start fresh as of tomorrow. How's that, eh? Here, let me." He removed the bag from her shoulder and placed it over his.

"That sounds good to me, Mr. Reynolds." She grinned.

They proceeded up the stairs to her room. He handed back the key and her bag, and made a speedy exit.

Everything was as she left it, except for a neat stack of phone messages on her night table. The top one was from Shiny:

Hi, Sarah, welcome back. Don't eat. I'll pick you up around 7 tonight for dinner, unless I hear otherwise from you.

Among the pink notes was a missive from Richard's assistant confirming the Monday court date. There was also a strange message from Earl White:

Mrs. Berman. This is Earl White. I wanna meat up about my story. There are some things you should no.

E. W.

Sarah shook her head and sneered at his spelling and how his initials formed her exact feelings about Earl White and his relatives.

At 6:50 p.m. Shiny called to let her know she would pick her up in a few minutes. "Oh, listen, come out through the back exit. I'll be in the parkin' lot, okay?"

Sarah was already there when Shiny pulled up. She jumped in the car, snapped on her seat belt, and took a generous sniff. "Is that fabulous scent your new perfume, Eau de KFC?"

Shiny shook her head and smirked as she drove away. "Nope. It's Eau de Chinese takeout."

"Great. So, how's everything?"

"Okay..." Shiny managed a smile that thinly-veiled some underlying tension.

"What's up?"

"We're goin' to my place for Chinese."

"Yeah, I figured that out." Sarah chortled.

"You like Chinese, don'tcha?" Shiny blurted.

Sarah shrugged cautiously, "Sure, I love Chinese, as long as there are lots of vegetables."

There was no wisecrack response. Sarah looked at Shiny, who hadn't said another word. "Are there lots of vegetables?" She nudged.

Shiny remained silent, with her eyes fixed toward the street ahead.

"I take your silence to mean that you've got nothing but a side of pork in that bag."

Suddenly, Shiny stirred. "What? No. There's lots of vegetables. A bucket of vegetables...and chicken, but no pork at all."

Sarah feigned relief. "Whew. Glad to hear it. Now, cut the crap, Shiny, and tell me what's bothering you."

"Let's have dinner, then we can talk," Shiny insisted as she tightened her grip on the wheel.

"You're starting to scare the crap out of me. Just tell me; is everyone okay?"

Shiny nodded unconvincingly.

Sarah crossed her arms over her chest. "I admire your feeble attempt at enthusiasm. Now for God's sake, what's going on?"

Shiny heaved a sigh, loosened her grip, and spoke begrudgingly. "Okay fine. There's some worrying news that Earl White's gonna go free."

Sarah responded with a burst of laughter. "That's the big worrying deal? I've been telling you all along, that would likely be the case."

"Yeah, but somebody's been lettin' us know they're not happy about it."

"What does that mean?"

Shiny shrieked. "It means, goddammit...we're being threatened!"

"Oh, for heaven's sake, give me a break."

"This isn't a joke, Sarah. It's for real." Shiny's face was now ghost white.

"What does 'it's for real' mean? What brought this crazy paranoid idea on?" Sarah shouted, shook her head then delved into silence.

The foreboding message spreading across Shiny's intense face was that this was neither a crazy nor paranoid idea. Sarah reached out and tapped the driver's arm. "Okay, Shiny, I can see you're getting pissed over this. I'm sorry, so please stop for a second and tell me why you think there's a Prescott Mafia Mob going around threatening chefs and waitresses."

Just two blocks from her home, Shiny pulled over.

"All right, thank you. Now please, tell me why you think someone's threatening you."

"Okay, but no interruptions and no jokes."

Sarah offered a perfunctory salute. "Go ahead, I'll be serious. I'm listening."

After a deep sigh and an intake of air, she began. "Okay, I found a shoebox on our front step when I opened the door to get the morning paper. Inside it was a Barbie type doll with its hands and feet bound with rope, and plastic wrap tied around its face and head."

Sarah's cinched brow demonstrated her incredulity. "So, a shrink-wrapped Barbie doll is a horrifying threat? Really? Come on, Shiny, either I'm missing something here, or this is even too paranoid, for me."

Shiny shook her head and continued. "Wes called to tell me he found a male version, hangin' by its neck from the door handle at the Journal office this morning."

Sarah shrugged. "Honestly, it's like a dumb prank, or a bad joke in need of a good punch line."

Shiny's jaw-clenching silence should have been a major clue that she was deadly serious. "Forget it, you're not ready to listen!"

"I'm sorry, but come on, it sounds ridiculous." Aware her friend's continued frustration, she offered another option. "Maybe it's a hazing stunt for some high school club or something."

Silence prevailed. Sarah's discomfort was becoming palpable. She exhaled a slight whistle through clenched teeth. She gazed for a second out the window, then turned toward her friend again. "Okay, Shiny, you're clearly not prepared to listen to reasonable explanations, so tell me why you've concluded that Ken and Barbie are such serious threats?"

"Well, I'm no English whiz or big-time journalist, but the messages that came with the 'gifts' were pretty specific. The letters were cut and pasted together from newsprint, ya know, the way they do it in those wacko movies. My note said: *Messing with the devil can suffocate you;* and Wes's said: *If Earl walks, you hang.* Whoever sent this shit is a real nutcase."

"Why would anyone want to hurt you guys?"

"I don't have a clue, but I'm pretty sure you're gonna wanna find one." With that, she reached behind her seat with a grunt as she grabbed onto something; "I believe you're also a part of this elite club." She lifted up a paper bag and placed it on Sarah's lap.

Sarah warily reached inside, as if it was a bag of spiders. She retrieved a long, black box with a rounded top. She cautiously opened the lid to discover a Barbie type doll, laid out in a white shroud and heavily made-up to resemble either a hooker or a corpse.

"Holy shit!"

Shiny nodded and mumbled. "Uh-huh. Now you're gettin' it. That painted dead hooker in a casket was left for you at the O'Brien."

Sarah took a healing breath and proceeded with whatever bravado she could muster. "Uh...I resent the likeness..." she shrugged, "but I guess I should be grateful that this nutcase didn't leave me any of his disturbing prose."

Shiny shook her head and snapped on the overhead light, "Turn over the box, Sarah."

Reluctantly, she turned it over. Each letter was crudely cut and pasted onto a slip of paper: *Here lies the remains of the late Sarah Berman.*

"The bag was left on the reception desk with your name on it, but no room number. Mitch wasn't sure if whatever was inside was perishable, so he figured he should take a peek. It freaked him out, but he was smart enough to think to drop it off at Wes's office. Wes asked him to take all your mail and phone messages directly up to your room. He figured, whoever these crazies are, it's not a good idea to leave your personal information lying helter-skelter around the lobby."

"Did you call the police?"

"It just happened this morning, so I wanted to wait for you. After your first reaction, it wasn't so dumb of me to feel weird calling the cops and saying I'm scared 'cause someone left a Barbie doll on my doorstep. I didn't tell Ron. I don't want him worrying. After Wes got one, he and I talked about calling the cops, but he said he was willing to wait 'til you got back tonight.

Look, Sarah, maybe I'm overreacting..."

"And maybe not. Maybe Earl's cousin, Zane, is sending us a message."

"Why him?"

"He did call me a whore. And he did stress how badly he wanted to share his cell with Earl. He even wished Laurie Cowan dead."

Shiny nodded slowly, "Yeah, but how do I fit in?"

"You drove." Sarah's eyes crinkled with her grin.

"That's not funny." With that, Shiny put the car in drive and headed for home.

"You know, Shiny, this is really creepy, but if it *is* Zane Fergusson pulling this stunt, I really don't think we need to worry too much. He's behind bars, and the dumb jerk he paid to pull this off, likely thinks this was the prank of the decade."

As the headlights announced their arrival, the women saw Shiny's grandchildren jumping up and down in front of the bay window.

Shiny cut the engine and pulled the key out of the ignition before turning to look at her passenger, "Listen, Sarah, let's both try to knock it out of our heads for tonight and just enjoy our evening. As you can tell, my grandkids are really excited to see you. They figure if you're around, they'll get something outta me they'd never stand a chance o' getting otherwise."

With effort, Sarah managed a genuine smile. "Okay then, let's go in and see what mischief I can bring to the Dumas family."

* * *

That evening, when Sarah returned to her suite, Mr. Reynolds called up with a message: "I forgot to tell ya earlier, but I thought you'd wanna know, that Earl White character phoned here more than a couple o' times this week. He asked when you were comin' back, and I told him I didn't know. I also told him since I was keepin' the room for ya for free, ya could take yer sweet time if ya wanted."

"Thanks, Mr. Reynolds. I appreciate your discretion."

"Yeah, yeah," he grumbled before slamming down the phone.

Just hearing Earl White's name, disturbed Sarah. The last thing she wanted to think about that night was a Fergusson connection of any kind.

Not five minutes went by before the phone began to ring again, and Sarah's fears heightened with each clang. She dreaded that it might be Earl White on the other end of the line. Finally, she resigned herself and picked up the receiver.

It was Saul's voice that enveloped her with a tsunami of revulsion.

"You come all the way to Toronto to sneak into my closet like a thief in the night? Did you think you'd catch me in some compromising situation? I don't know what you said to Cora, but she's leaving, and I'm pretty sure it's because of you. You really fucked this up. I just want you to know I've had it. I've met with my lawyer and there's no more postponing. I want this divorce finalized immediately. I suggest you get yourself a lawyer and let me make this perfectly clear: I don't want my future put on hold because you're too busy with some pathetic quest to save a child molester."

"Saul? What a pleasant surprise."

"I'm in no mood for your bullshit, Sarah."

"I thought it was a wrong number at first, but once you started dictating the terms of my life, I knew you'd dialled correctly. The thing is, Saul, I'm in the middle of something very important, and sadly, I can't adjust my schedule to accommodate your bimbo's due date! Little Johnny might have to end up being born a bastard...kind of like his middle-aged father."

Saul was silent for a moment, "What the hell? How did you know about this? I only found out myself, yesterday."

"Really? Me too."

Sarah hung up the phone feeling gratified that for once, she'd been a step ahead of her ex, who was

Reva Leah Stern

moronic enough not to notice a used pregnancy test sitting in his medicine cabinet.

CHAPTER THIRTEEN

"*You're listening to Andy's Oldies but Goodies on CKRL radio. We're bringing you a tossed salad of Elvis, the Everly Brothers, Bobby Darrin, and a garden full of other greats from the fifties and sixties. I'm your very own, well-seasoned D.J., Andy Madison, and we're here to spice up your Monday morning.*

"*Look out the window, folks. It's a sunny blue-sky day, and, for November, here on the shores of the beautiful St. Lawrence, it's a balmy forty-two degrees...*"

Monday had arrived, but Sarah was worried that she might get a call informing her that court was once again cancelled. As she headed out the front door, she got a friendly nod from Laurie Cowan as he was getting into his car, confirmation for her that court was on.

Hoping to bypass all the courtroom formalities, she drove in late, and just as she was about to park, she spotted Richard McCall and Laurie Cowan leaving.

She pulled up and shouted, "He cancelled again?"

Laurie Cowan sauntered up to her window, "No. It's just when a man pleads not guilty and is not guilty, justice is swift." He grinned.

"Are you saying the judge dismissed the case?"

"Oh, that would have been particularly nice, but no, he just informed us that the hearing starts on

Wednesday." He began to walk away, but turned back, "By the way, you didn't respond to my message. If you're still interested in talking about Earl White, I'm going to be around. The food's pretty good at the O'Brien, or there's a great French restaurant here in Brockville, almost as good as any in Toronto. Check your calendar, then call me and we can talk over dinner."

"I may do that, thanks," she quietly replied as she gunned the engine and sped away. Something about Laurie Cowan's penetrating blue eyes made her feel girlishly uncomfortable.

* * *

As Sarah headed out the door, en route to Tim's for her usual morning coffee and croissant, Mr. Reynolds called out to her, "Hold up there. Ya better come and get this before ya leave."

It was a message from Shiny.

Hi Sarah, the other night with my grandkids and all that Barbie talk, I didn't get a chance to tell you that Braydon and I ran that errand you asked us to take care of. We wanna meet at the Journal office at 10 this morning to give you an update of sorts...if you can make it. Wes'll be there too.

* * *

Sarah sacrificed the coffee run and headed directly to the office. Shiny arrived soon after, fully armed with caffeine and donuts for all. She placed a coffee into Sarah's eager hands.

The Prescott Journals

"Go ahead, Braydon," Shiny urged as she plunked herself down on the corner of his desk. "Tell her what we know."

Braydon nodded and took a deep breath. "Okay, here goes. The secretary insisted it would be impossible to retrieve records dating back thirty or so years, but Shiny went directly to the head of Hospital Administrations, Francis Murk, who she knows from her curling league. Francis told her to leave it with her for a few days and she'd see what she could do."

Sarah shrugged and offered a slight grimace at what seemed to be less-than-dire news. "So, I rushed my butt here for 'breaking news' about a curling buddy? Please tell me there's more?"

Braydon nodded, "Shiny suggested if Francis found out anything, she should send it to us at the Journal office; and sure enough, this morning a manila envelope with Shiny's name on it mysteriously arrived in our mailbox, without a stamp."

He handed the opened envelope to Sarah, who plunged into it as if it were a lottery cheque. "Holy crap," she blurted as she scanned the documents, "these are photocopies of Eleanor Miller's medical records." Sarah gasped as she inspected the pages. "Oh my God, you guys, these copies are gold,! Look here under general observations. There's the doctor's description of Eleanor's condition that night." She scanned the record a moment. "Oh, bloody hell! She was so messed up, it's a wonder she survived."

"I know. That report shook me like crazy," Shiny shuddered. "Did you see the doctor's note at the bottom?"

"Unbelievable. He actually put in writing that *no further action was intended!*" Sarah shook her head scornfully.

"Dr. Bond hasn't practised at St. Gabriel's for over fifteen years," Wes declared. "But he's still around. Maybe I can track him down if you need him."

Shiny added with childlike enthusiasm, "Guess what else, Sarah? The nurse on duty that night was Ket Martin's older sister, Bernice. She was a good six years older than Ket, so you probably don't remember her."

"Oh contraire, I most definitely remember her." Sarah's reply was infused with irony, as she laid out the conversation she had with Mitch about his mom, Ket, and his Aunt Bernice.

"Holy cow! Don't you think it's kinda cosmic that it was Mitch Martin who discreetly brought your Barbie doll to us here?" Braydon added.

"I asked Francis if Bernice still works at St. Gabriel's," Shiny continued, "and she said she does some on-call nursing for them, but mostly she does private at-home-care for the elderly."

The room grew quiet and contemplative until Shiny enthusiastically inserted her conclusion, "Now, it looks like a real competent lawyer can open up the case, eh, Sarah? I mean, you've got it all right there, huh?"

Sarah was hesitant to share the enthusiasm. "Shiny, this is great info, but honestly, I know we're going to need more than a decades-old hospital report to kickstart a cold case," Sarah heaved a heavy sigh. "Listen, I'm thinking if, by some slim chance, there's something to those insane doll antics, then we shouldn't be telling anyone what we're doing until we're sure we've got something definitive to present. Agreed?"

All heads nodded in agreement.

"You know what I'm thinking, Sarah?" Braydon's query elicited a smile from Sarah.

"I haven't got a clue. Please enlighten me." She quipped.

"Okay. If you could find out where the assault took place, I could check the land title records and find out who owned the property in the winter of '58," Braydon volunteered. "Maybe someone has a burning secret they'd be relieved to share before they die."

Sarah seemed distracted while Braydon continued. "Anyway, Wes and I looked through the Journal archives again, but came up with nothin'. Then I spent a few tedious hours at the *Brockville Standard,* going through their microfiches from 1955 to 1960. But we didn't find any sexual assaults. We found reports of fist fights at hockey games and drunken husbands smacking their wives around, but nothing that involved a teenage girl being beaten, let alone, raped."

Sarah offered a snippy retort to Braydon's revelation. "Well, since females back then were warned to crawl into a hole and hide, you can bet we won't find too many assaults reported."

Wes rose from his chair and sidled over to Sarah to have another look at the report. "Or maybe, Sarah, it's because, back in the '50s," he teased, "We didn't run to the press every time we slipped on the sidewalk, or got insulted, like they do today."

Sarah offered a wisp of a smile and a gentle elbow nudge to Wes's arm.

"Hey, Braydon mused, "I wasn't around back in those ancient times, but come on, Sarah, I mean, even though what happened to Eleanor back then was a disgusting miscarriage of justice, it doesn't mean that there wasn't any justice."

"He's right." Shiny muttered. "Maybe it was just a more civil time and there weren't as many violent incidents to report,"

Sarah stiffened and sneered. "Oh, please. People wore blinders, but you can bet, the violence was still there. Maybe the horror of World War II was still so fresh people needed to hide in the safety of denial to survive the pain and guilt. I'm just learning about how threatened many Holocaust survivors, who'd barely escaped the Hell of the death camps, felt after they'd settled in Prescott. There was plenty of violence directed toward them. In fact, I bet, you wouldn't have to dig too deeply to find out that most of the Jewish families who lived here during those 'fabulous fifties' would have plenty of horrific stories to tell about the rejection or abuse they suffered right here."

Wes placed his hand gently on Sarah's arm. "And what about you, Sarah?" He asked.

She responded with an indecisive shrug. "I was a kid...and I was born in Canada. What did I know?"

An absence of chatter suddenly invaded the space. All that could be heard was the shuffling of feet, sipping of coffee, and clearing of throats, until the tension was abruptly broken by a ringing phone.

Braydon answered, "Journal Office," and as he listened to the caller, a puzzled expression spread across his face. "It's for you, Sarah," he handed her the receiver.

"Hello?" Sarah answered with trepidation before becoming visibly relieved, "Oh, hi, Eleanor. Everything okay? Tomorrow night? Sure, for another of your culinary masterpieces? You bet I'll be there! Hey, how did you know where to find me? Of course, Reynolds. That guy manages my life these days," Sarah snickered. "But listen, Eleanor, I'd like to ask you a question. Is that all right? Uh-huh, great. I'm at the Journal office. Is it okay if I put you on speaker? Yeah, Wes...and Shiny. Good, thanks. It's about what we discussed the other night..."

"You don't give up, do you?" Eleanor lightly chided.

"Nah, I'm kind of like a deer tick. I latch on and just dig deeper."

Everyone in the room quietly nodded while they did their best to stifle a laugh.

Eleanor chuckled. "You have a strange itch for crawly things, don't you, Sarah?"

"Touché. That was pretty good for a novice." Sarah snickered.

"Thanks. So?" Eleanor invited the question. "Go ahead and ask."

"Okay. I have many questions, but for right now, I'd like the answer to just one." Sarah looked around the room to find all eyes and ears anticipating the question.

"All right, if I can," Eleanor warily agreed.

Sarah sighed in relief. "Okay. Can you tell me where the assault took place?"

The question and the pause sucked the air from the room.

"I'm sorry, Sarah. I can't." Eleanor breathlessly replied.

Sarah bent forward in her seat and whispered into the phone. "Please, Eleanor."

Another lingering silence followed.

"Honestly, you know I wouldn't ask if it didn't matter, but please, it's really important." Tension beaded on Sarah's forehead as she waited. The short, rapid breaths from the other end of the line was proof that she hadn't hung up. Quietly and hesitantly, Eleanor responded.

"Remember, I told you that I was on my way home from a 4H Club meeting?"

"Yes of course," Sarah replied.

"I didn't tell you it was at the old high school, and that I took a shortcut. I squeezed through the bushes that separated the Carsons' house from the Daniels', and I cut through the Daniels' backyard..."

"Oh my God," Sarah whispered.

Shiny's eyes widened as the reality sunk in; but she sat stalk still.

"It couldn't have been there." Sarah murmured. "Someone would have heard. Anna...her parents... someone."

Eleanor's prolonged silence reflected a resounding statement of dread while the revelation rushed at Sarah with unrelenting force. Her jaw was clenched, her fingers white as they tightened around the arms of the chair.

"What about the Carsons next door?" Sarah asked. There was still no response. Sarah's taut face reflected her shock. "How is it possible that no one heard anything?" She whispered.

"I've asked myself that a million times and I still have no answer! Sorry, I'm sorry, but I have to go." With a distinct sob, the call ended.

Sarah stared at the phone as if it was as much an enigma as the answer she'd just heard.

Shiny moved to Sarah's side and quietly asked, "The Daniels' backyard?"

In stunned disbelief, Sarah nodded as she slumped in the chair.

Shiny raised her hands in a gesture of hopelessness. "That's insane. Where were the Daniels? What about the Carsons? Oh my God, Sarah, do you remember how old man Carson used to go crazy when any of us would step one foot onto his front lawn? He had ears like a cat. He must have been a hundred years old even then, so he won't be helping us out now," Shiny mused.

Wes did a quick mental calculation. "That leaves the Daniels. And since both her parents are gone, I guess that means your friend Anna is the only possible lead."

The voices trailed off as Sarah became transfixed on something Anna had said in Montreal. Suddenly, she turned to Wes, "I have to make a long-distance call, right now. Wes, can I do it from here? I really need to call Anna."

"Of course, go ahead." He replied without hesitation.

Sarah's hand shook as she dialed the eleven digits. Her voice quavered as she left an urgent, message clearly indicating she needed a speedy fax reply.

The air was thick with apprehension as Shiny suddenly jumped up. "Listen, I have a thought. Why don't we head back to the Daniel's house, Sarah? It was dark and weird on Halloween, right? So, let's see how it looks in daylight, okay?"

Sarah smiled wanly, stood up, and took a revitalizing breath. "Good idea. Thanks, Shiny."

The two women hiked the nine blocks to the old high school, and from there, they followed the route that Eleanor had taken, and as they had unwittingly done on Halloween night. They passed between the bushes that separated the two houses and came through the clearing into the Daniels' backyard. They looked around, trying to determine which neighbours, if any, might have had a view of the yard.

"Since you already killed off old Mr. Carson, I don't see anyone else with a bird's eye view, do you?" Sarah chortled.

"Very funny, Sarah. But you're right. 'There's nothing to see here,' as they say."

* * *

When they returned to the Journal office, a fax was waiting for them.

Hey Sarah,

I looked at the entry you asked about, but there's no date on it. The entry on the previous page is all about a heart-shaped box of chocolates my dad brought my mom on Valentine's Day, 1958.

Not sure why you asked but I trust, for some bizarre reason, it means something to you. Let me know if it helps.

Anna

* * *

"I didn't understand what you were talking about when you were leaving the message, and I still don't understand what the hell you're talking about. Chocolates? Valentine's Day? What does it all mean, Sarah?" Shiny urged as she shifted in her chair.

"I can't really explain it, Shiny. I'm not sure I understand it myself yet. I mean, could such an atrocity have really happened in the Daniels' backyard? And if it did, and Mrs. Daniels witnessed it, why wouldn't Anna know about it." Sarah groaned.

Shiny looked at her quizzically. "What are you talking about? She was a teenager. She could have been anywhere that night: a movie, a school dance, making out in the back of a car...anywhere."

Sarah shook her head. "Not a chance. You'd have to know something about Anna's life to understand why that was likely impossible. The thing is, Anna's mother was deeply traumatized and depressed, and rarely ever left alone. Her husband worked day and night in their restaurant. Most of the time, it was Anna who looked after her. She stuck to her like glue." Sarah shook her head as if to dislodge an unwelcome tic. "I remember the first time I had dinner at their house. Mrs. Daniels had set a perfect table. I don't mean an attractive setting. I mean perfect. The tablecloth was perfectly aligned, as if she had measured it to the millimeter. The cutlery and dishes were laid out in precise order. After the food was set out, she sat down with us at the table...and then the strangest thing happened: She was breathing, and her body was seated at the table, but her soul or spirit or whatever crazy hippy surreal thing you want to call it, seemed to disappear." Sarah furrowed her brow and bit her lip. "It was as if the human being had been replaced with a wax replica." She trembled as she recalled the vivid images.

"I watched as Anna tied a napkin around her mother's neck, and fed her, one mouthful at a time. When the meal was over, I thought my heart would wither when I spotted an avalanche of tears streaming down Mrs. Daniel's face. I pointed it out to Anna, but she shrugged it off. I started to move toward her mother with a box of tissues, but Anna grabbed my hand and stopped me. She pulled me into the kitchen and explained that whenever her mother retreated into that catatonic state, she simply had to be left alone."

"That's pretty cold and unfeeling of Anna." Shiny scowled.

Sarah shook her head. "No, she was right. Within the hour, all three of us were listening to music, laughing, and having a great time. That was the first time I saw Sophie Daniels in that eerie state of mind, though it wasn't the last. But honestly? Most of the time, she appeared to be pretty normal.

"After school, when I was doing nothing useful, Anna was at home taking care of her mother and learning everything she could about the culinary arts. To many, it might seem that Anna was enslaved by her mother's affliction, but I would argue that, in a bizarre way, she actually became more independent because of it. On rare occasions, her father would close up shop early and stay home so that Anna could go to a school event or spend time with me. But she would always repay his good will by helping out extra at the restaurant while he stayed home with his wife. It was a tough life, but she never griped about it. Anyway Shiny, that's why I know that Anna was always close to home."

Shiny shook her head and whispered "Jeez, Sarah, I can't imagine a life like hers."

The 11 a.m. chiming of the townhall bell, jarred Shiny back to the present. "Oh, shit, sorry, but I gotta go, the grandkids are coming for lunch." With that, she buttoned her jacket, said her goodbyes, and left.

* * *

Braydon and Wes had remained silent throughout the tense discussion, but as Shiny headed out the door, they quietly slipped away to the back. Sarah remained at the desk, going over Eleanor's file and Anna's fax again and again. Suddenly, she grabbed up Eleanor's medical report and stared at the top line: 12:20 a.m. March 13th, 1958. Sarah's face turned crimson. Her adrenaline was pumping like a marathon runner on his last mile.

She reached for the phone and dialed frenetically. By the time she heard Anna's voice, Sarah could barely speak. "Anna, thank God you're there. Do you remember where you were on March 12th, 1958?" she croaked.

"Is this a joke? I don't remember where I was last Monday," Anna laughed. "But knowing the exciting life I live, I can assume that last Monday, I was either at the restaurant or at home. And come to think of it, I was probably in either of the same two places in 1958, except then, I was in Prescott. What in hell is going on?"

"Anna, do you know what March 12th is?"

"Are you crazy? First, it's 'Where was I on March 12th, 1958?' And now it's 'Do I know what March 12th is?' Where are you going with this, Sarah?"

"Do you remember the story you told me? It was so vivid I could picture every detail. You spent the day with my brothers, blowing up balloons, and we all spent the night running around bursting them. Does it ring a bell yet?" Sarah rocked in her chair as she waited for the answer.

"Ah, well, duh," Anna replied. "Sure, it was your surprise Bat Mitzvah."

"Bingo!" Sarah's face lit up like Broadway after dark.

"Oh, I get it," Anna mused. "It's your birthday. March 12th is your birthday. Come on. Give me a break, Sarah. It's been decades since I've rushed out to send you a belated birthday card. Anyway, March 12th is months away, so what's it got to do with anything?"

Sarah began to pace back and forth as far as the phone cord would allow.

"Anna, it's so complicated, I can't explain it to you properly on the phone, but for old-time's sake, just trust me and fax over a photocopy of the Yiddish entry from your mother's diary..."

"Jesus, Woman, it's almost all in Yiddish. Can you be a bit more specific?"

Sarah allowed herself a fleeting smirk as she got the point. "Sorry, you're right. I think it's the page after the one dated Valentine's Day 1958. And I need your best translation along with it."

"Okay, Boss. Will do." Anna joked.

Giddy with anticipation, Sarah jumped up and down, and silently raised her fist in the air Rocky style, before calmly adding, "Oh, and Anna, I need it as soon as possible."

* * *

A glass of curdled milk and a plate of sandwich crusts cluttered the night table while scribbled pages lay strewn about. In the midst of the chaos, the bespectacled Sarah sat cross-legged on her bed, examining the latest fax she'd received from Anna.

If Sophie's words were to be used as evidence that the *storm troopers* she referred to, were the same animals who had attacked Eleanor, then the translation of her log would require absolute accuracy.

In a late-night telephone conversation, Anna tried to offer some clarity to her mother's murky chronicles while Sarah shared her suspicions over the assault that allegedly took place on her family's property.

Could Sophie's unusual journal entry identify her as the only witness more than thirty-five years later? The periphery of the Daniels' yard was populated with trees and bushes.

"Anna, the reference to seeing 'arms glowing in the blackness' could indicate that your mother mistook the glint of a jackknife, for a gun," Sarah theorized.

"Gun?" Anna shouted. "Where in hell did you get a 'gun' from? I never mentioned a gun."

Sarah glanced at the phone as if it was the problem. "It's right here in your translation; in the fax. You said arms. That means guns."

"No," Anna protested, "I said arms. 'Orem' means arms. Not the kind that you point and shoot. They're the kind that are attached to your shoulders. The word for gun in Yiddish is 'biks'."

Although that clarification only served to further baffle the two, they agreed that the attack that Sophie Daniels recorded in her diary must have taken place under her bedroom window on March 12, 1958.

"My God, Anna, I think the night those bastards raped Eleanor, you and I were at my home celebrating my pseudo-Bat Mitzvah."

"Holy hell, this is nauseating and terrifying." Anna murmured. "And now, it's also personal. The terrible irony is that my father always wanted to put up a fence to keep people from using our yard as a shortcut, but my mother wouldn't let him. She insisted we'd seen enough of fences. My God, Sarah, if only my father hadn't listened to her."

CHAPTER FOURTEEN

Sarah booked a seven o'clock dinner reservation for two at the O'Brien Hotel, and then spent part of the day contemplating how to convince Laurie Cowan to look over the evidence that she and her collaborators had gathered.

* * *

Nat King Cole's buttery-smooth voice helped Sarah decompress as she flitted about her suite, preparing for her meeting. Close to 6:30 she heard a faint knock at the door. She smiled at the delightful notion that the blue-eyed gentleman had come by slightly early, to escort her to dinner. He <u>was</u> early, and she was wearing only a bra and panties. She needed to tell him she'd meet him in the dining room, so she quickly slipped on her bathrobe, turned down the music, and inched the door open. The unexpected glimpse of Earl White numbed her. She turned her face away from the gap in the door, took a deep, reviving breath, and queasily asked, "What are you doing here?"

"Ya didn't call back after I left ya a shitload o' messages so..."

She continued to speak to the wall "Uh, sorry, but I've been busy. And right now, I'm getting ready for another meeting," she stammered. "You can call me tomorrow and uh, make an appointment."

Having stated her position, she began to press the door shut, but with one sharp jolt, Earl White pushed the door open, forcing her to step back. He stomped into the room and kicked the door shut behind him. As his lascivious eyes surveyed her, she shuddered in disgust, then tightly folded her arms, held her head high, and glared at him. "Mr. White, you have no damn right to be here..."

"The hell I don't!" he barked. "The fuckin' story's about me! So, I wanna know how ya got time to go out to the Kingston Pen to talk to that scumbag liar, Zane, but yer too busy ta take my call?"

"If you have questions, Mr. White, you can ask me about them at your lawyer's office!" She persisted, while discreetly clutching the collar of her robe.

"I'm tellin' ya, right here 'n now, if ya wanna write about me, then ya better lay off talkin' to them assholes, 'cause that really pisses me off. An' trust me, lady, ya don't wanna see me pissed off!" His pink-rimmed eyes darkened with rage.

Sarah felt her temples pound and her fingers turn icy cold. She gritted her teeth and clenched her fists. "Let me tell you something, Mr. White. You should be more worried about *me* getting pissed-off. After all, I have the megaphone of the media on my side. So, pissed-off or not, I'd be very careful what you say next."

Getting those words out gave her confidence that she wouldn't fall victim to his bullying.

He cackled contemptuously. "You're actually tryin' to threaten me?" He roared. "I'd be real careful about doin' that."

By now, Sarah's fear had morphed into raw fury. "Who in hell do you think you are?" She railed. "I could bring charges down on your head for coming here like this and harassing me. I could even have you thrown in jail for unlawful entry!"

There was a brief pause before Earl regained his footing and smug confidence. "Really? Unlawful? Remember, you opened the door for me. If ya think ya can scare the shit outta me, then yer dumber than I figured." As he spoke, Sarah, strode forward in an attempt to get to the door. Startled by her resolve, he backed up to block her. He stood firmly and spat out yet another threat. "You listen to me, lady, I'm warnin' ya...you better not talk to them prisoners again or else."

"Huh? Or else what? Here's my warning...if you don't leave right now, I'll be forced to get a restraining order against you. I wonder how that'll sit with the judge? And how it'll read in the press?" At the mention of the press, Sarah watched his body language transform from aggressive to concerned, giving her the impetus to offer one more warning. "Yeah, now it's sinking in, right? Bad press would definitely affect your case, wouldn't it? So, Mr. White, I'd be very..." Her message was interrupted by a sudden knock at the door. Earl's face froze in a bulge-eyed mask of fear. The knock repeated, but this time, louder and more rapid. As Earl frantically calculated his way out of the dilemma, his face began to thaw but his smugness returned as he mockingly stepped aside, as if giving her permission to open the door. "I gave ya the message, eh? So fer now, our business is done."

Sarah pushed past him and opened the door, relieved to find Mitch standing on the threshold.

"Hi, Mrs. Berman, I came to look at the toilet. I understand there's a bad smell in there? Is it too late?"

She offered a grateful smile to her young hero. "No, your timing is perfect Mitch, thank you. Please come in.

And you're right, it does smell pretty foul in here." She sniggered as she gave a swift glance toward her unwelcome guest. "So, Mr. White, as I was saying, if I have a need to interview you further, I'll let you know. But I suggest you don't wait by the phone."

Earl, paused for a second, clearly wanting to share a less-than-kindly retort; but resisted and stalked out, slamming the door behind him. Sarah released a soul replenishing exhale as she dissolved onto the sofa. With a rather bemused expression, she looked up and asked. "Mitch, how in the world did you know?"

He smiled and shrugged. "Well, everybody in town knows you're gonna write about that crap-mouthed boor, so after Mr. Reynolds spotted him heading for the stairs, he sent me up."

Sarah smirked. "Wow, what a hero that Reynolds is to send a kid into potential danger. But, Mitch, you really are one gutsy guy."

He nodded in appreciation. "Thanks, Ma'am, except I didn't need guts. Mr. White's not a danger...he's just obnoxious."

She smiled playfully. "Okay, he's obnoxious, on that we agree, even though I think you're a tad naive. But all that aside, does your mother know what a great kid she raised?"

He shrugged and smiled. "Probably not, but I'll pay ya to tell her." He started toward the door. "Oh, I almost forgot," He turned toward her, "Mr. Cowan is waiting in the dining room for you," he winked and grinned, as he exited.

"Thank you," she replied, ignoring his cheeky gesture. She locked the door and hurried to finish dressing. As she did, she thought about the compelling argument she'd need to present if she wanted to persuade the big city lawyer to offer his professional expertise on the cold case. She decided not to mention Earl White's threatening visit, for fear Laurie Cowan would see it as a legal conflict for him.

Checking the mirror for any telltale signs of her unnerving encounter, she added a stroke of blush, a swipe of lipstick, grabbed her purse, and headed down the stairs.

* * *

As she entered the dining room, she felt a wave of relief to see that the lawyer appeared relaxed, wistfully listening to the dulcet sounds of Sinatra that filled the room. Being twenty minutes late for their dinner meeting could have led to him fleeing in frustration; but instead, he looked up, offered a warm, inviting smile, and stood gallantly as she approached.

"I'm so sorry to be late, I had to resolve a minor pest problem before I could leave." He smiled again and pulled a chair out for her. "So, did it get resolved?"

She returned the smile and sat down. "Thankfully, it did, and now I'm starving."

"Good. Me too." He returned to his seat, glanced at her, and asked: "Is it appropriate for a lawyer to tell a journalist that she looks terrific?"

Sarah's complexion evolved through deepening shades of pink as she tried to think of a witty response to ease her obvious awkwardness. "Well, journalist to lawyer, I confess, you look pretty good yourself." Her colour then turned crimson as the words hung in the air. "Are my cheeks as red as they feel from the inside?" She giggled. "I'm not all that used to compliments these days; neither receiving, nor giving them."

"I have an idea," he suggested with a wicked grin, "let's order wine and dinner and see if the colour fades."

It felt good to Sarah to sit across from an interesting and handsome gentleman. They shared a carafe of wine and ate their way to the final course without a lull in the conversation.

As Sarah pushed aside her empty crème caramel dish and poured herself a cup of tea, she proposed a kind of game. "Okay, Laurie, it's time for some unadulterated truth, with no consequences, okay?"

"Sure, go for it," He urged with a nod of his head.

"Okay, when I met you for the first time, I was confounded to find out you weren't a she."

He grinned. "Is that supposed to be some embarrassing blunder that'll turn me red like you? No chance, 'cause that mistake happens all the time. And yes, my name is Laurie, spelled like a girl."

"You can't stop there. I mean, how or why did your parents make that decision. Not that it isn't a lovely name, it's just unusual.?"

"I see you want the full Cowan version, huh?"

"And nothing less." She playfully insisted.

"All right. When my parents placed the birth announcement in the *Jewish Reporter*, it was supposed to read, *Sam and Eve Cowan proudly welcome their baby boy, Lawrie, into the family* The editor mistakenly corrected the ad to read *baby girl, Laurie* and I've used the confusion to embolden me my whole life."

"Then, it seems it was a useful karmic error."

He smiled and raised his glass in appreciation.

He never mentioned Earl White. Instead, they talked about their children (he had one) touched briefly on their mutual divorces (his was three years old, hers was pending) and shared their views on small towns (he had never spent more than a day in one before this).

Sarah made a valiant attempt to grab for the cheque, but Laurie got it first and insisted on paying, "You'll get it next time...maybe." He teased. That left Sarah wondering if the *maybe* was about her getting the cheque, or whether there'd be a next time. She dared not ask.

"Thank you so much, Laurie. It's good to meet up with a *landsman* in a strange land."

For the first time, there was a hint of blush on his face. "Yes, I agree. I wondered when I first saw you at the courthouse, what a nice Jewish girl from the city would be doing in the midst of a small-town sex scandal."

She reared back in surprise. "You did? I mean, you pegged me for Jewish from the other end of the hall?"

He nodded. "I absolutely did."

She looked dubious. "Absolutely?" He nodded again and took a sip of coffee while she continued. "Hmm, so, I guess assimilation is out of the question for me, huh? Maybe a nose job would help," She chuckled.

He tilted his head as he playfully examined her profile. "Nope, your nose is just fine. I think it was more about demeanour than Semitic features that convinced me you were from the tribe. I must admit that I was surprised when Richard told me you were originally from here. If you were as cute then as you are now, I can understand why your parents shipped you off to the city to meet Mr. Right Religion."

Sarah did her best to brush off Laurie's flirtatious remark with a flippant retort. "Actually, my parents sent me to Toronto to become a lawyer, but I botched it by getting married instead."

He cocked his head and asked. "Really? A lawyer?"

She shrugged and grinned. "Yup, a lawyer."

"Then it's my loss, 'cause we might have ended up in the same firm and history might have played out very differently for both of us." He mused.

She smiled and glanced at her watch. "Oh, jeez, it's late."

Laurie checked his watch. "Wow, it is late. Time actually did fly. I enjoyed this dinner meeting, but we clearly didn't cover your questions about my client, and I think that's what you had in mind. If so, do you want to leave me with questions I can answer at our next meeting?"

There was a lengthy pause as Sarah struggled to come up with a fitting reply. "Laurie, I do have some important issues I'd like to discuss with you, but I'm not sure I do my best thinking after a glass of wine. Do you think we could talk again, maybe on Wednesday? Same time and place...but my treat, and no wine?"

She'd never been so forthright, and now, she felt the sting of embarrassment at the thought he might see her as too aggressive. She held her breath and waited.

After glancing through his Day-Timer, he nodded, "Wednesday evening it is."

She heaved a calming exhale. "Great. It's a date then...I mean, appointment...meeting...to discuss some important issues."

He grinned. "Exactly right."

She attempted to stand up but teetered back into the chair.

"Sorry, I'm not very good at drinking."

He laughed and rose from his chair. "Never apologize for that. It's not a liability. I'm generally a two-drink-limit guy, myself. He moved to her side and offered his arm, then helped her to her feet. "Can you make it to your room on your own, or would you like a chaperone?"

She smiled and steadied herself, then removed her arm from his grip. She looked up at Laurie and affirmed. "I'm good. Thanks anyway. I'm tired, but otherwise, I'm perfectly fine."

Laurie's knitted brow was a clear indication that he was dubious about how "perfectly fine" she was. "Well, since you're okay, I'm gonna hang out in the lounge for a few minutes to catch the news. I don't have a working TV in my room yet."

Sarah controlled her wicked urge to snicker at the thought that even this big-city lawyer could get shafted by Reynolds.

* * *

The next evening, during Eleanor's delightful dinner, Sarah's thoughts comingled with her pleasant memories of last night's dinner meeting with Laurie Cowan. But as the evening progressed; Sarah grew concerned about a shroud of restraint that she hadn't felt since her first encounter with the dressmaker.

"Eleanor, I'm feeling like our conversation is kind of strained tonight. The meal was wonderful, but you scurrying around your kitchen and landing nowhere, forces me to ask: What's going on?"

Eleanor stared into her coffee cup. Sarah tried again.

"Listen, Kiddo, I don't want to cause you anymore pain. I realize you've spent years trying to forget the nightmare I made you remember the other night. I feel guilty as crap about that, but..."

Eleanor abruptly set down her mug. "Wait a minute, Sarah. After I opened up to you, did you take that to mean I'd forgotten it happened? There isn't a week that goes by that I don't think about that night. So, please...there's no reason for you to feel guilty."

"That's kind of you, Eleanor. I appreciate it; but if that's not the issue, then why are you avoiding eye contact with me? And why are we having such a hard time filling this dead silence with lively conversation?"

The hush continued. The only sounds were the sipping of coffee and clattering of mugs as they landed on the table. Finally, Sarah cut through the murky veil of silence. "Can I show you something, Eleanor?"

The hostess nodded reluctantly.

"Good, it's in my purse in the other room. Excuse me while I get it." Sarah headed for the living room to retrieve it while Eleanor brought a fresh pumpkin pie to the table and sat waiting.

Sarah re-entered with her purse and sat down. She removed a folded sheet of paper, straightened it out, and slid it toward Eleanor who chose not to look at it.

"Eleanor, please look at it. It's a faxed copy from Anna, of an entry from Mrs. Daniels' diary. It indicates that she was home that night."

Eleanor chose not to look. Sarah folded it and tucked it back into her purse. The two friends wordlessly nibbled at their dessert. Frustrated, Sarah took a deep breath, braced herself, and tried once again to unlock Eleanor's voice. "I'm sorry, but I have to ask. Did you hear anything unusual the night of the attack? Do you recall seeing anyone? Maybe a neighbour as you passed by?" Eleanor didn't reply, but the sudden pallor of her skin and the pulsing of her clenched jaw, were telltale signs that she had answers. Perhaps Sarah wasn't asking the right questions. She pulled her chair closer, placed her hand on Eleanor's wrist, and offered a comforting smile. "I know this is incredibly hard for you, but please try. Was there any chance you were followed?"

Eleanor tilted her head toward Sarah and offered a feeble shrug. "Honestly, Sarah, I saw no one. If I'd been followed, they would have had to pass by me before I cut through the bushes, then race around the block to head me off at the other end. It was a dead quiet night. If they were running, I would've heard ice crunching under their feet. I'd have thought it was skunks or wolves, and then I would've been too scared to take that shortcut."

Sarah interjected, "Could they have been waiting for you?"

Eleanor pressed her fingers firmly over her eyes for a moment. "No. Definitely not. I almost never took that route. And even though I couldn't see their faces, I'm sure I didn't know them."

Cautiously, Sarah asked, "So, why do you think you were targeted?"

Eleanor's body stiffened.

"Eleanor?"

Her lip quivered as she quietly murmured, "Please...please don't ask me..."

Sarah was undeterred. She sat stiffly and asked again. "Eleanor, please, you have to..."

"I can't!" Eleanor shouted. Her face flushed and her eyes brimmed with tears, but she remained eerily still.

The quietude was cacophonous. Sarah's heart pounded as Eleanor's voice screamed inside her head; then a faint whisper escaped. "It was a horrible, horrible mistake."

Sarah gasped. "Mistake? Eleanor, how can you call what happened a..."

"It was!" She shrieked. "It was a mistake!"

"Why would you say that? Why would you think that?" Sarah exclaimed.

Tears ran down Eleanor's cheeks. Her eyes pleaded for the inquisition to stop. "I just do. Please, Sarah, can't you just leave it be?"

Sarah paused to consider her answer, then slowly pressed on. "No, Eleanor, I can't."

Eleanor began to tremble and heave with each sob as if some alien monster was railing inside her.

Sarah edged closer, placed her hand gently on her friend's shoulder and whispered: "It's okay. Really, it's okay. You need to free yourself from this terrible weight. Please, tell me."

Crushed ice worked its way through Eleanor's bloodstream as she painfully waded into the vile bog of memory. "When they grabbed me, all I heard was gibberish. There was snorting and heavy breathing, but I hadn't processed a single word. I kept telling myself, 'They're bullies. They're just trying to scare me, they'll let me go.' When I heard, 'Who wants' ..." Eleanor paused for a desperate gulp of air. "'Who wants to...to...f- fuck her?' Those were the first words I understood, and that was when I heard one of them run away."

Her voice was barely a whisper, but Sarah winced at the deafening volume inherent in the narrative:

"After they threw me on the ground, one of them latched onto the St. Benedict medallion around my neck, and I heard him say 'What the hell is this? Maybe she's the wrong one.' but the others laughed at him, saying things like: 'What a jerk, it's a bloody key. You can't see shit in the dark.'

"Then one demanded they turn me over and 'feel if she's got a tail.' They twisted me onto my stomach, and looped my scarf around my throat, and tried to drag me like a dog. I choked and gagged on the filthy glove they'd stuffed in my mouth.

"'Killing Christ and chewing pigskin, huh, Kike? You're goin' to hell for sure, ya Jew bitch!' Have I told you enough yet, Sarah?" She spat out the question.

Sarah's heart was pounding, her head spinning. In stunned disbelief, she meekly nodded, and Eleanor responded. "Now, for God's sake, can you understand why I didn't want to tell you?"

Sarah slumped in the chair, drained, and shocked. "Eleanor, there were only two Jewish teenaged girls in the entire town...Anna and me!"

Eleanor slowly continued. "But Sarah...I swear, that fact didn't register with me until one night, many years later, during a blizzard. I slipped and fell on the ice right by my front door. My mother rushed out to help me, but I pushed her away. I was lying there reliving with horrific clarity, the absolute terror of the last words I heard on that gruesome night: 'Strip her, fuck her, and then nail her to a tree like the Jews did Jesus.' That must be when I passed out." Eleanor sank back in the chair, pale and spent.

Sarah stopped listening. Her mind had paused on the last thing Eleanor said. Her question came across stilted and monotone. "Eleanor, tell me again what they said about nailing you to a tree."

Eleanor appeared perplexed, but she robotically repeated the words: "Nail her to a tree like the Jews did to Jesus!"

Sarah's face evolved from blushed to ashen.

"Are you okay, Sarah? What's going on?"

Sarah rose from her seat and attempted a meagre smile. "I'm okay, but I'm not exactly sure what this is about. I'm gonna go back to the hotel and do my best to fall asleep and not think about it until tomorrow. When, or if, I get my head straight, I'll hopefully be able to answer your question." With that she headed toward the foyer. Eleanor, looking startled and confused, tentatively followed.

The two beleaguered friends exchanged a reassuring embrace at the door. Each feeling left with a flood of emotional baggage yet to be unpacked.

*　*　*

The midday sun, with its warm, pastel glow had deceived winter, and after the stomach-wrenching conversation of the previous night, Sarah was desperate to revel in the glorious and rare sensation of sun and warmth in November.

Loaded down with groceries, she sauntered along the street, soaking up the rays. Realizing that a sunburned peeling face would make an ugly impression at dinner, she dropped into the pharmacy for a tube of sunscreen. She'd never left a drugstore before with only one item, and today was no exception. The cashier glanced at her credit card before returning it with a smile.

"Can you manage all those bags on your own or would you like some help, Mrs. Berman?"

Sarah smiled warmly and returned the courtesy by noting the cashier's nametag.

"Thank you, Karen. I'm okay. I'm much stronger than I look, but I appreciate your offer."

The cashier smiled back. "Anytime, Mrs. Berman."

Sarah added the bags to her grocery burden and offered a cheery goodbye. As she started toward the door, she heard the pharmacist call out to her. "Mrs. Berman? Hi. I thought I heard your name. How was your trip?"

She backed up and turned toward him. "You mean last week?"

"Yup. Montreal, eh?"

Her face reflected the bewilderment tripping through her mind, but the last thing she wanted to do was become a fresh source of town gossip; so, she smiled and politely responded.

"Yes. Yes, I was...and in Toronto as well, and both trips were fine. Thank you, Mr. Cook, for asking. Oh, before I go, I don't suppose there's any word yet from the photo lab?"

He held up a finger to suggest she wait a moment. "I did call your hotel last week about those old negatives, but Mitch told me you were away, and you'd be back by the weekend. I tried again on Saturday, and you still weren't back, so I figured, you'd call whenever you could."

"That's okay, Mr. Cook, I was pretty sure the photos wouldn't turn out, so I'm not surprised." Sarah shifted the heavy bags in her hands and was about to walk away.

"Hold on a second, Mrs. Berman, that's not altogether true." The pharmacist declared.

She moved closer. "Huh? You mean, some of the pictures actually turned out?"

He nodded. "Well kinda."

She set the bags down on the floor and leaned against the counter.

"There are about three of 'em. Now, they're not good quality, but you can sort o' make 'em out. I mean, you wouldn't win a prize with 'em, but then I'm not an expert, eh? Oh God, here I am chattin' away, and I still haven't given them to ya."

Karen suddenly reappeared from somewhere. "Here's the envelope, Mrs. Berman. The negatives are in there, too. Can I slip it into one of the bags for you?"

"Sure, thanks, Karen. How much do I owe you?"

"Oh no, Ma'am," the pharmacist interjected. "I think the boys down at the lab felt bad they couldn't do a

The Prescott Journals

better job for ya, so there's no charge, Now, you go and have yourself a nice day."

"You too. Thank you so much!" She smiled, waved, and picked up her parcels. She hurried back to the hotel, anxious to have a look at the three surviving photos.

The grocery bags and drugstore purchases were quickly abandoned on the living room sofa. Sarah rushed to the window to look at the photos in the bright sunlight.

She squinted as she peered at the first dark and faded image of what looked to be a street scene. Disappointment painted her face when the next picture emerged as just another grainy landscape. She continued to stare at it for another few seconds. Suddenly she gasped, grabbed her key and bolted from the room, the door slamming behind her. She raced down the stairs to the front desk arriving short of breath.

"Mr. Reynolds. Do you have a magnifying glass I can borrow?" She gasped.

"Hell, I thought the place was on fire with you comin' down here huffin' like a huntin' dog. Yeah, I got a magnifier, but I'm not big on lendin' things out 'cause I never get 'em back in the same condition." He sneered.

"Sheesh! I'll pay you for the darn thing! What's it worth? Five bucks?" Sweat was beading on her radish-red face.

A tad embarrassed; he grudgingly handed it over. "No charge. Just bring it back in good condition, ya hear?"

She rushed back to her room and peered at the photo again through the magnifying glass. The image was clear enough to identify Fleischman's Grocery Store with its baskets and stands piled against a wall. The store name was partially visible between the shards of shattered glass that still clung to the window frame. Scribbled across the stone wall, in the centre of the photo, were the words "DEAD JEW" but, faded spots eliminated the rest of the phrase. It couldn't eliminate the outline of a swastika graffitied on the front door. The scene was just as the Fleischmans had described it.

    She placed the second photo on the bottom of the pile and studied the third. The edges of the last snapshot were cloudy but seemed to have been taken at the same location. Two fuzzy individuals were positioned near the wooden stands in front of the shop. One appeared to be wearing a cap, and the other, possibly sporting a buzz cut. The one with the cap stood in the street, pointing to the shop with one hand, and holding onto something with the other. He wore a bomber jacket with what looked like a faded crest on the sleeve.

    Sarah set down the magnifying glass and dissolved into a chair. She needed time to figure out what to do with her discovery. Where in the world had the negatives come from, and did she have the legal right to develop them?

CHAPTER FIFTEEN

"Listen, Sarah, any discussion about the Earl White case has to be completely off the record tonight, agreed? If not, then this will be a very quiet dinner from my side of the table." Laurie teasingly warned.

She offered a pretend pout and replied. "I have no note pad, no tape recorder, and will likely have no memory if I drink this whole glass of wine; therefore, you have my sworn word, any talk of Mr. White is off the record, so you may speak freely."

"Okay. I was geared up for court today and ready to meet a worthy adversary, but instead found a Crown Attorney who was absolutely vacuous and uninspiring."

"Oh, thank God, I wasn't the only one bored to death."

"Hell no. I've never been more bored by an opening from a prosecutor. In fact, the huge mug of coffee I downed before court, failed to keep me awake, I had to resort to biting the inside of my cheeks so I wouldn't nod off." He shook his head and smiled.

She returned the smile and proceeded to one-up him. "Well, I downed a double latte this morning and a bottomless cup of caffeine at lunch, so I was worried I'd flood the courthouse before he finished." She offered a 'wiping of hands' gesture before her final shot. "I gotta say, after your revelation, Mr. Cowan, I'm surprised your bladder held up so well."

Laurie smirked. "It's the super absorbent Depends I wear. You should try them."

She giggled.

As the first half carafe of wine led to a second, they both grew more comfortable peeking into each other's personal lives and comparing experiences. To an eavesdropper, their exchange might have appeared banal, but to these two diners, the conversation was extraordinarily revealing.

They discovered that they were, too insecure, personally too trusting, and both struggling to restore their dignity after being cast aside by their spouses.

"What was your ex hoping to find out there in the world, Laurie; the next Meshiah?" Sarah giggled at what she thought to be a hilarious retort.

By the bottom of the second carafe of Sauvignon Blanc, Sarah's unfettered candour began to resemble Liz Taylor's, *Virginia Woolf.* "What in hell was she thinking, for Christ's sake?" She sputtered.

Laurie tilted his head and looked toward his dinner companion who seemed suddenly dazed. "Sarah, I think you might be getting a little blitzed...so maybe we should get you some more coffee." Sarah appeared oblivious. Laurie caught Mitch's eye, held up his mug and two fingers.

As the two men were communicating over the coffee order, Sarah roused herself and continued as if there had been no pause at all. "My ex traded me for a pregnant nursh...He gets two babes w-with one shot. But you? I don't g-get it, Laurie. Your w-wife really thinks she could find b-better than you?" Mitch refilled the mugs and quickly exited, holding back a desperate urge to giggle.

"It's certainly crossed my mind that maybe I wasn't good enough for her." He retorted.

She was about to take a sip of coffee, when a snicker erupted. "Shorry, Laurie, but I can't g-get over that name. How can a m-manly man who is sho c-comfortable with the name Laurie, be inshecure?"

"Have a bit more coffee, Sarah...we'll both be glad you did." He smirked.

She complied. "I'm really shorry. I can ushually drink a little w-wine without feeling so...you know."

"A little wine maybe, but we polished off the equivalent of a carafe." He chuckled. She shrugged.

She gulped down the rest of the coffee before responding. "Can I have a m-minute? I'm uh, I gotta go to the g-girls room if you d-don't m-mind."

Laurie nodded and helped her to her feet. He watched as she ambled away along a rather circuitous path. He paid the bill and waited for her to return.

As she got closer, it was clear that her gait and the path hadn't straightened out at all.

"I'm f-feeling musch better now. Thanks, Laurie, I uh..." the sentence remained incomplete as she dropped wordlessly into her chair.

He stared at her in bemusement, then cleared his throat like a parent about to deliver a stern warning, or a professor about to discipline a student. "Sarah Berman, I think you will definitely need some help up the stairs, and I don't know if my accident insurance covers wine related injuries." He stood up.

Sarah feigned indignance and attempted to get to her feet while insisting; "No w-way! I can d-do it by myshelf. If I could drive all the way to M-Montreal by myshelf, I can n-navigate a few stairs." She made it to her feet and wobbled two steps toward the exit. "Oh no, wait, the bill didn't come yet." She moaned.

Laurie smiled. "Yes, it did, you're just too inebriated to remember, you took care of it." She looked utterly bewildered. He stood up, put his arm around her waist and steered her up the staircase. He took the key from her and opened her door. He placed her handbag on the coffee table, pulled down the duvet and eased her onto the bed before heading to the door. He took another look back and the vision brought a wry smile to his lips. He returned to her bedside and stood over her silently and curiously studying her as she slept. He sat down on the bed, gently lifted her smooth shapely legs onto his lap and carefully removed her stilettos.

* * *

A thunderous ringing reverberated through the cavern that was the inside of Sarah's head. It took a few minutes before she focused, and by then, the caller had hung up.

She squinted at her surroundings. She was in her room, on her bed, and to her relief, Laurie was nowhere in sight. As she pulled herself into an upright position, she was both relieved and embarrassed to discover that she was still wearing her little black dress. Her stilettos had been neatly placed beside her bed and her handbag was on the coffee table. She slowly got to her feet, dropped her clothes, and headed into the washroom for a much-needed shower.

Afterward, feeling refreshed, she donned her robe and exited the washroom. She let out a shriek when she spotted the backs of two males appearing to sneak out of her room.

Mitch froze on the spot with Laurie close behind. They turned to face a bewildered Sarah.

"I'm so sorry, Mrs. Berman, but Mr. Cowan called and then knocked a bunch o' times, and when you didn't answer, he got worried...and so did I...so I had to come and check. Then we heard the shower, but then we heard nothing, and we didn't know what to think, and then we heard the bathroom door open, and then we figured you were okay, and then we tried to get away before you saw us, and then we..."

"Okay, okay, hold it, Mitch, I've got this." Laurie snickered. "Listen, Sarah, don't blame the kid. He was just trying to be of service. I really gave him no choice. It's my fault."

Sarah shot a mystified glance at both men. "Really, well then, who do I tip? And for what service?"

Laurie tried to hide his relief, but his audible sigh was a giveaway. "Very funny, we were worried, okay?"

She shook her head and scoffed. "Worried about what?"

"Hey, you could have been dying all alone from alcohol poisoning."

"I'm fine, and I really appreciate your concern, but as you can see, I'm completely sober and not exactly comfortable having anyone seeing me unmasked." With that, Mitch turned and raced out the door, clearly not waiting for a tip. "If you don't mind, I'd like to get dressed without an audience."

Laurie smiled sheepishly before heading to the exit. "Do I get to vote on that?"

She playfully raised a threatening eyebrow. "Mr. Cowan, I awoke this morning, grateful that I was still fully clothed. During my invigorating shower, I was praising your gentlemanly ways, so please don't make me regret it."

"Okay, I got it. If you can handle breakfast, I'll be in the dining room for the next half-hour or so. Otherwise, I'll look for you later in the courtroom."

"Considering how much reconstruction I'll need to look presentable; a half hour isn't gonna cut it." She quipped.

As he turned to go, she added, "Wait, Laurie, seriously...thanks for doing the right thing by me last night...and this morning. It's been a long time since anyone's looked out for me."

His usual cockiness gave way to bashfulness. "Uh, no problem. Okay, well...yeah, see you in court then."

"Uh, about that...I may take a break today. I have some other stuff to deal with."

"Like how to rid yourself of a hangover?"

She shrugged and offered a mischievous grin. "Nah, the trick to that is getting nine hours of sleep, which I did and now I'm up and ready to go; but not to court."

He seemed disappointed "Do you really want to miss all that court action?"

Sarah smiled wryly. "If yesterday was any indication, I won't miss a thing."

He nodded. "Yeah. It's true. If I didn't have to be there, I'd skip it too. I'll call when I get back, to see how you're doing."

Sarah smiled pensively as she watched him saunter out the door.

* * *

A couple of hours later, Sarah was sipping breakfast tea and staring blankly out the window of the O'Brien dining room. Guilt clung like burrs to her conscience as she realized that another night had slipped by with Eleanor Miller's cold case still left on ice.

"Mrs. Berman? Another pot of hot water...or some dry toast maybe? That usually works for my mom." Mitch sympathetically suggested.

Sarah robotically turned away from her thoughts. "Oh, thank you Mitch. Yes, more hot water would be great."

As he returned with the fresh pot of hot water, she smiled. "As always, your service is excellent."

The compliment elicited a blush. "Thanks, Mrs. Berman, it's only water." He set the teapot down and was about to stroll away when Sarah tugged on his sleeve.

"Wait a sec, Mitch. How's your mom doing?"

His eyes twinkled with delight. "Oh, thanks for asking. She's doing great, With the weather getting colder, my mom and dad are lookin' forward to goin' ice fishing on the river."

"Wow, I remember doing that as a kid." Sarah smiled dreamily. "We used to take our rods out into the middle of the St. Lawrence and reclaim the holes the ice fishermen left behind. I used to pray I'd reel in a fish so big it would get stuck in the ice and everyone would come rushing out to see it." She stopped abruptly. "Sorry, Mitch, I got a bit carried away. I didn't mean to take you away from your duties. But it does go to show what a dumb kid I was. I never thought about the fact that a fish big enough to get stuck in that hole would've also been big enough to pull me right down into it." The two shared a quiet chuckle. "Tell your mom to be careful of those big fish." She added.

He smirked and leaned in, to whisper. "Mrs. Berman, don't ever tell my mother I said this, but it would take a really giant mammal to pull my mother down that hole."

"Boy, could I ever blackmail you, Mitch," Sarah playfully chided.

"Nah, my mother's a great sport. She's got the best sense of humour in town."

"Speaking of...um...how's your Aunt Bernice?"

Exhaling a giant guffaw, he replied, "You wanted to say, speaking of no sense of humour, how's my Aunt Bernice, didn't ya?"

A squeak of a giggle slipped out, but Sarah recovered. "I have to admit, there was quite a personality difference between your mom and her sister. What's your Aunt Bernice doing these days?"

"Well, she babysits these really old sick people 'til they croak. That's the only way they can get away from her. She's a kind of self-made Doctor Whatsis in the States, you know, the suicide doctor?" He snorted.

Sarah arched an eyebrow. "Kevorkian?"

Mitch nodded. "Yeah, that guy. But she doesn't have to put a plastic bag over their heads or anything. After spending time with her, they just pray to God, their hearts'll give out quickly. She has a perfect record of success 'cause every single one of them has died."

Sarah did her best to stifle a laugh. "Does your mom know you talk about her sister like this?"

Mitch picked up the empty teapot to make himself look busy. "Yeah, we joke about her all the time. But the truth is, Aunt Bernice is a good person who's really good at her job. I know Brockville hospital's always calling her to come back, but she likes being her own boss."

"Does she still live here in town?"

Mitch nodded. "Yup, she's been living with us since my uncle died a few years ago. Well, not exactly living with us. We've got a finished basement, so she's sorta got her own apartment down there."

"You know what, Mitch? I'd love to see your Aunt Bernice...and your mom. Do you think they'd be willing to come here and have brunch with me sometime? Like, maybe this Saturday or Sunday?"

Mitch's smile filled his face. "I could almost guarantee it. We can call Mom from the reception desk if you want."

"Absolutely. Let's do it."

With that, they headed to the front desk. Mitch dialed the number and handed her the phone.

After forty years of tobacco abuse, Ket Hall's voice was thick and raspy, but still familiar.

"Oh, Jeez Louise. I can't believe after all these years; I'm talkin' to Sarah Klein. You and me were real little farts in school as I recall. You, 'cause you were a smarty pants, and me, 'cause I was a big bag o' trouble. But we made the teachers laugh like hell, didn't we? Do ya remember?"

Sarah's wide grin rivaled the Cheshire cat's. "Of course, I do. You know, Ket, if you'd asked me before I got here, what I recalled of growing up in Prescott, I probably would've drawn a complete blank. But, ever since I've been here, all kinds of memories have come rushing back."

"Is that a good thing, Sarah?"

"I don't know yet. But I'm pretty sure I'm about to find out." She replied. As the conversation continued, Mitch became concerned that Reynolds might notice the phone wasn't being used for calling a cab. He gently motioned for her to end the call and Sarah caught the signal.

"Okay, Ket, sorry but I gotta go, So, you, me, and Bernice are on for Saturday breakfast at 9 am, in the hotel dining room, my treat, yes?"

"Sure. Absolutely. We'll be there. Lookin' forward to it."

"Okay then, bye for now."

With that, Sarah hung up and raised her thumbs in triumph, which inspired Mitch to raise his own in response.

"Great," he whooped and punctuated his excitement with a happy jig. "Yup. It so happens, I'm gonna be working that morning shift too."

"Hmm. That reminds me. I wanted to ask you about your schedule, Mitch. How can you work on weekdays, like today? Aren't you still in school?"

"I am, but when I have spare periods, I ask Mr. Reynolds for more hours 'cause I'm gonna need the money."

"Aha, I'm impressed with your dedication, Mitch." She sincerely stated, then added with a mischievous grin, "But what you're gonna do with all those zillions you're earning?"

He stretched himself up to his full five-and-a half feet, and proudly announced, "Law school." He then leaned in and whispered, "Do you really think I'd put up with that shithead, Reynolds, if this job wasn't my tuition ticket outta here?"

As they burst out laughing, Reynolds stuck his head out of his office and shouted, "Over here, Mister!"

Mitch warily ambled over to his boss.

"Now listen here, Kid, I'm not payin' ya to have a good time, eh?" he warned.

Mitch loudly whispered with no subtlety whatsoever, "No, you're not, Mr. Reynolds, and I wouldn't dream of it. But the handwriting's clearly on the wall of how important this big shot guest is to you, so I'm just bein' friendly is all." Mitch did his best to control the smirk that threatened to give him away.

"Okay then, I hear ya. Keep up the good work; and you'll keep workin'." Reynolds quietly grunted, then shouted for Sarah's benefit, "Did ya hear me loud and clear, young man?"

Mitch stood at attention, nodded, and replied. "Yes, Sir, I heard you loud and clear."

As Reynolds disappeared behind his closed office door, the two conspirators let loose the laughter they had been trying desperately to control.

* * *

Wesley sat behind his desk, carefully studying the photos, and attempting to explain to Sarah why he had left out the Antisemitic references when telling her about the Fleischman incident. "After telling you about the vandalism on the Orange Hall during your High Holy Days, you were really upset. And I didn't want you to falsely remember us as a town of bigots and racists, so I just left the graffiti part out. I'm sorry. I should know better. It was a disgusting incident, but one that was never repeated after that. For better or worse, Prescott just moved on after the Fleischmans moved away."

She grimaced. "But why in hell did such hate-fueled attacks happen. I mean, were they organized? Was there a neo-Nazi party living here?"

Wes looked at her in bewilderment, "What? Wait! Slow down, please. One answer at a time. First, there was never an organized fascist group in this town. Second, while there were some Antisemitic slurs from time to time, as your dad would've attested, there was no Nazi party operating in or near this area. It was just a bunch of ignorant, dumb-assed, bigoted hooligans."

"If that was the case, then why did they stop? Or did they?"

"Yeah, they did. My best guess is they either grew up or moved away."

Sarah shook her head. "Sorry, but I can't get past the fact that a pack of hateful animals hunted down, raped, and beat a young, innocent girl like Eleanor because they thought she was a Jew."

Wes slumped in his chair, hands in his lap and head down. A prolonged silence filled the space as the awfulness of it sunk in. "There are no words powerful enough to describe the evil of it." He quietly professed.

She inhaled a cleansing breath. "Well, I need to find some words...the right words...because Eleanor needs to see justice."

He looked at his former protégé with a wisp of a smile. "My dear, I can see you're making Eleanor your mission. You've moved a long way from wanting to make the potential Earl White case a steppingstone to a big journalism career, eh?"

"No, I still want to see that case through to its end. I feel for those horribly abused kids. The thing I dreaded most when I started this trip, was hearing all the sickening details surrounding those crimes; but what I didn't expect was to be shocked again by an old acquaintance's horror story. Anyway, if Earl White is innocent, then fine; all the guilty parties have been incarcerated and hopefully those child victims are getting the help they need to rebuild their lives."

Wes reached out and squeezed her hand. "That's the spirit. But this Earl White business isn't what's really haunting you, is it?"

Her eyes glistened with tears "No." She sniffed. "What really haunts me, is the idea of Anna and my family carrying on with that stupid Bat Mitzvah that night...while Eleanor was being viciously attacked."

"But if Anna hadn't been with you, then she would've been the one they attacked." He released her hand and turned her face toward him. "How would that have been any better?"

Sarah struggled to keep her tears in check. "It wouldn't. Of course, it wouldn't."

"This is a King Solomon dilemma. Do you remember that story, Sarah? He solved the problem by offering to split the baby in half. I mean, it was a clever, but pretty grotesque ruse."

She offered a diminutive nod. "Wes, that was one of the stories in that wonderful Hebrew book my aunt gave me, and it was the focal point of that ridiculous Bat Mitzvah night. Pure irony huh?" The thought elicited a momentary silence.

"I'll do what I can to help bring closure, Sarah. I'll think harder on it, starting tonight."

* * *

The candescent morning sun cast its shimmering rays across Sarah's duvet, luring her away from her thoughts. Since the glimmer of Saturday's dawn, she had been lying in bed, mulling over a quandary: was her life a pathetic mess or an exciting adventure?

She lazed under the covers, with bold colourful thoughts hovering then drifting away. *Why did she get herself mixed up in such an ungodly mess? Will Bernice Hall remember Eleanor Miller? What does Ket Hall look like now?*

Before heading to the dining room, Sarah checked herself in the mirror for the third time, finally feeling more assured that she would be recognizable. But would they?

* * *

Mitch bustled about the dining room, balancing decaf and regular, while Sarah positioned herself at her favourite table, waiting for a sign that one or both guests had arrived. Finally, Mitch cheekily crossed his blue eyes and gave a subtle head tilt toward the hotel lobby. Sarah made a mental note to double his tip; and then reconsidered as she saw him turn and head into the kitchen, leaving the guest standing alone at the entrance.

Now, Sarah was faced with the embarrassing dilemma of trying to guess which one of the sisters was about to join her. As Sarah was dredging up the gumption to get up and greet whichever sister had arrived, Mitch returned from the kitchen empty-handed, and offered his arm to the waiting Hall sister.

It was clear as they approached, that at least one of the formerly young and sexy Hall girls had burgeoned into a plump, grey-haired matron with robust cheeks, a bountiful bosom, and a strange, whistling wheeze.

"Mrs. Berman, this is my Aunt Bernice. Aunt Bernice this is..."

His aunt curtly interrupted. "I get it, Mitch. Now how about you hustle along and get us some fresh, hot coffee? I walked here and I'm damn near frozen." She barked the order to her nephew like a general in the field. With that introduction, it was clear that Bernice hadn't really changed. As Sarah recalled, she was always kind of grumpy, even at school dances she looked as if she was there under duress.

While they waited for Ket, they nibbled on warm rolls, sipped coffee, and began to chat.

All morning, Sarah had contemplated how to get Bernice to open up and share any details she might recall about the Eleanor Miller incident. So, try she did.

It turned out that she barely had to mention Eleanor's name before Bernice proceeded to share everything she could recall about that night at St. Gabriel's.

"Bernice, I'm so relieved that you remember her."

"Oh, that was a terrible thing. I was barely out of nursing school and only a few years older than her. I remember feelin' sick all over at the sight of that poor girl. The extent of the blood and bruises and lacerations on her body was a memory you don't easily forget, eh? No matter how hard ya try."

As she spoke, the sadness in Bernice's eyes supported her traumatic memory of that night.

"Did you know that the doctor told her not to report it to the police?" Sarah asked.

Bernice shrugged. "That was pretty much the standard back then. They all did that. Did ya ever see that movie *Town Without Pity*?"

"Uh-huh. I did, a hundred years ago. Why?"

"Well, Sarah, that was a perfect example of a girl who was raped once and then kind of emotionally raped again and again after reportin' it. First, the horrendous gang rape, then the town screwed her reputation, and finally, the justice system totally fucked her over. They all had a go at 'er. So, why bother reporting?"

Sarah gulped and twisted in her seat at hearing Bernice speak so casually about such a horror. "Yeah, but that actress got to go home after they shot the scene. She was safe and secure without a hair out of place. She wasn't a rape victim, she just played one on the screen. Eleanor was a real victim!"

Bernice stiffened and clenched her teeth at the seeming insinuation that she was unfairly defending the doctor. "I'm just sayin', I believe that Dr. Bond figured, why put a young girl through all that pain if it could eventually just heal over...like a war wound?"

Sarah gasped. "Eleanor Miller's wounds have never healed. She's kind of an emotional amputee, limping through life. Deep down, she's hoping to God that one day, they'll find and punish the bastards who did it so that maybe she can work on regenerating those severed emotions."

The response came soft and sincere. "I hope it happens for her, Sarah. I really do. Personally, nothin' would give me more satisfaction than to see all rapists neutered and sent into the prison population as eunuchs." Both women awkwardly chuckled at Bernice's grim quip.

As they regained their composure, Sarah spotted a tall, slender, athletic looking woman walking toward them. She was, by any standards, a knockout. Several thoughts flitted through Sarah's mind. *'Wow. This is Ket Hall? Really? This is my old school chum, the woman that her son implied would need a crane to move her?'*

She wore a navy-blue Pea Jacket, a pair of grey slacks, and a sky-blue angora sweater that matched her eyes. She waved a pert hi to her sister and smiled her warmest at her old school chum. She extended her hand to Sarah, who felt her fingers go numb under Ket's incredibly strong grasp.

"It's so good to see you, Ket. I didn't know if we'd all recognize each other." Sarah chortled. "Bernice and I got a head start. You have some catching up to do, so please sit."

Standing nearby, Mitch flashed Sarah a wink, and then headed to the table with a carafe of fresh perked coffee.

Momentarily, Sarah struggled in anxious silence with a tinge of guilt over the fact that it was really Bernice she'd wanted to connect with, and Ket was just a means to that end. But over home-fries and eggs Florentine, the three old schoolmates began to freely share stories of their most favourite and least favourite teachers, their team's basketball victories, and an array of colourful characters. Laughter, memories, and revisionism made for an amusing and interesting morning.

During a moment of raucous laughter, Mitch approached the table. "Uh, ladies, sorry to interrupt, uh, but it's been almost three hours and my boss was wondering if you're going to be staying for lunch. It's okay if you are, but if not, I'm supposed to get the table ready for the lunch service."

The women acknowledged the hint and reluctantly broke up the coffee klatch with the customary best-intentioned promise to, "stay in touch".

As the sisters exited, Mitch approached Sarah with the check, which she quickly signed and handed back with a well-deserved tip.

"Jeez, thanks a lot, Mrs. Berman. Ya know, it was a real trip to see my Aunt Bernice smile, let alone laugh. That's a rare sighting; like the Abominable Snowman or the Loch Ness monster."

Sarah gave Mitch a friendly shoulder punch. "You're pretty loose with your descriptions, Mitch. Like the one about your mom? A giant mammal, huh?"

Mitch shrugged and guffawed, "Come on, Mrs. Berman, she's female, five-nine, and strong as Mohammad Ali. She is a giant mammal."

Sarah snickered, "Boy, you've got that story-telling skill down pat, don't you? It's a good talent to have if you're going into journalism?"

"Nope. I told you, Mrs. Berman, I'm gonna be a lawyer."

* * *

The Hall sisters had just left, and Sarah was heading up to her suite when Mr. Reynolds called her over. "Mrs. Berman, phone for you, again," he grumbled. "It's Wesley Jackson."

She put the receiver to her ear, half expecting to hear bad news.

"How about having lunch with a couple of handsome, virile men?"

"Wes, I had no idea that Paul Newman and Robert Redford were in town, but if it's not them, my second choice would be you...and who?"

"Ray Connell."

With a furrowed brow and a cock of her head, Sarah asked, "Why is that name familiar?"

"Ray's father, Bill, was the Prescott chief of police when you were a kid. He was the one who caught those punks who vandalized the synagogue at the Orange Hall."

Her eyes opened wide. "Oh, wow, yeah, I remember Bill Connell! Is he no longer with us? I mean like...dead?"

"No! No, he's still around. Didn't you ever hear that old cops, like old soldiers, never die, they just fade away? He lives in that Catholic seniors place your nun works at."

"Holy Trinity?"

"That's the one. His body doesn't work too well after decades of cigarettes, donuts, and booze. He had a mild stroke, so he's pretty much confined to a wheelchair now. Anyway, his son, Ray, is the chief of the Brockville police, and since he's not out there on this sunny Sunday, chasing bad guys, he's willing to have lunch with us good guys. I'd ask Shiny to join us, but she's off babysitting her grandkids for the day. So, will we see you at the Best Service in a half-hour?"

In spite of the fact that she'd just gotten up from a marathon breakfast with the Hall sisters, she agreed to meet over lunch as long as she had time to change into a pair of expandable-waist pants.

CHAPTER SIXTEEN

As she tramped through the chill air en route to the Best Service, Sarah's memories rolled back to the fifties and the images of a handsome Chief Connell in his dark blue uniform, astride a motorcycle, clearing the streets so her school band could march along uninterrupted. It suddenly dawned on her that she never knew his kids because, although they lived only a few miles outside of Prescott, they were bussed to school in Brockville.

David Klein was the uniform supplier for all the police within a twenty-mile radius. He would measure each cop, send the data to Ottawa, and six weeks later, spanking-new uniforms would arrive. He was always careful to lock up the uniforms until they were claimed, for fear someone might steal them, impersonate an officer, and commit a crime.

He also kept the size of a cop's waistline a secret. Occasionally, some nosy neighbour would hint, "Jeez, David, I noticed that Bill Connell's puttin' on a few pounds there. What's his waist size now, 'bout a forty-two?" David Klein would raise an eyebrow, sometimes offer a disappointed shake of his head, and change the subject. A policeman's girth was privileged information that he would never reveal.

* * *

While her hosts feasted on bacon and eggs, Sarah sipped tea and talked. She described the recent events that included the Barbie Doll "threats," her meetings with

Eleanor Miller, and her revelations while in Montreal. She was careful to avoid mentioning that Shiny had acquired Eleanor Miller's medical file.

Although intrigued by her stories, Ray was quick to respond; "Mrs. Berman, I can't launch an investigation without actual evidence that a crime's been committed. In all likelihood, the dolls are a prank by some dumb-ass kid trying to impress his buddies. As for the Miller situation, you're talkin' about somethin' that allegedly happened thirty or more years ago...and the alleged victim chose not to even report it."

Although Sarah simmered with fury and her palms were sweaty, she managed to keep her storm under control. Steadily and patiently, she disclosed the details and the photos, while studying Ray's reaction.

He couldn't recognize any of the characters in the photograph, but Wes insisted that the images supported Sarah's contention of a further look. Ray offered a skeptical grunt, then, with less-than-wholehearted enthusiasm, he offered a bizarre proposal: "Why don't we all drive out and talk to my dad? If these guys lived in Prescott back then, you can bet he knew 'em. But I'm not so sure he'll remember?"

Wes enthusiastically agreed, and since Sarah felt she had little choice in the matter, she nodded. The trio left the restaurant.

A frigid gust of wind groaned in protest against the dark, threatening mood that had overtaken the day. The shiver that ran through Sarah was as much a reaction to her second-thoughts about the plan, as it was to the biting cold.

The chill did wake her up to the reality that if there was information to be revealed, it could be a game-changer.

She smiled and played nice. "Hey guys, right now I'm dressed more for Miami than Prescott, so before we head out, I need to stop at the hotel and throw something around me that closely resembles a bear."

They scrambled into the police cruiser and circled back to the hotel.

"Give me five minutes and I'll be right down," she vowed as she exited the car.

In record time, she was bundled up in scarf, gloves, and Alaskan parka. As she was about to leave her suite, the phone rang. The frantic voice on the other end was Shiny's. "Oh my God, Sarah. Where in hell have ya been?"

Sarah pressed the phone tightly to her ear and took a deep breath. "Hey, hey, calm down. What's going on?"

Between short gasps of air, Shiny's voice quivered. "I...I had just walked in my front door...when someone...threw a rock...through my living room window. There's shattered glass everywhere...and...my nerves are shredded. Ron dropped me off and left to drive the kids home, and...I can't reach him. I tried calling Wes, but I couldn't reach him either...I'm freakin' out."

As Sarah listened, her fear rose from her gut to her throat. She suppressed her anxiety and did her best to calm the situation. "Listen to me, Shiny. I'm getting in the car with Wes and Ray Connell right now. Just wait by the front door. We'll be right there."

The threesome was stepping over the threshold when Ronnie pulled up behind the police car. He rushed in to find his wife looking eerily pale. He stood beside her, staring at the hole in the picture window.

"What in hell happened?" he shouted.

"I-I, uh...I was uh, hanging up my coat when I heard the bay window shatter," she shuddered. "Thank God, I wasn't standing there. Uh, oh, here...this is what they threw." She placed the object in Ray's hand.

It was a jagged rock, about the size of a grapefruit, with a headless doll duct-taped to it.

Ray looked it over, set it down on a nearby table, and shrugged. "It looks like a bunch of punk kids are havin' some tasteless fun."

"Fun?" Shiny squealed.

"Yeah, to some asshole kids, that's fun," Ray added.

Ronnie heaved a sigh of relief. "He's right, Shiny. I mean, why would anyone want to scare the crap outta you?"

Shiny's eyes narrowed and her hand trembled as she snapped up a slip of paper from the hall table and dropped it into Ray's hand. "This was also taped to the rock."

If he woks...your JEW frend DIES. was printed in red marker.

Ray stood quietly, glancing from window, to rock, to the note. He cleared his throat and turned to Sarah. "Ironic, isn't it?"

Sarah's face was crimson with rage. "Ironic? That's your conclusion? It's ironic?"

"Yup, ironic! We were just sittin' there eating eggs and tryin' to figure out how we could initiate an investigation without an actual crime; and suddenly, a crime comes flyin' through that window."

Sarah grabbed onto the officer's arm. "Oh my God, Ray, I'm so glad you said that. It's great news then, right? I mean not great that Shiny almost got stoned...well you know what I'm saying. I mean, what happens now?"

"Now? I think we should start by findin' out what lunatic bought all these dolls. Hell, there can't be too many shops in town that could sell a mess o' these things without it bein' noticed." He pulled out a handkerchief and reached for the doll. "I'll take this little doll cadaver along as evidence. No, ya know what? I'll take the rest of 'em as well."

"Oh, thank God! You can gladly have mine, coffin, and all," Sarah sighed.

Ray nodded. "Good. Thank you, Sarah. And if ya wanna reach in your handbag there and leave those old pictures and negatives with me, I'll send them to the crime lab in Kingston to see if they can do any better."

The surge of optimism that engulfed Sarah prompted her grateful smile. "Sure, absolutely, thank you so much," she enthused as she handed over the envelope.

Wes swayed anxiously. "Shiny, listen, if you're okay, maybe the rest of us should get goin'? Ronnie's here anyway, and we were on our way to Mallory Town to do a little nosin' around."

"Yeah, about that," Ray interjected. "It's after four. It's too late to head out to my dad's place now. We'll do it another day."

Certain that Ray's mind was made up, but concerned with losing momentum, Sarah suggested that

Ray drop into St. Gabriel's Hospital on his way home. "Maybe you can check and see if they can dig up Eleanor's old medical records."

"Not a bad thought. Any of you have any idea an approximate year we should be lookin' to start?"

Shiny rushed to answer. "Yeah. Maybe around March 13th, 1958, a little after midnight."

"Maybe March 13th, 1958, a little after midnight, huh? A wild guess, eh?" Ray smirked.

* * *

Sarah returned to her hotel room with thoughts of an investigation top of mind. She placed a call to the front desk. Two seconds later, she opened her door to find Mitch standing there, poised to knock.

"Come on in, Mitch. Glad you could make it." She stated as she drifted toward her front window.

Mitch stepped inside and closed the door "Ya know, Mrs. Berman, if you'd called down three minutes later, I'd have been on my way home. Maybe you're psychic."

Sarah wasn't listening. She was looking through the glass and contemplating her next move. Mitch raised his voice a notch, "Uh, so, what can I do for ya, Ma'am? Do you need me to take a tray back or somethin'?"

She turned slowly toward him. "No, Mitch. I called you up here to ask you if you're really serious about wanting to be a lawyer."

He took a few steps in and cocked his ear as if he hadn't heard correctly. "That's it?"

She smiled and moved a bit closer. "Yes, that's it. So, are you, serious?"

His face lit up like a child meeting Santa Claus. "Oh, for sure, eh? It's what I've wanted since I was about eight. And judgin' by the excitement we've had around here for the past few years, and knowin' they had to import a criminal lawyer from the city 'cause there isn't one for miles, I want it more now than ever."

She moved to the table and sat down and pushed another chair away from the table. "Have a seat, please." She insisted and he cautiously obliged.

"I've been thinking, a good criminal lawyer also needs to be a pretty good detective. So, how would you like to earn a few dollars and get some practice doing a little undercover detective work for me?"

He seemed momentarily paralyzed.

"Well?" She urged with an awkward laugh.

He abruptly thawed and stared into her eyes, "Are you kiddin' me? 'Cause that would be a really cruel joke."

Sarah waved a finger at him. "Not kidding, Mitch. I need help from someone young, smart, and discreet, and I think you fit that description."

"Really? Sure. I mean, yes, I'll be glad to help." His eyes widened with excitement.

"Good. Okay, so here's the challenge. I need to know where those dolls came from; like who bought them and sold them? And when and where were they purchased? I want you to explore local convenience stores and toy shops to see if some clerk might have found a bulk purchase of Barbie-type dolls to be a little unusual. That's it. What do you think?"

"I'd die for the chance, Mrs. Berman, but most of the stores will be closing in a few minutes, so I wouldn't get to finish up until after school tomorrow. Is that okay?"

She stood and extended her right hand. "Perfect." He extended his hand in response and they shook. She then asked one more thing of him. "Whatever happens, Mitch, this assignment requires absolute discretion. Do you understand?"

He nodded and placed his hand over his heart. "Yes, absolute discretion, for sure. I promise." One more handshake sealed the agreement.

As he reached the door, he turned and offered an eager boy scout salute before making a grand exit.

* * *

Another dinner invitation from Eleanor was a surprise that Sarah was eager to accept.

Course after course, Sarah was delighted with the chef's haute cuisine, beginning with an eye-catching caviar soufflé, then a chilled papaya-cream soup, and followed by a risotto-stuffed Cornish hen in a truffle brandy sauce. Throughout the feast, Sarah praised each dish, and Eleanor humbly soaked up the acclaim.

"Maybe we should sit for a while and have dessert and coffee later, if that's okay," Eleanor suggested.

Sarah turned toward her, feigning a childlike pout, before relenting with a smile. "Yeah, I probably need time to organize some space in here anyway." She giggled as she patted her stomach.

Their last dinner conversation had been taken up with the disturbing revelation over where Eleanor's assault had taken place. This time, Sarah had promised to share the details of her Montreal trip. "But, Eleanor, I think it's best that I skip over the horrific Holocaust details..."

Eleanor interrupted. "No. No, Sarah, if we're going to do this, then you need to be open and honest with me. Listen, I've seen many movies and documentaries about Antisemitism and the Holocaust, and it always turned my stomach; but over the years, I've read a lot of books by survivors like Eli Wiesel, and I learned to look beyond the horror of it and be in awe of the courage and determination of the Jewish people to survive. It makes you wonder how those who did survive were able to put it behind them and go on. I mean look at what the Fleischmans, and Anna's family endured." She shook her head. "I could never have that kind of strength."

Sarah crinkled her brow in bewilderment. "You, Eleanor? You don't have the strength? You must be kidding."

Eleanor lowered her head. "I don't. Honestly. Look how I've hidden myself away all these years. Strong people don't hide. Strong people live their lives, no matter what."

"Which is exactly what you did. You never stopped living. You've mastered amazing skills while running your own business and a beautiful home."

An awkward silence came over the room as a blush spiralled from Eleanor's neck to her cheeks. "Jeez, Sarah, we'd best get back on topic before my ego explodes."

The comment came as a relief to Sarah who was beginning to worry that the topic might once again be bypassed. "Okay. Listen Eleanor, maybe I'm nuts, but I have this gut feeling that the animals that attacked you could have been the same bastards that tried to burn down the Fleischmans' grocery store. Do you remember Bill Connell?"

"Bill Connell?" Eleanor quietly repeated the name. "Yes, of course, I do," she confirmed. "Every kid in this town knew him. He was your typical Irish do-gooder cop, like Spencer Tracy in those old black and white films."

Sarah smiled and nodded. "Yup, the friendly, dependable, neighbourhood cop."

Eleanor smirked, "When he wasn't drinking, that is."

"Oh, please don't shatter my illusions," Sarah quipped.

"No, no. Bill wasn't a bad guy or a mean drunk, and I doubt he ever drank on the job. But the thing is, after his wife died, he was kind of sweet on my mother. I think she enjoyed the flattery, but she was a confirmed widow. He was really kind to me and very funny too. She would welcome him in for dinner or coffee and conversation in the evening. But if he came by after having a couple of beers with the boys, she wouldn't let him in the house. She had a real aversion to the smell of alcohol. Eventually, I heard that some woman in Brockville fell for him, and I figured that's why he stopped coming around. I couldn't tell if my mom regretted it or not at the time, 'cause I was too young to know about that stuff. Anyway, yes, I do remember Bill Connell. Why?"

"Well, this is a really freaky coincidence, but today, I had lunch with his son, Ray, who's now the police chief in Brockville. We'd just finished eating when I got a terrified call from Shiny asking me to come over right away. I did, and Ray came with me."

As Sarah shared the "Barbie doll adventures," Eleanor remained riveted.

"At first, I thought they were just stupid, desperate pranks from folks who don't want to see Earl White walk free, but the message delivered by that flying rock changed my mind. The words were very clear. It said, 'If he walks, your Jew friend dies'!"

As the words registered, Eleanor's body became rigid, and her face grew ashen. Since Sarah was gesturing dramatically with her hands, she failed to notice her friend's reaction and continued on with enthusiasm. "I told Ray the whole story about you and Anna, the attack, all of it, and he's convinced that we're onto something, particularly because of today's incident. He believes there might be a chance of opening an investigation; but it'll be up to you to make that decision. You should also know that since Earl White's got a great lawyer, there's a good chance his case will be dismissed. That means, before long I could be heading back to Toronto."

Eleanor sat motionless, her face, a chalky mask.

"Come on, Eleanor. Listen to me. I'm here now, and I'm willing to do whatever I can to help get it started. Please? If they're still alive, let's find the bastards."

Eleanor turned toward Sarah with a feeble smile, took a deep breath, and offered a sideways nod. Sarah took it as a promising sign and headed home, happy that hope was alive.

* * *

Sarah went about her bedtime rituals while trying not to think about the fact that she hadn't heard from Laurie Cowan in several days. She shuddered at the thought that he could have been put off by her drunken antics. She had hoped at least, he'd give her some guidance as to whether or not Eleanor had a case worth pursuing. Now, she worried that all could be lost because of her inability to hold her wine.

As she was about to slip into bed, there was an abrupt rap at the door. Her skin prickled at the sound, as memories of Earl White's unwelcome visit played in her head. Her heartbeat sped up, as did her breathing. Panicking, she grabbed up the phone and called the front desk. No answer. Before she opened the door, she left the receiver off the hook and tossed it on the living room sofa hoping to give the visible impression that someone was waiting for her on the line.

There were two more demanding knocks before she got to the door. She rubbed her damp hands on her nightclothes and squeaked, "Who is it?"

"It's me, Mrs. Berman."

At the sound of Mitch's voice, she sucked in a deep breath, exhaled with relief, and threw open the door. Mitch was effervescent. His face was glowing, and he could barely stand still.

"I have to get to work, Mrs. Berman, but I wanted to report to you first. You're never gonna believe it! There were four Barbie-type dolls all bought on the same day and paid for with cash. The clerk didn't know the guy, but he told her he might be back for more. She remembered him because they had to look through their whole supply to find dolls that looked just the way he wanted them. There were only four he was happy with, but he wanted two more; so, she told him that she would ask the supplier if they could exchange the remaining two evening-gown-type dolls they had in stock, for two of the business-suit dolls he was after."

Mitch paused for a breath, and Sarah jumped in. "That's bloody excellent, Mitch!"

He held up his hands. "Wait a minute, wait a minute, Mrs. Berman. It's better than excellent, 'cause this is what I figured," he held up a finger to pause, "but if you don't like it, I'll forget it. You just say the word."

She clapped her hands together and repeated, "'Better than excellent?'"

"Yeah. Now remember, the clerk said he bought four, but he wanted six. So, maybe he'll come back for more, especially if there's a trial and it drags on. Now, here's my idea: I'll get her to tell him, if he comes back, that there's a store promotion happening, and with one more purchase, he'll have bought five dolls and that would entitle him to get the last one for free."

Sarah's face glowed as brightly as her young detective's. He continued. "Of course, you'll have to pay her for the free one. Then, listen to this. She'll tell him that the store policy won't allow her to include it with the sale, but if he leaves his name, address and phone number with her, the freebie will be mailed to him. What do you think?" He stepped back proudly as if he'd just delivered the valedictory address.

Sarah raised her hand for a pause and then with a glimmer of doubt she responded. "What do I think? I think it's potentially a clever idea, Mitch, but, if this guy committed a crime, he'd have to be pretty dumb to leave his name and address."

Mitch smiled. "That's exactly the thing, Mrs. Berman. The clerk said that the main reason she remembered him was because 'he seemed pretty dumb.'"

"How old was he?"

"She figured late twenties. She couldn't really describe him, other than 'kinda ordinary.' Average size, average everything." He sucked a bit of air through his teeth. "To tell the truth, it was a definite surprise to me because I imagined a guy with a doll fetish would be some disgusting old pervert who was anything but average looking. In fact, I would expect he'd be hideous looking."

Sarah smiled fiendishly at the description. "You're quite the character, my young Detective Colombo. Thank you for your excellent work and I encourage you to go ahead with your creative plan as long as it won't get you or the clerk in trouble."

The blush returned to his cheeks. "Nah! She's been working there since she was tall enough to see over the counter and, since the owners are her parents, you don't have to worry; she'll make up some story to keep them happy."

"But I don't want to turn a young, innocent girl into a criminal in order to catch one, Mitch," She smirked.

He swayed aimlessly for a few seconds as his face turned rosy red. Finally, he spoke up. "Ya know, Mrs. Berman, it's funny, I go into that shop all the time, and she's never looked at me before. In fact, she's always seemed real bitchy. But now, all of a sudden, she's lookin' at me like I'm a stud, and I'm thinkin' she's pretty hot."

Sarah raised an eyebrow. "Bitchy, huh? Is this clerk by any chance Cindy, from Perkins Gift Shop?"

"Bingo." Mitch yelped. "You've met her?" Now Mitch was anxious for his mentor's opinion. "Well?"

"Uh-huh. I've met her, and it wasn't the most pleasant encounter I've had in this town. However, my young P.I., I have faith that you can lighten her mood."

He chuckled. "Oh, you can bet on it, Mrs. B."

He checked his watch. "Three minutes to spare. Gotta go. Don't wanna be late or Reynolds'll kick my ass." He craned his neck and squinted. "By the way, your phone's off the hook." He grinned and rushed out the door.

CHAPTER SEVENTEEN

An unnerving exchange with the judge was still swirling in Sarah's head as she rushed from the courtroom and collided with Ray Connell. "Oh jeez, Sarah, I was late, so I didn't get to see the whole action in front of the judge, just the last, few, memorable minutes. But didn't you say you were gonna be there simply as an impartial observer.?" He snickered.

"Yeah, well, I tried to do exactly that." She hissed.

"Ah, come on, own up. What was it about? What did I miss?"

Sarah unclenched her teeth. "Okay, you're gonna be relentless, aren't you?"

He folded his arms, leaned forward, and whispered a firm, "Yup."

"Fine. Here it is. Near the end of yet another frustrating experience of listening to that obnoxious Crown Attorney drone on, the judge asked Laurie Cowan 'if the defence would like to begin,' and Laurie said, 'Your Honour, since there's only fifteen minutes left in the day, I would like the court's permission to wait until tomorrow.' It sounded like a reasonable request to me, but it was obvious the judge didn't agree 'cause he said: 'Well, there is no tomorrow, Mr. Cowan. As a matter of fact, court won't resume until Monday morning, so if you want these fifteen minutes, they're yours. If you don't take 'em, then don't complain when you're on your way back to the big city and you realize you needed 'em.' Then, I blurted out,

'Well that's not fair!' I didn't even realize I'd said it out loud."

Ray, shook his head in amusement, and weighed in. "You actually interrupted Judge MacMillan, the grouch?"

Sarah shrugged. "Yup, I did; and because the judge chose to ignore me and I'm a stubborn goat, I had to push some more. 'Excuse me your Honour,' I bleated, 'may I ask, why court won't be in session tomorrow?' He told me, I could ask...if I wished to be permanently removed from the courtroom; and then he said: "However, for any other nosy parkers in the room, I won't be here because I have an appointment at the hospital.'

"'Again?' I heard myself say. 'And again, I'm hearing from you,' he said. Then, suddenly, Laurie Cowan jumped in. 'Your Honour, this young lady is Sarah Berman, an enthusiastic journalist from Toronto, who's here to cover these proceedings. I'm sure she meant no disrespect. It's just journalistic curiosity.'

"And then the judge asked: 'Okay, just what are you curious about, Ms. Berman?'

"'Um, I, uh, was just concerned about your health, Your Honour.' I nervously lied, while he peered over his glasses at me like a sullen schoolteacher about to deliver corporal punishment; but instead, he offered a reply. 'Ah, well thank you for your concern, Miss, but hopefully, after my medical procedure, I'll be quite ready to handle the stress of even someone like you.'

"*What a smartass*, is what I was thinking, but I decided to be nice. So instead, I said; 'You know, Your Honour, today with all the new advances in medical technology, there's so much they can do. My father had a pacemaker installed that we credit with prolonging his life.' But that damn judge couldn't just accept my stab at compassion. He had to have the last word: 'Ms. Berman, even if they could install a pacemaker to fix my problem, I'd have one hell of a time sitting on it. It's because of people like you that I have hemorrhoids as big as apricots. And now that you've managed to waste the court's valuable time, let's hope Andy Warhol is right, and your fifteen minutes are up.' With that, he slammed the gavel, stood up and waddled away."

"I came in at the hemorrhoids big as apricots part," Ray said, relishing every humiliating word.

She shook her head and released a feigned sigh. "Uh-huh, I see, this is Brockville's finest, huh? Taking pleasure in other people's pain...shame on you, Chief Connell." She snickered.

Ray chuckled, regained his composure, and suggested they sit for a minute. "Sarah, I got those photos back from the lab."

Her head jerked toward him, her mouth agape. "Wow, that was fast!"

Ray winked. "If you want something done fast, it pays to be on the right side of the law."

"Okay, we've established, it was fast, but was it productive?" Her tone was now more urgent.

"See for yourself." He carefully withdrew the photos from the envelope. "Here, as you can see, they're enlarged to eight by ten, and in duplicate." He handed them over and she rifled through them.

"Jeez, Ray, these are clearer. Is this real or did you tamper?"

Ray covered his heart in mock disdain. "You could go straight to hell for such a suggestion! No tampering. These are the real deal."

Although the graffiti on the building was more visible, it still wasn't legible. But the pale letters on the sleeves, against the dark background, stood out: **SS.** Sarah shivered.

"Remember in the original photo," Ray prompted, "this guy's left hand was doin' a Vanna White gesture toward the shop? Now look," Ray pointed to the man's hand in the photo. "You can see he's actually holding a flip-top lighter in that hand. I guess now we know how they lit the fire."

Sarah continued to stare intently at the photo. "It's too bad that with all their state-of-the-art equipment, they still couldn't improve on the clarity of the faces."

"There's something else. I also put our fingerprint unit to work on the original envelope just in case." He proudly declared.

Sarah lowered the photos to her lap and looked up at Ray with admiration. "Wow! Way to go. Oh crap, my fingerprints will be all over that envelope. I'm such an idiot." She fumed and stamped her foot in frustration.

Ray smiled. "Okay, if you say so; but we already figured on that; not the idiot part, the, 'your prints on the envelope' part."

Sarah smirked and gently punched his arm.

"Now, before I have to arrest you for assaulting a police officer; I just want to tell you that you'll eventually need to come down to the station so we can print and eliminate you."

Sarah jumped to her feet. "Why not now? Oh, but first, can you drop me off at the car rental place? They promised to have this little turquoise Chevelle gassed up and ready for me."

"I'll take you, but I'm gonna tell Buzz he should be arrested for pawning off a piece of crap like that on a hometown gal."

She pouted in jest. "No way, Buddy, I rented that little beauty a few of weeks ago and we bonded all the way to and from Montreal."

He shrugged. "Okay, if you want to drive around in an un-cool car, be my guest. But for now, you'll get to drive in a luxury cop car en route to be fingerprinted. I'll bet no one's ever made you that offer before." He opened the passenger door for her.

Before she stepped into the car, she tapped on the roof and declared. "Ray, I want it on record what a huge sacrifice I'm making, 'cause I gave myself a manicure last night and now my fingers will be covered in black goop."

* * *

Looking like a mobile feather bed in her heavy, down coat, Sarah strode along the overheated hallway that led to her suite. As she arrived at her door, she found Mitch curled up beside it, snoozing. As she jiggled her key in the lock, his eyes popped opened.

With a casual smirk, she asked, "Late date last night, Mitch?"

"No such luck Mrs. Berman...late-night studying." He rose to his feet. "I've only been here a few minutes, but my mom says I can sleep like the dead anywhere." He glanced at his watch. "Listen, I only have seventeen minutes before my shift begins, so can we talk, I mean now?"

Sarah offered a nod. "Sure, come inside and we'll talk."

Once they were seated, Mitch began to transmit like an out-of-control ticker tape.

"So, here's the thing. I heard from Cindy, and my plan worked. The guy came in to buy another doll, and she told him that he was entitled to a freebie. She said he cheered as if he'd just won a lottery. Then, quick as you could say *Barbie doll*, he wrote down his name, address and two phone numbers: one for home and one for work. Take a look."

He handed the paper to Sarah, who squinted at the name scribbled on the form. "Ben...Gil-len. Ben Gillen," she repeated. Perplexed, she looked at Mitch. "Do you know him?"

"Never heard of him."

He pointed at the scribbled paper. "But see here? It's a Brockville address. Cindy asked why he came to Prescott to shop. And believe it or not, he said he heard the Barbie dolls in Prescott are better quality than the ones in Brockville. Sorry, Mrs. B, but no kidding, he really said that." Mitch exploded with laughter. Noticing that Sarah didn't join in the hilarity, he paused to get a grip on himself. After a couple of deep breaths, he continued. "Okay, I'm good now. Anyway, Cindy said she almost lost it, but she pulled herself together and said, 'I guess it takes a pretty sharp guy to have figured that out.' He puffed up like a blowfish and let her know that he was a class act and, if she was lucky, he might even ask her for a date sometime.

Well, that pretty much freaked her out, so she excused herself to answer a phone that hadn't rung. He left. She was bloody relieved to see the back of him go through that door." He looked up at Sarah as if waiting for some sign that she was impressed. Sarah appeared to be more bemused than impressed.

"Oh wait, wait, I didn't finish. This is the best part. I called his home number. There was no answer and no machine; but then I called the work number, and you're not gonna believe what I heard."

"Mitch, I'm enjoying the show, but your shift begins soon, and I don't want you leaving me with a cliffhanger, so please just tell me, okay?" She ended with a heavy sigh.

"Okay." Mitch held his hand to his ear in a mock phone call. "Good afternoon, St. Gabriel's Hospital. How can I help you?"

Sarah gasped, "St. Gabriel's?"

Mitch nodded and released a frustrated whistle. "Yeah, but come on, Mrs. B. You aren't really thinking that moronic *doll man* could actually work at St. Gabriel's. Really? I mean, this guy wouldn't know a hypodermic needle from a tongue depressor, or a bedpan from a dinner tray."

With an arched brow, Sarah asked, "Do you think your opinion might be a tad jaded because this *doll man* was making moves on Cindy?"

Mitch glowed red again and lowered his eyes.

Sarah changed the subject. "Listen Mitch, you did a great job. I'll happily do business with you anytime. And speaking of business, as promised, here's payment for your first assignment." She handed him a twenty-dollar bill, which he gratefully accepted.

"Thanks Mrs. B. I get that this information is really important for you, but I don't understand why...and I'm pretty sure you're not gonna tell me either." He chortled.

"You got that right. See how smart you are, Mitch." She offered her young detective a warm smile in return.

"Well, I better move my butt and get down to the desk." He paused on his way out. "So, Mrs. B, do you really think this *doll man* might be Brockville's top brain surgeon?" He giggled as she playfully pushed him out the door.

* * *

"It's good to hear from you," Sarah confided as she twirled the phone cord idly around her fingers. "I thought my inebriated condition may have scared you off. But then, you did try to rescue me again in the courtroom. I seem to be causing trouble wherever I go these days." As the conversation continued, she giggled from time to time. "No. No actually, I haven't had dinner yet...Sure, I'd love to...Seven it is."

She hung up the phone and flew around the suite, trying to decide what to do first: jump into the shower, choose the right outfit, or take a nap.

* * *

At 7:01 p.m. she drifted toward Laurie Cowan's table. As she approached, he stood and handed her a bouquet of peach roses. The gesture left Sarah momentarily dumbfounded. "Wow, Laurie, they're gorgeous."

"I figured these may help take the sting out of the bite you got in court today."

"Then, I should make a fool of myself more often."

"If you were a fool, the judge would have thrown you in jail for contempt before you got that second chance to speak. But that old coot actually enjoyed the exchange. It's probably the only fun he's had since he developed those bloody hemorrhoids." They both burst out laughing.

As the laughter petered out, Laurie remained fixed on his dinner date. "Sarah Berman, you certainly are an unpredictable woman. One day, you're a passed-out drunk freshman, and the next, you're a combative courtroom inquisitor."

Feeling both embarrassed and flattered, she reached into her reserve of humility, looked him in the eye, and stood her ground. "Laurie Cowan, I can assure you that one glass will be my limit this evening. I've learned my lesson well."

"We'll see about that." He offered a flirty grin and gestured for her to sit.

"Seriously, Laurie," she began in earnest, as she settled in her chair. "There's something weird about this town. Ever since I arrived here, I get woozy on a glass of wine, nauseous at parties, and scared half to death in my dreams."

"Hey then, please don't dream about me. I don't want to be your bogeyman."

At 9 pm, the snippy new waiter hinted that they were holding him up. She missed Mitch.

"Don't take this the wrong way, Sarah, but I have a feeling you haven't gotten to your questions yet. Do you want to go up to your suite to continue the conversation?" He tentatively asked. "I mean...I only suggest yours because it's a decent size, with a sitting area, and a real coffee maker. Mine on the other hand, is basically a closet with washroom facilities. I leave it to you to decide."

Inside Sarah's suite, the coffee was brewing and so were her thoughts. "Laurie, there's something I've wanted to ask you. I hope it's not inappropriate, but I don't know how long we'll both be in town..."

CHAPTER EIGHTEEN

The beautifully manicured parks and beachfronts that had offered Sarah so much joy as a child, now insinuated irony as she and Ray Connell drove by, en route to the Holy Trinity Retirement Home.

Once inside, Sarah noted that the cordial nuns she encountered were very different from the somber sisters of torture that her childhood friends had relentlessly complained about.

* * *

Dependency on a wheelchair didn't seem to alter Bill Connell's feisty character. With a mischievous glint in his eyes, he eagerly journeyed into his past, regaling Sarah with stories of his colourful experiences.

Before heading out to see old Chief Connell, Ray and Sarah had agreed they would drop in, show the photos, and leave quickly. After an hour of lively conversation, Ray had to remind Sarah to bring out the pictures. She removed the eight-by-tens from the envelope and placed the Fleischmans' shop photo in front of the chief. He glanced at it and grunted his disapproval. Next, she handed him the graffiti shot. As he stared at it, his face tightened, and his eyes narrowed.

"Goddamn bastards." He barked.

Sarah was surprised by his intense reaction. "Officer Connell, do you remember this incident?"

He snarled and seethed. "Do *I* remember? I doubt you were even born then. So how in hell would you remember? How would you even know about this shit?"

Sarah explained how and why she knew about the incident, and then watched in nervous anticipation as Bill carefully studied the photo of the two men she hoped he could identify.

"Dad, do you remember Earl White?" Ray asked.

"Christ, Son. How could I forget that lowlife? If you're askin' if he's in this picture," he waved the photo, "the answer's no. These smirkin' faces may not be real clear, but I have a hunch I'd know that ugly mug if the picture were twice this bad." He drew the photo close and stared intently. Suddenly, he shouted, "I knew it!"

Ray put his hand on his father's shoulder and leaned toward the picture. "What is it, Dad?"

Bill tapped his pointer finger at the photo. "See there? Those two figures? See the SS on the sleeve? I knew it was those stupid, bastards. Those slimy rats used to slink into town, do their damage, and then slink away again."

Sarah pressed her palms to her temples to try to calm her anxiety.

"What rats? Where did they come from?" Ray asked.

"They lived north o' the woods, about ten miles or so."

"There were neo-Nazis near Prescott?" Sarah shrieked as her thumping heart beat a deafening cacophony in her ears.

Aware that his anger was upsetting his visitor, Bill attempted to quell his rage. "No Miss, they were rotten like Nazis, but they weren't Nazis."

Sarah sat in paralyzing confusion. Ray shook his head and scoffed. "Dad, come on, if they weren't Nazis, then why would they be wearin' the SS insignia on their sleeves?"

"Jesus, Son, you're a cop. Use your head. Ya think SS can't stand for somethin' else. It could stand for someone's name, like Sam Smith or Stan Scott, ya know? But it doesn't! It stands for school letters."

Ray and Sarah exchanged stupefied glances. "What the hell are you talking about, Dad?" Ray's question was rife with cynicism. "The old high school was *Prescott High* and the newer one is *Grenville District High*. Where do you get SS from either school?"

This was a significant moment for a once important man who'd been set out to pasture. For the first time in several years, Bill mattered. He calmly turned his sights toward the large bay window with the view of the river. After a pensive moment, he returned to his audience and began to explain. "You're sniffin' along the wrong trail, Son. This has nothin' to do with Prescott. Those letters stand for Stutstown Secondary. I don't know why they ever called it secondary, 'cause it barely went past grade nine. It was a one-room-schoolhouse with a ramshackle outhouse at the back. There were only a couple o' kids that ever got as far as grade nine, so they didn't even hire another teacher for 'em; they'd just hold 'em back instead. A couple of 'em were goin' on eighteen and still in grade nine. I remember one Halloween when those stupid bastards burned their own schoolhouse down. Nobody investigated, so nobody was punished for it. Instead, they bussed the whole damn lot of them to Grenville District High for the rest o' the school year." He grunted in disgust, then offered an afterthought. "I'll tell ya, Prescott was a hell of a lot healthier after that pile o' crap finally went back to their cesspool."

Sarah's mind was rapidly reviewing snippets of stories and experiences from the people she'd encountered over the many weeks since her journalistic expedition began. *Stutstown Secondary?* The name wasn't even vaguely familiar to her. She looked to Ray, who offered a bewildered shrug. "Where is Stutstown?" She asked.

Bill placed the photo on the table and offered an open-handed gesture of resignation. "It doesn't exist anymore," He replied. "Even when it did, it never really did. At its height, it had a population of maybe at best, a hundred and fifty, and they were spread out like manure over two miles of dirt fields, trailers, and dilapidated clapboards. It was a town that amounted to a corner store, a beer hall, and a gas station; and reported more robberies in one year than the whole town of Prescott did in a decade. Most of the assholes moved away years ago, and now there's nothin' left there. That rebuilt ramshackle of a school they called Stutstown Secondary has been gone for ages."

A rush of determination prompted Sarah to ask. "Officer Connell, there's gotta be a record somewhere of who attended the school, maybe even school pictures?"

"Ask about Knight!" Bill demanded.

"What night?" Sarah asked.

"Knight! I don't remember his other name. He was the...Ray, you know, damn it. Speak up."

Ray quickly wiped away his smirk before his dad could catch a glimpse of it. "Yeah, I know. You're talking about Harold Knight, the former mayor of Prescott, right? Well, yeah, he was mayor for many years...but he's also been dead for many years. So, asking him would be a problem."

Bill hissed through his teeth. "I know he's dead, for Christ's sake. Do ya think I'm senile or somethin'? Knight ain't here, but there's a mess o' boxes in the basement o' the Prescott library they're callin' the 'Knight Archives'. O' course the family paid some bucks, to get his name nailed to a plaque on that cellar door."

"Yeah, I know, but what the hell can a library do for us?" Ray grumbled.

Sarah placed a calming hand on Ray's arm. "Listen to him, Ray, it makes sense. If you want historical information, the library's the place, right, Bill?"

"Yeah, and if ya want current information, ya ask Sister Mary Margaret. She knows everybody's business. Don't swear at her, though, 'cause she'll take your cigarettes away," Bill warned.

"But *you* can swear all ya want, 'cause you don't smoke anymore, do ya, Dad?" Ray smugly queried.

Bill lowered his head and mumbled. "That's 'cause that bitch keeps takin' my cigarettes away."

"Then maybe you oughta save your cursing for those times when you really gotta let loose," Ray grinned.

"Around here, that's all the time," Bill muttered, "Because they're always takin' my goddamn cigarettes away."

On the return trip from Holy Trinity, the pair decided to detour to St. Gabriel's Hospital on the chance they might get to visit with the "doll collector," or as Mitch labelled him: Brockville's top brain surgeon.

Having investigated an endless number of bar brawls and traffic accidents over the years, Ray was well-known and well-liked at the hospital.

When they arrived at the information desk, Ray was disappointed to find a new receptionist manning it. The smiling civil servant did a doubletake at the sight of the handsome cop leaning against the counter. She smiled, flipped her hair, and asked: "What can I do for you, Mr. Law and Order?"

It took Ray a few seconds to gather his wits. "Ma'am, we're lookin' for an address or phone number of a staff person who works here. Does the name Ben Gillen ring any bells?" He scribbled the name on a pad and handed it to her.

"Uh-uh. I don't think so, Chief, though I'm kinda new here, but I'll definitely check that out for ya." She opened a file drawer and shuffled through a row of folders. "I'm sorry, I don't see any Ben Gillen, but I can give ya my number, if that interests ya," she suggested with another flip of her hair.

He shuffled his feet and blushed, but soon recouped his dignity. "Well, Ma'am, for right now, I just need one for Ben Gillen. Do ya think you could take another look in those file drawers for me?"

Sarah whispered to Ray. "Listen, I'll head over to find Francis Murk in Administration while you continue to exercise your charms on the receptionist here." She winked and left.

* * *

Sarah smiled warmly and thanked Francis for the envelope she'd left at the Journal office. Francis pressed a finger against the half smile on her lips and quietly whispered, "Shh."

Sarah felt a wave of relief and proceeded to ask about Ben Gillen.

"Hmm, Ben Gillen. It's kinda weird. Ben Gillen doesn't ring a loud bell, but it does seem vaguely familiar." Francis mused.

"Could he be a physician? A surgeon?" Sarah asked. Francis assured her there was no Dr. Ben Gillen on the medical staff there.

Sarah handed Francis the paper with the doll collector's info and signature on it. As the administrator looked it over, a mild chuckle blossomed into a full belly laugh.

"Was it something I said?" Sarah asked, wearing a muddled expression.

Blotting tears, Francis beckoned for Sarah to come closer.

"His name is Bern Giffen, not Ben Gillen." Francis deduced as the laughter continued.

Sarah squinted as she looked closer. "Oh crap, so it is." Sarah shook her head. "Kids and their lousy penmanship. Look, I don't mean to be rude, but why is that so funny?"

The Prescott Journals

Francis's case of the giggles broke out once again. She did her best to regain her composure. "Aw, Sarah, I'm so sorry, but the picture in my mind of Bern Giffen in surgical greens with a scalpel in his hand just finished me. When he isn't cleaning the wards, Bern works in the cafeteria washing dishes, dumping garbage, that sort of thing. And the thing about Bern is, he does strut around here like he's the chief of surgery. He's delusional, but not certifiable. You know the stories about patients in mental institutions believing they're Napoleon or Shakespeare?" Sarah nodded. Francis continued, "Well, he believes one day people will be entering those institutions claiming to be Bern Giffen. You'll see what I mean when he gets here."

Francis leaned toward the intercom and instantly, a hollow, toneless echo emanated from the loudspeaker and crept along the hospital corridors. "Paging Bern Giffen...Bern Giffen to Administration."

When the announcement was completed, Francis eyed Sarah and grinned. "He's gonna be real grateful to you 'cause he's always claimed that one day everyone in this hospital will hear his name, and this is his lucky day." She punctuated the absurdity with a mock salute as she headed toward the door with Sarah following behind. "No, stay here, Sarah. Use my office. I've got a meeting in the boardroom anyway, so make yourself at home."

"That's really generous of you, Francis. I owe you."

"Nah, I owe you, 'cause this is gonna be Bern's best story yet, about how he's buddies with this big city journalist. And by the time the story gets around the hospital, it's likely you were here to write a best-seller about all his accomplishments and next he'll be up for a Nobel Prize."

The two women shared another laugh as the administrator made a spirited exit.

Sarah nervously scouted the room trying to decide on her most advantageous position. She avoided the temptation of sitting in the executive's seat and instead, settled on a straight-backed chair facing the open door to be sure she'd see the visitor arrive.

Suddenly, Bern Giffen loped into the office, greasy hair, crusty overalls, and filthy fingernails. Imagining this man as a doctor, nurse, or orderly was impossible, and the blatant clue as to what brought on the administrator's bout of laughter. He remained standing by the door, confused or alarmed to find a stranger in the administrator's office. Sarah motioned him to enter.

"Mr. Giffen, please come in and have a seat."

He looked around the room, then judiciously chose a chair and plopped into it. Sarah was grateful for the coffee table that separated them.

"My name is Sarah Berman and I'm working on a story about collectors. I understand you're a collector. Can you tell me if that's true?"

"What are ya talkin' about, lady?"

"Let me cut to the chase. You're maybe twenty-five or twenty-six, am I right?"

He crinkled his nose and peered at her as if he was peeking over spectacles. "So, yer some kinda age-guesser? You with the circus or somethin'?" He guffawed.

She caught herself before a snide chuckle could escape. "No. No circus. I'm just curious as to why you're buying up all the Barbie dolls in the area."

A flush of blood red edged its way up Bern Giffen's cheeks while globules of sweat dripped from his brow. "I don't have to talk to you, and I'm not gonna. Ya hear me?"

It was an effort for Sarah to hold back her urge to snicker. "Come on, Mr. Giffen, help me out here. I just have a few questions."

"Well, you can't just walk in here and question me, 'cause I got seniority in this place." He crowed.

"I'm not questioning your seniority, Mr. Giffen. I just want to know what you did with your dolls."

He angrily pressed his chafed lips together. "They ain't mine. I ain't got no dolls! I ain't no damn queer!"

The word was as revolting as he was, but she felt obliged to ignore it and keep him talking. She gritted her teeth and continued. "Okay then, who did you buy them for?"

He crossed his arms and clenched his jaw in a determined stance of non-compliance.

Sarah leaned forward in her seat as if to share a secret. "Bern, I gotta tell you, I've heard, from some pretty high-up people, that you know what's what around here which makes you a pretty important guy. I'm impressed. So, come on, tell me what you know, and I'll be even more impressed." She sat back, quietly allowing time for her words to percolate. She spotted Ray taking a surreptitious peek inside. He gave her a nod which she subtly acknowledged.

She watched as Bern lowered his eyes in a kind of creepy James Dean gaze and repositioned himself side-saddle with one leg slung over the arm of the chair.

She stared into Bern's glassy eyes and tried a more direct approach. "Mr. Giffen, I'm giving you a chance to come clean before the police get here. If I know the truth, then I can protect you."

"Let 'em come. They can torture me, but I'll never talk."

"Answer the question you little cockroach!" Ray bellowed as he slammed the door shut behind him. Bern jerked his head around to see who owned the voice. The confident smirk that had etched its way across his face froze instantly at the sight of the six-foot-two cop.

"Who told you to buy 'em?" Ray seethed.

A shudder rolled through Bern as a muffled gasp escaped his lips.

"I'm askin' ya, one last time, Giffen! Who told you to purchase the dolls?"

All the trembling little man could manage was a feeble grunt.

"Did you say something?" Ray asked as he approached Bern's shrinking frame.

Bern nodded effusively.

"I didn't hear you, so, say it again." Ray remained solidly planted inches from Bern's chair.

"Doug." He croaked.

"Doug what?" Ray demanded.

"Doug...I don't know," Bern whimpered as he slunk down in his seat.

"Ya know what I think? I think you just dug yourself a hole deep enough to bury you! What do you think?" Now Ray was hovering over him like an ominous thunder cloud.

"Wait! His name is Doug...I-don't-know-his-last-name. He comes into the cafeteria almost every day. And sometimes he talks to me and tells me wild stories and I like listenin' to 'em. So, one day he tells me, if I pick up some dolls for 'im in Prescott, he'll let me hang around with 'im. When I ask 'im what the dolls are for, he says he's part of a big drug ring. He says they ship the dolls to Colombia, they fill 'em with cocaine and fly 'em back. But I knew that weren't true, 'cause, on television, I seen them cocaine-sniffin' dogs at the airport, so I know they ain't never lettin' any cocaine dolls into this country."

Sarah's mouth was agape, while Ray's eyes narrowed on Bern who he mentally labelled, witless.

"Are you aware that you could be arrested for drug trafficking?" Ray threatened.

Beads of sweat now detoured along Bern's nose.

"Listen, wait a minute...wait. I knew Doug made up the cocaine story, thinkin' I'd believe it, but he never thought I'd know about them cocaine-sniffin' dogs, eh? When I told 'im he was full o' shit, he admitted the dolls weren't for cocaine. But he never said what they was for. I bought them 'cuz he wanted 'em...and I liked bein' around 'im. But he never talks to me no more anyways, so why should I give a shit about 'im?" Having confessed, Bern sat back bearing a cocky smirk and a lackadaisical posture.

Ray glared at the smarmy witness and took a deep breath of resolve. "Listen carefully to what I'm gonna tell you, Bern Giffen. Are ya listening carefully?"

With an exaggerated motion, Bern farcically cocked his ear toward the cop.

Ray began to deliver his message through gritted teeth. "I get it wise guy. You think you're some smart operator, but what ya really are, is a dumb twit. And I'm tellin' ya, if ya don't want to end up on the wrong side of prison bars, you'd better listen real close. Don't you ever tell a living soul about this conversation we just had. Do ya hear me?" Bern nodded frantically. "Okay, good, 'cause I know where to find you. So, for now you're free, but get goin' before I change my mind." Ray stepped back, and the terrified janitor raced off as if he was already being hunted.

* * *

On Francis's return, Ray relayed the information he'd garnered from Bern, and asked if she could check her human resources files for an employee with the first name Doug.

"Not a problem," Francis cheerily replied. "This actually makes my day far more interesting," She unlocked the cabinet and rifled through her files, placing several on her desk. She had found three Dougs who worked in the hospital. The first was a gynecologist...a family man in his late fifties. The second was a male nurse who'd been working the night shift for over twenty years.

"The third Doug," Francis said, "is an orderly, mid-twenties. He's been here for a couple of years." Francis turned over the page. "This'll interest you: this Doug came to us through a social services jobs program. I'll write down the specifics for you; um, most recent address, phone number, and last name...Fergusson."

* * *

It was midafternoon when Ray and Sarah left Francis's office and headed for 217 Brock Street, to check on Mr. Doug Fergusson.

Ray parked his green Plymouth a block from the house, and they walked the rest of the way.

Several yards from the address, Sarah stopped abruptly, tugged on Ray's arm, and looked up at him. "Listen Ray, I'm thinking, if he sees a cop, it might spook him, so why don't you hang back a bit. I'll go to the door, and when he answers, you can step in. Okay?"

The cop shook his head. "Now, why in hell would I let you do that?"

Sarah stiffened her neck and folded her arms to demonstrate her determination, "Why? Because I need to show a little moxie, or I'm never gonna be taken seriously as a journalist; and with you at my back, I can afford to be ballsy. So, please do me this favour. Don't worry. He's not Freddie Kruger."

Ray raised an eyebrow. "You sure about that?"

Sarah nodded and unfolded her arms. Ray, though still dubious, offered an exaggerated sweep of his hand, indicating she was free to go ahead. She edged closer to the building with Ray following behind. The crumbling concrete steps that led to the basement door were littered with all manner of disgusting debris. The pigeons that straddled the overhead wires had tendered their opinion of their neighbour with their overly generous fecal offerings. Sarah maneuvered around the trash and filth that decorated the path to the entrance. Ear-shattering honky-tonk music seeped through the walls. She stepped up to the door and knocked.

"Come on Sarah, if you're gonna do it, put a little muscle into it. He can't hear that little tap over all that noise," Ray muttered.

She sneered at the cop for implying weakness; but to prove him wrong, she pounded on the door with her tightly clenched fist.

The music stopped abruptly, and the door opened. Inside the frame stood Doug Fergusson; average height, average weight, and not monstrous looking, but Sarah noted, he did have a sparse hairline for such a young man.

This is too easy, she thought as she gazed past him into his flat. There, strewn across a dinette table, along with beer bottles and KFC buckets, were scissors, glue, scraps of newspapers and several doll-display boxes.

"Hey, who ya lookin' for?" He growled.

Sarah was fascinated by the rigid lips that barely moved as he shouted.

"Lady, I asked, who ya lookin' for? Are ya deaf?"

"Uh, no, sorry...I'm not sure I have the right house. I've uh, been looking all over the place and uh, asking everybody." She stammered.

Still holding onto the door, Doug shook his head, leaned forward and hollered, "Jesus Christ, Lady, for the last time: who...in hell, are...you...lookin' for?"

As Sarah's knees began to quiver, Ray's voice boomed from the shadows. "We're looking for Doug Fergusson."

Anticipating Doug's reaction, Ray stepped in front of Sarah, shoved his foot in the door, and flashed his identification. "We'd like to have a little chat with ya, Doug. So, invite us in."

"I don't have ta, do I?" he anxiously asked.

"Well, for your sake, I'm hopin' you'll be hospitable, Dougie," Ray casually replied while targeting him with a steely glare.

Doug Fergusson nodded and took a cautious step back, allowing the visitors to enter. Sarah lingered by the door, ready for a quick getaway. Ray strode inside, jerked a chair away from the table, and shoved it toward Doug. "Sit down," he ordered. Doug remained upright and stiff as stone.

Ray's face changed from determined to livid as he hollered. "Sit the fuck down, Dougie! Or do you need my help?"

Doug plopped into the chair, without assistance. Ray paced in silence for a minute before firing the usual W5 questions at the suspect (i.e., "*Why* did you want those dolls? *Where* did you buy them? *When* did you get them? *What* did you plan to do with them?" *Who* are they for?). The cop watched the jittery suspect dance wildly around the questions, refusing to answer. Like a mouse on a glue-trap, this rat was sinking deeper into the ooze.

Ray turned toward Sarah and offered a discreet wink and a subtle grin in the hopes it would reassure her that he had everything under control. He stepped behind Doug, and asked another question.

Receiving the same bristling non-response, Ray's jaw pulsated with frustration. He tried another tack. "Doug,

I'm trying to help you out here, but you've been caught with all the evidence we need right there on your table; so, arresting you is my only option, unless you cooperate." Doug's scowling silence continued. Ray clenched his fists and grunted. "I'm done dancing around this shit. You got two minutes to decide!"

With raging eyes, Ray stalked away leaving the edgy doll collector in silent limbo to reconsider his options.

Ray dragged a chair to the door, then nodded to Sarah, indicating it was safe for her to sit. She obliged.

The moment of silence proved effective. Suddenly, Doug had something to say. "Officer, I- I didn't know that buyin' those dolls was a crime. I just did what my Uncle Zane told me I had ta do."

Ray approached the table, faced Doug, and straddled a chair,. "Keep goin'. I mean, who did he say they were for? His grandkids maybe?"

"No, he just told me to buy them."

Ray huffed a lung-full of oxygen before continuing. "So, Doug, you bought 'em and then what?"

The suspect fidgeted and mumbled. "Uh, then, uh, nothin. I don't know what he did with them."

Sarah watched Ray's thread of patience shred as a shudder of fury rumbled through him.

"Listen, ya little turd, 'cause I already know the answer, I'm only gonna ask you this once. You threw one of them through a plate glass window. And I know about the rest, too. So, here's your last chance to help yourself. What did you do with the goddamn dolls after you bought them?" With that, Ray rose from the chair like a monster from a lagoon and hovered over his prey.

"Okay, okay. I bought 'em. Yeah. And I stuck a note on that car; but I never threw nothin' through anybody's window. Look, I still have a doll left, see?"

"I do see. And now, you listen carefully to me, Dougie boy. You better not get rid of that doll or even one scrap of that wrapping material. I'm comin' back with a warrant, and if the stuff's not here, I'll arrest ya on the spot. And you better remember exactly what ya did with every one of them, so you'll be telling me the absolute truth when I ask again. Meantime, I want ya to put it all in one of those neatly folded garbage bags over there. Got it?"

Doug nodded vigorously as his guests exited.

As they walked away, Ray whispered to Sarah, "Did you see that supply of jumbo garbage bags?"

"Uh, huh." She nodded. "What's the big deal? I used to buy them in bulk from the Price Club. Does that cast suspicion on my judgement?" She smirked.

"There's no way they came from the Price Club, Sarah," Ray insisted with a sneer. "I guarantee they're stolen from the hospital's supply closet."

"Why would he do that?" She interjected. "And how?"

"How? He likely shoves a few in his pants every day, and away he goes. I doubt a gallon jug of bleach would fit down there quite as well." He chortled.

"I don't get it. What good is a big pile of trash bags?"

"I don't know. It works for me though, 'cause if I need leverage, I'll arrest him for stealin' government property."

"Come on, Ray, seriously, why take them? It doesn't make sense."

"It doesn't have to make sense. Maybe he has a trash bag fetish." Ray chuckled. Sarah did not.

Once they were back in the cop car, Sarah continued her push for answers.

"Ray, he's obviously never used them for cleaning up. I mean, why go to all the trouble of sneaking around and risking your job, or an arrest, over a plastic garbage bag?"

Ray shrugged and started the engine, "He's a thief. They don't need a reason to steal, just an opportunity."

Sarah nodded and sighed before asking: "Hey, listen Ray, if we get back in time, do you think we can stop by the Prescott Library before you toss me outta your car?"

The cop smiled and stepped on the gas.

* * *

The librarian, Miss. Evanson, was titillated over the importance granted her by the Brockville police chief and the "big city" journalist. Sarah employed her most innocent and manipulative plan. "Miss. Evanson, would you possibly have any yearbooks or student photos from Stutstown Secondary, from around say, 1956."

"Oh, my goodness! I'm not sure about that. I need some time to check that far back," the librarian declared as Sarah stifled a groan of frustration. The librarian continued. "But I'll do my best."

"Oh, that's great. When do you think we could pick them up?"

"Well, if and when I can find them, I'll bring them to you. So, let me get back to work and you have a good day." The librarian stipulated. Catching Sarah's grimace and shoulders slumping, she continued. "Or, Miss, if you're in a real big hurry, you could hang around for a while to see what I can find." The librarian smirked as she sat down in front of her computer. Her fingers danced over the keys as the name, age, and grade level of every student who attended Stutstown Secondary from early 1900's 'til its closing, rolled across her screen. The name Fergusson appeared on the roster running the gamut from A to Z: The first was Arvin and the last was Zane.

The librarian rested her hands on her lap and looked up at the serious faces of the two anxious visitors and offered a thought. "Actually, as far as I know, there were no Stutstown yearbooks ever produced. But there could be some student photos, boxed and stored down in the Knight Archives. Now, most loose pictures weren't labelled, so we never did anything with them; but if it's important, I can try and find the time to locate them after the weekend, if it doesn't get too crazy busy around here."

Ray nodded his appreciation and, as they turned to leave, Sarah offered a sincere "thank you" and an appreciative smile.

Once out on the street, Sarah wondered how quickly the librarian would get to the task. Ray flippantly remarked "Listen, since we seemed to have been the only two visitors in the hour we spent there, I'm sure she'll find the time." He grinned, said goodbye, and jumped into his car. Sarah waved and headed back to her hotel.

Exhausted but exhilarated, she picked up her messages and trudged up to her suite. Among the short stack of pink notes was an uncharacteristically reasonable, but somewhat illiterate, missive from Earl White:

Mrs. Berman,

I'm leaving this note so I won't be buggen you on the phone. I'd like to mete with you on Monday. If you don't mined please call me.

Earl

* * *

The next day, Ray called Sarah to ask if she wanted to join him on a follow-up visit with Doug Fergusson.

"Listen Sarah, first thing this morning, I drove out to Kingston to see Zane in the pen, and let me tell ya...I've been around enough liars, drunks, and thieves to know if they're snowin' me, and believe me when I tell ya, Zane didn't have a clue about those dolls."

Sarah gasped and tightened her grip on the receiver. "What are you talking about, Ray? Doug said Zane told him to do it. Why would he lie to you?"

"Lesson number one, Sarah: lowlifes lie. Do you want me to pick you up or not?"

* * *

Ray called out: "It's the police," but received no response. He was about to kick down the door when Sarah intervened. She twisted the knob and found the door unlocked. She moved back. Ray stepped inside and looked around. He spotted Doug slumped in a chair, motionless, with his back to the door.

Sarah remained in the doorway, waiting for a safe sign from Ray.

A long, low groan reverberated through the space.

Ray shouted, "Put your hands up and turn around." There was no reaction.

"I said, turn around and look at me, you little weasel." Ray rested his hand on his weapon.

Doug grunted but didn't comply. "I'm telling you to turn the fuck around so we can talk here in the company of this fine lady journalist. Or we can do it down at the station with my less civilized buddies present. It's your choice, but I gotta see your hands, in the air, now!"

Slowly, Doug raised his hands and shifted around in the chair. Confident there was no threat, he turned and nodded to Sarah.

Ray moved in, with Sarah following behind. As they approached, they could see that the right side of Doug's face bore an unsightly purple welt, a starburst of lacerations from forehead to jaw, a deep, oozing cut above his left eye, and the right side of his mouth was torn and bloodied. It was clear by the rips and blood stains on his clothing, that there were hidden wounds as well.

Sarah wasn't sure what to do. Should she offer first aid? Walk away? Was there a protocol for a naïve journalist who happened to arrive on the scene of a serious assault? "Can we drive him to the hospital, Ray?"

"No! No cop car." The battered young man rasped.

"Then I'm gonna call an ambulance." Sarah insisted.

"No! No ambulance. Just leave me alone." He pleaded.

"What in hell happened here for Christ's sake?" Ray barked "Who did this to you, Doug?"

Doug pressed his lips shut, lowered his head, and barely whispered, "Nobody. Nobody did it to me. I fell down...outside...on broken glass. Go away."

"Okay, we'll go. But I wanna know why you lied about who told ya to buy the dolls?"

The pummeled suspect slowly raised his head and bellowed; "Get the hell out of my house! I didn't let you in, so yer illegal here. Get out...Now!" Doug shrieked.

Ray grunted in frustration. Sarah rushed out the door without waiting for Doug's second command. Ray knew that this time, Doug Fergusson was within his rights. Without a warrant or permission from the victim, Ray had no legal alternative, but to leave. He turned on his heel and started toward the door, then paused; "I advise you to get yourself to your workplace and let them tend to your wounds, Doug, 'cause infection or gangrene can cost ya your life. But then, it seems someone has already tried to take that from you, and you don't seem to care enough about it to try to save yourself. So good luck with that."

Doug kept his eyes fixed on the cop as he walked out. Once the door was shut, Doug closed his eyes and winced as salty tears stung at the open gashes on his face.

CHAPTER NINETEEN

The following afternoon, Sarah, enthused with a grand idea, knocked on Eleanor's door, The dressmaker opened the door with scissors in hand, and a length of rayon fabric slung over her shoulder: "Hi, Sarah, what can I do for you?"

"Well, I was thinking we might jump into my turquoise limo over there and take in an early movie in Brockville."

Eleanor's flushed cheeks were evidence that she still wasn't ready to venture outside of the town boundaries. "Oh, thanks, Sarah, but as you can see, I've got work to do."

The response didn't surprise Sarah who had come prepared to try and convince her. "Aw, come on." Sarah wavered for a moment, then in an excited rush, she blurted out her plan. "The truth is, Eleanor, I was thinking that on the way, we might stop by and visit Bill Connell."

At the drop of the name, Eleanor's face lit up like a toddler tempted by ice cream. "Um, oh. Maybe I can finish this up later. Well, okay, why not?"

* * *

The November sun mockingly dashed between the clouds, offering periodic respites from the gloomy, grey sky. But gloom was certainly not what Eleanor was feeling. Sarah watched her friend smile lazily as she gazed out at the changing landscape along the St. Lawrence shoreline.

For a few minutes, Sarah drove in silence except for Eleanor softly humming some abstract tune.

Eventually, Eleanor listened politely as Sarah updated her on her recent introduction to the world of crime. However, Eleanor was clearly preoccupied with the anticipation of seeing her mother's old friend, Bill Connell.

If Sarah had learned nothing else from her last visit with the veteran police chief, she had definitely grasped the fact that this senescent John Wayne could still roar like a tiger. Still, she was daring to wrestle with fate by arriving unannounced with a new visitor.

Sister Catherine Grace escorted them into the salon and pointed toward an enormous picture window. There, resting in a wheelchair, gazing out at the rolling, crystal water of the great St. Lawrence, sat the old town hero.

Reminiscent of a kitschy Thomas Kinkade portrait, tangerine sunrays streamed against the cerulean sky and brushed against Officer Bill's pale, weathered profile.

"Bill, I brought you something," the sister announced.

"If it ain't smokes, I don't want it," the craggy cop grumbled.

"No, it's something much better, you old coot." The nun giggled.

The two women headed toward him. He squinted, then focused on Eleanor as she drew closer.

He inhaled a measured gulp of air.

"H-Holly?"

Eleanor smiled softly and bent down beside him.

"No, Officer Bill, it's Eleanor, Holly's daughter."

Bill fixed his gaze on Eleanor while he struggled to find words. His eyes filled with tears, and a humble sob erupted from his throat.

"I'm sorry," he said, trying desperately to reclaim his dignity. "At my age, ya leak outta places ya don't expect ta. But ya look just like her...except for the hair colour."

Sarah pushed a chair forward for her friend and then invisibly retreated to the kitchen with Sister Catherine.

Eleanor smiled and sat, "Yes, I know. My mom wasn't much older than me when she died, but her hair was still as black as coal. As you can see, I'm not that lucky."

"I guess not," he mused, "but if you weren't grey, you'd be just as pretty."

Eleanor offered a shrug and a shy smile over the unintentional insult. But it reminded her that Bill was still, the candid, unscripted man she remembered; and as it turned out, a gratifying connection to warmer memories of her mother. Lost in a vacuum of time, Bill and Eleanor remained absorbed, exchanging ardent reminiscences.

In the meantime, Sarah remained in the kitchen, intermittently entertained by two humorous nuns. The People Magazine Sarah had stashed in her purse, kept her occupied whenever the nuns had to step away to tend to their duties.

As time ticked by, her hunger overcame her desire to take in the movie they had planned to see. Mouth-watering visions of egg drop soup and lemon chicken tormented her. Could she really interrupt Eleanor's happy reunion, just so she could bite into a hot, crispy spring roll?

The rumbling in her stomach echoed the answer.

"Sister Catherine, to be honest, I'm starving and dying for Chinese food. Do you know a place, not too far away?"

The nun had a quick answer. "Sure, there's the Sun Lo Chinese restaurant in Brockville. It's been there forever, and the food is delicious."

"Hmm, I'm salivating." Sarah enthused.

After a brief pause, she sidled up to the nun and asked, "Sister, they've been catching up for almost three hours...that's probably long enough, right?"

The nun offered a dubious squint, but casually replied. "I guess so."

Sarah clapped her hands with delight. "Okay, so you agree. Then, how can I get Eleanor to leave without me looking like a selfish jerk?"

The nun raised an eyebrow and grinned. "Come with me and I'll show you."

With that, Sister Catherine Grace marched off with Sarah close behind.

The nun stepped between the visitors. "Sorry to cut your visit short Bill, but it's time for dinner. And I don't want to hear you asking, 'what's on the menu', because you know you're gonna give me a hard time even though you're gonna clean your plate no matter what's on it."

Bill held back a smirk as the nun turned to Eleanor, "Sorry to interrupt, but please come back anytime. It seems you can do the impossible and subdue this old grouch."

Eleanor rose from her chair, leaned over, and kissed Bill on his forehead. Once again, he teared up. "Don't be a stranger, eh?" He whispered.

"Not a chance, Bill." She touched his shoulder and smiled wistfully. "You take care now. I'll see you soon."

As the two women headed to the parking lot, Sarah stopped to take a breath before offering a proposition. "Listen Eleanor, I was wondering how you'd feel about forgetting the movie...and going into Brockville for Chinese food instead."

Her response was a blasé shrug that dampened Sarah's plan.

"It's okay, Eleanor, if you don't want to. Sister Catherine said they have great food at Sun Lo, so I figured that was a pretty solid recommendation. But I get it. If you're set on a movie, no problem."

Eleanor grinned and nodded enthusiastically. "No, it's a great idea. Let's forget the movie. I'm starving and you must be too. So, let's go." With that, she opened the door and slid gracefully inside.

Sarah smiled broadly, jumped into the driver's seat, and headed toward the Sun Lo eatery.

As they drove along the nine-mile stretch, Eleanor chattered without reservation.

"I was very young when Bill used to drop by, but I think I suspected that my mother was sort of dating the police chief. Years later, she confessed to me that Bill had proposed to her. She said that, although she was flattered, she'd refused. She said she might have loved him a little, but she had this dream; I think it was more like a crazy delusion, that one day my father would walk through our door, and they would pick up where they left off. I guess loyalty was both her strength and her weakness." Eleanor paused and gazed dreamily out the window for a moment before returning to her monologue. "Bill was a widower back then, raising three kids on his own. I guess when my mom refused his proposal, his kids still needed a mother, and he needed to move on. Judging by his reaction when he saw me today, I have no doubt that he really did love my mom."

She returned to window-gazing with a sigh and a wistful smile. Sarah glanced at her friend, then drove along, humming quietly to herself.

After they were escorted to their table at the Sun Lo, Sarah excused herself and headed for the ladies' room with a quick detour to the payphone.

"Hi Ray, listen, we just visited your dad, and I have a feeling that Eleanor might be more amenable to the idea of talking to the police, and this might be the perfect time to meet. We're here in Brockville at the Sun Lo Restaurant, and we're about to order dinner, but I'll stall if you're free to join us for a *chance* meeting. Emphasis on *chance*, okay?"

"Sure thing," he replied. "I'll be there in a flash."

"When you get here, please do your best to act surprised."

"Hey, I'm no Paul Newman, but I'll try."

The two women lingered over green tea and free egg noodles for much too long. Eleanor heaved a weary sigh. "You know what, Sarah, now I'm really starving. How about you? Maybe we should order dinner before we're full up on noodles."

Sarah was figuring out another delay tactic when she spotted Ray making his entrance wearing jeans, a hockey jersey and bomber jacket.

"Wow! I don't believe it!" Sarah exclaimed and placed a hand dramatically over her heart.

Eleanor's face was scrunched in confusion. "Huh? Believe what?" She muttered.

"Believe who just walked through the door." Sarah confidently replied. She extended her arm as if she was flagging a cab and cheerily called out, "Ra-ay?"

Ray engineered a pitiful double-take, with a poorly contrived look of surprise. He ambled over to the table doing his awkward best to play his part. "It's great to see you, Sarah. I just came in to order some takeout for myself and uh, here you are."

Sarah picked up her cue. "It's good to see you too. Oh! Eleanor Miller, this is Ray Connell."

Eleanor's mouth was agape, but she managed to utter four words. "You're Bill Connell's, Ray?"

He offered a casual nod and a warm smile. "That's right, Ma'am."

A hedge of silence was maintained for a few seconds before Eleanor's voice broke through.

"Ray, uh...we haven't ordered yet. Would you like to join us?"

After that, Sarah only needed to sit back and listen as the conversation jumped from, Eleanor's warm memories of Chief Bill, to the sad fact that Ray and his two kids had been deserted, several years ago, by his ex-wife.

Dinner lasted far longer than Sarah had planned, but the scene was too charming to say "cut." It came to an end when Ray got a dispatch call from headquarters. "I'm really sorry, ladies, but I gotta go." With that, he said his goodbyes and left with Eleanor watching intently as he disappeared.

* * *

After Eleanor exited the car and waved goodnight, Sarah drove off, trying to remember if there was ever another day when so much conversation had taken place and she'd personally said so little.

* * *

On Monday morning, Sarah arrived for the scheduled meeting in Richard's office with Earl White. She immediately sensed something different about Earl. As the meeting got underway, he seemed hesitant, even depressed. He avoided eye contact with her, and actually let Richard do all the talking. There was one thing that Sarah knew for sure; the lawyer wasn't going to offer any useful information, so she needed Earl to talk. She leaned toward him.

"Listen Earl, your cousin, Doug, for some bizarre reason, purchased a load of dolls which he delivered to certain individuals in town to threaten and terrify them. But when Doug was questioned by the police, he accused his Uncle Zane of creating the creepy plan. The truth is, the cops don't believe a word of Doug's story. In fact, they know it wasn't Zane who planned it, so now they're intensifying the investigation."

Having set the scene, Sarah sat back, awaiting his response. It took an uncomfortably long time for the news to penetrate, but finally, after a few grunts, grimaces, and shakes of his head, Earl spoke up. "If it ain't Zane, that means there could be some other nutcase out there waitin' ta get me...or any of us." Earl's face was awash in a profusion of sweat. "Jesus Christ, yer sayin' I'm in real danger, aren't ya?" His screeching voice reverberated like a threadbare violin string.

Sarah shrugged and subtly nodded, suggesting he could be right. "Well, Mr. White, whoever this nutcase is, the cops think he got to Doug after they were there the first time, 'cause when they went back the next day, he was sporting a face full of cuts and bruises and a deep ugly gash over his eye. So, if the same people that pummeled Doug come after you, then yeah, you'd definitely be in danger."

Earl, slid forward in his seat and nervously offered a hunch. "Listen, I ain't never been that close with Doug, but I know when he was a kid, he was always fallin' on his face 'cause o' some kinda health problem he had; so, he coulda just taken one of them tumbles o' his and wanted it to sound smarter than trippin' over his own stupid feet. I'm sayin', he coulda made up the whole story."

Earl's explanation might have sounded absurd to Richard. But Sarah was recalling her visit to Doug's trash laden property, and wondered if an accidental fall near his front door was possible. She planned to share Earl's "falling down" theory with Ray.

* * *

She returned to her room to find a message from Richard's office, letting her know that court would proceed the next day with Earl's hearing on the docket. The news left Sarah relieved and excited.

* * *

Sarah arrived at the courthouse on time and seated herself with notepad and pen in hand. Anticipation grew as the gallery came alive with the court buzzing like a beehive in the summer heat.

She noted that the Crown's three Fergusson related witnesses, gloomily clad in prison garb, were paraded into the courtroom, past the defence table and lowered into their designated seats. What Sarah looked for and didn't see was Earl White. She quickly scribbled her next note. *Where is Earl White? Could the thugs who beat the crap out of Doug have done likewise to Earl?*

As the minutes ticked by, each prisoner took the witness stand. While they displayed the vulgarity and buffoonery she'd anticipated, they actually surpassed her expectations. Although they were sinfully entertaining to the gallery, Sarah found herself fixated on the fact that there was still no sign of Earl White. She scrawled, *Shouldn't someone mention that the accused or suspect or whatever Earl is, is missing?*

It didn't require a Clarence Darrow to cast doubt on the credibility of the witnesses. Each convicted pedophile took the stand and spewed testimony that was clearly fabricated and rehearsed with no objection from the Crown Attorney, who seemed to be concentrating on staying awake.

Sarah stifled a groan and jotted another note: *Crown Attorney Dunn's indifferent questioning of his own witnesses was outrageously inadequate and incompetent.* She sat back pensively tracing her lower lip with her fingertip while reading and wincing at her note. She thought about Wesley's notion of good *lawyering*; "Sarah, a good lawyer needs to have a fire in his belly that inspires him to fight for justice all the way to the door of the proverbial death chamber, if need be."

She also recalled his assessment of Crown Attorney Dunn's lawyering ability. "I tell ya, Sarah, if Dunn ever had a spark in his belly, it cooled by the time he passed the bar. He has no enthusiasm or talent for the profession. The only thing in his favour is longevity. If you wait long enough, in a small place like Brockville, you get to be anointed Crown Attorney 'cause you're the only one left in line."

With renewed determination and a wry smile, she added a postscript: *If the charges are dismissed, it might not be due to Laurie's brilliant defence, but because of the ineptitude of Dunn. And that would be a real shame!*

Laurie had finished with the three loathsome prisoners and was waiting for Dunn to bring on his last witness when the Crown Attorney rose to his feet. "May it uh, please the court, uh, we've removed our last witness from the list. We're ready to wrap up."

The judge peered over his spectacles looking completely baffled but wasted no time in responding to the Crown's request. "I see. Well then, if it pleases the defence, court will recess until tomorrow morning at ten."

Laurie nodded and replied. "Without objection, your Honour." With a rap of the gavel, court was dismissed.

Sarah was puzzled by the Crown's decision to wrap up. According to Richard, Dunn's final witness had been a major concern for Earl's team. Whoever it was, that person was touted to be the Crown's star attraction. Sarah had two burning questions now: What happened to that star witness; and where was Earl White?

Laurie hurried out before she could reach him, but she managed to grab hold of Richard as he rushed past. "Richard, I have a couple of questions..."

His reply was swift: "Sorry. Laurie and I have an important meeting down the hall. I've gotta go. Your questions will have to wait."

She headed back to Prescott and parked her turquoise Chevelle in front of Richard's office, drew a deep breath, picked up her pen and notebook, and exited the car.

With the contrived cunning of a seasoned journalist, she entered Richard's reception area hoping to come away with the name of the dismissed witness. "Hi Joannie, I didn't get a chance to speak to Richard after court, 'cause he was rushing off to another meeting; so, can you please write down the name of the Crown's last witness. I must have missed it, somehow."

Without hesitation, Joannie printed the name, then put her finger toward her lips and whispered. "Of course, I didn't give you this." She grinned. Then her mood shifted a bit. "Listen, Sarah, the name from the witness list is supposed to be public anyway, but you know I can't give ya the contact information, right? But I'll tell you what you can lawfully do, ta get it. Head over to the town hall with that name and they can point ya in the right direction. Good luck."

Sarah smiled warmly as she folded the paper and shoved it in her purse, "Joannie, I owe you lunch."

Joannie winked and whispered, "Forget it. Giving you that name isn't illegal, but still...we never had this conversation, okay?"

Sarah stifled a smirk. "Then I won't say a word. Thank you so much."

Sarah, thrilled with her success, headed back to her car with a hop in her step and a grin on her face.

A quick check of the county register at the town hall produced the phone number and address of the witness.

With paper in hand, Sarah rushed back to her hotel room where she paced like a caged tiger as she tried to muster courage. Like Goldilocks, she sat on a chair, leapt from it; sat on her bed, leapt from it; then paced some more. She berated herself for being weak. "What's wrong with you, Sarah Berman? You had the guts to walk into Earl's lawyer's office and get the witness's name, and you got the damn phone number too. So, what in hell are you waiting for?"

She sat on the bed and dialed the number. Her heart pounded in her chest as she waited for the first ring, but all she got was a busy signal. She dialed several more times, to the same end, always a busy signal. Her next try was interrupted by an incoming call.

"Hello? Oh, hi Laurie...Uh-huh. Um, yeah. Yes, I did ask Joannie for the name. I hope I didn't get her into trouble...Oh good, that's a relief. Why? I was just curious why that witness was dropped? In fact, I was trying to call to ask for an interview when you rang...What? Okay, I guess I can do that. No, I won't try to make contact until after court tomorrow, I promise.

"Wait, before you go, how did you know I'd asked Joannie? Oh really? No, it's not a problem. I'm glad she told Richard. Wait a sec, Laurie, I know you're crazy busy, but can you just tell me why Earl White wasn't in court today? I mean, doesn't the accused have to be there for a preliminary hearing? Yeah, sure! I'll meet you down there in ten minutes."

* * *

Warm muffins and a fresh pot of coffee were already on the table and Laurie was sipping from his mug as she took her seat.

He poured her a cup, and she wrapped her fingers tightly around it to warm up. "Thanks. Hot coffee's exactly what I needed to offset the chill that followed those creepy witnesses into court."

He chuckled. "Remind you of the hillbillies in that movie *Deliverance*?"

"Oh my God, exactly. That's what I was thinking when I went to see Zane in prison, but I couldn't remember the name of the film." She offered a theatrical shiver, and he smiled.

"Sarah, I only have about twenty minutes; is that gonna be enough time for you?"

She nodded. "Probably. Oh, first, I want to tell you how impressed I was with your lawyering skills."

"Thanks, but unless Dunn has a surprise in store, it doesn't take much skill to go up against an opponent who mostly sleeps through the hearing." He chuckled.

Sarah giddily tossed her hair and proceeded. "Laurie, I was surprised to see that Earl wasn't in the courtroom with you and Richard. I mean, isn't that protocol?"

Laurie nodded hesitantly. "Generally, that's true. But there are always extenuating circumstances if you have the right judge. In that, we were very lucky. Here's the thing, Sarah. You've met White, you know what kind of a character he is."

She grunted, "Hm-mm."

Laurie grunted in agreement "Hm-mm. Exactly. Well, Richard and I felt that having him in the courtroom when his prison buddies were testifying wouldn't have done anyone any good." He paused, took a bite of muffin then continued. "Listen, I can continue, but only if it's off the record. Agreed?"

"Agreed." She nodded and gestured for him to continue.

"Earl would have exploded in a barrage of profanity and threats and maybe worse. You may have heard that he's not a man who takes criticism well." He snickered. "So, we presented our case to the judge, explaining that it would cause delays and unnecessary disruption to the court, the judge, and the Crown. He listened carefully and granted permission for Earl to be allowed to remain out of the courtroom during the witnesses' testimonies. Since the Crown declared he's done with witnesses, Earl will be in court tomorrow for the closing arguments. How about you?"

"I wouldn't miss it." She raised her cup in a toast. Laurie obliged, then rose from his chair. "Sarah, I'm glad we had a chance to meet up, and now I've gotta go; important meeting. See you in court tomorrow. Don't you be late. I think it's gonna be interesting." He smiled and rushed away.

* * *

The court formalities were already completed by the time Sarah got to her seat. She was surprised to see Earl's chair still empty, though Laurie was standing and addressing the Judge:

"Your Honour, we call Bindy Fergusson ..."

The words set Sarah's thoughts spinning as she wrote. *Neither on the phone nor during our coffee chat did Laurie even hint they had garnered the Crown's former star witness for themselves. But he did say he had to rush away to an important meeting.*

Sarah was riveted as she watched a tiny, sparrow-like woman slowly rise to her feet and move tentatively toward the witness box.

She was frail with brittle, colorless hair, and a well-worn face. Her sad eyes offered a glimpse into her tortured spirit while her gnarly hands exposed the physical manifestation of a wretched life.

It seemed bitter irony that Laurie might have to break down such a heart-rending soul in his attempt to salvage a despicable one.

He approached the witness cautiously and spoke softly.

"Mrs. Fergusson, you're the wife of Zane Fergusson. Is that correct?"

She quietly grunted and turned her face away.

"Mrs. Fergusson?"

"I ain't sayin' nothin' to you." She spat out the words like poison darts.

The judge frowned and peered at the witness. "Mrs. Fergusson, you must answer the questions, or this court will have no choice but to hold you in contempt. If you don't want to find yourself sitting in a jail cell, I suggest you answer. Do you understand?"

"Uh-huh, but I was told last time, I didn't have to do no testifyin' against Zane 'cause I'm his wife." She folded her arms and scowled at the judge. Laurie stepped back and waited while the judge resolved the dispute.

"Madame, that'd be true if it was your husband on trial here, but that's a dog that was put down a while back, eh? This hearing isn't about your husband today, Mrs. Fergusson, so you must answer the questions."

Bindy glowered at the judge and snorted her disapproval.

The judge emitted a restrained sigh, then nodded toward Laurie; "Mr. Cowan, you may proceed." Anyone watching closely would have spotted the smirk that flashed across the judge's face.

As Laurie approached, the witness abruptly spun around in her chair and turned her back on him. It was a ludicrous reaction that caused the gallery to break out laughing.

"Settle down! And you, Ma'am, turn yourself around!" The judge shouted. It was loud and aggressive; though the room complied, it was clear by Mrs. Fergusson's back that she wasn't about to.

Laurie took a breath. "Your Honour, permission to treat this witness as hostile?"

"Permission granted." The judge turned to the witness with another warning. "Mrs. Fergusson, again I caution you that it's in your best interests to turn around and answer the questions. Do you understand?"

With the scornful persona of a black crow, the witness stiffened her back, turned to face the court, and through tightly pursed lips, muttered, "Uh-huh."

"I didn't hear that. Was that a yes?" The judge asked as he bent forward.

"Yes!" She snapped.

The judge nodded and turned his attention to Laurie. "Mr. Cowan, you may proceed."

"Thank you, Your Honour. I'll repeat the question. Are you the wife of Zane Fergusson?"

The witness nodded.

"Mrs. Fergusson, the court recorder does not recognize a gesture," the judge cautioned. "I repeat, you will have to answer aloud. Yes, or no?"

Her shoulders slumped and her eyes began to water. She slowly pulled a tissue from her sleeve. "Sorry. Yes."

Laurie continued. "And isn't it true that your husband is in prison for crimes related to this case?"

A murmur rumbled around the courtroom and through the frail woman's body. She lowered her head and replied. "Yes, he's in prison, like ya said."

"Okay, Mrs. Fergusson. Now I want you to think very carefully before you answer. Can you remember if you've ever seen Earl White, in your home?"

There was a pause, and then almost inaudibly, "Uh-huh."

"Speak up. Again, the court must hear your reply," the judge sternly prompted.

"Yes, Judge. Yes, I seen him."

Laurie nodded and calmly continued. "Okay, thank you. Now, could you tell the court when that was?"

"Yup...once a month...I made him breakfast."

Laurie paused and looked at her quizzically for a few seconds before proceeding; "Breakfast? That was it, Mrs. Fergusson? He came by once a month for breakfast?" Laurie patiently repeated.

"Yes. Yes, he did." It was a noticeably more confident reply. Suddenly, her bearing appeared less rigid and the taut expression on her face softened.

Laurie carefully watched the transition evolve. "Mrs. Fergusson, I know this is difficult for you to have to think about, but please, tell the court if you ever saw Earl White interact inappropriately with the victims in this case?" A tense hush hovered over the courtroom. He waited patiently, allowing time for her to think. She closed her eyes and twisted the tissue in her hand. He waited a few beats, then pressed further. "Mrs. Fergusson, did you not hear the question?"

"Yes, b-but I-I don't know what I'm supposed to say."

Sarah squirmed in her seat and quickly scribbled a note. *If the witness refuses to answer, judge could take it to mean she knows or maybe has proof Earl's guilty?*

Laurie continued. "Mrs. Fergusson, let me ask it this way. Did you ever see or hear Earl White make lewd or sexual advances at anytime, toward any members of your family?"

"Y-yeah."

The gallery was pulsating with spectators' babblings. "Silence! Or I'll clear the courtroom!" The judge shouted as he hammered down the gavel. He glowered at the crowd until the din receded.

"Continue, Mr. Cowan." The judge urged.

"Thank you, your honour. Mrs. Fergusson, to whom did he make those unwanted advances?"

She shook her head rapidly, as if trying to shake away a demon. Suddenly, she stopped, leaned toward Laurie, and whispered. "Please, I don't wanna say."

Laurie stepped back and repeated. "Mrs. Fergusson, you must answer."

She lowered her head and mumbled, "Me...It was me."

The room once again was alive with gasps and groans, but another dour glare from the judge ended the clamor.

Laurie paid no attention to the chorus of mutterings. He was intent on keeping the momentum moving forward. "Mrs. Fergusson, when Mr. White made these advances toward you, what did you do or say?"

She spat out the bitter words. "I told 'im to take his goddamn money and git the hell out."

Laurie pressed on. "What money are you referring to, Mrs. Fergusson?"

"The damned rent money...first o' every month."

"So, when Mr. White came by to see you, they weren't actually social visits were they? They were business calls from a landlord collecting his rent. Don't you think that by inviting him in for breakfast, you might have been sending the wrong signal?"

She offered a one shoulder shrug and a toss of her head. "Maybe...but I had ta. Zane said I had ta give

Earl breakfast...an'...uh...He said, we needed that old house, for Christ's sake. We couldn't afford ta be thrown out. We had no place else ta go."

Laurie moved cautiously to the witness box and leaned in. "Mrs. Fergusson, I know this is going to be a difficult question for you to answer, but I have to ask: Did your husband demand that, in exchange for a place to live, you offer Earl White sexual favours?"

Insidious excitement permeated the crowded courtroom. Laurie walked to his table, took a sip of water, scanned the crowd of spectators, then turned back toward the witness. Instantly, his confident demeanor was shaken at the sight of the crushed wisp of a woman who was drenched in tears and desperately trying to swallow her sobs.

Laurie approached the judge and asked with more emotion than he'd intended. "Your Honour, um, I'd like to withdraw the question."

The judge nodded, cleared his throat, and replied. "Granted. Now, can we get on with it?"

"Yes, thank you, Your Honour. Mrs. Fergusson, I need you to think carefully before you answer my next question."

She cast her eyes away from her interrogator. Her face was tense, and her clasped hands moved stiffly from her lap to her chin as she waited in terror for what he signaled would be another dreaded question.

Laurie tried unsuccessfully to make eye contact. "Mrs. Fergusson, did Zane instruct you to come here today and tell the court that Earl White was the mastermind behind the crimes that sent your husband to prison?"

She glanced briefly at the witness box door, perhaps hoping it was an escape hatch. Then suddenly, she straightened up, looked directly at the lawyer, and answered. "Yeah, yer darn right, he did."

"And did he tell you to stand before this court and claim that Earl White was inside that house of horrors, committing those unspeakable acts on children?"

She began to fold into herself once again. Tears streamed, her head bowed, and her body shook. "Please. You don't understand. Your Honour, I can't. Please...don't make me answer."

The gallery erupted once again. The judge slammed his gavel causing the witness to recoil. "You must answer the question! Perhaps you need to hear it again?"

She shook her head but wouldn't look up.

Laurie nodded toward the judge and continued. "Mrs. Fergusson, did your husband threaten that he would send someone to hurt you or your children if you didn't tell the court, it was Earl White who organized the horrific crimes?"

Bindy covered her face with her hands and released a long guttural moan.

The judge's tightly pursed lips and knitted brow indicated that his patience was rapidly dissolving. "Answer the question! Ask again, Mr. Cowan."

Laurie took a deep, agitated breath and exhaled. "I'll rephrase. Mrs. Fergusson, did your husband, Zane

Fergusson, order you to lie to this court? And you must answer!"

She cried softly but remained motionless. Before Laurie could push further, the Crown Attorney stirred from his stupor and apathetically objected.

"He's badgering the witness, Your Honour."

The judge exhaled a weary sigh as he looked toward the droopy-eyed prosecutor. "I'm delighted to hear your voice, Mr. Dunn. I thought for a moment you might have left us permanently. Objection sustained. And Mr. Cowan, I suggest you take extra care not to badger your own witness."

"Thank you, Your Honour. I'll try again. Mrs. Fergusson, are you afraid to tell the truth here today?"

A strange metamorphosis began as the witness slowly stretched herself to full seated height and spoke through clenched teeth.

"Am I afraid o' the truth? You betcha! In my house, the truth can kill ya faster than a bullet. But maybe dyin' wouldn't hurt as much as livin' the kind o' life I been stuck with." She leaned forward in her chair, placed her intertwined hands on the ledge, and looked directly into the lawyer's eyes, "Ya wanna know the truth? Here's the truth! I couldn't stomach what they was doin'...But every time I opened my mouth to try to stop it, I'd take a beatin'. Ya get used to the pain after a while, so's ya don't even notice no more. I'm tellin' ya the truth when I tell ya I don't know who came to the house. I don't know, 'cause after Zane'd beat the bejezus outta me for tryin' to stop 'im, he'd lock me up in the barn. Night after night, I slept in that miserable hellhole with rats and bugs and filth. So, the truth is, if Earl came to the house that night or any other night, I never seen 'im."

Beyond the gasps that resonated around the room was Laurie's own shocked reaction. He gently placed his hand on hers. "One last question. I'm sorry to have to bring this up, but...your young grandchildren were called to testify in the trial that sent your husband to prison, correct?"

"Yes, Sir, but we was all promised they'd never have to do it again. All o' them kids is in school now and gettin' help and doin' well, eh. Some don't have them awful nightmares no more, either. Even the welfare folks say they're satisfied; so please don't make 'em talk about or think about this filthy stuff again."

"I promise you, Mrs. Fergusson, that's not my plan. But I would like to know whether you asked any of them if Earl White ever sexually abused them?"

She nodded her head in short quick bursts before quietly uttering, "Yes..."

A collective loud gasp spread through the courtroom. The judge's gavel came thundering down again. Unflustered by the commotion, Laurie continued. "I'm sorry, Mrs. Fergusson, I don't think you were finished. Please go on."

"I was sayin' yes! Yes, I did ask all of 'em kids." She paused.

Laurie waited for a beat or two. "Okay, good, you asked them. And what did they answer?"

She looked up defiantly. "Don't get me wrong, I want nothin' more than ta see that bastard, Earl, put away with the rest o' them animals; but every last one of 'em kids...all of 'em, said no!"

"Mr. Dunn, no objections to this line of questioning?" The judge shouted. The Crown Attorney briskly replied, "Uh, yes, uh, I object. It's hearsay."

The judge offered a gruff, "Good to hear it, Mr. Dunn. It is hearsay. Objection sustained." He offered an exasperated sigh and then turned toward Laurie, "Mr. Cowan, another warning. Watch it."

"I have no more questions for this witness, Your Honour."

"All right then, the court will recess for lunch." He struck the gavel, and everyone headed for the exit.

Laurie rushed toward Sarah. "Listen, I have maybe thirty minutes for lunch. Would you like to join me in the meeting room for a stale boxed lunch from the cafeteria?"

Sarah, delighted to have a chance to ask him a myriad of questions, was quick to accept. "Sure. Stale or not, I'll bet it won't be pastrami on rye, huh?" She snickered.

"More likely ham and cheese on Wonder bread." Laurie countered.

In truth, Sarah was less concerned about the menu, and more anxious to probe the lawyer for answers. What she didn't foresee, were Richard McCall and Earl White joining them. In spite of that disappointment, Sarah still saw it as an opportunity, too good to pass up. It was her chance to get some inside information. She wanted to know why Earl White was at lunch but not in court. Was he going to be in court?

And if so, wouldn't that intimidate Bindy Fergusson during the Crown's cross-examination?

The meeting room had a musty smell, like the root cellar of old stone barracks.

The dark paneled walls and shuttered courthouse windows prevented even a meagre trace of fresh air or light from invading the sanctity of the bleak fortress. Sarah wondered how many souls had been forced to communicate the ugliest, most intimate details of their lives in that stark, barren room.

As the unlikely foursome sat around the oak table, opening their boxed lunches, the lawyers were silently engrossed in thoughts on the hearing. Meanwhile, Sarah was picturing a Michener Award for journalism in her future.

While the others were deep in thought, the alleged offender was fixated on his lunch. He removed a sandwich, carrot stick, and apple from the box. His odious mien told the tale, but he nevertheless felt the urge to comment. "This is it? No dessert? Not even a chocolate bar? Jesus, Dick, why didn't ya tell me we was getting' lunch from the local food bank." He snickered like a Grimm's fairy-tale witch. Surprisingly, Richard didn't let the insult pass. "Earl, you're bloody lucky to get that. In our late-night strategy meetings, Laurie and I've had our fill of stale sandwiches and bruised apples. Anyway, you agreed not to be present in the courtroom until the witnesses were all heard and gone, right?" Earl ignored the question and focused instead on unwrapping his sandwich. "You also had the choice not to show up for the closing arguments. But you're here, so I advise you to be grateful that you were allowed to be free as a bird. And...a thank you would be nice."

Earl ignored Richard's sarcasm and gnawed at his cheese sandwich like a gluttonous rodent. Unintentionally glancing over at the nauseating spectacle, caused Sarah to hastily push away her tuna sub.

In a flash, Earl had polished off his meal and headed out the door, presumably to find a vending machine to satisfy his junk food urge.

In his absence, Sarah began her own interrogation. "Listen, I'm not sure what you guys are free to say, but how do you feel things have gone so far?"

The lawyers grinned and replied almost in unison, "Sorry, we can't talk about it."

"Okay, I respect that, but how come Earl's here now? Does he know that Bindy Fergusson's on the stand?"

"He insisted he only wanted to be present for the closing arguments, and we're not there yet. Bindy was our last witness, and knowing how he might react; we didn't mention her to Earl." Richard declared.

"But aren't you worried that he might overreact when he sees her testifying?"

Laurie scoffed. "Oh, it's doubtful he'll see her."

"I'm completely confused now. Please explain..."

"Okay, I'll try..."

Any explanation he was about to offer was interrupted by a PA call to return to the courtroom. "Uh-oh, sorry, Sarah, but I think they refer to that as 'saved by the bell.'"

Sarah offered a playful pout and followed the men out of the room.

The crowd reassembled; Sarah found her seat; the attorneys took their respective places...and then, surprisingly, Earl White strutted in. Sarah was quick to write: *Earl symbolically tipped his hat toward the gallery before taking his seat beside Richard. Perhaps he's assuming it's filled with his adoring fans; but from my perspective the spectators' expressions reflect derision not adoration!* She added a large exclamation point before laying down her pen.

The bailiff announced the judge's arrival, and everyone rose to their feet. The judge sat down, and the bailiff continued, "You may be seated."

The judge took a quick glance around the courtroom, finally focusing on Earl White. "I see you managed to join us today, Mr. White." The courtroom was silent, and surprising as it seemed, so was Earl White. The judge pursed his lips, stroked his chin, and spoke. "The defence stated, they had no more questions for the last witness, and I was informed during the break that the Crown had no questions, therefore, the witness was dismissed. The closing arguments will be heard at a later date. Please check the dockets in the next few days. Court is dismissed."

The judge exited the courtroom, leaving everyone bewildered.

Reva Leah Stern

CHAPTER TWENTY

The Chevelle pulled up at the Prescott train station just as the Montreal express screeched to a halt. Sarah watched Anna slowly step off the platform and slog toward the car.

She jumped out and embraced her friend before relieving her of her travel bag and tossing it in the trunk. She spotted trepidation in her friend's eyes. "Whoa. Whoa there, Anna. You weren't sentenced to life in San Quentin, ya know." Sarah teased. "Ease up, this is gonna be a fun weekend," she gushed. Anna offered a skeptical smirk, then slid onto the passenger seat. Sarah settled in, turned on the radio, and began to sing along with Elvis as she sped away.

* * *

Mr. Reynolds blathered on congenially, as he escorted the pair to Anna's room. "Ya know, around here, we got a real soft spot for Montrealers. Thankfully, we get a lot of 'em up here. You're gonna love the room I gave ya, Miss." He punctuated his assurance with a wink, and opened the door onto a clean, bright space with a spectacular view of the St. Lawrence River. He handed Anna the key, tossed a smug nod toward Sarah, then jauntily strode down the hall.

"What the hell?" Sarah fumed.

Anna looked perplexed. "What did I do?"

"You? Nothing. It was that smug jerk, Reynolds. He treated you like visiting royalty. Me, he treats like a boil on his ass."

Anna smiled coyly as she gazed out at the sparkling river, "Sarah, my insecure friend, you could learn a lot from me about how to charm your way to success; and more importantly, how to discreetly slip the manager a twenty-dollar bill."

* * *

The dressmaker was usually in the front room sewing by window light, but this time, her paraphernalia was tucked away, and she was nowhere to be seen. The door, as always, was unlocked.

"Hey, Eleanor, it's Sarah. Where are you?" She hollered.

"In the kitchen. Come in. I'll put on the kettle. I'm glad you came by, 'cause I need help." She shouted.

Anna stayed out of sight while Sarah giddily entered the kitchen, only to be taken aback by the sight of Eleanor seated at her table wearing a flowered mu-mu and fuzzy slippers. Her hair was clipped up haphazardly, and her face was covered in a green, gloopy paste.

Sarah stopped abruptly and sputtered. "Uh, jeez! I'm so sorry Eleanor, although I can see this is a bad time for a surprise visitor, it's too late to change plans now. So, 'visitor' come on in!"

With that, Anna stepped forward wearing a gut-busting smile. "Eleanor Miller, it's me, Anna Daniels. Oh my God, you haven't changed a bit." Anna joshed.

"Anna? Holy cow, Anna Daniels!" Eleanor gasped and rose slowly to take in the sight. "I would never have recognized you. You look so...um, grown up."

Anna snickered and waggled a finger. "Uh-uh. First lesson in diplomacy; when greeting an old face from the past, whatever their condition, you're supposed to say, like I just did, 'You haven't changed a bit.'"

Eleanor shook her head in disbelief. "Oh, good gosh, Anna, what're you doing here?"

"What? Well, I actually came to surprise you and maybe relive some lost days of my youth. Why should Sarah be the only one having fun?"

"This is so weird...but definitely a surprise." Eleanor gripped the edge of the table to steady herself.

Anna shot her a wicked grin, "I can't tell if you're in good health or not; 'cause you do look kinda green."

A spontaneous titter erupted. "I don't know about good...but my life has really changed, thanks to our relentlessly determined friend here." She asserted with a nod toward Sarah.

"Yeah, she can be a real pain in the ass, but then, we must be masochists, 'cause we're not complaining, are we?" Anna chortled.

All three women paused for an uneasy second, until Anna happened to notice the green mud cracking and flaking around Eleanor's shy, tentative smile. Anna suddenly rushed forward and clasped her in a gripping bear hug. Eleanor found herself softening under the startling embrace. She tentatively placed her hands on Anna's back and patted gently before pulling away.

Anna giggled, "I've hugged an illegal alien or two in my life, but never a green one," she mused.

"Don't make me laugh," Eleanor muttered through clenched teeth, "or my face might fall off."

"What in the world are you doing anyway?" Sarah asked.

"I think I'm giving myself a makeover; but this facial stuff is so foreign to me, I'm not sure what I'm doing. Does it look like I've messed up here?" She nervously asked, clenching her jaw.

"How long have you had it on?" Sarah asked.

"About thirty-five minutes."

Anna and Sarah shared a look of alarm before Sarah begged the question, "Why, thirty-five minutes?"

Eleanor gave a defeated shrug. "Well, it said 'leave on for twenty,' so I figured an hour would be three times as good."

Anna rolled her eyes. "I suggest you wash it off right now before your skin is permanently bonded to the masque. And what's with your hair?"

"I was about to try to dye it. But maybe I'll leave that for another time along with my attempt at a manicure."

The two old friends looked on bemused. "Where did you get the dye?" Sarah asked.

"Cook's Pharmacy. They have everything there; polish, files, this masque, I even bought a portable hair dryer."

Anna peered at Sarah who glanced back and nodded. Sarah took the initiative. "Eleanor, relax; between Anna, me, Miss Clairol, and whatever brand of nail crap you've got, you're going to have the best beauty treatment

Prescott has to offer. But only if you promise, when there's a break, we can have tea and some of your homemade goodies."

That was a deal that Eleanor couldn't pass up. The tasks were quickly assigned. Sarah became the colorist, while Anna took the role of manicurist.

As they worked, they talked, and Sarah finally eased into a burning question. "What suddenly prompted this makeover, Eleanor?" She casually asked as she brushed goopy dye onto long strands of Eleanor's pepper-grey hair.

Eleanor flushed a little before answering. "Uh, no special reason," she replied. "I've always wanted an excuse to do it, but a good one never came along, before now."

"That's my point: why now?" Sarah asked as she leaned over to look Eleanor in the eye.

The fact that Eleanor hesitated too long and fidgeted too much before answering, did not go by unnoticed by her beauticians.

She continued. "Well, I've been giving it a lot of thought since we visited Bill Connell. Remember, I told you he made that crack about my grey hair?"

Sarah rolled her eyes. "Come on. Bill Connell's a doddering, old curmudgeon."

"Yeah, that's partly true. But I'm not really crazy about the grey myself, so I figured why not try it?"

With coloring brush in hand, Sarah struck a pose and declared, "I salute you, Eleanor Miller, I think it's great. And since we're all going to Shiny's party tonight: *if not now, when would be a better time?*" Sarah reasoned.

"Okay, *Rabbi Hillel*," Anna quipped. "Enough with the Jewish philosophy. If we're all going to this shindig, let's get this beauty thing done here, so I can get back to my room and make myself look fabulous, too." She squinted at the two other women and continued. "Besides, why should you skinny bitches get all the attention?"

Two hours flew by as the beauticians completed their tasks. The manicure was done; Eleanor had paused to take a shower and wash out the dye, while Sarah and Anna relished their early afternoon tea and cookies.

She hurried back to the kitchen in a terry robe, so that Sarah could roll her damp hair in curlers. All that was left, was for Eleanor to sit patiently for an hour or so, on her own, under her plastic blow-drying cap.

The visitors said their goodbyes and rushed back to the hotel to get themselves ready.

Sarah had offered to pick up Eleanor on their way to the party; but she declined. "Ladies, it's a refreshing two-minute walk to Shiny's. I'll meet you there."

* * *

The invitation said 7:30, but just like the old days, Anna was late, Sarah was miffed, and the pair arrived at 7:55.

A big crowd created a congested living room. However, amid the chattering throng, Sarah managed to spot Eleanor. She nudged Anna and the two women watched their friend approach through the maze. A picture of glamour in her mauve silk knit designer dress. Her rich, golden chestnut hair bounced and floated as she glided toward them.

"Holy shit, she looks like a Clairol commercial!" Anna gasped. "How does she get her hair to do that without a slow-motion camera? I want hair that makes me ooze sexy like that."

"I think her *oozing* might have less to do with her hair," Sarah replied. "Look closely and you'll notice another detail of Eleanor's ensemble."

There, alongside her, wearing a grin and unapologetically holding on to Eleanor's arm, was Ray Connell.

"So, Eleanor, I turn my back for thirty years, and before I know it, you've gone and gotten yourself this gorgeous guy, and never even mentioned it? Hi, I'm Anna Daniels. And you are?" She confidently extended her hand, which Ray shook while carefully sizing her up.

"I'm Ray Connell. You're Sarah's friend from Montreal, right?"

"I am, exactly. Now, nobody told me about this situation, so I'm kind of in the dark here. I have a laundry basket of questions for you, Ray Connell!"

Sarah playfully groaned as she recalled how brash, and candid Anna had always been and how clear it was that nothing had changed

Ray chuckled. "Okay, let's empty that basket. I'm an open book, so, ask away," he happily agreed. "But please, just remember, this isn't an inquisition, it's a party."

"Okay, so let's start with, what do you do for a living? Are you, or have you ever been married? And if so, what's your present status?" She stood firm and waited.

Ray shook his head and grinned. "That's the best you've got? I can do better than that, 'cause I question people for a living. I'm a cop. I was married. I'm divorced. And I'll throw in a couple for free...I have two terrific kids, and a father who used to date Eleanor's mother. And that's kind of how Eleanor and I got to be here. How's that for cooperation?"

The foursome broke into laughter which subsided as the message rumbled through the crowd that the buffet was now open. En route, Anna clumsily apologized to Eleanor.

"Hey, Kiddo, you might recall that I have a knack for putting my foot in it. I'm, sorry if I embarrassed you. I just didn't know you were dating anyone."

"Oh my God, Anna," Eleanor whispered. "It's not like that. Ray offered to walk me over on his way and I took him up on it. I was sticking with him 'til you two got here. That's all there is to it."

Anna sucked in her cheeks and raised her eyebrows in a demonstration of disbelief.

The night flew by as Sarah and Anna found themselves surrounded by people they didn't recognize or barely remembered. Still, there was something fascinating about being among old schoolmates who had stayed and thrived in Prescott.

When Sarah approached Ray to say goodbye, he discreetly whispered: "Eleanor's decided to file charges."

It was all Sarah could do to hold back a scream of delight, but the smile that spread across her glowing face told the tale. "That's amazing news, Ray! My God, I didn't even know you two were in touch until tonight. I'd ask how you convinced her, but I'm guessing that would be privileged information." She dramatized her innuendo with a perky wink.

Ray ignored the inference. "Look, if we want this thing to go forward for Eleanor, we'll need to take it nice and easy, so we don't shut her down. We don't want her to be disappointed again, now do we? So-o, we'll just deal with the situation one step at a time."

Sarah smiled softly. "Which situation are we talking about here, Ray? Come on, did you really think I was done?"

The officer blushed. "Okay, fine, maybe I could be looking at two situations, Sarah, but I know for sure that I have to take care of this one before I can ever hope to move on to the next. Maybe I can gain an advantage if I start with a little legwork and a lot o' luck. I'm gonna pick up Doug Fergusson in the morning and take him down to the police station. Let's hope he's had a recent memory surge."

* * *

The short drive home was filled with a flurry of conversation as Sarah and Anna traded stories about the people they'd encountered that evening. It became a rapid-fire game of "Do you remember so and so, and such and such?"

They continued their chat in Sarah's suite, until pending delirium forced Sarah to give in and call it a night. Anna dragged herself up to her room after finally admitting that 2:00 a.m. didn't feel as great as it used to.

* * *

Early the next morning, Ray rapped on Doug Fergusson's door and waited 30 seconds before putting his hand on the knob to find the door unlocked once again. He stepped inside and over a tangle of sleeping boozers who reeked of sweat, urine, and stale beer. In the far corner of the room, a mouse was eagerly devouring a putrid leftover, while Doug Fergusson lay sleeping nearby. It was a disturbing scenario in light of the fact that Fergusson's job was to help keep Brockville's main hospital microscopically clean. Pounding on the door at seven in the morning hadn't roused the sleeping herd, but the cold air that followed Ray into the room spurred a few to blink and grumble. As the drunken bunch began to stir, Ray dragged Doug outside, pushed him into the back of the patrol car, and chauffeured him to the police station.

By 9:30 a.m., Doug was returned to his address along with Ray's harsh warning: "Listen carefully, Fergusson. I'll be droppin' by on Monday to inspect your place. And, if it isn't as clean as the maternity ward at St. Gabriel's, you'll be brought in again and charged with neglect and endangerment to human life!"

CHAPTER TWENTY-ONE

As always, Anna, averse to backing down from any challenge, agreed to join Sarah on a one-mile jog along the crisp, snow-packed streets of Prescott. She disliked exercise in any kind of weather but was too stubborn to admit her shortcomings. While Sarah was prepared with fleece-lined, boots for snowy days, Anna tied up her sneakers and hauled herself along in a desperate attempt to keep up.

The two women were approaching Eleanor's house when Sarah stopped suddenly. A mischievous grin appeared on Anna's face as she caught her friend's scrutinizing eye. "You're looking to see if Ray's car's around here, aren't you? Sarah Klein, you're still a secret voyeur hiding in a prude's clothing. You haven't changed a bit!"

"Neither have you, Anna Daniels. You're still a horny old teeny bopper who's not getting any." With that, Anna signaled the start of a snowball fight with a direct hit to Sarah's butt cheek. Each snowball crumbled into flakey clumps that continued to accumulate inside Sarah's boots weighing her down.

Cold and giddy, they reached the last leg of the run with Anna in the lead, which meant she'd soon be back in her toasty warm hotel room. She began to walk backward, watching for any attempt by Sarah to catch up. "Come on *Myrtle the Turtle*, this *hare's* winning the race. In a few more steps, I'll be on my way to a steaming hot shower and a delicious pancake breakfast.

"No fair, Anna." Sarah whined, "My boots are full and so is my bladder!"

"It's your own fault. You should ditch those fancy boots and stick to sneakers like me; and by the way, menopausal women, like toddlers, should always pee before they leave home. I did."

While enjoying her momentary triumph, Anna noticed a car edging slowly along the curb. "Do you have an admirer you haven't told me about?"

"Little ole me?" Sarah hammily joked. "I've got dozens of them!"

"Well, there might be one of them in that car behind you."

Sarah paused, turned, and squinted as she tried to see who was inside. The car abruptly stopped. The door flew open, and Earl White slithered out of the driver's side. Attempting to step over the crusty snowbank, he slipped on a strip of ice and coiled himself around a lamppost, hanging on for security. Sarah stood immobile and aghast.

"What the hell are ya doin' out here?" he shouted. "Ya could have a fuckin' accident walkin' on this ice, ya know. I don't want ya laid up before ya finish my goddamn story."

The heat that emanated from Sarah's fury could have melted the icy embankment. She took a deep breath before calmly responding. "Did you actually come looking for me, or was this merely a happy coincidence?"

"Nah, I was just passin' through and saw ya, so I thought I'd stop to pay my respects, it bein' Sunday, the

Lord's Day, and all. I do that from time to time, ya know, like the Good Samaritan, eh? I even went by to see how my little Dougie was doin'. I was worryin' about 'im 'cause of that beatin' ya told me he took. But, when I got there, he was all freshly banged up again. He told me it was a cop beatin' on him, so I guess he'll be pressin' charges on that cop real soon, eh?" Earl sneered and clenched his teeth as he struggled to release his frigid grip from the icy lamppost. Finally freed, he skidded back to his car, grasped the handle, and offered a strangely ominous goodbye. "Well, you be careful now, eh. We wouldn't want nothing harmin' yer precious ass now, would we?" With that, he stumbled into his car and drove off.

"What in hell kind of creature was that?" exhaled Anna with her jaw agape.

"If I had my wish, it would be the extinct kind." Sarah answered with a slight tremor in her voice. "Let's go before I wet myself."

A subtle snort turned into a full out belly laugh as Anna wiped away a tear.

Sarah stood, hands on hips, shaking her head and smirking. "Okay, 'Eddy Murphy,' you got jokes. I don't see it, but go ahead, let's see what you've got."

Anna gulped back a snigger. "No big deal. I was just thinking, if you were a guy with a full bladder, you could have whipped out your hose and froze that creep to the lamppost."

The two grown women let loose and giggled their way back to the hotel.

* * *

That evening, Sarah asked Ray to join her and Anna for dinner at the Best Service, to trade stories about their intimidating meetup with Earl White, and Ray's confrontation with Doug Fergusson. Over dinner, they traded trivial niceties with no mention of either incident. However, when pie and coffee arrived, Anna jumped in to tell Ray about the disturbing encounter she'd witnessed with Earl White. "So, Ray, there we were, racing back to the hotel, after I already beat the boots off her; and this creepy, reptilian guy pulls up, slithers out of his car and starts nattering at Sarah like he's some Hillbilly Mafia boss or something. I can't believe that's the asshole she's decided to write about to make her mark in journalism. Sarah, for God's sake, that guy isn't worth the ink."

Throughout the telling, Ray said nothing. When Anna finished, the cop suddenly rose to his feet and excused himself. Sarah was dismayed as she watched him dart away. She turned toward Anna whose face was awash with confusion. Sarah shrugged it off as if it was typical of Ray. "Pay no attention to him, Anna. If you think he's bewildering, then you haven't met his father." She smiled and sipped her coffee.

The two friends sat a while longer, stuffing as much conversation as they could into the last few hours of their visit. Since Sarah insisted on driving Anna to the train station for 7 a.m., Anna reminded her they'd need to be up really early. So, they left the restaurant, returned to the hotel, and offered each other a reluctant goodnight before returning to their suites.

While getting ready for bed, Sarah was preoccupied with anticipation of Monday morning, Laurie's summation, and the judge's decision. She couldn't help but think that her journalistic inauguration into the big time would be irresistible if the twist at the end of her article turned out to be the forthcoming trial and conviction of Earl White. Of course, that outcome would be contrary to the general view of Prescott residents that, even though Earl White was an obnoxious boor, the flimsy evidence, vengefully motivated charges, and obvious capability of his big-city defence attorney was assurance that he'd never face a trial.

* * *

The next morning was sadder than Sarah had imagined when she said goodbye to Anna at the station.

En route back to her hotel, the sleet and dreary sky invoked pangs of loneliness. She returned to her suite feeling restless and anxious. She spent the rest of the day making notes about the Earl White hearing, ordering up meals and snacks, and viewing mindless TV shows. After watching the eleven o'clock news reports about fires, thefts, and accidents; and with sleet still slapping against the icy windowpane, she finally headed to bed.

Not even a long sip of brandy could quell the disturbing images that invaded Sarah's dreams throughout the restless night. The fragments of her continuing nightmares were becoming larger and more vivid, but they still didn't form a clear picture.

She awoke several times during the night, each time with an urgent need to empty her bladder. By 5:00 a.m., after repeated visits to the toilet, she realized that sleep was impossible. Something had been nagging at her ever since her chilly morning run with Anna.

She remained in bed mulling; the eerie encounter with Earl White, her frigid, snow-filled boots, and how bewilderingly difficult it was to say goodbye to her friend. Those thoughts led to bits of memory from her trip to Montreal, and all the wonderful people with whom she'd reunited.

A sudden sense of déjà vu bolted Sarah from bed. She grabbed the phone, then promptly set it down as she caught the neon glint of 5:35 a.m. on her digital clock.

By 6:45, Sarah was showered, dressed, and willing the clock to advance to 9:00 a.m. Five minutes later, Sarah's self-restraint was waning and, at the stroke of 7:00, she dialled.

On the other end of the line was a warm, welcoming smile in Esther Gorman's voice; "There's no need to apologize, my dear. I'm always up by dawn. It's an old habit. It's fine to call early any morning, but woe betide, if you call me after nine at night. 'cause there's never any good news to be heard that late at night. Anyway, Sarah, dear, I'm sure you didn't call long distance to talk about my sleeping habits, now did you?"

"No, Ma'am," Sarah chuckled.

"Well, go ahead then, Dear. I'm listening, and I'll try not to talk too much."

"Oh no, I want you to talk, Mrs. Gorman. Please. As a matter of fact, that's why I called. I've been thinking about something you said when I was leaving the Fleischmans' apartment that day. Do you remember when I asked to use the bathroom and you joked that you wouldn't want me to have an accident again?"

"I'm so sorry, Sarah." She emitted an uneasy sigh. "I didn't mean to make light of that predicament."

Sarah's anxiety escalated; "Honestly, Mrs. Gorman, I'm completely baffled. What predicament? What accident? What did you mean?"

Sarah heard a slow, steady exhale of breath before the voice continued. "Oh, my goodness, Sarah, have you really forgotten?"

Sarah looked at the phone as if it were an alien. "I promise you; I have no idea what you're talking about."

"You know what, Dear," Mrs. Gorman quickly interjected, "I shouldn't have said anything, and it's really not worth mentioning after all this time."

"Please Mrs. Gorman, whatever it is, I need to hear it."

Another tense pause. "Well, let me gather my thoughts for a minute, 'cause I'm not sure where to begin."

Sarah remained anxiously silent. After gently clearing her throat, Esther Gorman began. "I don't know how well you remember my husband, Albert, but when we lived in Prescott, he sold groceries door-to-door. It was mostly on the outskirts of town where it was too hard for folks without a car to get into town to shop. He'd load up the old van from the stock we kept in our garage. Oh, my goodness, I can't tell you how many times thieves broke in and stole from us...but Albert would never go to the police." She tsked.

"One evening, when he was returning from his late afternoon deliveries, he flew over a bump and groceries went tumbling. When he pulled over to straighten up the mess, he heard shouting. He looked out and saw a bunch of hooligans chasing a child down the cliff. Albert was getting ready to help...but just then, a school bus pulled up and the hooligans all went racing to get on board. That's all I know." She ended the account with a heavy sigh.

Sarah's complexion was ashen. "No, Esther, we haven't gotten to the accident thing yet."

A quiet moan filtered through the phone line, louder than was intended. "Ugh, yes, yes...the accident. Well then...a minute later, Albert saw a child scramble up the hill. He was truly shocked to see that it was you."

"Oh my God," Sarah moaned, "The blinding light. The deafening noise...in my dream."

Mrs. Gorman paused in bewilderment. "Blinding light? Noise? I'm not sure what you're talking about, Dear. I know, of course, you tried to ignore Albert at first. You were quite naturally afraid. But once he got out of the van and approached, you recognized him. He helped you gather up your scattered things; but when he tried to help you into the van, you began to sob. You begged him not to tell your parents that you'd had a...an accident."

Sarah's voice all but disappeared. She barely whispered into the phone, "I remember, Mrs. Gorman, I remember. He promised he'd never tell my parents I'd wet my pants, if I vowed to forget it happened, and never, never tell anyone he'd driven me home." She reached for a glass of water on her nightstand and took a sip, then a deep breath. "Mrs. Gorman, your husband would be relieved to know I kept my word. In fact, I'd completely forgotten." She shrugged. "I think a psychiatrist would have a field day with me. But why on earth would your husband ask me to make such a promise?"

Mrs. Gorman released a mournful groan. "Life's so complicated, Dear. There's no simple answer to your question. I just know that when Albert got home that night, he was terribly upset. After he told me what happened, he asked me never to bring it up again; so, I didn't. To me, it didn't seem like such a critical matter, but to him, it clearly was. He'd been through so much in his life and he asked so little of me, it wasn't hard for me to keep such a small secret for him. It sounds a bit crazy; I know. I'm sorry."

For a moment, it seemed as if the line went dead, but the pause was due to Esther Gorman trying to rally the courage to share something that had long ago been assigned to a burial place in her mind. Slowly and deliberately, the nightmare that her husband had lived through during his internment in Buchenwald began to unfold. "Every day, with an armed Nazi soldier riding shotgun, Albert was forced to drive a truck to a wooded area, miles from the concentration camp, to offload its cargo."

"Cargo from a concentration camp?" Sarah repeated as the horror of possibilities stormed through her mind. But she needed to know. "Esther? What kind of cargo?"

In the quietest possible voice, she murmured "Jews...dead Jews. He was ordered to remove all those poor souls that had died or, more accurately, were murdered overnight in the camp."

"Oh my God! That's absolute evil." Sarah shrieked.

"It was that absolute evil that forced my husband to drive at the point of a rifle, held by someone who needed no excuse to use it on Jews. There were live Jewish prisoners chained together in the back of every truck. Their job was to unload the pile of corpses when they reached their destination. Albert was forced to help the prisoners dump the naked, emaciated bodies into a pit and cover them with lye."

"Oh my God." Sarah gasped, "How did he not go completely mad?"

"I think maybe...it was because of one sliver of light..."

"...Light?"

"A sliver, Sarah. Only a sliver. It might not seem so illuminating to people today, but for those prisoners, there was a spark of hope the second that Albert signaled them to make their critical move."

"To do what?" Sarah whispered.

"*To save a life!*" She proclaimed.

Sarah shook her head in confusion. "But they were all dead!"

There was a hollow twinge of pride in Esther's voice as she recounted the eerie plan: "On each trip, the corpses were heaped on top of a single, naked, frightened-but-still-living soul whose role was to play dead. Once they were en route, the survivor would cautiously fight his way out from under the crush of what the Nazis classified as human trash. When the guard would nod off, in the actual shotgun seat, Albert would slow the truck down to avoid hitting a pre-set log or branch he 'happened upon' in the middle of the road. That manoeuvre would allow just enough of an advantage for the survivor to be quietly rolled off the truck and rescued by the partisans who had carefully placed the obstruction there.

"Measured against the six million lost, the numbers may be small, but not small to those whose lives were saved. After the war, many of the survivors found Albert through Jewish reunification organizations. They just wanted him to know they were alive and grateful. But he couldn't bear to think about it, so I wrote to them, for him, and he was free to keep his memories buried."

"I don't know what to say, Esther. All those years, all those wonderful happy stories you told us; all the candy and treats your husband gave us...I would never have known your lives were anything but magical."

"Being married to Albert, life was magical for me; but for him, the Holocaust was always there. So, you can imagine what went through his mind when he saw those bullies go after you and heard their hateful taunts. His fear of being caught helping a victim was too familiar. But he stayed and watched...and in the end, he came forward. He never would have let them hurt you."

Now, Sarah's disturbing dream fragments morphed into a more complete picture of Albert Gorman who had rescued her and protected her dignity through all those years.

"I really wish your husband was still here so I could tell him how grateful I am for his courage and compassion."

Sarah felt warmth and kindness filter through the phone line as Mrs. Gorman offered her sage advice. "You go ahead, my Dear. Tell me how grateful you are, because I intend to see him long before you do, and I'll be sure to let him know."

CHAPTER TWENTY-TWO

The question on many minds in the restless courtroom: 'Will the elucidating words of Laurie Cowan's closing remarks, determine Earl White's future?'

"The facts are there before you, Your Honour, etched in stone like the faces of Mount Rushmore. I've taken you on a trip through the crags and pitfalls of the Crown's inadequate attempt to indict my client..."

The judge frowned. "I'm giving you some rope here, Mr. Cowan, but you'd best avoid tightening a noose."

"Thank you, Your Honour. I'll keep that in mind. We showed you pictures of my client as the businessman, the family man, and other such Kodak moments, but do those pictures honestly represent who Earl White really is? When you look at him, what do you see? I'll tell you what I see:

"I see a man whose personality and character has likely alienated most everyone he's ever encountered in his lifetime. I would describe Earl White as vulgar and boorish. And I'll wager that many here would agree with that description and add a few adjectives of their own."

A muffled snigger rumbled through the courtroom, followed by gasps as Earl White attempted to scramble over the table. Richard latched onto the back of Earl's jacket and pulled him into his seat.

As the courtroom clamor escalated, the judge shattered the racket with an ear-piercing rap of his gavel and a verbal warning to the defence: "You, Mr. Toronto counsellor, are running out of my patience and your luck."

Laurie Cowan remained unflappable, "I apologize Your Honour, but if you will indulge me, I'll show you that I'm travelling in the right direction and will get there safely."

After releasing a loud and weary groan, Judge MacMillan muttered his permission for the defence to proceed.

"...Your Honour, I want to reiterate your own words when you described your job here, as 'having to make an informed decision based on the evidence presented.' If you do that, Sir, then given the unreliable testimonies offered by the witnesses, and the lack of any physical evidence presented by the Crown, then I'm confident you will allow my client to return to his work and the community that needs him."

The judge grunted, lowered his glasses, and squinted at the counsellor. After a quiet moment of deliberation, he leaned back, and motioned for Laurie to continue.

Laurie nodded, then proceeded. "Now, we can probably agree that Mr. White doesn't fit the kindly image of Santa Claus, Moses, or Mother Theresa, but that doesn't make him guilty of the alleged charges. We are a civilized people, Your Honour, with a precious duty to uphold our laws. We don't have the luxury of locking up an individual just because we don't like or trust him. If that were the case, then half of our dentists and most of our politicians would spend their golden years in prison."

The courtroom vibrated with laughter while the judge managed to suppress his own impulse to join in. "Alright, alright, settle down. Continue, counsellor." He muttered.

"Thank you, Your Honour. We all watched as three of the seven convicted child molesters were paraded in here one-by-one from the Kingston Penitentiary, to serve as witnesses against their relative, Earl White. Their motivation was simply revenge against the one member of their family who had achieved incredible financial success in the business world. And after decades of living free off of the charity provided by Earl and his wife, the property on which they have squatted all this time was to be sold. It meant that the families, of those particular prisoners who still lived there, would have to leave. This, and only this, was the basis for the unfounded accusations against my client and the sole reason we are all in this uncomfortable position today. There was no evidence, no reliable witnesses, and no reasonable or probable grounds presented to justify an indictment of Earl White on these erroneous charges."

A low murmur spread through the room.

"In conclusion; I trust, there's no need for me to reiterate to this court, the tenet that: 'there's no tolerance for vengeance in the courtroom.' And that is because, we wisely leave that kind of payback to fate. So, Your Honour, when you review the lack of evidence presented by the Crown during this hearing, I know you'll consider the facts...and then the law. When you do that, Sir, then, with the words 'Mr. White you are free to go,' I believe the law will have prevailed."

All present assumed that Judge MacMillan would dismiss the court early, but instead, he called for a lunch break and ordered the court to reconvene in a half-hour.

* * *

Thankfully, there was no invitation for Sarah to break bread with Earl White during the recess. She wanted to be able to grab a quick bite and digest it. However, by the time she cleared out of the courtroom and emerged from the ladies' room, there was only enough time left to devour a stale granola bar she found at the bottom of her purse. After one bite, she tossed the inedible bar into the trash and headed back toward the courtroom. On her approach, she found Wesley leaning against the door frame, wearing a smug grin. "I love to see you speechless, my dear." He chortled.

Her delight was confirmed by the spontaneous bear hug she delivered. "How did you get here, Wes?"

He emerged from the hug, still smiling, "I drove."

"On your own?"

"Yup. I wanted to hear this fancy-pants lawyer, and there was no way I was paying for a taxi, so I drove. And you know what? It was easy. Thanks to my kids, I've become such a coward about driving. They almost had me convinced I'm too old and feeble to drive. I think, they'd honestly feel more comfortable if I was in a nursing home."

"And miss all this fun?" Sarah giggled. "You did get here in time, I hope?"

Wes nodded. "Yeah, I was here for the whole thing. I heard Richard's illustrious Toronto barrister sullying the good name of Earl White," he offered with a wry chuckle. "I was sitting in the gallery upstairs during his closing. I could see the Crown Attorney struggling to keep his head up, and I watched a Rorschach test pattern of sweat develop on the back of Richard's jacket."

The clanging courthouse bell signified that the break was over.

Everyone was in place except for the judge. Suddenly, the clerk marched in and announced: "Hear ye, hear ye, all parties. The judge is in his chambers weighing his decision. You have permission to leave the room; but you are asked to stay nearby."

Sarah growled like a wounded lion. "You've got to be kidding me!"

Wesley leaned in and muttered. "I know it's annoying, Sarah, but all we can do is wait. Wanna go down to the cafeteria for a quick cup of tea?"

Sarah smiled. "That's the best offer I've had all day. I only hope they have some edible food to go with that tea, 'cause I'm starving."

"Yeah, actually, me too. I guess driving here burned some calories."

The pair shared a chuckle as they rushed through the doors and down to the cafeteria.

Two cups of tea and a shared egg salad sandwich later, they heard the call over the intercom for all interested parties to return to the courtroom.

* * *

"All rise," The clerk shouted.

His Honour ambled to the bench and took up his position. He peered around the gallery, scanning the faces, finally focussing on the defence table where Richard, Earl, and Laurie sat stone silent. The judge hunched his shoulders and exhaled a gust of air before proceeding. "With due deliberation, I was able to arrive at a decision."

* * *

After a bit of a struggle, Mitch popped the champagne cork, poured four glasses, and politely made his exit.

"A toast," Richard announced, "to a topnotch lawyer."

"With a stomach of steel," Sarah added. "Laurie, may all your future clients be innocent."

"I'll drink to that," Laurie drolly agreed.

"Are you implying that our client isn't?" Richard asked without a hint of cynicism.

"Isn't what?" Sarah asked.

"Innocent," he replied.

Wes couldn't resist the impulse to join in. "Come on, Richard, you know full well that just 'cause the judge found insufficient evidence to proceed to trial, doesn't make Earl innocent!"

Sarah attempted to quell the smouldering fire she'd lit. "Richard, all I meant was, wouldn't it be nice to defend someone who doesn't make your teeth itch and your stomach turn? I'll bet even Laurie had repugnant feelings about his client, and yet he still did an admirable job."

Richard shrugged and offered a cock-eyed grin. "Okay, I get it, Sarah. But a little more compassion and a little less judgement would be appreciated. I think Earl's been vilified enough."

An uncomfortable pause hovered over the foursome for several minutes while Richard silently and slowly twirled his champagne glass between his palms. Finding his voice once again, he stammered. "Um, Sarah, uh, I know, no matter the decision, Earl still wanted you to interview him. But now that there's no blockbuster story for you, maybe we should just tell him, it's not worth your while. What do you think?"

Sarah studied him a moment. "Thanks, Richard. You could be right. But let me sleep on it."

Richard grew pale and sullen. "I'd feel better if I had your decision now. I'm sure Earl would want to know, one way or the other."

Observing his twitchiness, she crinkled her nose and replied. "Ya know, champagne goes directly to my brain, Richard; so, I can't think clearly about it right now. Hopefully, tomorrow the fog will lift, and I can let you know."

"Hey," Wes interjected, "I haven't made a toast yet, and tomorrow, Laurie will be on his way back to Toronto. So, I say tonight we should drink to Laurie and Richard for getting this thing over with... and more important, to the O'Brian, 'cause I'm starving and that tray of sizzling steak dinners coming our way is looking damn good to me..."

During dinner, Richard confided that he'd been representing Earl White since the day he graduated law school and planned to continue representing him.

As the evening was coming to an end, Sarah was working up the courage to ask Laurie if he would stay behind, because it would be her last opportunity to talk to him about Eleanor's situation. As fate would have it, just as she rallied the courage to ask, she heard Laurie's voice speaking her words. "Glad they've all left. Now, do you think we could stay and chat over a decaf or two?"

Thankfully, the influx of goosebumps that marched up her arms remained concealed under her long sleeves. She inhaled deeply and replied. "Sure. If you insist, I guess I could stay for a little while."

"Okay," he smiled, "in that case, for the record, I insist." With that, he raised his coffee cup toward the waiter, who rushed forward to refill both mugs before making a hasty exit.

Realizing this would likely be her last chance, Sarah drew a motivating breath and began. "Laurie, I've wanted to bring this issue up for a while, but the time was never right. However, since we're talking and you're leaving, could we talk about a legal issue that's time-sensitive, and not related to Earl White?"

He placed his clasped hands on the table and nodded. "Sarah, I'm happy not to even mention him, and we can talk about anything you like...as long as I also get to put an item on the agenda."

She stitched her brow, studied his face, and then extended her hand. "Great, it's a deal." They shook on it.

She spelled out the strange connections she'd made since her return to Prescott. She outlined the facts concerning Eleanor Miller's assault. She even ventured into accounts of the traumatic childhood revelations she'd been discovering through visits with old contacts and her unnerving dreams.

Laurie listened without comment until she finished. "I get the feeling that this Miller case is as much about you, as it is about your friend. Surely, this isn't about you imagining some guilt over this because that would be absurd!"

She shut her eyes, but her sadness was still discernible. She gathered her courage and plodded on.

"I know, guilt doesn't make logical sense. But nevertheless, I need to try to make it right for her. Laurie, I know in my gut, if you would take on the case, the outcome could be so promising."

He placed his hand on hers, shook his head, and offered a visceral shrug. "I'm sorry, Sarah, I want to help, I honestly want to, but I can't in good conscience make that kind of commitment. I've spent more time away on this Earl White hearing than was ever intended, and I really need to get back to make sure that my firm is still on solid ground."

Although she managed to conjure a feeble smile, words escaped her. He squeezed her hand and offered a wry chuckle. "Listen, kiddo, I can't afford to let my practice slip. Remember, I've got alimony to pay, and that brings me to my agenda item. Remember, we had a deal? I get to ask a question as well. So, here's mine: Can you afford to take all this time away from your writing and still pay your bills?"

She nodded and took a slow sip of coffee before responding. "Uh-huh. I've been writing my pieces for the Sentinel and faxing them from the Journal office every week, and odd as it may seem, I've been given more by-lines since I've been three hundred miles away than when I was three miles away."

He released a rich and sincere laugh that made him even more attractive. "So, Ms. Berman, notable journalist, you're actually richer for not being at work."

With a grin and a nod, Sarah concurred. "Of course, there's still the mess of my divorce to deal with when I get back; so, I guess you could say, I'm doing my best to avoid the inevitable."

"Well, my dear, many of us have lived through that hellish experience. On a scale of evil, from mayhem to murder, how bad can it be?"

She playfully stroked her chin like a cartoon villain. "Hmm, well, I don't like to measure...but if forced, I'd have to go with *Jeffrey Dahmer* bad." She quipped.

"That's quite the yardstick, Sarah," Laurie noted as he flashed a fleeting smile and continued. "Still, in all seriousness, I've found that really good friends can help you gain perspective on the situation."

She slowly lowered her hand. "Well, I haven't really opened up to anyone about my separation... except for my friend, Madeleine, who, by the way, saw my ex coming out of Simon Nathan's law office a few weeks ago. As you probably know, when it comes to divorce lawyers, Simon Nathan's more of the *Jack the Ripper* kind. I've been getting scary letters from him for weeks."

"Really? And what do these scary letters say?"

She shrugged and grunted. "Ugh. I have no idea what they say, 'cause I don't look at them. I just dump them into my briefcase, unopened. Come on, Laurie, do you think a legal-aid advocate could ever win against a *Jack the Ripper* lawyer?"

He leaned back in his chair, silently contemplating how to advise her without upsetting her. He forged ahead. "Sarah, please believe me when I repeat, you need friends to help you through this."

She shook her head decisively. "No. I don't want to drag people I care about through all this misery. Even my own kids chose to close off communications, rather than deal with it. And I don't want to find out that some of my friends have gone over to the dark side with my ex...or maybe worse, they don't really give a damn. I hear that nothing weeds out friends like a dirty divorce. And in the end, it's always the spouse with the deepest pockets and the deadliest lawyer that wins. That is definitely not me. The truth is, Laurie, after seeing you in court, I'd be begging you to help me...if I was a rapist, thief, murderer, or a victim of any of those crimes; but thankfully I'm not...and since you're not a divorce lawyer..."

"No, I'm not." He reaffirmed. "But we have a sharp, young divorce attorney in our firm. Let me speak to him and see if we can do something for you that won't cost you your organs?"

"I really appreciate the offer, but I can't think about that right now. I have too much to deal with." She lowered her eyes to focus on her clinched hands.

Laurie shrugged in exasperation.

She glanced up for a second. "I'll be okay," she implied with little conviction before returning her gaze to her knuckles.

"No, Sarah, you won't. You're hiding in that denial place, and you know it's a temporary residence. If you don't open and respond to the lawyer's letters you've been getting, no matter how scary you might think they are, I assure you, you'll find out the hard way that in-denial isn't a safe place to hide."

Sarah remained silent as she continued to study the anatomy of her fingers.

He placed his hand on top of hers again. She warily glanced at the entwined hands, then met his eyes.

"Please, Sarah, let me call Jason Fine and see if he'll act on your behalf. He's young, but he's going to be the best damn divorce lawyer in town, and he could use the rehearsal. Let me call him."

With a subtle shake of her head, she stood her ground.

"Damn it, Sarah, do you want to see your ex take everything?"

Her eyes began to fill with the tears she'd been attempting to hold back. "He already has!" She woefully lamented.

Laurie shook his head sorrowfully and leaned forward. "You think so? You have no idea what he can take from you. He's just getting started. Have you tried to reason with your kids?"

She shook her head and looked down again. "Not really."

"Yeah, I thought as much."

She picked up her coffee spoon and studied it, as if there were answers hiding deep within its polished bowl. "Well, Rona's been in Israel for over a year...and Jordie stayed at Dalhousie, 'cause he had a summer job there before his fall semester began...and I only moved out of the house a few months ago, so..." she shrugged as she surreptitiously wiped away a defiant tear.

"Sarah, your kids may be on the other side of the world, but if they're not communicating with you while he is, they're only getting one side of the story."

Catching and disposing of another tear, Sarah murmured. "You're right, they are. Saul flew around the world to see them and make sure they heard it all from him first. Since then, I barely hear from them. I call, but they often don't answer. I leave messages and they don't reply...or they'll leave monosyllabic messages at my Toronto apartment even though they know I'm here, and they know how to reach me. So, what in hell can I do?" She asked as she tossed the spoon onto the table and folded her arms in defiance.

Laurie allowed a slight snicker to escape. "Ya know, Sarah, they don't give out Nobel Prizes for achievement in divorce; and God didn't send down a divorce manual from Sinai either. But people get through it, and so will you. Hey, who knows? Maybe it won't end in divorce. Maybe there's a way you can still work it out with him."

Sarah barked out a guffaw. "You think? And who'll get custody of Saul's lovechild?"

"Huh? what?" Laurie's stunned expression might have seemed comical had the situation been less dire. "There's a love-child?"

She lifted her chin to reveal a smug sneer. "Oh, yeah, that was the big surprise I discovered on my last trip home. Still think we'll work it out?"

He leaned in close to offer his advice. "Please listen to me. I'm more convinced now, than I was a half-hour ago, that you need to get that bastard before he gets you! Please do us both a favour and call Jason Fine. And then call or write your kids again."

She nodded and smiled and patted away another determined tear. "Okay."

He smiled broadly and toasted her with his empty cup.

She raised hers to meet his. Then as an afterthought, she asked, "By the way, Laurie, what was the question on your agenda?"

"We just covered it. But I do have another one."

"Uh-uh, we agreed on one." She simpered.

"I just want to know; are you really okay?"

She wobbled her head and chuckled. "Sure, of course I am."

"I'm trying hard to believe you." He jibed.

"To be frank, I think this bizarre small-town adventure just caught up with me tonight. But honestly,

I'm fine." She replied in as cheery a voice as she could muster.

"All right then, I'll take you at your word. Listen, it's after ten and I have to leave early tomorrow, so I better say goodnight." With that, he smiled, politely kissed her cheek, and exited.

As she watched him leave, Sarah felt her heart sink as her blockade against an assault of tears crumbled, and the flood surged.

* * *

A rapping at a hotel room door after midnight is an unnerving event, especially when the door doesn't have a peephole.

Do I ignore the tapping and hope the intruder will move on to the next suite? And if he does rob or rape my neighbour, can I live with that? Or do I ask who it is, thereby letting the interloper know I'm here?

Sarah rose from her bed and slipped on her robe, She picked up a large ginger ale bottle and raised it above her head as she shouted at the locked door: "Yes?"

"I'm sorry to bother you, Sarah. Should I go back to my room and call you instead?" Laurie whispered.

"No, of course not...can you wait two minutes?"

"Sure."

She ran to the washroom, sloshed a mouthful of Listerine, pinched her cheeks, fluffed her hair, and returned.

"Come in," she whispered as she held the door open.

"I know this is really insane. I tried to sleep, but I couldn't shut my brain off. I really have to talk to you."

A wave of excitement rippled through Sarah as she nodded toward a chair at the table. He sat and she settled into another across from him.

"You have unresolved issues you need to address before you can get through this divorce, Sarah. I'd hate to see you destroyed by your ex. You have so much potential, but you can't reach it while you're dealing with the marital terrorism you're going to face. Please, let me talk to Jason for you."

His offer was like a splash of ice water that froze Sarah's romantic fantasy.

"Please, Sarah. I would hate to see you get screwed."

Her mind was swimming with cheeky comebacks, but instead, she addressed his generous offer.

"You're right, Laurie. I do need help. So yes, a thousand times yes, and I thank you from the bottom of my heart."

"Okay, then give me the lawyer's letters you've been stashing away, and anything else you have on hand concerning the pending divorce. Then you won't have to think about it 'til you get back to the city. In the meantime, I'll have Jason look them over and get a head start. He'll likely need to call you. Is that okay?"

She nodded and proceeded to toss the correspondence into a shopping bag and hand it over. Laurie wrapped his hand around the handle.

"So, now that we got that out of the way, would you object to me kissing you goodbye, properly? Because I've also been thinking about that all night. I mean, none of that cheek-brushing stuff, okay?"

She blushed. "Sure, um...I mean..."

He placed the bag on the chair. The two stood gazing into each other's eyes, motionless for seconds. Slowly, and gently they were drawn into an embrace that culminated in a tender and lengthy kiss. Sarah couldn't recall ever feeling such a thrilling impact from just one, lingering kiss.

The embrace ended, and her Harlequin hero started toward the door. He turned back and smiled. "I don't want to appear greedy but...how about 'one more for the road?'"

Thrown by the thrill of it all, she tried her best to appear coolheaded. "Sure, as long as I don't have to sing it."

He stepped closer and smiled. "I have confidence in you, Sarah, I'll bet you could sing the hell out of it."

"I'm afraid you'd lose that bet." She shyly whispered.

Inch by inch, he drew her toward him. She gazed into his sapphire blue eyes and ultimately melted into his comforting embrace. While the refrain of *one more for the road,* played on a loop in her mind, his fingertips gently traced her lips. Every cell in her body tingled with excitement.

Long after he'd left, Sarah still felt the imprint of his warm hands on her back. She inhaled the faint scent of his cologne on her robe and recalled his resonant whisper: "I've thought about holding you like this since the first day we met, but I had to stay focused. Honestly, it was worth the wait. Goodnight, Sarah Klein."

Many panicky questions dive-bombed her brain as she closed the door behind him and realized she might never see him again.

CHAPTER TWENTY-THREE

There was a palpable shift in the tenor of Prescott as morning approached.

Sarah slipped out of bed and over to the misty windows, only to discover that the milky coating was not erasable. Through the night, a dense fog had cast a grey patina over the entire town, obscuring even the orange neon Perkins sign across the street.

Nevertheless, the opaque haze brightened Sarah's outlook for the day as she assumed that Laurie would be grounded in Prescott until it lifted. She showered and applied her makeup, ready to join him for breakfast whenever he got around to calling.

At 7:45, as she glided the last brush stroke through her hair, the phone rang.

With a racing heart, she snapped up the receiver.

"Hi there." She purred.

"Mrs. Berman, it's Earl White." Assaulted by the unnerving sound of his voice, Sarah twisted and tightened the sash on her robe.

"I called a few times last night, but ya didn't answer and there was some new guy at the desk, and he said to call back in the mornin'. I think you and me should get together 'n talk about my story yer writin', okay?"

Her spine stiffened as she delivered, her response. "Mr. White, since it's all over, I just can't devote any more of my time to your story."

"It ain't fuckin' over. Now ya really got somethin' to write about. I mean, them assholes thought they could ruin me, but they didn't do shit to me, did they? So, now it's my turn, and I wanna give ya a real good story about how them animals tried ta take revenge on an innocent man."

An eerie shiver motivated her to bring the call to a speedy end. "I really need to think about it, Mr. White."

"Wait just a minute would ya?" he snarled. She didn't respond but remained on the line during the tense pause. "My wife wants ya to come by our house for a drink. She'd like to meet ya."

"Well, thank your wife for me. I have your number, so I'll try and get back to you."

He growled, "Suit yourself," and abruptly hung up.

Sarah put down the phone and took a deep breath.

She gazed through the front window and spotted a sunbeam waltzing between the clouds, lifting the fog like a venetian blind. It was closing in on 8:00 a.m. and there was no phone call from Laurie. Sarah lamented, *"Now he's on his way back to his wonderful life and out of my questionable one."*

A hot chill rumbled through her as she removed her robe, pulled on her socks and sweatsuit, and dissolved onto the bed.

Who could she dare to share her personal soap opera with at 7:58 in the morning? Madeleine wasn't a morning person, and up until now, Sarah hadn't bothered to confide in any of her other friends back home. She hadn't even told Anna that she was separated. Airing her dirty laundry with new-found acquaintances in Prescott didn't feel comfortable. So, Laurie was right again. She had isolated herself, and now needed the very friends she'd excluded.

While she waited for room service to deliver her breakfast, she removed her notes and files and spread them out across her bed.

From the day she arrived in Prescott and experienced her first fragmented nightmare, she'd developed the habit of jotting down notes about every odd experience, strange comment, terrifying dream, or unfortunate mishap that occurred each day. The majority were related to Eleanor Miller or the Earl White case. Still, there were also the revelations she experienced in Montreal, but they were mismatched ramblings that seemed to go nowhere.

She continued to stare blankly at the notes until she was interrupted by a knock at the door. An unfamiliar voice called out, "Room service, Ma'am."

The fact that a strange new face delivered her muffins and coffee added to Sarah's sense of isolation and sadness. She missed the chitchat she shared with Mitch, and now she felt deprived of even that small pleasure.

The same stranger returned later to take away the tray with the uneaten muffin and pot of cold coffee.

He stopped short of her door, returned, and handed her two folded pink notes. "Sorry, Ma'am. I forgot to give you these before."

She nodded, accepted the messages, and closed the door behind him.

She flipped open the first message.

Hi Sarah.

It's 5:45 a.m. The fog will be lifting soon, so I'm getting a head start. Please call when you need to, or even just want to talk. If I don't hear from you, I have your number.

Thanks for opening your door.

Laurie

P.S. I care about you, so be careful out there, and please...try your kids again.

* * *

She grinned, closed her eyes, then threw open her door and shouted down the hall, "Hey, hold up a minute. What's your name?"

"Uh, Freddy."

"Well, Freddy, can you bring that tray back? I'm feeling kind of hungry now. No, you know what? Take it away, please, but when you get the chance, bring me a fresh pot of hot coffee and a couple of soft-poached eggs and buttered burnt toast."

She glided to the sofa and flopped down, suddenly awestruck by the idea that her mood could change so drastically in the time it took to open her front door.

She stopped rereading Laurie's note just long enough to realize she was still holding a second message in her hand:

Mrs. Berman,

I've located the Stutstown school pictures you were after. You can drop by and pick them up later this morning if you're still interested.

Helen Drummond,
Head Librarian

* * *

By eleven o'clock on that brightly shining morning, Sarah was cruising toward the Prescott library. Upon her arrival, Head Librarian Helen Drummond held up a package labelled, Mrs. S. Berman. "Ma'am, 'll need your signature and at least one piece of photo identification before I can hand it over," she insisted.

"But Mrs. Drummond, you know it's me. I was right here with the police officer. Don't you remember?"

"I'm not senile, Ma'am. Of course, I remember." The librarian groused as she pushed a document across the reception desk toward Sarah. "I follow the rules, Mrs. Berman; if that's who you are." She quipped.

Sarah rapidly scribbled her name, flashed her driver's license, picked up the package, and scurried back to the hotel.

She opened the thick envelope and withdrew a stack of student photos and a paper bearing a list of students' names.

She scrutinized the rogues' gallery of mugshots from Stutstown Secondary, moved the images around like puzzle pieces hoping that a pattern, a name, a face, some clue would emerge. She slid an enhanced photo of the Stutstown gang into place beside a headshot. She took a sip of water, inhaled, and turned the photo over. The faded name on the back was, Zane Fergusson. The "flame thrower" in the infamous snapshot was Zane Fergusson!

Sarah rifled through the rest of the pictures, desperate to find a mugshot that would match the second figure.

"Bill Connell has to be wrong about Earl White. He's got to be in the snapshot!"

She muttered. A raw shudder unnerved her as she suddenly realised, she would have to bear another encounter with Zane Fergusson.

* * *

Standing tall behind Sarah, Ray cast an imposing shadow; but Zane Fergusson showed no sign he was intimidated. With ghoulish eyes, he ogled Sarah like one might view a stud horse on the auction block.

"Hah! Yer back. Ya couldn't help yourself, eh, Lady? Yer jist dyin' fer a piece o' old Zane, huh?" His diabolical laugh waned as Sarah ignored his taunts. Still, it didn't keep him from trying.

"Are you screwin' this big dick? Or did ya jist bring 'im along ta make me jealous?" He slapped his hands together and guffawed like a donkey. In spite of his vile efforts, Sarah remained remarkably calm.

"Obviously, I have no authority to offer you any deals, Mr. Fergusson, but I have something you might like to hear. Are you interested?"

His expression changed from smug to curious as he leaned forward expectantly. "Well, Lady, I ain't heard nothin' yet."

"Okay, here it is. You've made it perfectly clear that you despise Earl White. Well, I have solid information that tells me, if you were to cooperate, there's a chance he could still become your cellmate. Isn't that right, Officer?"

Ray nodded and grunted: "Mm-hm."

A tantalizing image of Earl being dropped like a rat into his trap elicited a wide, putrefied smile from the prisoner.

Acting against her conscience, Sarah proposed a modest Faustian bargain. "Mr. Fergusson, if you cooperate, and tell me what I want to know for my story, I'll agree to keep secret whatever parts you don't want me to make public."

Snot spewed from Zane's nostrils as he erupted in fury.

"Not a fuckin chance that secret's gonna land that asshole in here?" He rubbed his hands together like a gambler about to toss the dice; then he folded his arms and sat back ramrod straight. "No deal. No way in hell!" He Hollered.

The dumbfounded look on Sarah's face, both assured and amused the offender. He chortled as a surge of power rushed through him. "Ah, yer not so smart now, are ya, Lady? Go ahead, ask your cop buddy there, he'll tell ya, I'm already in fer a long stretch, and I ain't got nothin' to lose. So, all what I tell ya, ya damn well better use against 'im. No fuckin' secrets! Now, turn on that goddamn tape machine or there's no fuckin' deal!"

"Okay, you win," she agreed while stifling a sardonic grin. She turned on the tape recorder and iterated. "I promise, Mr. Fergusson, at your insistence, it's all going to be on tape. Nothing you tell me will be kept secret, am I right?"

"Yeah, yer absolutely right about that. No secrets! That's more like it." Zane crowed into the recorder. "Now we know who's boss around here."

Sarah ignored his misogynist gibe and held a photograph up against the glass.

"Recognize anyone?"

"Sure. That handsome guy right there, that's me; and don't waste yer time lookin' for the guy standin' beside me, that's my cousin, Dwayne Berger. He died some years back. They say it was from a heart attack when his house burned down, but I say his innards got pickled from all that goddamn rubbin' alcohol he was pourin' down his gullet. He was lucky he dropped dead, 'cause that asshole sure as hell woulda been the first one they dumped in here. Funny, eh? That there picture was probably one o' them few times Earl was the one snappin' 'em instead o' me."

A tremble coursed through Sarah as a stunning revelation hurtled through her mind. *Earl White was in the picture after all*!

Without a pause, Zane continued to unload his arsenal of information while a new boost of empowerment bolstered Sarah's confidence.

"Yeah, big shit Earl was the head honcho, and I was stuck with the camera, 'cause he always wanted pictures of hisself. He used to brag...one day, they'd make a big iron statue o' him, and everybody'd be kissin' his metal ass. I never thought much of it before, but takin' pictures is part o' why I got sent up, so I owe the bastard fer that, too."

Sarah waded cautiously into the morass that was the Eleanor Miller incident. "I take it, Earl's quite the leader huh? So, was he also the head honcho in the rape of that Miller girl?"

A smarmy grin spread across the prisoner's face. "Sure, you bet he was. But ya don't know why he did it, do ya?"

She utilized super self control to maintain as objective a reaction as possible. "Nope, I don't. Do you?"

Without hesitation and with insidious relish, the offender spit out the tale. "Ya see, Berger and me used to go with Earl to that Jew restaurant, ta check out that slut's huge knockers, an' razz the owners. We'd ask 'em for a glass o' hog juice or pig testicle stew, just to piss 'em off. It was hilarious. But jist when we'd start havin' some fun, that big-mouth, Jew-bitch'd give us a hard time. Her folks knew their place. They kept their mouths shut. But she always had ta start up: 'Leave us alone.' 'Get out of our restaurant.' 'I'll call the police.'" He mocked, in a shrill, whiny voice.

"We had about enough of her shit. Earl and Berger weren't takin' no crap from no Christ-killer Jew, that's fer sure. We watched her a lot. We knew when she headed home. But we didn't go there that Saturday night. Nope. Around nine, we waited by the bushes in her backyard. Earl said it was our duty ta let them Jews know whose country they was livin' in. He said, we was gonna push her around a bit. Ya know, scare the bejezus outta her, eh? It sounded like fun ta me." He snorted like a bull. He leaned back in his chair, inspecting his grungy fingers while the visitors sat stone-still, waiting for him to continue. His eyes remained fixed on them while he chewed on a craggy hangnail and spat the dead skin onto the floor.

"Oh yeah, I got lost there fer a second, but I remember now. She came by, and things got crazy. I was scared shitless, 'cause I didn't have no flash bulbs with me, which meant Earl was likely gonna beat the crap outta me again.

"I guess Earl thought she was gonna scream, so he shoved his fuckin' glove in her mouth ta shut 'er up, and then I pulled the sack over her head like he said ta.

"Now, soon's we grabbed 'er, I said, we had the wrong bitch, but Earl swore it was her. I tole 'em, when I was pullin' that sack down, I thought I felt a goddamn cross hangin' on her neck. But asshole, Berger, says, it's just a key." Zane paused and turned his attention back to his fingers.

Sarah, edged forward in her seat, preparing to urge him on. Anticipating her move, Ray tapped her on the back and gave a quick, subtle, shake of his head. She shimmied back in her seat and waited.

The convict slowly raised his head, revealing a pale and twitchy guise. "Jist so's youse know, I helped hold her down; but I didn't fuck 'er. I told Earl straight out, 'I did the bag for ya, but I'm not doin' nothin' else, 'cause I'm thinkin' we got the wrong one.' Earl laughed and tole me 'That's why we put the bag over her head, asshole, 'cause then it don't matter.'" Zane shook his head, slapped his knee, and laughed as if he'd just heard the funniest joke ever told. Neither Sarah nor Ray moved a muscle.

"Oh yeah, man, after Berger got done with her, Earl got on her again. But that time, she weren't kickin' or squirmin' no more. Nope. All of a sudden, big honcho Earl sounds freakin' terrified. He jumps up...zips his pants...and croaks, 'she's dead as dead gets!' That's when we all took off like piss in the wind.

"But we heard a rumour later, she weren't dead. Maybe, she passed out from all the excitement." Zane Fergusson's crude cackle reverberated in Sarah's head like a scream to a migraine.

"And in case you're wonderin', I didn't get no pictures o' the night Earl and Berger did that bitch, 'cause it was pitch black and, like I tole ya, I forgot the flash bulbs." He offered an innocent shrug, like a kid who forgot to pick up milk at the corner store for his mom.

"Oh, and don't think I didn't get my ass kicked by Earl fer that. Ya know how many pictures I snapped for that prick? But it was never enough. I took piles o' pictures o' Earl. Ya want 'em? I got a whole shit load of 'em he don't know nothin' about. Ya remember my loudmouth wife, crowin' in the courthouse? Well, if you get out there ta my house, them pictures is all yours. She'll have 'em waitin' for ya, I guarantee it. If I find out that Earl got free, 'cause o' that stupid bitch, she better do everythin' she can to get 'im convicted now, if she knows what's good fer her."

* * *

Ray and Sarah inhaled deeply as they headed back across the prison yard. Even the exhaust fumes that lingered over the parking lot smelled better than the toxic stench that surrounded Zane Fergusson.

On the way back, they listened to bits of the gruesome interview on the tape. It was demoralizing to have to admit that their evidence was based on the word of a convicted child molester who had repeatedly sworn vengeance on Earl White.

"I doubt that any judge in the country would open a thirty-five-year-old cold-case with Zane Fergusson's testimony, as the only evidence," Sarah asserted.

"Maybe. But his wife was a credible witness, wasn't she? I think the eviction notice gives her until mid-December to move out, so let's call her up and pay her a visit before the moving trucks arrive." Ray urged.

* * *

Ray's squad car drove along the country road while Sarah tried not to show the fear bubbling up inside her. Two fresh, young Rookies, Dan, and Wally, sat in the back, quietly taunting each other, just for fun.

The dilapidated old house was inconveniently situated at hell's end of an infinite dirt road, several miles north of Prescott. The crumbling stone dwelling loitered shamelessly on a barren field that resembled a junkyard, complete with heaps of rusted-out farm machinery, broken appliances, and a battered, old pickup truck.

The car came to a stop on a patch of gravel. The Rookies jumped out and stood by dutifully, waiting for orders.

Before opening his door, Ray turned to Sarah; "Listen, you don't have to come in if you're feeling nervous. I can run in, get the stuff and be back in a jiff. You can stay in here, or out there with Laurel and Hardy. I mean, I understand, this might freak you out."

Sarah scowled at the audacity of the suggestion. "Hey, if I can sit across from the likes of Earl and Zane, that sad guttersnipe of a wife isn't gonna devastate me." With that, she gathered up her handbag, hoisted it onto her shoulder, and reached for the door handle.

"Wait, Sarah, I gotta ask: Ya don't know, do ya?"

"Know what?"

"Sorry, but I think, you really don't know what I'm talkin' about."

Sarah felt her heart drumming more rapidly. "Why are you acting so weird? What don't I know?"

"Uh, this is the house where the S & G crimes took place."

"Holy crap. Oh my God! Okay, this is definitely creepy...and a little fascinating...but more... creepy." Sarah confessed.

He raised his eyebrows, waiting for her to remove her hand from the door handle, but there it remained.

"You sure you're good to go?"

She opened the car door, turned her face toward him and replied. "Absolutely! This is how I begin to earn my journalist's stripes." She stepped out confidently and closed the door as Ray emerged from the driver's side.

"You two newbies, stay out here and watch for any incoming traffic. I mean we don't want any surprises, understand?" Both novices responded with a sharp salute and a, "Yes, Sir."

As Ray and Sarah trudged up the rickety steps to the front door, they saw Bindy Fergusson waiting in the entranceway, looking even more frail than she did in the witness box. Once inside, she shuffled along the shabby corridor, looking back to make sure they were following. She halted at a slagheap that might once have been a living room.

"Why don'tcha both have a seat?" She timidly suggested.

The visitors surveyed the space, looking for a safe place to sit. They each found a wooden seat that wasn't piled high with clutter and hopefully wasn't infested with bugs or rodents. Seeing that the visitors had settled on an orange crate and end table, Bindy Fergusson sat on a well-worn fabric chair bursting at its seams with dirty, yellowed wadding. They all sat in silence for several uncomfortable seconds before the lady of the house spoke up.

"Would youse like a drink? I made hot chocolate when you called ta say ya was comin'. I just have to heat it up if ya want it."

"Oh, that's kind of you, but no thanks, Mrs. Fergusson." Sarah hastily responded. "I'm sorry, but we don't have a lot of time. Your husband said you might have something to give us?"

"Yup, I'll get it...but I can't get it down from the attic on my own. The cop better go up there with me."

Sarah cringed as every horror-film-trailer she'd ever seen, flashed through her mind. She cast a bewildered glance at Ray as he rose and quietly followed the woman to the staircase leaving Sarah alone and contemplating what horror show she might face in their absence.

* * *

Outside, in the biting cold, officers Dan Murdoch and Wally Brown were being entertained by three vicious, skeletal cats that were brawling over a small, roundish object. When Officer Dan attempted to approach the battlefield to get a closer look, two fierce mangy cats hissed at him while the other emaciated tabby snatched up the object in its snaggy teeth, and carried it like a prize catch over to the woodshed.

Wally seemed amused by Dan's keen interest in the action sequence, but not curious enough to walk his pudgy girth across the yard. He stayed back at a safe distance, unwrapped a *Milky Way* bar, and entertained himself chewing, and taunting from the bleachers. "Hey, Dan, you that hard up for action that you get off on watchin' mangy pussies fight over a piece o' trash? Listen, if you're really desperate for a thrill, we'll try and find ya a kinky hooker or maybe a cockfight, later."

Dan waved him away. "Wally, shut up! I'm studyin' the situation."

Wally rolled his eyes. "Oh, pardon me, Sherlock."

"Can-it, asshole." He looked back at Wally and frowned. "Seriously, what does that thing look like to you? It's not a golf ball, it's not round enough. A marrowbone maybe?"

Wally licked the chocolate wrapper and tossed it on the ground. "How in hell should I know? Do I look like a butcher?"

"Nope. More like a hind o' beef. Git over here an' look closer, for shit's sake! Don't be such a pussy. It won't bite ya."

Wally stood his ground and refused to budge. Dan moved in closer.

"Jesus, it's really creepy. It looks more like a nose with a beard attached."

"A nose? Are you shittin' me?" He waddled hastily over for a closer look.

"Murdoch, you're such a jerk. That's one o' them troll thingies that the kids hang from their rearviews like dice. Are you afraid o' the big bad troll?"

Just as Dan was about to lunge for the object, the vengeful tabby swatted it toward the shed with a powerful right paw, while another scruffy cat propelled it into a small, black hole.

* * *

Bindy emerged from the attic balancing a grey shoebox and panting, as she shakily maneuvered her way down the ladder. Ray followed close behind, lugging a large, sealed, wooden crate, and breathing more heavily than his fit physique would have predicted.

Ray followed Bindy back to the living room, where they each rested their cargo in the middle of the floor.

Catching Sarah's bewildered look, Bindy explained. "Most o' the crap up there, came from Arvin's place. That's Zane's brother. When Arvin went to prison with the others, his wife got thrown outta their house, so he told her to store any stuff they didn't need over here. Then, this place became the dumpin' hole for everybody. Even his cousin Berger's, broke-down furniture and shit ended up there after he was gone, 'cause none o' his family had a house to keep it in. I didn't wanna be caught messin' with any o' their crap. Listen, Zane said to give ya the shoebox, but ya may as well take the crate too. I sure as hell don't need no more junk to have ta move around when we leave. Just do me a big favour and don't bring any of it back."

Ray smiled and assured her, "Don't worry, Ma'am, Zane promised it to us, and we won't be returning it."

Sarah lowered her head to hide the cheeky smile that crossed her lips. "Well, we better get going, Mrs.

Fergusson. Thanks for your trouble. You take care now." She bent down and picked up the shoebox. Ray hoisted the crate onto his hip and nodded to the hostess. "Good day, Ma'am."

There was no hiding the hint of a genuine smile that appeared on Bindy's lips as she bade the visitors a warm, "Goodbye now. It was nice ta have company for a few minutes, ya know," and she led them out the door.

When Ray whistled for the Rookies, the cats scrambled for cover as if it was hunting season in the Ozarks.

Before submitting to the whistle, Dan took one last look toward the black hole that had sucked up the troll-like object. By the time Walley reached the car, Ray had handed the crate over to Dan and was starting the car. Sarah settled into the front seat with the taped-up shoebox on her lap. When Dan opened the trunk to set the crate inside, he spotted a box of dolls tucked away in the back corner. He scratched his head, smirked, then closed the trunk and quietly slid into the back seat next to Wally.

They had barely travelled a few yards before Dan's silent curiosity became vocal. "Ray, what the heck are those dolls doin' in the trunk?"

Ray offered a very abridged version of events surrounding the dolls. As he spoke, Dan's ruddy complexion turned ashen.

"Stop Chief. Pull over, please." Dan howled.

Ray did as asked, then turned to his Rookie. "Newbie, I hope you have a better than good explanation for this.

"Yes, sir, I think I might. Me and Wally saw a bunch o' cats brawlin' over 'a toy troll.' But after seein' whatcha got in the trunk, I'm thinkin' it could be that doll's missin' head."

At sonic speed, Ray spun the car around and headed back to Bindy Fergusson's.

All four intruders sneaked past the stacks of firewood piled high against the woodshed. Ray shone his flashlight into the tiny, dark hole before casually dropping something into it. "Oh hell! See that? I accidentally dropped my key fob down there. Jeez, we're gonna have to dig it out." He theatrically declared.

The men pounded at the rigid ground with their nightsticks until it started to give way. Then, with great care and speed, they dug their fingers into the chilled earth and removed enough debris to make the hole big enough to investigate. Ray shone the flashlight into the space again, to be sure there were no unwelcome guests lurking inside. Satisfied that it was safe to engage, he reached in and retrieved his fob and the dismembered doll's head. They carefully filled in the hole, and, with the head in hand, returned to Prescott.

* * *

Later that evening, Ray arrived at Sarah's suite with a hot pizza and a cold six-pack of Pepsi most of which, they polished off in short order.

"Ray, since you've been so generous in providing my favourite *food-for-the-gods*, I'm prepared to martyr myself by looking through Zane Fergusson's shoebox of memorabilia...but no way am I doing it on my own. So, if you'll join me..."

Within seconds, Sarah had cleared away the greasy residue from dinner, Ray had opened the taped-up shoebox and began to deal the photos across the table like a game of "Go Fish."

There were black and white shots showing a teen-aged, Earl, applying a Karate kick to a garbage can, graffitying a window with profanity, and straddling a motorcycle while holding a beer and striking a pseudo-Brando pose. There were several shots of Earl and others cozying up to bimbos, or posing like Charles Atlas, but nothing jumped out as incriminating. They got to the bottom of the shoebox without a single revelation.

Sarah pouted and slumped back in her chair. "This was a total waste of time, Ray."

He nodded sympathetically. "Yeah, maybe. So, what do you say I bring up the wooden crate now?"

Sarah looked over at Ray, about to offer a feeble thumbs up, when a second thought occurred to her. "Wait. Nope. Uh-uh. First, you have to tell me what happened with Doug Fergusson. You rushed away, leaving me to wonder if maybe Earl was right? I mean, maybe you did lose it with Doug?" The words fell out of her mouth unplanned and unintended; and with one glance at the stoic cop's downcast eyes, she knew she'd perforated his pride. "I didn't mean to offend you, Ray, but try and see it from my position. There we were, having a deeply serious conversation, when you up and disappeared without so much as a 'see ya later.' I know the guy's objectionable, but you did take him in for questioning and then avoided telling me about it. So, what was I supposed to think?"

He rubbed his hands together, snuffed up a deep intake of air, and shrugged.

"Okay, I get it. You're pissed with me, but here's the thing; Yes, when I heard that Doug had been roughed up again, and I knew I didn't do it, I had to get back there before someone cleared away the evidence."

"Why didn't you just say that?" She pouted.

"Why? Because, if I told you, then you'd want to come with me, and I didn't think it was safe for you to be there. Anyway, when I got there, the door was open, and the place was as black as a skunk's ass. I found Doug cowering under the table...a total mess. I got him over to St. Gabriel's. He had a slew of lacerations, a bunch o' broken ribs, and gonads the size of baseballs. For sure, you didn't need to be there."

She cringed. "Whew! I couldn't agree more. Oh my God, the poor guy. Why would anyone think he deserved that kind of beating?"

"If Doug had just talked when I questioned him that morning, it probably woulda saved him a lot o' pain. Oh, and you were right, Doug says he's gonna press charges...but not against me."

"Then who?"

Ray scratched his head. "That's the sixty-four-dollar question. He's not ready to talk yet, but he promised that he'll call and tell me as soon as his balls are back to normal."

Sarah sat quietly chewing on her lower lip while she gathered her thoughts. "Okay, now what do you suggest we do?"

"I say we wait for breaking news on Doug's balls."

CHAPTER TWENTY-FOUR

Rising from another fitful sleep, Sarah dragged herself to the window to check on the weather. She was delighted to see virgin snow covering the streets like a candy floss eiderdown. In the sunlight, ice crystals burst into a milliard of ephemeral diamonds as shopkeepers filled their shovels with the sparkling treasure and stockpiled them at the curb.

In short order, Sarah was bundled up in winter attire and stepping sprightly along Main Street, crunching icy jewels under her Uggs.

Once inside the Journal office, her winter fantasy melted as she caught a glimpse of her limp hair and smudged mascara in the mirror.

"Hi guys. This damn, miserable slush...I'm a complete mess," she muttered as she grabbed a tissue and wiped the dark stains from under her eyes.

"You've gone soft on us," Wes teased. "Big cities can do that to ya. They turn robust, country folk into shiverin' wimps."

He continued his monologue while Sarah remained in front of the mirror, attempting to make herself presentable.

"Hell, even a hearty, old broad like Estelle McCall isn't fazed by a little snow. She made it down here with her walker first thing this mornin' to ask when I was gonna write a front-page story about how her clever son got his good friend, Earl, off scot-free." Wes recounted.

"Hey, you said Richard and Earl could never be friends, Wes, but clearly, Estelle disagrees. And doesn't mother know best?" She removed her coat and hung it on the hook. "I mean if age is an indicator of wisdom, then she should be a genius, right?" Her cheeky slight elicited a wide grin from her mentor. "Let's face facts, Wes," She asserted as she plopped into a chair beside an empty desk. "Richard has a brain and can put logical sentences together without using profanity as punctuation, whereas Earl is an ass..."

"Ah, Sarah," Wes interjected, "Can you believe that Estelle still runs her own house at ninety-somethin'? Anyway, here's some good news. She invited you and me to join her there for tea this afternoon." He paused and took note of Sarah's sober face. "Now, I didn't commit, 'cause of course, it's up to you...although, truth be told, you're such a grinch, I don't know what would possess you to say yes." He smirked as he settled back in his chair.

Sarah suddenly bobbed up and down in her seat and clapped with glee. "Yes!"

"What? Yes? Are ya kiddin' me?" Wes lurched forward and squinted at her as if he'd come upon an alien.

"Nope, dead serious. Let's pick up some chocolates and go have afternoon tea with the lonely, old busybody. Come on, Wes, for me? Call her, please."

He shrugged and nodded. "Uh, okay. Since you insist. I'll call her." He held back a grin as he placed the phone in front of him. "Now, I'm just going along to get you in the door. Once inside, I'm gonna sit quietly, drink tea and eat muffins, or whatever she serves. So, young lady, I hope you've got a bloody-good reason for pushing for this visit, and a damn good plan." He teased.

Sarah leaned forward slipping into a confident grin. "Oh, I do have a bloody good reason. I'm thinking; she's poked her nose into skeletons in this town's closets for decades, so maybe she can tell us where they can be found. And my plan is to bring along an array of those archival photos that'll hopefully trigger a memory or two."

"Flowers would work better." Wes mused.

* * *

"How thoughtful of you to bring me gifts," Estelle purred. "You go ahead and take off your damp things and hang 'em up on the hooks there an' wait just a minute while I run these goodies into the kitchen. Be right back."

With that, she gathered up the flowers and chocolates, and carried them away.

The guests followed her instructions and waited.

The hostess promptly returned, inspected her guests, and then instructed: "This way." With that terse order, they followed her into her elite, but antiquated. parlor.

"Now, you both take a seat an' make yourselves comfortable while I go and arrange your lovely flowers, Wesley."

"Can I help you with anything, Mrs. McCall?" Sarah courteously asked.

"No, Dear, I'm quite able to do for myself. But thank you for asking. Although, since you're the tallest one here, maybe you could take down that crystal vase from on top of that breakfront?"

"Certainly." She replied. She rolled up onto her toes, brought down the vessel; and carefully handed it to Estelle, who clasped both hands firmly around it and exited to the kitchen.

Sarah let out a sigh of relief and rolled her eyes toward Wes as she seated herself on a Victorian loveseat. Wes countered with one of his own audible sighs as he settled into a tapestry wing chair.

The hostess's absence gave the visitors the freedom to check out the space without appearing gauche. The room was festooned in doilies, bric-a-brac, and faded cut velvet, all of which reflected the age and financial stratum of its resident.

A framed photo on the mantel caught Sarah's eye. She rose to take a closer look at the image of a bespectacled young nerd.

"It's hard to tell, Wes, but that must be Richard." She proposed as she returned to her seat.

"Oh, yes, that certainly is my boy," Estelle burbled as she re-entered the room. "He was such a brilliant young thing, eh?" She preened as she placed the bright, yellow mums beside the photo. "But he was always too shy. Not like his older brother, Christopher, who never shied away from anybody. Nope, he'd talk to anyone, king, or peasant. I used to worry about Christopher gettin' in with the wrong kind, but I never had to worry about Richard. He was a real homebody."

"He may have slipped a tiny bit a time or two, but he was always a good boy." She shouted en route to the kitchen. She returned immediately with the chocolates on a beautiful, Wedgewood candy dish which she placed on the coffee table. "He knew to stay away from certain types. You know what I mean, right, Wesley?" She cast her eye in his direction and winked.

Wes shifted in his seat and bowed his head as he pondered how to respond without offending. "I'm not sure I do, Estelle. But please, enlighten us."

Fearing she understood exactly what Estelle meant, Sarah braced herself.

The old lady's shrill voice trailed behind her as she traipsed back to the kitchen. "I doubt you'd remember, Sarah, but years ago, there were lots of ungrateful newcomers that came to our town and tried to change things around here. It probably started back before you were even born; but they were here when you were growin' up, that's for sure."

Re-entering the parlor, pushing a rolling tea cart, Estelle paused and smugly pursed her lips at the sight of Sarah whose hands were clasped and pressed tightly under her chin.

The hostess stopped the cart beside Wesley's chair and fussed with the tea service. "Now, my dear, I don't want you to get the wrong impression. I'm quite sure your family was different. They were likely born in this country, and they probably worked hard for everything they got. And, as a matter of fact, it seemed they did pretty, darn well for themselves." She poured a cup of tea. "Actually, it's a well-known fact that the Jewish people always do well for themselves. But there were other types who never wanted to accept their position in line behind true Canadians. That's who I'm talkin' about." She handed Wes the cup and pushed a bowl of sugar cubes toward him. He politely refused with a subtle wave of his hand. He did, however, take two shortbread cookies from the plate she brandished.

The plate was then passed to Sarah, who sucked back her outrage over the bigoted drivel, and briskly replied, "No! Thank you."

A tactical smirk flashed across Estelle's face. "Suit yourself dearie. Just so you know, I made 'em myself...and it sure looks like Wesley's enjoyin' 'em."

Estelle returned the plate to the cart and offered Sarah a cup of tea. The visitor gave a wary shake of her head which did not go unnoticed by the hostess. "It's Earl Grey, my dear. Very British." Sarah managed a fixed smile as she reluctantly accepted the tea. "You know, Sarah, I've always felt that those Jewish people that came to our town after the war, were bloody lucky this country took 'em in. And I'm guessin' that's why they understood their place."

Sarah dropped two sugar cubes into her cup and stirred belligerently. "Other 'types?'" Sarah spat out the words. "Here, in Prescott? Just what other 'types' are you referring to?" She insisted.

"Hmm, other types, eh? Let's see." The old lady tapped her chin with her spindly finger while contemplating her answer. "Well, there was the Chinaman who ran the restaurant. Those people always pretend to be so accomodatin', but soon as ya turn your back, watch out. Then there was that Negra teacher who came here with his wife and those piccaninnies of his. Of course, he only lasted about a year. I heard the schoolboard had a real good talk with him, and he moved on. I'm sure there were others, but this old brain isn't as swift as it used to be."

In an attempt to head-off an angry escalation, Wes fabricated a frozen smile and cagily entered the conversation. "Estelle, I've been around near as long as you have, and I wanna help ya out here, but no one's readily coming to mind. Oh, wait, there was another immigrant family living here. I think the name was, uh, Panasar?" He casually tossed the hook, and now, it was up to Estelle to swallow the bait or let it swim by.

Her brows lifted and her cheeks turned rosy with delight. She bit. "That Indian family?" she managed to simultaneously sneer and grin as she spat out the words. "Hah! Some poor, white Canadian had to get fired from RCA Victor so that foreigner could take his job. There were lots of families that came over here after the war. They never even tried to speak our language, and there were plenty of people who thought that was plain disrespectful. But one-by-one, they moved away, and it was for the best. Those people never fit in."

Reva Leah Stern

"Did you ever have to deal with any of 'those people' in person, Mrs. McCall?" Sarah inquired, feigning wide-eyed virtue.

"I never had a reason to, my dear. I don't care for Chinese food. I always worry what they might be puttin' in it. My kids were both outta public school already when that Negra was teachin' there, so I never had to deal with that nonsense. I didn't really frequent the other two Jew-owned stores. No special reason, o' course. They just didn't ever seem to have the quality of product I was lookin' for. But I sometimes visited your father's place. His prices were surprisingly fair for a...a small town."

Sarah remained determined and focussed. "And the Indian family?" She continued.

"Oh, them? Never really met them." She shrugged but was unable to resist the urge to expound. "I'll tell ya what I think, though. I'd bet they were here for one reason only: and that was to make certain their daughter'd marry some unsuspecting white boy with big prospects, so her parents would be taken care of forever. That's how those people operate, ya know. They marry off a daughter to some rich Canadian, and then they move in with them for life." Satisfied with her revelation, she took a few silent sips of tea.

Sarah calmly broke the stillness. "Ah, I can see you were concerned about your sons falling into that trap, huh, Mrs. McCall?"

"Ah-ha, there it is, plain as day. Yup, it's clear you already got a hold o' the story. I can't imagine how, but I guess that's what journalists do." She looked at Wes, "Right, Wesley?"

"Oh, yeah, that's what we do alright, Estelle." He raised his teacup in a mock salute; a gibe she completely missed, as she raised her cup in compliance.

"Well, if the truth be known, my husband and I near died when we found out that Richard was seein' that girl behind our backs. Don't think we didn't put a stop to that real fast. As soon as he finished high school, we shipped him off to Montreal to live with his grandmother. Oh yeah, we settled him in early so he could get a head start on law school. Thank Jesus, we had the presence of mind to do that, or who knows where he'd be today! Any real Canadian would understand that."

Wes cleared his throat and attempted to shift the mood. "Estelle, you haven't changed a bit in all these years. Still a, a feisty broad."

She took a sip of tea. "Well thank you, Wesley. I just call 'em as I see 'em, that's all."

That's all? Sarah repeated in her head.

"So, Estelle," Wes continued, "Richard was actually steppin' out with that East Indian girl then, huh? Daisy, was it?"

"That's what she said her name was, but I can guarantee her real name was something no one could pronounce or spell. And yes, he was seein' her; behind our backs, of course."

"Hm, I never heard about that, Estelle."

"Well, of course ya didn't hear about it, Wesley. That was the idea. It was a terrible embarrassment, and not somethin' ya wanted to see in the town paper. I still can't figure how your young friend here heard about it." She grumbled.

Wes ignored the reference to Sarah and continued to probe. "Well, they were really young at the time."

She snorted, "Young and stupid is what they were. And how do you know how young they were?"

"Well, I know that the summer she turned fifteen, she was supposed to swim across the St. Lawrence in a race against an American, but she never made it, 'cause she drowned. So, fifteen would have been the oldest she ever got to be."

The old lady paused for a second; then decidedly, without a filter, continued to prattle on. "Yes, it was a terrible tragedy and I'm glad Richard was already in Montreal when it happened, so he didn't hear about it 'til all the hullaballoo died down. Ya couldn't help but feel sorry for the parents though...no matter who they were. You know, that Indian girl woulda made two hundred dollars if she'd won the race; and that was a fortune back then, eh Wesley? It sure was enough incentive for her parents to let her go out into the river alone to practice her swimmin'. Just so ya know, as a good Christian, I wouldn't have wished such a terrible end on anyone. It says in the scriptures, 'Jesus mourns the loss of any life...even beasts of burden...and we must too' no matter how we really feel."

Sarah's teacup began to rattle. Wes took it from her and set it on the table. Of course, the action didn't escape Estelle's watchful eye.

"Maybe your sugar is low, Dear. Would you like a cookie?"

"Oh, no thank you." Sarah replied with a paltry smile. Then as an afterthought, she added, "But, maybe you're right about my sugar, Mrs. McCall. I'll just have one of these." She zeroed in on the chocolates and selected one.

After a couple of nibbles, Sarah continued. "Huh, that seems to have done the trick. I guess you were right. I just needed a little sweetener to steady me."

Estelle smiled and nodded. "Well, emergency averted then, eh?"

"It seems so, Mrs. McCall." Sarah shifted in her chair and glanced over at Wes, hoping he'd jump in with his usual curmudgeonly candor and get the nonagenarian to open her floodgates. Wes pressed his lips together and folded his arms across his chest. The message was not lost on Sarah. She was on her own.

"I was wondering why you wanted to see us today, Mrs. McCall. I mean, I appreciate your time and the lovely tea you fixed for us, but if there's something you wanted me and Wesley to know, please don't let us leave here without telling us." Sarah reached for another chocolate while she waited for an answer.

Estelle set down her teacup, raised her head, and leered at Sarah. "You're quite correct, my dear. There is somethin' I want you to know." She sat up stiffly, never shifting her eyes from Sarah. "My Richard says you're writin' a story about Earl White. I found that ta be interesting. I'm hopin' we can count on it bein' a positive one, eh? That Earl is a wonderful man. He's been a good friend to Richard since...well, I can't even remember since when."

The old woman momentarily interrupted her glowing endorsement with an indignant harumph. After an uncomfortable moment of amplified tea sipping, she continued.

"Sorry for that little lapse there, but it just struck me that Earl was Richard's very first client when he graduated law school, and he's been loyal to my son ever since. I know there are people around here who don't like Earl; but that's 'cause they don't know 'im." The old lady shifted her focus to Wes, who was doing his level best to avoid eye contact. "Hmm, I'm sorry to say this, Wesley, but I'm beginning to think you're one of 'em, and that hurts me."

Unflinching, he offered a grin and some wry advice as he reached for another shortbread. "Estelle, it's best you leave me outta this. I'm not the one writing the article. I'm just along for the tea and goodies." He sat back and bit into the cookie.

She tsk-tsked at him like an old clucking hen. "Oh, sweet Jesus, Wesley, that's the point. You should be writin' it. Earl's one of us, and I got the feelin' this morning, that you have no intention of even reporting in the Prescott Journal about how he was almost railroaded and how my son saved 'im. Doesn't that deserve the full front page?"

"I assure you, Estelle, there'll be something in the paper. But I can't promise a full or front page. Listen, Earl got off scot-free, and now, Sarah here might be writing about it for a big national newspaper. Isn't that reward enough?"

Estelle grimaced as she struggled to keep her indignation under control. "Wesley, I mean no disrespect to this lady journalist." She shifted her focus to Sarah. "You may, at one time, have lived in this town, but you're not one of us." She sniffed the air as if searching for an odor before shifting her focus back to Wesley. "We have a certain code we live by here, and comin' from where she does, she no doubt has a very different code."

Sarah's red-hot cheeks and slow hissing between clenched teeth were indicators of a volcano about to erupt. Wes threw her a merciful glance; and after a few slow deep breaths, her temperature began to level off. In a quieter but higher octave, Sarah managed to squeak out a query, "And where is it I come from, if not here? And what code would that be, Mrs. McCall?"

"I just mean you're a city girl now. And Earl...well, he has strong Christian values. Not everyone's comfortable with that. That generous man donates plenty o' money to our church, and he comes to services whenever he can." Estelle shook her head in despair, "To accuse that good soul of bein' mixed up with those perverts, is a real crime. Richard says Earl's been nothin' but charitable to those unfortunate families, and this is how they repay him. Now, that's a tragedy. All I ask is for ya to be fair to Earl and to my son. You might want to talk to Richard about the real Earl White. Ya may see a very different side of him, and your story may take on a whole different point o' view."

Sarah forced a smile, lifted her bag from the floor, and wriggled to the edge of the seat. "Well, I'll take it under advisement." She stood up and hoisted the strap of her bag onto her shoulder. "Thank you for your hospitality, Mrs. McCall. You've given me a whole lot to think about. Wesley needs to get back to the Journal office now, and I have work to do as well."

With that, their hostess escorted them to the front hall where they bundled up in their winter attire, offered a cordial goodbye, then ventured back out onto the chilly, damp street.

Wesley huffed as he struggled against the cold wind that chased them en route. He rubbed his gloved hands together to warm them as he mused aloud. "I can't get over the fact that Richard dated Daisy Panasar. That was good investigative journalism, Sarah. I mean, Estelle upchucked that information like it was Montezuma's revenge. I still can't believe that no one ever found out about Richard and Daisy 'til now." Wes looked at Sarah quizzically, "But, I gotta ask, how did you know?"

Sarah stopped for a second and squealed with glee. "I didn't have a clue! I just picked a random key, so to speak, to see if a door would open, but I didn't expect her to blow it off its hinges. I *do* know that gossips can dig crap up and spread it like Ebola, but to protect their own turf, they can also dig down and hide it. That's just what gossips do." She began to jog in place, in line with Wes, who trudged slowly and cautiously along the frosty street. "What I don't get is how no one noticed in ninety-whatever years, what an out-and-out racist that woman is!"

He halted and removed one of his crisply ironed hankies from his coat pocket. He wiped icy tears from his cheeks and blew his nose while he collected his thoughts. On the move once again, he replied. "Every small town has its bigoted busybody, Sarah. Didn't you ever watch *Little House on the Prairie*?"

She gave him a playful punch on the arm and giggled. "I did. And I can say with certainty, Estelle McCall is no Harriet Olson. I'm sure of it, because, by the end of every episode, Harriet always got her comeuppance, which made me very happy. I doubt that Estelle McCall has ever had to face the error of her ways."

Wesley smirked, "And I take it, you'd like to hang a scarlet letter around her neck and send her into to a raging mob?"

Sarah snorted. "I'd have to find a raging mob in this town first."

He placed his hand over his heart and feigned an attack. "Oh, that's a low blow, Sarah. Just be at a hockey game when we lose, and you'll see plenty of raging goin' on. I think you're mostly upset because you put a package of photos together to help prod her memory and you didn't get to pull them out."

"I should have brought something sharper than a photo to prod her with," Sarah laughingly lamented.

Wes shook his head. "No need. My heartfelt gift of flowers obviously pried her open like an oyster shell. And look at the pearls that fell out." He teased.

* * *

Within seconds of their return to the office, Richard was on the line asking for Sarah. Brandon placed his hand over the receiver and whispered. "This is his second call."

She took the phone out of his hand and inhaled some courage. "Hello?"

She paused, listening. "Sure, I'd be happy to meet with you, Richard, but it'll have to wait until tomorrow."

There was a long pause and some negotiating, from the 9:00 a.m. appointment (his preference) to her 11:00 a.m. time slot, that he eventually agreed to. Then, there was the change of venue, from her suite to his office (her preference) which he grudgingly accepted. What he did stand firm on was his insistence that Wesley not join them.

"I'm not sure I understand why, but hopefully, Wesley will understand. I'll see you tomorrow. Bye for now." As she hung up the phone, she turned to her mentor with a puzzled look on her face. "What in the world was that about, Wes? We didn't even have time to take our coats off, and there he was."

Wes chuckled like a fraternity brother enjoying a private joke. "Think about it. In the time we took to get from Estelle's house to here, she managed to call Richard and tell him all about our teatime chat; and I'd bet he knew nothing about it beforehand. So obviously, he's anxious to clear up her torrent of misunderstandings and bull-puckey. Oh man, she must've scared the bejezus outta him."

Sarah crinkled her brow in bewilderment. "Damn, how old does Richard have to be before mommy lets go?" Wes hung his hat and scarf on a hook while pretending to ignore the remark. "Or, Wes, is he just waiting for her to...you know?" She snickered as she signalled a dramatic thumbs down.

He scowled. "That was a low blow, Sarah. Pretty damn dark."

She shot him a dubious glance. "Is it really, Wes? If we're being honest?"

He shook his head and tried not to grin. "Okay, I admit...it was kinda funny. Now, let's move on. I take it he doesn't want me at the meeting?"

She pressed her lips tightly together and sniffed, then groused, "Nope, he doesn't. Now that's plain weird, isn't it?"

He tilted his head and shrugged. "Yup, but then, nothing surprises me much anymore. Do you want me to drop by anyway?" He asked as he unbuttoned his coat. "I mean, just in case he needs verification..."

"Of what?" She sucked air through her gritted teeth. "What? That he has a racist nonagenarian mommy? I'm sure he knows that. My bet is that he simply wants to try and purge the crap she spewed."

"Sarah, remember the code I taught ya about journalism?" he asked as he hung up his coat.

"We already played that game weeks ago, Wes."

He gave her a stern, fatherly glare.

"Okay, okay. I remember...In a nutshell? *Don't confuse truth with fiction.*"

"Right." He leaned in and lowered his voice. "Although, if you were to slip in a little fiction here and there, in order to get to the truth, you might very well clear up a lot of confusion." Sarah squinted vacantly at him. "Okay, Kid, let me try it this way: now that Earl's trial is over and he's a free man, you could suggest you've had a change of heart about your assignment. That you want to switch to a *human-interest* story about how *the poor guy's* been misunderstood." She stared blankly at him. "What I'm getting at, my dear, is that empathizing with him, no matter how sickening it may seem right now, could open a peephole to Earl's ego, so ya could ask him direct questions about his upbringing, his relationships...all of it, any of it." Wesley sat back, looking smug while Sarah's eyes widened as the scene played out in her mind.

A satisfied smile spread across her face. The idea had sunk in. "Yeah, okay, Wes, I get the gist. But let's get real. I could never use 'poor guy' or 'human interest' with reference to Earl. I'll never be that great a liar. You on the other hand seem to have had no problem coming up with this devious little plot." She snickered.

He flashed her an impish grin. "Not me, actually, you can thank Estelle. She's the one who was insisting you write a kindly tale about Earl and Richard's loyal and enduring relationship." He chuckled. "I'm just saying, to do that, you're likely gonna need to use a little fiction to get to the truth. The police do it all the time."

"I'll think about it tonight, while I'm reviewing the material I have on hand. And hopefully tomorrow, I'll be ready to talk to Richard about a heart-warming tale that I'll likely never write. Thank you, thank you, thank you, Wes."

She jumped up, gave him a hug, and giggled as he blushed.

* * *

Morning came, and along with it, Sarah's realization that, thankfully, she hadn't been counting the minutes until daybreak. She'd slept soundly and couldn't recall having any nightmares.

She was lingering over her first cup of coffee in the O'Brien dining room when Mr. Reynolds shuffled in with a message.

"I tried callin' yer room. I didn't know you were in here 'til I spotted ya just now, Mrs. Berman." He seemed unusually civil. "Officer Connell phoned about twenty minutes ago and I wrote down his message for ya."

The note was as vague as Mr. Reynolds:
I'm heading to Eleanor's. Meet me there.

* * *

It was only 8:45 a.m. Sarah had plenty of time to drop by Eleanor's and then head a few doors down to Richard's office.

Ray answered Sarah's knock and ushered her inside, too quickly for Sarah's comfort. "Jesus, I'm so glad you're here." He panted and spoke with a tremor in his voice.

Sarah felt a cold wave of tension wash over her. "What's going on, Ray? Where's Eleanor?"

He took a deep inhale. "Follow me." He headed to the kitchen with the journalist close on his heels.

Eleanor was seated at the table, looking frazzled. She barely raised her eyes as Sarah slid onto a chair beside her.

"I should never have teased you, or doubted you, Sarah. But now I know what it feels like and I'm so sorry."

Sarah stared blankly. "I'd say it's okay, Eleanor, but I don't have a clue what you're talking about."

"And the parade marches on," Ray declared as he held up a Barbie doll. The anatomical oddity was naked except for a tiny slipcover over the head and a string noose around the neck.

"I found it this morning when I went to get the mail. It was in this brown paper bag." Eleanor's voice trembled as she slid the item toward Sarah.

Sarah's knees quivered as she read the words scribbled on the paper bag. The message was illiterate, yet clear as ice.

Intersted in a nuther date, Elner? It can be arangd.

Sarah dissolved onto a seat and placed her hand on Eleanor's trembling arm. "Oh my God, Eleanor...I'm so sorry this happened to you! Are you okay?"

She exhaled slowly. "I, uh...I think so."

Sarah looked up defiantly at Ray. "Still think this is a prank, Ray?"

"Hell no," he affirmed. "Sure, I was figuring this was about Zane and his buddies payin' someone to scare you and Wes into writin' some crap that might influence the judge. But then, Shiny got that rock through her window, and then we found that doll's head at Bindy's place..."

"But why in hell scare the bejezus out of Eleanor?" Sarah shrieked.

"Exactly my point, Sarah. Zane may be a dumb shit, but having someone plant evidence at his own home? And now this? What's there to gain? It doesn't make sense!"

The room was silent except for Ray's rhythmic pacing and the pounding of his right fist into his left hand.

Watching his torment build, Sarah quietly responded. "You're right, Ray. It doesn't make sense."

He stopped abruptly; "No, it doesn't, and that's why I'm gonna head out to the pen and have another face-to-face with Zane."

"Really, Ray, don't you think you should stay here with Eleanor?"

Eleanor shook her head and gazed steadily at Sarah and Ray. "Look, guys, I panicked. But honestly, I don't need babysitting. Ray, please do whatever you need to do."

"I've arranged twenty-four-hour protection for you. I'll be takin' the night shift and Officers Dan and

Wally will share the daytime duty. Sarah, if you can stay 'til they get here, I'd appreciate it."

"Of course, I will." Sarah agreed.

Eleanor protested, claiming too much was being made of such a cowardly and obnoxious prank, but Sarah held fast. Ray continued to think out his plan. "Dan'll be here any minute and I'll be heading into Brockville first to pay Dougie Fergusson that little visit he owes me. He promised to tell all when his balls were back to normal, whatever normal is for that little weasel. But whether his balls are balloons or walnuts, I don't give a flyin' ya-know-what. I'm about to make damn sure he delivers on his promise. And I can tell ya, if he doesn't have that one last doll still in his possession, he's in for a shitload o' more hurt."

"Ray, if it looks like you went there for revenge, you can get into a lot of trouble," Eleanor warned.

"She's not wrong, Ray. You know better than me, that you can't afford to confront him again without a witness. There were already rumblings of police brutality from your last visit. So, whether you like it or not, I'm coming with you." Sarah insisted.

"You need to stay right here!" Ray demanded.

Not a moment too soon, Dan arrived, and Ray headed for the exit. "Keep a close eye on things here, Dan," Ray warned as they crossed paths.

"No problem, Boss."

Ray stopped in the archway and called out, "Well, Sarah, you comin' or not?"

With that, Sarah gave Eleanor a hasty hug, a wave to Dan, and fell in line behind the policeman.

CHAPTER TWENTY-FIVE

On the drive to Doug Fergusson's slum-shack, Sarah decided, this time, she was going to stay several paces behind the strapping officer. The dash of courage, she'd previously managed to conjure, had now dashed away.

* * *

There wasn't a shred of garbage, a fragment of broken glass, or a cigarette butt to be found outside Doug's door. It looked as if the concrete had been scrubbed with a floor polisher. Next to the door, which now housed a peephole, was a newly mounted intercom with a plastic sign above it: *Please ring bell. If you hear a buzz, press, and hold intercom button, and speak.*

Ray did as instructed, and waited to hear the buzz.

"Doug, this is Officer Connell. Open up, please."

The door slowly opened with Doug peering from behind. Ray entered and carefully scanned the room before waving Sarah in.

The place looked and smelled spotless. Everything was in its rightful place. There was even a bowl of polished red apples on the table.

"Is it okay, Officer?" He anxiously asked.

"Sure. That's what I'm talkin' about, Doug," Ray gushed. "You got this place lookin' clean as a hospital operatin' room. Good on ya."

"Now...how're the balls, Dougie? Have they shriveled enough so you can talk?" Ray asked as he took a step toward him. Doug, still heavily bruised, flinched like a rabbit from a fox. He cautiously backed up to a chair and sat. Ray watched with a dour glare. "I'm waitin'. Start talking!"

Doug shook his head in defeat. His voice rose in pitch as he spoke.

"Officer, please. I'm not tryin' to piss ya off. I really didn't know all this crazy shit was gonna happen. My life's hangin' on this dangerous line you want me to cross. I wanna tell ya everythin' I know...but ya saw what happened last time I talked to ya, and the time before that. I'm not the smartest guy in town, but I'm not the biggest idiot either. I swear to ya, if I talk, the only thing that'll be messin' this place up next time you drop by, will be my corpse."

Clearly, the young man was terrified. Ray's demeanor softened as he dragged a chair over and sat down next to him. "Listen to me, Doug. I don't wanna make your life any harder, but we started out with a minor crime that's escalating here by the day. If we don't stop it, I don't wanna even think about how serious it may get, and what could happen to you and a shitload of innocent people."

Sarah cautiously took a seat near Ray and offered her plea. "Doug, I can see you're a good guy who just got mixed up in something awful. But if there's anything you can say that won't endanger you, please say it. Other people's lives are also being threatened."

Doug rose and began to pace. Sarah and Ray sat quietly, watching, and waiting.

Doug, sweating profusely and breathing heavily, stopped in front of Ray, but said nothing.

Ray stood up, placed a hand gently on Doug's shoulder, and quietly repeated Sarah's request. "Please, tell us, Doug. Come on, let's resolve this for everyone's sake."

Doug slowly crumpled into his seat. "Okay, I'll tell ya something...but only if you don't hound me for more questions later."

Ray sat and offered a humble smile and a two-finger salute. "Scout's honour," Ray vowed. "Go ahead."

Several seconds passed while Doug weighed his options. "Okay. First off, I gotta come clean and tell ya that Uncle Zane had nothin' to do with this. I swear. Zane never asked me to do nothin'. I ain't even seen or heard from him since way before he went to prison." An involuntary shudder traveled through his battered body as he continued. "The truth is, I never wanna see that animal again. I just wanted to blame him for the beatin's 'cause o' what he did to the kids." He lowered his head to hide his despair. "My father had took off...ya know...before all this crap went down."

"Your father is Arvin?" Sarah exclaimed.

Doug nodded. "Yup...and when he left, my mother got thrown out o' our house, 'cause she couldn't pay the rent. She wanted Aunt Bindy to let us stay with her, but Bindy said no, 'cause she wasn't gonna see my little sisters handed over to Zane. She told my mother what was goin' on, and then...maybe it was just luck...but only a couple o' weeks later, those guys all got arrested. We didn't know my father was one of 'em 'til they arrested him too. Now, he's in prison with Zane and the others where they all belong.

"I was barely seventeen when the bastards got arrested, eh? But I got myself a job, and this place, and I moved my mom and sisters in with me, and then the government came to help, and got me some trainin' and the job at the hospital. They got my mom and sisters a safe place ta live too. Now, I send them money ta help. So, ya see, I can't lose my job."

It took surprising restraint for Sarah to hold back her tears. "I'm truly sorry you've had such a rough time, Doug. But helping Officer Connell put another bad guy away can only make life better for you."

He sniffed and rubbed his eyes. "It ain't never gonna be better for me. Every time I have ta say my last name, they look at me like they just ate a spoonful o' shit. My father and those other bastards may be locked away, but I'm the one in prison. Aunt Bindy tells me they got it pretty good up there in the Kingston Pen: colour TV, basketball court, music videos, you name it. And it's all for free. They even got people comin' ta entertain at Christmas. They get clean clothes and good food...and that's more than Zane ever gave Aunt Bindy and his kids...or my father ever gave us. So, I wanted to blame Zane, figurin' he'd get pissed off and cause trouble in prison. And maybe the whole bunch of 'em...includin' my ole man would lose some of those cushy privileges, or maybe even get the crap beat out of 'em so they'd know what it feels like."

"I kinda see his point," Sarah muttered to Ray, who was squirming in his seat.

"Yeah, I get the point." Ray stood abruptly, knocking over his chair, and causing Doug to flinch. "I get it, but for Christ's sake, Doug, I still need to know who's behind this crap." Ray bent over and grabbed up the chair.

Fearful as he was of the cop, he still wasn't ready to name names. "I told ya, Officer. I can't say no more."

"Where's that last doll gone, Doug? I got a feelin' it's the same one I picked up at another crime scene."

Doug suddenly spoke up with a renewed confidence. "Listen, Officer, if ya got questions about the family, ya really should be askin' Aunt Bindy."

"And which esteemed Fergusson should I ask her about?"

"None. He's not a Fergusson."

Ray and Sarah looked puzzled. "Then it must be Earl." Ray concluded.

The statement drew an audible gasp from Doug. "You're kiddin' right? Earl? I'd beat the shit outta that slimeball before he'd get his money-grubbin' finger outta his nose. No way Earl did this to me." Doug shouted. He eyed the chief and Sarah, then pathetically dropped his face into his hands and muttered, "Aw, shit. I'm such a screw up." He raised his head and looked pleadingly at the chief. "See that! Now I'm talkin' and getting' myself in deeper and deeper."

Ray retained his cool as he tried one more approach. "Here's the thing, buddy...you've already dug yourself into one hell of a deep hole, so you may as well stop diggin', step out, and tell me who it is we're lookin' for."

"Why? There's no point. You'll never find 'im. He's like an invisible man," Doug lamented as he slumped down in his chair, "But he'll find me, alright. And next time, he'll finish the job." He looked up at Ray with pleading eyes. "Is that what ya want? Because me dead is what'll happen, if I tell ya."

In that moment, all Ray could offer was a deep, guttural sigh, and finally some advice. "Well, we're outta here for now...but don't leave town. And Doug, keep this door locked, although I don't think it'll be much protection against an invisible man."

* * *

Spotting the gnarly old pick-up truck perched at the top of the hill was a relief to Sarah; evidence that the owner of the wreck was home.

Bindy Fergusson seemed slightly bewildered by the reappearance of the cop and the journalist, but she led them inside without hesitation.

Ray got right down to business. "Thanks for that crate, Mrs. Fergusson...and also for the shoebox. We haven't had a chance to go through it all yet, but we will. I have a few more questions for ya if that's all right?"

She offered a half-hearted shrug. "I don't know what more I can tell ya but go ahead and ask."

"I'm sure ya know that Earl is free o' the sex crimes accusations?"

She reacted with a sardonic grin. "Yeah, I know only too well."

Ray offered a nod of understanding before moving ahead. "Well, Bindy, you should know, that doesn't mean Earl's out of the woods yet." Ray watched as her lips transformed from grin to grimace. "We also know that your husband is in prison with a few relatives and some losers who aren't related. Isn't that so, Bindy?"

Her body stiffened and her eyes narrowed. "Yeah, everyone knows that, so why ya askin' me? I mean, ya came all the way out here to ask me what ya already know?"

Sarah jumped in. "You may not know this, Mrs. Fergusson, but I'm working on a story about Earl White, and we're looking for anyone who may have been damaged by his behaviour over the years. I know you're only a Fergusson by marriage, but there are probably other relatives that have been affected by Earl's, or even Zane's, behaviour. What we would like to know is: Are there any other relatives of your husband's we could speak to who aren't in prison?"

"I know ya spoke to Dougie, but I can tell ya, ya ain't gonna talk to any of our other kids, that's fer damn sure. The children's services wouldn't let ya anyhow. Them little ones is safe and doin' real well now...and soon, we'll be gettin' 'em all back. The big ones, like Doug, got help too. He's a good boy. He was there for his family even after the disgusting things his filthy bastard father did to him and his little sisters."

As her words confirmed that Doug was a victim of paternal sexual abuse, Ray's fists clenched like stones as he tried to keep hold of his fury.

"Did Doug's abuse ever come out in court?" Ray seethed.

She shook her head sorrowfully, "Nope. He begged us to keep his secret. He was maybe fifteen in high school when the crimes went public, and the name Fergusson was splashed all over the papers. He'd just make a joke of it, eh? He'd say he weren't no relation. It was just his cursed luck to have the same name as those crazies. It took years before the sons-o'-bitches were all tried and sent to prison. No one knew the truth about Dougie. And now, I'm suddenly feelin' like crap 'cause I'm thinkin' maybe you guys didn't know neither. I was figurin' since he's so scared o' the law, he woulda told ya everythin'."

With honest humility, Ray took a replenishing breath and declared, "Jesus, you've walked through more hellfire than Satan himself, Mrs. Fergusson. I swear on my honour as police chief: as long as what I'm hearin' here is the truth, I have no need to mention Doug's secret outside your door. It won't serve any of us to put his family through more pain."

A spark flickered in Bindy's cloudy eyes at hearing Ray's promise; but her years of abuse and manipulation overshadowed her urge to trust anyone. "And why should I believe you?"

"You're gonna have to trust someone, Bindy, and it might as well be the guy who's on the right side of the law."

A long, breathless silence filled the room...a stand-off of sorts that neither Ray nor Sarah wanted to break for fear of disrupting a powerful dynamic emerging in the hush.

"Well, uh, maybe I can help, a little," Bindy tentatively suggested. "Tuth be tole, there's a relative o' Zane's, uh, who didn't go to prison. God only knows why, 'cause I woulda sent that bastard to the gallows. But I'll bet my life, ya haven't talked to him yet."

Goosebumps ran up Ray's spine as he posed the question. "And who would that be?"

Without looking at him, she uttered, "Berger..."

The name registered, and Sarah stammered "Dwayne B-Berger?"

A mix of shock and concern was reflected in Bindy's face as she asked. "I wanna know who in hell told ya bout Berger? Ya hear? I wanna know!" The whisp of a woman trembled as she spoke.

The reaction stunned Sarah for a moment, but she rallied. "It was your husband when I talked to him in prison. He said Berger died in a fire." A tense silence drifted through the room. Finally, Sarah broke through. "So, Zane was lying yet again?"

The feisty matron suddenly appeared sapped of any will. "Nope. Fer once, he wasn't lyin'. The truth is, Zane don't know, 'cause no one's seen Berger for years. There's only two of us knows for sure he's alive."

Sarah gasped. "Alive? But he died in a fire. What about official records of deaths? You can't just make something like that up."

"Ya can't, eh? Well, that never stopped Berger. He owed Earl a lot o' money and couldn't pay up, so Earl sent his thugs to beat the livin' daylights out of 'im. During the fight, a fire broke out, and the thugs ran off. Berger got burned up pretty bad, but he saw his chance to disappear. That way, he'd never pay Earl a cent, and he wouldn't go to jail with them other perverts either. So, he hides out until his burns heal up, then he gets someone to pay a guy to say he was cremated. They even delivered ashes to his wife, Gladys. She wouldn't o' thought ta ask for proof he died. She just believed that the ashes was Berger's. That was a good day fer Gladys, 'cause she was finally free." Bindy released a wry snigger. "Heh, she even had a church service for that sick bastard. Then, to take care of her family, she starts workin' at the hospital, cleanin' five days a week, an' cleanin' people's houses two other days. And after more than a year o' freedom, Berger calls her out o' nowhere and says if she tells anyone he's alive, she and the kids are dead." Bindy wiped away a stream of tears, with her sleeve and continued. "Ever since then, the bastard phones...not 'cause he gives a damn; it's all about mailin' money to him. She does it 'ta keep him away from her and the kids, every two weeks is when she gets paid. She don't know where he is, an' she likes it that way. All's she's got is a payphone, an' a post box number."

Ray offered a proposal. "Mrs. Fergusson, if you can get me those numbers, I'll do everything I can to make sure he's out of her life forever."

She looked up at him with entreating eyes and whispered. "Is that a true promise?"

Ray placed his hand on his heart and nodded.

She smiled weakly at her visitors, wiped her eyes, and stated clearly. "I'll do what I can for ya, but please, ya can't be buggin' Gladys. She's got worries enough just keepin' her family together. And ya gotta promise ya won't ever tell Dwayne, 'cause he'd be pissed enough ta kill us all."

As soon as Ray and Sarah pledged their discretion, Bindy picked up the phone and dialed Gladys Berger.

* * *

"Things have been quiet and uneventful," Wally reported when Ray and Sarah returned to the dressmaker's house.

Eleanor had gone about her business: cleaning, cooking, and sewing, while her rotating protection squad spent the day watching soap-operas and talk shows on TV. She even managed to bake a thing or two for her houseguests. It all felt pretty peaceful in the Miller household, but Ray took no chances. He opted for the night shift, as promised.

* * *

Wally dropped Sarah off at her hotel and headed home.

Reynolds peered over his spectacles as Sarah pass by. He shouted after her. "Hey, Mrs. Berman, ya might wanna get back here and pick up your messages."

She stopped, heaved an exasperated sigh, and trudged toward him. The smirk on Reynold's face told Sarah that he enjoyed hassling her. He stretched out his hand and waved the notes at her. She snatched them and offered a disgruntled, "thank you."

As she headed up the stairs, she quickly scanned the notes. All three were from Richard. She dropped her head and groaned as she realized that, in the frenzy of dealing with Eleanor's crisis, she'dforgotten all about her scheduled meeting with Richard. But she thought, *'It's late and he's likely already gone.'* So, she went to her room and left him a message, apologizing, and asking to reschedule for the morning.

* * *

There was a tentative knock on her door.

Twice shy, Sarah approached and officiously demanded, "Who is it?"

"It's me, Dan, Mrs. Berman. I'm just droppin' somethin' off for ya. Sorry to bother ya."

Sarah opened the door to find the young red-faced officer awkwardly shuffling on the spot. His uneasy silence was a sure sign that he'd rather be anywhere but there.

Sarah offered a warm smile and a curious tilt of her head. "Well, hi there, Dan. I'm sure there's a reason for your unexpected visit, but I'm not quite getting the message."

"Huh? Oh, sorry, Ma'am, one second." He leaned over and picked up the wooden crate. "Ray asked me ta drop this off to ya tonight and said he'll come by in the mornin' to wade through it with ya."

Sarah winced at the sight. "Oh, no, no, no, Dan listen, I'm not in any hurry to see that crate opened, and I hate to do this to you, but it kind of creeps me out. Lately, I've seen more photos of creepy characters than you'd find on the Jerry Springer show. So, I don't even want to think about what's in that box. Could you please take it back?"

Officer Dan shrugged and chuckled. "No problem, Mrs. Berman. I wouldn't want it hangin' around my bedroom either."

As he turned to walk away, she asked him to deliver a message to his boss. "Dan, if you're speaking to Ray tonight, please tell him, I'll be paying penance at Richard McCall's office in the morning. But when my meeting's over, I'll see him at Eleanor's."

He nodded and replied, "No problem. I'm gonna take this scary box back to him now, and I'll tell him." He grinned, shifted the crate to his hip, and marched jauntily along the corridor.

* * *

The scream of an unrelenting fire siren in the middle of the night jolted Sarah from her sleep. Terrifying thoughts raced through her mind as she struggled in the dark to find the lamp. Having won that battle, she called down to the front desk desperate to find out the meaning of the alarm. Was she in danger?

Was the town in danger? The phone rang endlessly, but no one answered.

She bundled up and ventured out into the frigid night. The stench of dense smoke swallowed Prescott, but she saw no flames. She followed the foot traffic to the front of the Journal office. There were no flames, no ladders, and no drama. But there seemed to be a lot of people milling about across the street. Sarah snaked to the front of the crowd and stared at the battalion of firemen marching in and out of Richard McCall's office.

The onlookers were either muttering angrily to themselves or shouting at each other: "It's a bloody false alarm, right?" "Does anyone know what the hell's goin' on?" It soon became clear to Sarah that the crowd had arrived, ready for a gripping drama that didn't unfold.

A fireman approached the assembly.

"Okay, it's all over, folks. It was just a big trash fire that got outta control, but we got it in time. That's what happens when you stash open bags o' dried leaves outside instead of takin' 'em to the dump like you're supposed ta. You can all get along home now."

"Hey, Sarah," Ray called out. "I didn't take you for a fire-chaser."

"Well, I see you're out here too, huh?"

"It's kinda hard to ignore when you're just a few doors away,. Besides, I'm still a cop, and with what's been going on around here, I felt a duty to check it out."

"Okay, then tell me, Ray, do you think it was spontaneous combustion or was there a little assistance?"

He feigned astonishment at the question and took the opportunity to lighten the mood. "Boy, your paranoia knows no bounds, eh, Sarah?"

She grinned and gave him a playful shove. "Come on, Ray, seriously; do you really think Richard would leave a pile of dried leaves right by his front door? Think about it. Earl got off scot-free, and there are a lot of pissed off townsfolk who aren't happy about it, and likely blame Richard."

"We'll see what the fire marshal says after he has a chance to sort it all out."

"I think my meeting with Richard this morning is gonna be very interesting." She paused and looked around, taking in the stragglers slowly leaving the area. "Speaking of Richard, where the hell is he? It's weird that half the town's out here, but not him. At least, I didn't see him."

Ray patted Sarah's shoulder and declared, "I'm gonna get back to Eleanor's. Good luck with your meeting. I hope you're not allergic to smoke, 'cause it's gonna take a long while to get that smell outta his office."

Sarah smiled wryly. "It'll be an improvement over the stink of Earl White. I bet even thick smoke can't hide that stench."

* * *

In the morning, Richard arrived at Sarah's suite with coffee and donuts.

He removed his coat and gloves and placed them on the sofa. "Sorry we had to change the venue, Sarah, but you likely heard about the fire last night?"

She nodded. "I did. I confess, I ran down there at two in the morning to see what was happening. Luckily, the damage seemed pretty minor, but you'd know best about that. Thanks for the treat." She smiled and pointed to a chair. "Please, sit."

They sat down at the table and began quietly sipping coffee and munching on donuts.

After a few minutes of inaction, Sarah set her coffee cup down and broke the stalemate. "So, Richard, I guess you got a good look at the damage this morning?"

He nodded and squirmed in his seat. "Uh-huh, I stopped by on my way here. Joannie's taking care of everything. She said it's just a matter of sanding and repainting the front door, cleaning the windows, and probably laying new sod in the spring. It's no big deal...except maybe for the smell."

"Jeez, Richard, if it was my place, I would've been the first one there last night. I can't believe you're so cool about it."

"Speaking of cool, Jeez, they keep this hotel room like a steam bath." Richard dabbed a bead of sweat at his temple.

She looked at him quizzically. "Really? Step out of the shower, shivering like I do in the morning, and say that. But Richard, how did you not hear that od-awful siren?"

He shrugged again. "My wife and I are really sound sleepers. It was actually the bedside phone that woke my wife up, not the siren. That was when Joannie called to tell us there was a grass fire at our office. She assured us she was taking care of everything and said, 'go back to sleep.' And that's just what we did." He shrugged, "Hey, Prescott's a small town. Thank God a grass fire is about as exciting as it gets around here these days. Lots of people go running to have a look...I'm just not one of them." He sniggered.

Sarah raised an eyebrow as she responded. "Not the curious sort, huh?"

"I've found it's generally safer not to be. I always hope that if I mind my own business, others might do the same."

"It's an interesting way of thinking; but as a journalist, I gotta say, not being curious is foreign to me." Sarah took a gulp of coffee, settled back in her chair, and got down to the essentials. "Richard, you wanted to meet, so why don't you start with your questions, and then I'll ask a few of my own." She kept her eyes on him while she waited and hoped her patience would endure.

She gritted her teeth as she watched him stuff chunks of donut into his mouth in what seemed to be a childish ruse to silence himself. After the last bite was washed down with a gulp of coffee, he dabbed his mouth with a tissue, and began to speak. "Sarah, I want to talk about the article you're planning to write, on Earl." As Sarah leaned forward to speak, he held up a hand like a stop sign. "Earl is still my client; so, before we get into it, I need to have your word that any discussion we have at this meeting, about Earl, will be off the record. Do I have that assurance?"

Perhaps it was her abundance of curiosity, or her lack of experience, but without hesitation, she agreed to the terms of the meeting. "Okay, Richard, it can't do any harm to have a conversation. So, for this meeting, any discussion about Earl is off the record."

"Then let me cut to the chase, Sarah. What would it take for you to walk away?"

Her jaw dropped in astonishment. "I don't understand."

Richard squirmed in his chair. "Well, let me clarify. If you can sell the story to a major newspaper, you'd make a fair amount of money, true?"

She laughed mirthlessly, "I wish it were. But the truth is, I doubt it would do much more than cover my expenses for this trip."

"In that case, you may be very interested in this proposition. How would you like to earn five thousand dollars without uncapping a pen?"

She stared at the lawyer in disbelief, tilting her head one way, then the other. Finally, she swallowed a gulp of air and replied. "I'm speechless."

"Well, that's a good beginning." He reflexively concluded.

She hunched her shoulders in bewilderment, "No Richard, It's not a good beginning at all. I'm really confused. Just a few days ago, Earl stopped me on the street, totally pissed because he assumed I wasn't working on his story..."

This time, Richard interrupted by waving his finger at her. "Okay. About that. He got the feeling you won't be writing a favourable story. And surely, you can understand why he can't afford more negative media right now. For one thing, he's got a big land deal about to close and we're both worried that things could change if he gets bad press."

"Why are you so sure it would be negative?"

"I wasn't, until I spoke to my mother yesterday. Naturally, she's assuming that the story would include me as his lawyer. But moreover, she thinks you don't care for Earl. Therefore, she's worried you won't place me in the best light either. I tried to assure her that you'd play fair, but she's tough to convince, as you probably gathered."

The two shared a genuine chuckle before Sarah explained. "The truth is, Richard, five thousand dollars, not to write, is a big enticement for me..."

Richard perked up, "I'm relieved to hear you say that."

"Wait." She blurted, "I'd pretty much decided to set the Earl White article aside. But now I have a gut feeling there must be something deeply swampy hidden under some rock he doesn't want lifted." Her eyes twinkled with excitement, "And *that* is irresistible to me. Look, I'd love that money, but then I'd probably never sleep peacefully again. So, I'll have to pass on Earl's generous offer."

As her words penetrated his ear, Richard appeared stunned by the refusal. "Really? Are you serious?"

She nodded, smiling. "Yup, really Richard. Dead serious."

He wiped away a cascade of sweat that was hurtling down his face. "Okay, well...I made the offer. I guess it's yours to refuse."

She twirled a lock of hair around her finger as she contemplated her next move. "Uh, Richard...if it's okay with you, I'd like to ask a couple of questions, on the record, and they're not about your client. I mean, it's better for both of us if I get my information directly from you, rather than your mother. Don't you agree?"

Richard affected a skittish smirk, sucked up a lung of air, and complied. "I guess. Okay, yes."

As his words met her ear, a surge of power raced through Sarah's body. "Great. Thank you. For a start, your mother mentioned you dated Daisy Panasar in high school. I'd like to hear a little more about that."

The flush of his cheeks and erratic twitch of his eyelid were proof that the question had caught him off guard. "Uh...um, there isn't much to tell, really. I guarantee my mother made it out to be much more than it was. My God, high school? Who can remember that far back?" He tried to lighten his response with a casual guffaw, but it fell flat. "Come on, Sarah, my mother's lonely and looking for anyone who'll listen to her long tales."

Sarah disregarded his explanation but managed an empathetic smile. "I know, but please, humour me, anyway." She broke off a piece of donut and popped it into her mouth...and waited.

He crossed and uncrossed his legs, then reached for, but decided against, another donut. He coughed and cleared his throat, and finally, running out of impediments, he continued. "It was kid stuff. You know, a movie here, a soda there...That's about it. We were babies." He lowered his eyes and stared at his hands for a wistful moment before raising his head once again and asking, "Why the interest in Daisy anyway?"

She shrugged ever so casually. "I don't know. It came up in conversation with your mother and she fascinated me..."

"My mother, or Daisy?"

Sarah snorted, "Your mother's intriguing, but I was actually referring to Daisy."

A flicker of anger lit up his face. "Why Daisy? Because she wasn't one of us?" He seethed.

So, it is genetic, Sarah mused. "Well, to be honest, your mother did imply that."

"Yeah, leave it to my mother." He spat out the words. In an effort to shift the focus, he straightened his tie and brushed crumbs from his trousers. "I mean, she's old, and half the time, she doesn't know what she's talking about. But you're obviously not discounting any of that."

"I'm sorry, Richard. It came up and I was curious. I'd recently noticed the plaque at the beach, so I guess Daisy was on my mind. Now, if I may, I do have a few unrelated questions..."

He casually removed his pocket hanky and wiped the sweat from his forehead. "Good. That works

Reva Leah Stern

for me. But you haven't asked one question about Earl, and I thought he was the subject of your story."

CHAPTER TWENTY-SIX

Minutes after Richard left Sarah's suite, Wes called her for an update.

"How'd you know my meeting was over?"

Sarah heard the smile in the old man's voice. "Old newsman's intuition, my dear; and the fact that I just saw him walking by. Anyway, I want to hear everything...but later. Now, I'm calling to tell ya that while you were busy chattin' it up with Richard, I was paying a visit to the library. I had Helen look up a birthday for me and I found somethin' kind of interesting."

She blinked and smiled sceptically. "Okay, Charlie Chan, cut the intrigue and tell me."

"Okay, when Daisy was fifteen, Richard was eighteen."

She shook her head and clucked her tongue. "Hell, Wes, I was engaged at eighteen. But then, yeah...it's true, fifteen's a whole other bucket of concern."

After a curious pause, Wes quietly asked, "Did Richard say anything about that drowning incident?"

Sarah's brow crinkled. "I didn't bring it up, Wes. But you have to wonder how terrible news like that would've affected an eighteen-year-old with a forbidden crush, especially after Momma had him exiled."

She sat on the edge of the bed, twirling the phone cord around her thumb as she tried to make sense of his news. "It's a fact that some of us never get over our first crush, which could be why he got so squirrely when I mentioned Daisy. Maybe it had nothing to do with a genetic propensity to racism, and more to do with a broken heart."

She paused while Wes pondered the possibility. "That's true. But if they sent him away before her accident, that could be partly why the poor kid drowned. I mean, going out at night without a trainer is pretty dumb, but her emotional state could explain why she was so reckless."

She lowered her head despairingly as she voiced a dark thought. "I hate to say this, but a teenage girl with a seriously broken heart can go to some crazy extremes. I mean, did anyone ever consider it to be a suicide rather than an accident?"

"If you'd brought it up last week, I woulda thought you'd gone over the edge, but now, I'm actually thinking about it. So, let me ask you, Sarah: how many investigations do ya think you can juggle in the brief time you've got left here? Right now, you've got a cold rape case and a creep who managed to weasel out of a pedophile trial. And now, you're looking for more crimes to write about?"

Her wry snicker couldn't be contained. "Nah, when I leave here, you can take them all on with Shiny and Ray. And when they're ready to prosecute, they can call on Mitch. He'll probably have graduated law school by then." She joshed before turning her focus back to her topic. "Getting serious now, Wes; who do you think might have some insight into the drowning?"

He retorted with a long, low groan. "Ach, I can see you're not gonna let this go. Fine, we can try and find out if Helen has anything more in the archives."

With the phone now cradled on her shoulder, Sarah used both hands to silently applaud his suggestion. "Wonderful, thank you, but you have to talk to Helen, 'cause she seems to need to screen me through CSIS and the RCMP before she'll talk to me. But maybe I can start with the Prescott funeral home, if there is one."

"It's Keith's Funeral Home, and it's been around for as long as this town's been here. Old man Keith always kept the records, and now his kid, Devyn, runs the place. I'll bet their ancestors were recording deaths all the way back to the War of 1812. Fortunately, we won that one, so it won't require any further investigation." He snickered.

She rose and paced as far as the phone cord would allow. "How about we each go and find out what we can and then meet up at one o'clock for lunch at the Best Service?"

"It's a deal. See you there."

* * *

The pungent odour of lilies punctuated Sarah's disdain for funeral homes. She hated those ghostly blooms. When she was a young student, her class was required to view a deceased schoolteacher who was laid out in a luxurious casket, under a thicket of gargantuan calla lilies. As the students stepped up to the coffin, each was expected to kiss the forehead of the corpse. Since that day, Sarah associated the sickly scent and sight of calla lilies with that repugnant kiss.

* * *

The funeral parlor was empty except for a woman in a dark suit, leaning over an oak casket that Sarah hoped was an empty floor model.

"May I be of some assistance?" The lady asked with the slow, resonant, tone generally projected by those who serve the gravely ill, mentally challenged, or the dead.

"I'm looking for the funeral director."

The woman extended her hand. "That would be me." Sarah gazed at the woman in disbelief as she politely shook her hand.

"You're Devyn Keith?"

She smiled at Sarah's confusion. "I am. I get that puzzled look a lot. Devyn is my father's revenge for not having a son."

"I'm sorry, it's just that I recently met a man with a traditionally female name, so I find it a little odd."

"It is odd," the woman laughed, "but I give my parents credit for the confusion. They spelled it D-E-V-Y-N. They were absolutely sure that the Y would resolve the confusion."

"Good thinking." Sarah snickered; then, in an awkward moment of self-consciousness, she pointed to herself. "I'm Sarah Berman, by the way. Can we talk?"

"Sure. I'm pleased to meet you, Sarah. Let's go to my meeting room. It's much livelier there." That was probably an old undertaker's jest, but Sarah fell for it and laughed a little more robustly than she intended. Moving to a meeting room meant more distance between herself and the malodorous lilies.

The room was tastefully decorated with warm lighting, comfortable furnishings, and a coffee niche. "Please, have a seat." Sarah chose the rose brocade chair closest to the exit. Once she was settled, Devyn sat down. "Now, what can I do for ya?"

"I hope this isn't too big a problem, Devyn, but I'm working on a story for a Toronto newspaper, and I'm looking for information on a decedent that goes back to the summer of 1958. Is that an impossible request?"

The director's eyes opened wider, a sure sign she was intrigued. "Not impossible at all, just give me the name. It'll take a few minutes, but most everything is programmed into this computer."

"You have a computer that does that?"

"Sure does...And it won't be long before this machine here'll be as obsolete as the corset. But in the meantime, it does a great job. Let me get us some coffee before we begin, and then we'll put her to the test."

Sarah offered an appreciative smile. "That would be super. Thank you so much."

"You have the date and the name of the deceased, I hope?"

"I absolutely do."

* * *

The chill and snow hadn't kept the townsfolk from dragging themselves out of their homes and into the Best Service for lunch.

Sarah was late and expected to find Wes comfortably seated in their favourite booth by the window, but instead, he was waiting in line. Shiny was serving the famished crowd and had no time to even glance up. Of course, the longer the line got, the more anxious the duo was to sit, eat, and share information.

While Sarah shifted from foot to foot and stared out the front window, Wes focused on an eagerly-waving hand in the distance.

Wes nudged Sarah. "Don't look, but we're being summoned to the corner booth by Earl White. I can't see who he's with, but that's the big booth, so maybe we should join them, so we don't have to wait? I'm starving."

"In spite of the stunning revelation that he's very likely a rapist, have you ever eaten a meal near that guy? It's like dining with a cave man." She shook her head. "No, let me correct that, 'cause that would have a human element to it. It's more like chowing down with a hyena. I could never be that hungry. But I *am* that curious, so once we get a booth, of our own, I'll drift over there with you for a nanosecond. Is that fair?"

"Definitely fair." He agreed.

As bad luck would have it, the first table to open up was directly across from Earl and Richard. Shiny rushed forward with menus in hand and nodded toward the empty table. "Sorry guys, but it's all I got, unless ya wanna wait another twenty minutes or more." With a shake of his head, Wes relieved her of the menus and headed toward the open booth with Sarah reluctantly following.

Earl hooted as the pair approached. "Ooh will ya look at that. We was just talkin' about ya; so, how's that for a *coinkidink*, eh? We just finished eatin' when Dickie told me you agreed you're gonna write my fuckin' story after all. Damned if I weren't glad as hell ta hear that. An' then, we're just about ta leave, I look up, and shit, there ya are." Earl punctuated his revelation with a chortle, while Richard cast his eyes anywhere but at Sarah, who was sliding into the furthermost corner of her assigned booth.

Finally settled and having used those seconds to process Earl's announcement, she responded. "Mr. White, I'd say *agreement* is premature, I actually haven't made up my mind yet. But I'm puzzled, 'cause I understood you didn't want me to go ahead with the story?" Sarah's raised eyebrows and derisive smirk were intended more for Richard's mendacity, than Earl's foolhardy assumption. "I mean, sure Mr. White, the five thousand dollars you offered is incentive, but like I just said, I haven't made a decision yet."

Before they could get embroiled in a debate over Richard's deception, the lawyer executed an exaggerated glance at his watch, grabbed his jacket, and timorously stammered, "Uh, sorry, but I gotta get going. Uh, I can't meet clients in my office for now with the smoke and all, so, I meet them at Tim Horton's. And Earl, you have to come by my office to pick up those papers from Joannie." Earl acquiesced and rose from the booth. Richard watched as Earl pulled on his coat and toque, nodded to Wes and Sarah, and strode past. "Good to see ya, both," he said as he hurried away.

With that, the devilish duo headed for the door.

"That was weird," Sarah mused. "I would've thought that Earl would try to hawk that mega-dollar offer like a carnival hustler, but instead, he kinda folded like a tent."

Wes offered up a Cheshire cat smirk. "So, are you ready to admit now, he's more complicated than ya thought?"

Sarah snorted. "If insanity is complicated, then all right, he's complicated."

Wes slapped his hand down on the table with the aplomb of a judge's gavel. "Okay, agreed! Now, change of subject. Can we talk about our investigations?"

Sarah nodded. "Okay, Wes, go for it. What did you find?"

"Me? I came up with nothing. How 'bout you?"

"Me?" She grinned and perked up. "Well, I'm glad you asked. I had an enlightening visit. Did you know their computer can actually spit out information going back before the War of 1812? Not that I needed to go back that far, but I thought you'd like to know. Anyway, Devyn found Daisy Panasar in there, and you wouldn't believe how much information they have on her in their archives! Most of it's on computer, but there's also some paper reports and photographs in a file cabinet. There's a black and white of her on the beach posing in a swimsuit, and I can see why Richard had a thing for her. She was adorable. There are photos taken of her before the embalming and after she was made up for the viewing. They also have records of her physical condition when they brought her into the funeral home. And believe it or not, they still have a decades-old, visitor's book."

Wes set his menu aside and leaned forward. "Whew. Now tell me, do ya think any of it's useful?"

"Oh, I sure do...very much so. I discovered a couple of unusual facts." With that, Sarah leaned in and spoke, *sotto voce*. "Did you know that if you wanted to pay your respects to the deceased after hours, you could ring the funeral home bell any time up to midnight, and the assistant would allow you in? But you had to sign the afterhours visitor's sheet first. Do you know who signed-in, five times that week?" She studied Wes's pinched brow before answering herself. "Richard! It was Richard! That begs the question: Was he really living in Montreal at the time?"

Wes released a low groan as Sarah eagerly continued. "And wait, do you know who else was on the list?" Sarah was verging on giddy. "Earl White! What would Earl White be doing visiting Daisy Panasar, dead or alive?"

Wes grimaced and shrugged. "It's a creepy thought, but maybe he and Richard are better friends than we realized."

Sarah leaned back and shook her head. "No. I'm considering there's something far more reprehensible about this than friendship between Richard and Earl."

"Sarah, please, drop the TV lawyer dramatics." He pouted like a temperamental teenager. "My patience is..."

At that moment, Shiny interrupted. "Sorry for the wait guys, but we're just so damn busy today. Can I get ya the usual, hot beef special?" The two nodded in unison. Shiny responded, "Will do. But be patient, 'cause we're runnin' behind." With that, she scurried away.

Wes, hunched over the table and squinted at Sarah. "I know you've got something ominous floating around in that brain of yours, so please, get on with it."

"Okay! The hospital report showed that she was terribly battered and bruised. Think about it, Wes. There were no crashing waves on jagged rocks to knock her around. It's the St. Lawrence River, for God's sake! The highest wave it can produce couldn't toss a puppy." She scouted the room for eavesdroppers before cautiously continuing. "I'm thinking she may have been assaulted. And maybe because of her family's strong, cultural beliefs, she chose to take her life rather than face the humiliation."

The wave of Wes's hand and his incredulous frown was a clear indication of his skepticism. "You're getting way too Hollywood on me here, Sarah. It's too much intrigue for me to grasp. It makes for good fiction, but please, let's find some corroboration before we implode this town again."

Sarah pushed herself back against the padded seat and threw up her hands in frustration. "Why in Hell is this town so afraid to get to the truth, and so willing to accept bullshit?" She growled through clenched teeth.

He casually scratched his head, "I don't know what to tell you, Kid. I'm not saying you're wrong to be pissed; but before we go upsetting the good people of this town again, I just want to be sure we've got undeniable, unassailable, proof."

She indignantly replied. "That's exactly what I'm trying to do."

"Listen, Kiddo, this is a small town, and, until this pedophile case came along, we never suspected there were dark villains lurking so close to our town. Anyway, deep probing, investigative journalism was for city folk or war correspondents, not for small-time guys like me. The worst that happened here was, like you said, the occasional Halloween prank, a barroom brawl, or maybe some shoplifting. Yeah, the worst of all were those terrible Antisemitic incidents you and I've talked about. And yes, there were rumours about Eleanor that were never reported to police and so were never followed up, but this is..." He stopped mid-sentence, clearly unnerved.

Silence hung in the air like toxic pollution, until Sarah attempted to clear it away. "Wes, you had no idea about Daisy. Don't do that to yourself. This isn't on you."

"Honestly, Sarah, I didn't know." With every laboured word, he became more unsettled. "The reports seemed logical." He shook his head as if to rid himself of decades of haziness. "It seemed clear to everyone, that going out there at night without her trainer, and against his orders, was nuts. Her seeming, but rare, disobedience and recklessness made it reasonable for everyone to conclude her death was just a terrible accident."

Sarah offered a brief, comforting smile. "I need to have another conversation with Richard. But this time, I'm not gonna hold back."

After a pensive moment, Wes spoke up. "Listen, maybe you should start with Earl? I mean, he's the common denominator. Like you implied, what reason would he have to show up at the funeral home? If you already have a witness who tells you that Earl raped Eleanor, then is it really a stretch to believe he's somehow responsible for whatever happened to Daisy?"

She nodded confidently. "I have little doubt that Earl was involved, but for now, I need to dig deep. There are still a lot of dark corners we'll need to shine a light on."

"You know, Sarah, for a girl who barely had the confidence to call herself a journalist a few of months ago, you're surprising the hell outta me. Now, you're daring to go where the press, including me, the police, and the courts; never dared to go." He laughed, "You're quite the detective."

She snickered. "Ah, well, when you raise teenagers, you learn all about sniffing out suspicious behaviour. Every mom has a little detective hidden inside."

"So, Detective, have you considered that if Earl committed crimes against Eleanor and Daisy, he might have also sent those dolls?"

She shook her head again. "I don't think so. He seemed genuinely scared out of his pants when he heard about them. He acted like his wretched life was also in danger. I don't think he's capable of being that good an actor."

* * *

Wally clocked in for protective duty at Eleanor's, relieving Dan, who then headed out on assignment with Ray.

Before leaving, Ray called Sarah with instructions. "Do me a favour. Since you're goin' over to keep Eleanor company, you might wanna bring along Zane's black and white photo collection and try and get her to look through it with you."

The perplexed frown on Sarah's face couldn't be seen, but somehow, Ray could hear it.

"Hey, drop the scowl, and just do it, okay?"

Sarah smiled and acquiesced. "I can do it...and without the attitude."

Ray snickered. "Yah, well, we'll see about that."

* * *

Ray tracked the phone number and mailbox info that Bindy had given him. The first lead was to a payphone fifty miles to the East of Prescott; the other, to a town forty miles to the west. Ray and Dan tossed a coin, then headed east.

* * *

Without a word, Sarah pulled the Stutstown pictures out of the shoebox and, one-by-one handed them to Eleanor, who looked carefully at each one before dismissing them.

"I'm so sorry, Sarah, but I don't recognize anybody."

Sarah slid her chair closer. "Come on, let's keep going. It's too early to quit."

Eleanor smiled wanly and picked up another photo. Partway through the pile, Eleanor hesitated, leaned over a particular snapshot, and remained focussed on it for several seconds.

Sarah glanced at the photo and shrugged. "I'm seeing nothing remarkable, so what are you seeing, Eleanor? And don't tell me nothing when it's clearly something."

"I honestly don't know. I'll get my magnifying glass." She ran to her sewing kit and returned, wielding it like a trophy. She barely glanced at the photo under the glass before pulling back in alarm.

"O-oh my God, Sarah!"

Wally jumped to his feet, turned off the living room TV and ran into the kitchen.

"Who is it?" Sarah hollered.

"I have no idea," She murmured as her eyes remained fixed on the photo.

He peered over Eleanor's shoulder. "I'm confused." He scratched his head and asked. "If you don't recognize the guy in the picture, then what was the shouting about?"

"It isn't about the guy." She tapped her finger on the photo while Wally and Sarah looked on in bewilderment.

Wally pulled up a chair next to Eleanor. "Let's sort this out. If you know it isn't the guy, then what's got you all worked up?"

"He's right, Eleanor, you're trembling like waves in a storm, and all I see in the photo is some guy you don't recognize, standing on a bed."

Eleanor took a deep, measured breath. "Here, look here, at this scarf." Sarah looked at the photo and back at her friend and offered a bewildered shrug.

"My God, Sarah, it's the scarf. It's the one my mother knitted for me."

Sarah remained perplexed. "Come on, Eleanor, we all had hand-knitted scarves from our moms or grandmothers when we were kids, and they were all pulled from the same pattern book. Why would you possibly think that one's yours?"

Eleanor shook her head, "I don't think it is, I know it is! It was one of a kind. You won't find another like it anywhere. It was my mother's own unique design. Look closely, right there." She held the magnifying glass over the scarf. "See the flowers? She crocheted every one of them and stitched them down the front of the scarf...And there...along the length of the scarf on both sides is a border of crocheted leaves and branches. My mother made it especially for me that Christmas, and I know it wasn't with the mess I gathered up that night. She asked me about it some months after, and I told her I didn't know what happened to it. I couldn't tell her they'd looped it around my neck and tried to drag me across the yard like an animal on a leash. And I didn't want to think about it...or where it might have gone. But, Sarah, that's *my* scarf. I'd know it anywhere."

* * *

Around 9:00 p.m., Ray and Dan returned, looking exhausted and discouraged. Eleanor, conversely, had become strangely energized by the scarf revelation. She sprung to her feet, straightened her apron, and unflappably asked. "How about I put on a pot of fresh coffee. You guys look like you could use it." They both nodded. "Maybe a bite to eat as well?" She added.

Dan bobbed his head eagerly. "Sure thing. Now, yer talkin'."

"In the meantime, Ray," Wally was quick to suggest, "Maybe you guys can fill us in on your highlights today, I mean, if there were any."

Ray shook his head. "Our day had no highlights. Nobody remembers seeing a guy with that name, or fitting Berger's description at either location. If he exists, he's a phantom."

Dan added with a sneer. "Yeah, and I'm beginnin' to wonder if the info ya got from Bindy isn't just a bunch o' crap."

Ray flinched at the suggestion. "Nah, I don't think so, Dan. Anyway, tomorrow, we'll check out the Brockville Funeral Home to see if her story holds up."

Dan dropped his head in exasperation. "I know you want to believe her, Boss, but I gotta say, it sounds pretty far-fetched, payin' somebody to fake a cremation. Maybe it works in the movie world, but not in this little corner of reality."

Up to that moment, Sarah had remained silently outside the conversation. "Listen, I wouldn't rule anything out. Before you guys got here, we were combing through those old photos, and something bizarre turned up, right Eleanor?"

Eleanor walked toward the group, carrying a basket of pastries. "She's right. I'm not sure how it's of any use, but I'll tell you, and then you guys can figure it out. You're Brockville's finest, right?" With that, she placed the basket on the table, sat down, and picked up the photo.

* * *

The next day, Ray discreetly shopped the black and white photo around town to see if anyone would recognize the guy with a beer bottle in his hand and a Confederate flag behind him.

Neither Wesley, the librarian, Mrs. Perkins, nor Mr. Reynolds had any idea who it was. However, there was one more possible witness he wanted to question.

* * *

Driving out to the nursing home to ask his father anything at all was generally an irksome exercise for Ray. He knew it wasn't easy for his once-strong, capable, and fearless father, to now be bound to a wheelchair, no longer feeling relevant...and maybe worse, replaced by his own son. Sometimes, Ray was met by a storm of derision, and other times, a light shower of pride. Unfortunately, he never knew which emotion would greet him upon arrival.

Today was a toss-up.

"Do ya really expect anyone to make out anythin' from this lousy picture? I can barely see the guy." Bill grumbled.

"Here, try this, Dad." Ray placed a magnifying glass in his father's hand.

"Jesus, Son, why didn't ya give me the damn thing in the first place?"

The old cop removed his eyeglasses and scanned the photo with the magnifier.

"There's somethin' about this that's naggin' at me, but I can't put my thumb on it," Bill grumbled.

"I know it's a lousy photograph, but if by some chance, a name comes to you, give me a call at the station, okay, Dad?"

Bill set his fiery gaze on Ray's face and pointedly asked, "Is he the one that attacked Holly's kid? Is that why yer askin?"

Ray shrugged and tried to look unconcerned. "No. I mean, we don't know. Eleanor saw somethin' about the picture that's bothering her, but she doesn't know who he is either."

A momentary silence chilled the room. Finally, Bill looked up at his son and smiled sardonically. "Listen, Kid, if he's a skunk, then ask that other skunk, Earl, if he knows him. Ya know what you kids used to say. 'It takes one to know one', right?"

Ray gently rubbed his dad's shoulder and sighed. "Ya know what, Dad, I just might take your advice and ask that skunk."

Bill looked up at his son and smirked. "Good, and if ya find out that scumbag is involved...do us all a favour and castrate the bastard before ya take him in. Better yet, let Holly's daughter do it." Bill clapped his hands and chortled, "Now, that'd be the right thing to do."

A fresh snowfall had blanketed the police cruiser. Inside, Dan sat warm and cozy, listening to Johnny Cash. The moment he spotted Ray exiting the home with a glower on his face, he jumped out of the car and rushed to brush the snow off the windshield. He continued sweeping away the snow as Ray approached. "So...uh, Ray, how'd it go?"

Ray shrugged and mumbled, "Not sure."

"Did your father recognize the guy?"

"Again, not sure."

Dan stopped brushing and looked at Ray quizzically. "Huh? He either did or he didn't, Sir."

"Things aren't always so black and white as you'd like them to be. He couldn't say he knew the guy. But I could see there was somethin' buggin' him. I told him if he thinks of what it is, to call me. So, when ya get done with the snow groomin' there, I'd like us to head to the funeral home." With that, Ray slid into the passenger seat and closed the door.

Dan opened the trunk to toss in the brush, and spotted Bindy's crate. "Hey Ray, did ya forget ya still got that box back there?" he asked as he slid into the driver's seat.

"No, I'll get to it."

"Yeah, well I hope ya do it soon, 'cause if there's a dead Fergusson stashed in there, it'll stink almost as bad as when they're alive."

CHAPTER TWENTY-SEVEN

The Brockville Funeral Home looked more like a resort for the living, than a final destination for the dead.

It was a postcard-perfect sight with its cross-gabled roof, wraparound porch, and classic Greek columns. The snow-capped trees that graced the immense property added the final brush strokes on the stunning winter scene.

There were no cars on the lot which meant there was no funeral in progress, therefore no need for the undertaker to have to explain a sudden police presence to a grieving family.

The funeral director was a small, grey-haired man who seemed shaken by the sight of two live police officers standing in his office doorway.

Before the man could utter a word, Ray began. "Sorry we didn't call first, but we were in the area. You're the funeral director?"

The director nodded and rose from his chair. "Wh-what uh, can I uh, do for you, officers?" he spluttered.

"Glad you asked. I've got this document here dated February 18, 1988," Ray began, "so could you please look up that date and tell us the names of the deceased you had possession of, on the premises that day?"

The director obliged and entered the date into the computer.

"Uh, it seems, according to these records, there was neither a receiving nor transferring of any deceased person on that day. I can check my personal date book to see if there's anything that shows up that somehow didn't get recorded...although that would be almost impossible."

He flipped through his personal date book from 1988, stopping for a moment at February eighteenth. He flipped back several pages, and then forward again.

"Ah, you see here. no entry." He resolutely snapped the book shut and jutted out his chin. "There was no entry, 'cause I was on vacation with my family in the Bahamas that week...and for another week after that."

Dan grimaced and cocked his head. "So ya just close up shop, 'cause ya figure no one will die if you're on vacation?"

"Not at all, Sir. We always leave word that another funeral parlor will be providing care for the deceased and bereaved in our absence. We leave a name and contact number clearly visible on our front door and in the newspaper as well. It's never been a problem." The director paused, took a deep breath, then proceeded. "May I ask why you're inquiring about that particular date?"

"We have reason to believe that, on that date, someone cremated a body on these premises."

The director unwittingly released a snicker. "Well, now I know for sure it's a mistake. We have no crematorium on this property. All bodies for cremation are sent to a facility away from these premises."

"But the death certificate comes from this place. Look, it has your logo, address, everything." Dan handed the document to the director.

The director looked at the paper and shook his head, "This isn't a death certificate. Only the province can issue a death certificate. What you have here is proof of death," he pointed at the signature line and scribbled his signature on a note pad. "And if you look here and compare, you'll see that's not my signature." As he continued to study the document, he became agitated. "I don't recognize that doctor's signature either. Also...it's signed in red ink. The law says it must be signed in blue. Officer, every funeral administrator knows that." He dropped the paper on his desk and sat down. "I'm sorry, officers...but I never saw or signed that ridiculous paper, and I can assure you that no crematorium would accept anything less than full, proper, and legal documentation before they would ever proceed. So, what in the world is going on here?"

Ray smiled warmly and politely asked, "May we sit?"

The director nodded and waved an open hand toward two chairs across from his desk. The officers sat down. "I think we got off to a bad start here, Mr. uh...I didn't even get your name. I'm really sorry. Please, let's start there."

"Well, thank you for that. Yes, I'm a bit taken aback by all this. I'm sure you can understand. I'm

William Riggert, and I'm the director and owner of this facility."

"Pleased to meet you Mr. Riggert. So, did you leave someone behind to take care of the premises while you were away?"

He nodded. "I always leave a caretaker here to make sure the driveway gets shoveled, and the plants get watered, that kind of thing. I couldn't tell you offhand who was working here at that time...I've had many caretakers over the years. I could look through the employee files and let you know. They're not in the computer, so I'll have to go through a load of paper files. It may take a day or two to dig them out, but if it'll help, I'd be happy to do it."

Ray offered a perfunctory nod and rose to his feet. "That would be a great help to us, and thank you, Mr. Riggert." He handed the funeral director a card, "This has my home and station number. If I don't answer, just leave a message and I'll get back to ya."

Ray tipped his hat to the befuddled man, and Dan followed suit.

* * *

While Ray hopped out at KFC to pick up chicken for dinner at Eleanor's, Dan drove to her house and parked the cruiser in front.

"Shh," Eleanor warned as she ushered Dan into the front room. "Don't wake him."

It was a tempting sight for Dan to see his rotund partner spread out on the easy chair, snoring like a weed-whacker, and filling the front of his uniform with a puddle of drool. It was a platinum opportunity for a prankster like Dan, but Eleanor caught his devilish grin and interrupted his ill-conceived plan. "Forget it, Dan. I've seen this scenario on TV sit-coms. I know you're thinking of doing something dopey, and I'm asking you to forget it. Wally's suffered enough today listening for odd sounds and watching for shadows...all with my sewing machine whirring in his ear. This was a tedious job, so give the poor guy a break."

Dan whispered. "Well, he had a choice and he said he didn't wanna be drivin' the cruiser through slush and sloggin' through snow drifts. So..."

Ray shouted as he came on the scene. "Everyone doin' okay here, Wally?"

Wally clumsily stumbled to his feet; an action that didn't go undetected by Ray, whose scowl was set in stone. "If you're sleepin', you're not watchin' and you're not listenin, and not noticing that door was left open'. Ya get my drift?"

Wally squirmed in his boots. "Yes, Boss. It won't happen again."

"You're damn right it won't, 'cause tomorrow you're in the driver's seat. Got it?"

Dan gritted his teeth as he grasped the fact that. having stupidly brought attention to Wally's blunder, his punishment now was to spend the next day inert and bored. He plucked up a bit of courage, cleared his throat, and took a stab at the truth.

"Boss," Dan mumbled, "Uh, I'm the one who left the door unlocked just now. I figured ya were comin' in behind me soon, eh? You shouldn't blame Wally for my screw up."

Ray silently and methodically removed his gloves and hat and placed them on the shelf of the coat rack while Dan continued. "So, Boss...I was just wonderin'...don't ya think it might be better to leave the schedule as is since you and me have kinda got this 'on the road thing' worked out, and Wally really knows the lay of the land here?" Dan shifted from foot to foot as he waited for an answer.

Ray removed his coat and hung it up, rubbed the cold from his hands, then paused and replied. "Yeah, well, Wally obviously knows the lay of it too well. So no, Dan, I don't think it's better. If I did, I wouldn't have suggested we change it. Ya hearin' me?"

"Yup." Dan sheepishly replied.

Wally offered up a long, animated stretch of his ample frame before adding. "Well, I guess I better get on home and get some rest. It could be a big, excitin' day out there tomorrow behind the wheel." He pulled on his coat, flashed Dan a cheeky grin, and headed out the door singing *"You can't always get what you wa-ant."*

Dan buttoned his coat preparing to make his exit. "Well, folks it's been a blast, but I've got places to go and cheerin' crowds to see...In other words, I'm playin' hockey tonight."

"Playin' or sittin' on the bench? Ray chuckled. Dan smirked and turned to exit.

Eleanor suddenly called out to him. "Oh Dan, wait a minute. Would you mind dropping Sarah's briefcase off at the hotel on your way? She forgot it, which is no surprise," she mused with a shake of her head. "Last time she was here, she forgot her appointment book, and the time before that, it was her gloves. I called her hotel, she isn't back yet, but she should be there by now."

"No problem." He assured her.

Eleanor pensively pulled at her ear lobe. "Oh, and please ask her how she's feeling. She seemed a bit out of sorts today. I don't think it gets this frigid in Toronto, so she may be coming down with something."

He gave a curt shrug. "Will do. Anyhow, I'll be on my way and let you two get reacquainted with the Colonel before it gets cold."

Ray nodded to Dan. "Yeah, like you said, the colonel's waiting, so..." He motioned toward the door. Dan grabbed the briefcase and headed out.

As Ray was unpacking the KFC, he commented, "Ya know what, Eleanor, I think I bought too much. I sort of expected Sarah to be here.

"She left a few hours ago, 'cause she had some errands to run."

Ray smiled and shrugged. "Okay then, that means a lot more chicken for you and me."

* * *

Dan called up to Sarah's room from the front desk. There was no answer. He summoned Reynolds who told him he hadn't seen her all day. He then tried Wes and Shiny but struck out on both calls. He left messages for them, but his gut was telling him not to walk away. He called out to Reynolds again. "Okay, I get it. Ya haven't seen her, but can ya check to see if there were any messages or packages left for her?"

Reynolds grunted as he turned to look. With raised eyebrows, he walked back toward the officer and handed him a sealed envelope.

Dan read the name, *Sera Klein*. "Who delivered this?" Dan growled. "And when?"

Reynolds squinted at the envelope. "See there, it was stamped as received at eleven this mornin'. Now, I wasn't here this mornin' so I wouldn't know who delivered it. Freddy was on the desk 'til I got here around one. I can call and ask him if ya want."

Dan hissed. "Call him...now!"

Reynolds scowled as he reached for the phone. Dan chewed a couple of Tums, shook the envelope, held it up to the light, and finally, unable to stand the pressure, he opened it. The message was brief:

Sera I no hoo you are an wen we meat you will no hoo I am an that will be suner then you think. We have lots to talk abot. Ill be waitin an wachin for you. Don't dare tell yer cop frends abut this. This is abot me an you.

Since the envelope had remained sealed until he opened it, Sarah couldn't have seen it. He watched while the manager listened, grunted into the receiver, then hung up.

"Well? What's the story, Reynolds? Does he know who left it?"

"Freddy says it was on the desk when he got back from a bathroom break. He didn't see nobody around. He wasn't even sure it was for Mrs. Berman, 'cause it said Klein on the front, but it had a room number, so he stamped it anyway..." He paused, remembering something, "Oh wait, he also said when he went to put her mail in the box, he saw that both keys were missin'."

Dan felt gastric acid rise to his throat. "I need your passkey. Now!"

* * *

Dan entered the room cautiously, searching every corner and under the bed before he moved warily into the bathroom. He flung back the shower curtain to find a sparkling clean tub. He exhaled an enormous sigh, then sat on the side of the bed, grabbed Sarah's phone, and dialled Wally's home number and waited anxiously. He picked up on the fifth ring. "Hello?"

Dan blew an exhale of relief. "Wally, it's Dan. Thank ya Jesus, you're home. Listen, ya gotta get back in the car right now and meet me at the hotel...I don't care if ya just walked in. Just do it for Christ's sake. Do I sound like I'm kidding? No, I'm not tellin' the Boss, until I got more than indigestion to prove that somethin' doesn't feel right here. Just get over here, okay? And don't try scoring points by calling Ray first, neither."

As he waited, Dan thought about the fact that the past few nights, when either he or Wally had driven Sarah home from Eleanor's, they stopped at the green grocers or the drug store so she could pick up a few things. But he saw nothing in her room that indicated she'd stopped to shop that evening. The room was intact...neat, clean, orderly...nothing suspicious.

* * *

Wally hurried into the lobby to find Dan pacing. "Christ, Dan, I was plannin' to settle in to watch the

Leaf's game at my brother's place in Maitland, but lucky for you, I was too tired and went home instead. Why're you actin' so weird. What's up?"

Dan's expression was grim as he pulled Wally aside. "Come on, let's go."

"Go where? What the hell's goin' on, Dan? You look like you just shit yourself."

"I think Sarah's missin'. Eleanor said she might not have been feelin' well, but she's not upstairs. I called Wes and Shiny to see if they'd talked to her, but I had ta leave messages. Shit, I just realized, it's gonna scare the crap outta them, what with those stupid doll threats escalatin' an' all. I get the impression; Sarah doesn't know anybody else here in town. A couple o' hours ago, she told Eleanor she was gonna run some errands and go home, and no one's seen her since." Wally was frozen to the spot. Dan demanded through gritted teeth "Let's go. What in hell are you waitin' for?"

Wally stood there, pale and shaking, "Oh Christ, Dan...like an asshole, I was sleepin' away there at Eleanor's. I should've driven Sarah home. If something's happened, it's my fault and the boss's gonna have my badge, and he'd be right ta take it."

"Jesus, will ya get movin'!" He hissed as he pushed his partner through the open door. "We'll throw a pity party for ya after we find her, Asshole. Right now, we've gotta figure out what to do. We'll stop by Archie Reid's Groceries to see if she's been by...or maybe, if she was feelin' sick, she stopped in for some meds at the pharmacy. You take Archie's and I'll talk to Tom. I'll meet you back at your cruiser in five minutes."

* * *

Dan heard Wally wheezing from half a block away. He shouted up the street to him. "Anythin'?"

Wally continued to trot his sizeable girth back to the car, where he reported, in a halting series of gasps, "Yeah...She was there...Late afternoon...He didn't notice what she bought...but...he noticed she wasn't...her usual...perky self. That's it. How 'bout you?"

"Nope. Tom said he didn't see her at all today."

"But at least we know she was at the grocery store not that long ago. So, why the big worry? I mean...she's not legally...missing."

Dan handed him the note. As he read it, sweat dripped down his face. "Holy shit, Dan, we've gotta tell the boss! We can't chase around the town like a couple o' amateurs."

"Fine. You go into the O'Brien and call him, fast. Tell him to be waitin', and why we're coming to get him, and I'll go warm up my car for ya."

Wally took a couple of steps, stopped, and turned to Dan. "Don't kill me for this Dan, but it just hit me that Sarah didn't even drop by Eleanor's 'til well after lunchtime today, and then she left early. So, if her friends didn't see her and she wasn't in her room, then where was she all mornin'? Where in Hell would she go?"

* * *

Dan pulled up in front of Eleanor's house. Wally bolted from the car and passed Ray as they exchanged places. Wally stepped inside, closed, and locked the front door. The chief buckled up his seat belt and doled out orders. "Turn around and head north."

"Ya got it, Boss." Dan began to squirm in the uncomfortable silence, searching for an appropriate conversation starter. "Boss, I hope I didn't overreact on this. I mean, Sarah coulda just been invited out by someone and didn't think to tell anybody."

Ray shot him a puzzled glance. "Why in Hell would she keep it a secret from Eleanor?"

Dan shrugged and slapped his forehead. "You're right. It's a really stupid idea. Why keep that a secret?" Silence resumed. "Uh, do you wanna at least tell me where we're headed?"

Ray offered a half-assed grin. "Wanna bet five bucks on who I think is mixed up in this?"

"Depends on who you're thinkin."

"My money's on Earl."

"Don't ya think that's a bit paranoid, Boss? Come on, even Earl's not that dumb." Ray offered a blasé shrug.

"Ya know what? I'll take that bet. I can use five bucks."

"All right. Let's see who collects." Ray settled in with a smug look on his face and drove into the bleak countryside.

* * *

The barren forest that surrounded the sprawling White property twinkled brightly while flood lights beamed in all colours, and in all directions from the rooftop of his palatial home.

"It looks as if Earl's 'freedom celebrations' are still goin' on." Ray observed.

"Man, if this is what being a sleazebag gets ya, I might try me some sleaze," Dan cracked. "This place is like hillbilly Hollywood. So, tell me, Boss, why should we hate this guy?"

Ray inhaled a fortifying breath. "We don't hate him. We're the police. We just document asshole behaviour for future reference, and then, when the asshole turns out to be a criminal, then we can hate him. For now, we're just visiting a random asshole, okay?" He glanced sideways at his deputy.

Dan nodded. "Got ya, Boss."

"When we get inside, watch, and learn. Keep your cool, be civil...and remember, we're guests...unless we've got a warrant, which we haven't."

* * *

Mrs. White seemed curiously unsurprised to see the officers at her door. Dan couldn't help but notice that her eyes lingered uncomfortably over Ray's six-foot-plus physique. She extended her hand, which Ray dutifully shook. "Well, now I've met big Chief Connell; but you're new. I'm Ruby, Earl's wife." She reached her chubby, bejeweled hand forward to shake Dan's naked, sweaty one. She tendered a roguish smile, "Oh, a shy one, huh?" She grabbed his hand, squeezed, and released.

The "lady of the manor," adorned from ear to wrist with gaudy jewelry, and clothed in a pink and turquoise velveteen track suit, offered a flirtatious wiggle of the shoulders as she motioned for the men in uniform to follow.

She escorted them from the marble foyer toward a large room with a vaulted ceiling, granite floors, and burled walnut cabinets. The house was beautifully built, but the furnishings were garish and tasteless, more suited to a brothel than a home. The place was crammed with gilded cabinets, a glittering mirrored bar, oversized cut-velvet furniture, and huge, ostentatious pieces of kitsch "art", leaving little space to maneuver through the room.

She motioned for them to sit. They remained standing.

"Okay. Well, this is a nice surprise, officers. My husband'll be down in a minute. He has to put some clothes on, eh? Can't come down here in his natural glory now, can he? He wouldn't wanna get our officers all worked up. Can I get ya guys a beer, bourbon, a Bloody Mary or somethin'?"

"Thanks, we're fine." Ray replied, shaking his head.

"You sure?" She asked. They nodded curtly. Ruby stepped up to the bar and poured herself a drink.

"So, you're Earl's surprise tonight, eh? He'll love that you drove all the way out here to apologize, in person," she smiled smugly.

Ray squinted in bewilderment "Do what, Ma'am?"

Her smile widened. "Apologize...for wrongly accusin' him." She turned toward him with a glass of booze in hand and raised it in a grandiose toast. "To Brockville's finest...for apologizin'."

Dan's eyes widened, but he found himself at a loss for words. In fear of committing another faux pas, he waited wordlessly for his boss to respond.

"No, Ma'am, that's not why we're here." Ray calmly exhaled the words. "We just need to talk to him for a minute, in private."

Ruby threw back the rest of the drink, shot a scornful look at Ray, and then slammed the glass down on the bar.

"Private huh? Well, yes, Sir. I'd best just run my ass up the stairs and get King Earl down here for ya right away, eh?" She mockingly retorted and scurried away.

While the cops waited, they discreetly checked out how these *nouveau rich*e lived. A giant-sized painting graced the far end of the room; a weird and twisted pastel portrait of a tuxedoed, Earl, standing beside his bedecked and bejewelled wife.

"It's a masterpiece, eh? That guy's a genius," Earl boasted as he crept up behind the cops. "Yup. I paid him a fortune for that piece o' art...more than you guys earn in a year." Earl punctuated the insult with a scurrilous chortle.

Ray gritted his teeth but said nothing as Earl continued. "Ruby tried ta tell me yer not here to apologize, and I told her, she's full o' shit." He stared intensely at the two officers. "The truth is, you wouldn't be dumb enough not to apologize for what ya put me though. So it's pretty hard for me ta believe you could show up at my home for any other reason," as he crowed, his face contorted into a sardonic grin.

Ray straightened himself to his full height, which greatly exceeded Earl's, and moved forward one long step, which initiated a few quick steps backward by Earl.

Ray managed a tight-lipped smile before responding. "Too hard to believe, huh? Well try, Earl, 'cause we need to get that settled right away." Ray took another step toward Earl, who stepped back again. "So, let me repeat what I told your wife...we're not here to apologize, for anything. You got that?"

Earl failed to reply, instead he turned and affected a slow saunter to the bar. "Okay, there's still plenty o' time. I'm a patient man. In the meantime, can I fix ya guys a drink?"

The men shook their heads in unison. Earl shrugged then poured himself a shot of bourbon. He turned and took a quick sip. "So then, what do ya want?"

Ray "Have you seen the lady journalist today?"

Earl stepped away from the bar, this time, taking a lengthy sip before offering a smug grin. "Not yet. I invited her to come to my party tonight, but she never told me yes or no. That's kinda rude, don't ya think?" Inside, Ray was roiling with red hot fury but outside he still managed to maintain an expression of cool indifference. Earl continued to taunt. "I guess there's jest no accountin' for class. But we're big-hearted people, so we're still hopin' she'll turn up. We want her to see the real me. We're thinkin' she got a bad impression, but once she sees how I live, that'll change." He strutted about the room like the lord of a manor. "Nobody can walk outta here without bein' fuckin' knocked out by all this."

Dan whispered through clenched teeth. "Is that a cue for me to let him have it, Boss?" Ray ignored the crack.

"Did you speak to her today?" Ray asked again, crossing his arms over his chest.

Earl sneered, downed the remaining dregs, and headed back to the bar. "I just told ya, I didn't hear from her, I didn't see her, I didn't talk to her, I didn't have nothin' to do with her today...Are ya fuckin' deaf?"

Ray rested his hands on his belt and stepped to the bar. "You said you invited her to your party tonight. When and how did ya do that without talkin' to her?"

Earl backed away again leaving the empty glass behind. He clumsily pushed his shaky hands into his pockets. "Didn't ya ever hear o' leavin' a message? I left one at the desk last night and she never got back to me." Earl took an exaggerated look at his watch. "I hope yer done, 'cause I got guests comin' at nine." He tapped his watch and continued. "It's getting' close to that time now, and my wife and me gotta get our party duds on. So, if there's no apology, then yer not my entertainment, in fact you're boring as hell...so you need to get out, now." He motioned for them to leave, much like one shoos away a pesky fly.

* * *

As the door closed behind them, Dan couldn't resist commenting. "I bet Earl's thrown plenty of people out of his house before us. But what he could never grasp is that, like me, they probably couldn't wait to get away from him. I know I sure couldn't." Dan waited for a response, but Ray scowled and silently stalked to the car.

Dan began to ponder the possibility that his boss's grimace might be an indication he was doubting whether the junior officer had checked for messages. "In case you're wondering, Boss, I swear, I looked through her messages, and there was definitely no invite from Earl among 'em...and Reynolds never mentioned one either."

Ray nodded. "Okay, if there was one, she must have picked it up first thing in the morning before the shift change. I'll call Mitch and find out who was on duty." As Dan took his seat behind the wheel, Ray pulled out his address book and his flip phone. "Okay I've got Mitch's home number, now let's hope we've got cell service in these godforsaken Boonies."

As the car left the White estate, Ray dialled and waited, then breathed a sigh of relief as Mitch's voice came through loud and clear. "I swear Officer, I didn't take the message. The night clerk handed it to me to give to Mrs. Berman this morning when I delivered her breakfast."

"Did you see her after that, Mitch?" Ray shouted into the phone.

"No, Sir. I went off shift at ten, and Freddy took over." Mitch paused. "Hello, Mitch? Can you hear me?"

"Yes, Sir, I can. Is there a problem?"

"Yeah, there may be, so do us a favour, don't go anywhere. We'll be at your house in about a half hour."

CHAPTER TWENTY-EIGHT

Mitch was outside pacing when the police arrived. Ray lowered the passenger window and called out to him. Mitch scurried over, looking apprehensive. Ray assured him he'd done nothing wrong and suggested, he jump in and close the door to warm up. The nervous young man did exactly as asked.

The car remained in park as Mitch hunched forward and began to chatter. "I swear, Officer Ray, I wouldn't ordinarily have read the invite, but seeing it was from Earl...well, I think ya know what I mean. Anyway, it was a simple note with the time and the address; but then, I got squirrelly 'cause it said *don't bring a guest*...and *don't tell anybody about it,* 'cause they invited a big crowd, and they don't want any party crashers."

Ray became ominously silent which set the rookie on edge. Dan squirmed in his seat, sighed, and finally reached for the radio dial. Ray slapped his hand away.

Dan sat, stone still, mustering the nerve to pierce the silence and defy his boss's mood. A sudden rush of confidence motivated him to speak up. "Listen Boss, I've been thinkin', I don't suppose Earl's got a big circle o' friends, eh? I mean, all his relations are in the pen, right?" Ray grunted and offered a perfunctory nod. Dan began to gesture wildly as he continued.

"Seriously, Boss, who do ya suppose he'd invite to his shindig? I mean, think about it."

Ray pinched his brow, "Maybe his lawyer, the local one, 'cause I can't see the other one comin' all this way to celebrate Earl."

"Yeah, that's for sure." Mitch piped up from the back seat.

Dan was still mulling; "But listen. Wouldn't ya figure that even a lowlife like Earl might've at least arranged a lift for Sarah? It's not an easy place to find. I mean it's in the middle of nowhere, for Christ's sake." He snapped his fingers as a dark thought crossed his mind. " Shit, I mean, what if she was ta run into a snowstorm or get a flat tire? She'd be stranded for sure eh?" He paused for a beat, then with a smile of relief, he continued. "So, let's say that same thought even occurred ta Earl. Then maybe he asked Richard ta bring her to the party." Dan raised his open hands and shrugged. "Whadda ya think?"

Ray's eyes lit up. "I think, ya got something there, Rookie. Let's go see if Richard's left for the big event yet."

* * *

Dan's unmarked car rolled quietly down Elm Street. It seemed as if the entire neighbourhood had already closed down for the night, leaving the area draped in darkness, except for the faint glow from a forest of television screens visible through sitting room windows.

Down the block, the sound of a coughing engine motivated Dan to pull over to the curb. The officers got out of the car and, while Dan approached the passenger side of the Pontiac, Ray knocked on the frosted driver's side window. As the window slowly lowered, the chief shone his flashlight inside. "Hi, Mr. McCall, we were just comin' to see ya. Havin' a little car trouble, are ya?"

"Yeah, these damn American cars." He grumbled as he looked straight ahead.

"Do ya need a boost?"

Richard offered a relieved half smile. "That would be a big help, Chief. I'm running kind of late."

"Yeah, we know. Unfortunately, Dan doesn't have his jumper cables with him. I mean, what kind of Canadian doesn't keep jumper cables in their trunk, huh?" Ray chuckled. "Oh Jeez, I hope you've got some?"

Richard offered an embarrassed and guilty shrug.

"Okay, sorry about the crack, but never mind. Just give me a minute." Ray offered an assured smile and walked around to the passenger side of Ray's car, hopped in, and lowered the window. Dan remained outside within hearing range, as Ray began to chat with Richard. "So, you're not taking the Missus with ya to the big celebration? By the way, we just came from payin' Earl a visit. Young Dan there was sayin', that's quite a little castle he's got out there in the sticks. Talkative guy, that Earl. Fascinating, didn't ya think, Dan?" He shouted toward Dan, who was dancing to keep warm.

Beads of sweat bubbled up on Richard's brow as he cleared his throat. "Earl? Really? W-what did he say that was so fascinating?" Richard asked in a tightly-pinched voice.

Ray, trying not to notice the lawyer's twitchy reaction, turned his attention to Dan. "Hey Rookie, you must be freezin' your ass off standing out there. Here's ten bucks. Go pick up your jumper cables, take Mitch over to Tim Horton's, both of you grab a coffee and warm up. But bring me back my change, huh? And drop over to the O'Brien to see if maybe 'the cat's come back.' In the meantime, Richard and me will be havin' a chat. I'll see ya right here, with the cables, in about twenty minutes, or so."

Dan took the ten and nodded. "Sure. No problem, Boss."

Ray didn't miss a beat. "Listen Richard, since you can't get the car moving yet, would ya mind if we went inside and warmed up while I ask you and your wife a few questions?"

Richard sighed and slumped his shoulders. "My wife's at her bridge club tonight, but yeah, we can go inside."

"That'd be great."

Ray exited Richard's car and watched as Dan drove off with Mitch.

The two men trudged inside, shed their overcoats, and settled down at the kitchen table.

Ray stared intently at Richard's face, but Richard avoided his eyes--much like a five-year-old looks away when caught doing mischief. "Did ya see Sarah Berman today?" He asked.

The lawyer stared at his hands, gazed at the ceiling, shuffled his feet, and finally replied. "Uh, yeah, I did."

"Can you tell me when and where, and what ya talked about?"

"Uh, well, uh, she called up this morning and, uh, asked to meet with me, around eleven..."

Richard's thin, gasping pause allowed Ray a few seconds to consider his follow-up questions. "Well, Richard, that only answers the *when*. What about the *where*, and *what* you talked about?"

Richard squirmed in his chair as if he was sitting on plum-sized hemorrhoids.

"Oh yeah, sorry. Well, when she got to my office, I was dealing with the stench of smoke, and workmen hammering away at the front entrance and all, so I wasn't in the best of moods, but then neither was she." He cast a glance toward Ray, who glared back.

"She wasn't in the best mood? How do you know that?" Ray snarled.

"Well, she seemed pretty riled up." Ray's scowl remained fixed on Richard who lowered his eyes and rested his clasped hands on the table. "Uh, anyhow, Chief, that's about it."

Ray sniffed up a lung full of air, then reached out and placed a heavy hand over Richard's stiffly entwined fingers. "No, Richard. That's not even close to 'about it'."

Flop sweat ran down the sharp curve of Richard's nose. Ray removed his hand just as the droplet landed. The lawyer unlaced his hands and wiped away the perspiration with his sleeve. He slowly nodded as reality sank in. "You know already, don't you, Chief? That's why you're here, isn't it?"

"Yup, you said it." Ray flawlessly lied.

"That louse." He muttered almost inaudibly. "She went ahead and told you everything, even though she promised she wouldn't. I should've known better than to trust a damn journalist." With an almost comical childish pout, he slumped down in his chair.

Ray smirked, and boldly drummed his fingers on the table. Suddenly Richard bolted upright in his seat. "Wait, if you already know, then why in hell are you asking me?"

"Because I need to hear it directly from the source."

Richard rolled his eyes and sighed. "Fine. She wanted to know why I offered her five thousand dollars not to write the story, and why I said the offer came from Earl. That's it, the end."

The police chief's rigidly pinched brow was an indicator he was running out of patience. "No, that's not the end, Richard. It's just the goddamn beginning. Now talk, before I lose my temper. You sure as hell don't want that happening."

"Jesus, Ray, I really don't want to talk about it. Why can't you just leave it the hell alone?" The sweat was now cascading from Richard's scalp like a waterfall.

"Look, Richard, you already mouthed off to a journalist, so how long do ya think it'll take before word spreads? Maybe if you talk to me, I can stop it."

Richard looked up at the police chief with pleading eyes. "Ray, please. I don't want my family to know. That's all I care about."

Ray settled back in his chair and nodded. "Then let's get on with it before your wife walks in."

The stink of body odor, dry mouth, and fear permeated the room. Richard took several deep breaths and cleared his throat. "This is so tough, Ray."

"Not as tough as it'll be if you don't get started!" Ray snapped.

"Okay, okay. It began, in the winter of '58. That's when I fell for Daisy Panasar. But our differences were uh, well, visible and abundant. I was eighteen and she was barely fifteen, and she was East Indian. My family was whiter than white. Her parents wanted her to merge into Western society while mine wanted me to shun anyone who wasn't born and bred, a white Christian.

"We'd been secretly seeing each other for several months when we were spotted together one night by a gang of thugs. I was terrified my parents would find out, so I agreed to pay the bullies to keep the secret. Over time, my fear of the blackmailers grew beyond any fear I had of my parents. But I was so damn in love with Daisy, I took part-time jobs, borrowed from my brother, even resorted to stealing money out of my mother's purse just to be able to meet the blackmailer's growing demands, so I could hang on to

Daisy." Richard dropped his head into his hands. "No, Ray. Oh Christ, no. I can't do this. I won't!" He looked up defiantly.

Ray calmly pressed on, "Yeah, you can, and you will. You said it yourself; you don't want your family to know. Well, if I bring ya up to the Brockville jail for questioning, what do you think the chances are that it won't leak out? But hey, the choice is yours. Do we do it here or shall we..."

Richard's hands trembled as he raised them in a gesture of submission. "Okay, okay. The threats escalated, and, from time to time...I...oh shit, I can't."

"Here or jail, Richard?!" The police chief's ominous tone left the terrified man no choice.

"Just give me a second." With that, Richard arose and poured two glasses of water. He handed one to Ray and took a sip from the other as he sat back down. Ray remained stoic and silent while the frightened lawyer haltingly continued.

"I, uh...I was threatened and coerced into tagging along with that gang. They got perverse satisfaction out of forcing a nerdy bookworm like me to watch as they menaced neighborhoods. They operated in the darkest of nights, and then...then they scurried back to their rat holes, leaving me standing there alone and petrified that someone would find me and accuse me of whatever awful thing they'd just done.

"One night, I finally found the courage to walk away. That was the night Earl and his gang waited to scare Jesus Christ into a young Jewish girl." He shuddered at the thought.

"I never knew for sure what happened that frigid night, 'cause the minute they snatched the girl, I ran. I never asked what happened. I didn't want to know. That's it!" He curtly slapped the table as a sign he was done.

Ray sat listening with clenched teeth and rigid fists, mustering the strength not to beat the coward into a throbbing pulp. "Don't you even think about stopping now." He commanded.

The lawyer began to shiver as if he'd just transferred the bitter cold from outside to his insides. "I'm not stopping, honestly. I just need a breather." After a few more sips of water, he resumed. "Look, I was scared they'd find me and maybe kill me for running away. But after that night, they actually left me alone. I thought the terror was finally over. Then one summer night, Daisy and I were, you know...uh." He stopped abruptly, red-faced and head down like a bashful teenager.

Ray wasn't moved by the reaction. "No, I don't know. Daisy and you were doing what?"

"Just necking...at the beach. It was late and already dark outside. We were alone...or we thought we were. But then Earl and his gang came running onto the sand like wild animals, flashing lights in our faces, hooting like monkeys, squealing like pigs. Berger and Arvin nabbed me and tied my arms around a post so I couldn't move, and Earl grabbed Daisy by her hair..." His words faded as low, guttural moans erupted in their place. Tears and snot dribbled toward his chin. Suddenly and defiantly, he pulled out a hanky and wiped the fluids away. He found his voice again. "Earl...dragged her along the sand shouting, he was gonna nail her to a cross.

"A cop car pulled up at the top of the street and parked. Your dad, Officer Bill, got out, I guess, making his usual rounds. But by the time he shut the car door and ambled down toward the beach, those bastards had run off like scared rabbits, and Daisy had untied me. When he asked what we were doing out there so late, we made up a dumb story about collecting data on water temperature in preparation for Daisy's big race that summer. I guess he believed us, 'cause he said if we had all the data we needed, he'd drive us home. I was petrified that someone might see me and Daisy together in the cop car and tell my parents. He dropped Daisy off, but I walked home alone, scared out of my mind that I'd get jumped...but nothing happened."

He gulped down the rest of the water before thumping the glass on the table like a gavel, as if to declare the interrogation over.

Ray rose steadily and stood tall behind his chair with both hands tightly grasping the top rail. "That's not where the story ends, Richard. So, enough stalling. Get on with it. I'm losing my grip here."

Richard hung his head and slowly exhaled. "Yeah. You're right, it's not where it ends." He drew a redemptory breath, pressed his fingers together, and tucked them under his chin. "Maybe it started when Zane snapped a picture of me and Daisy together on the beach that night and one of them sent it *anonymously* to my mother." His voice broke as the words wafted out like a bad smell. "In a matter of days, I was on a train headed for Montreal to visit my grandmother. I'd already been accepted at McGill for the fall semester, and was to start in a month, so, I just didn't come home." The pain of the memory was as obvious on his face as a keloid scar. He was worn and weary, but he continued without a prompt.

"That same summer, I heard the news of Daisy's horrific accident, and it nearly finished me." Another tear ambled along his cheek.

"About six years later, I had a law degree, and a wife. We had a kid on the way, but no law practice. My dad had passed on, so I moved my family back to town to stay with my mother 'til we got settled. That's when Earl came to see me. He told me, he was deeply sorry for what he'd put me through when we were kids. He needed to make it up to me. He told me he was building a business empire and he wanted me to represent him." He shrugged and offered a wan smile. "And the truth is, that's just what happened."

Ray sat back down. "So, you had no problem working for a possible rapist...and no problem having him socialize with your wife and kids?"

Richard shifted in his chair. "Once I started to represent Earl, I found it hard to believe he could ever do what the gossips claimed. Yeah, he's crass or vulgar or uncouth or any term you want to use, but the fact is, he's been my biggest and most loyal client. However, to be clear, I've never considered him a friend. My kids and grandkids have never met the guy. And if my wife would rather play bridge than go to his party, you can pretty much tell how she feels about him. So, I haven't needed to worry about his influence on my family. My mother and Earl get along just fine. She admires him because he shares her questionable views. If the party wasn't so late tonight, she would've begged to come along. My home, my office, and my kids' education were supported, for the most part, by client fees from Earl's legitimate real estate investments. So, am I sorry?" Richard looked at the officer and shook his head as he answered. "No. Why would I be? Maybe now you can understand why I didn't want Sarah digging into my life. At least by telling her about it myself, I know she can't use the information I shared with her, 'cause we agreed it was off the record; and I can't see a journalist with any integrity ruining my family and possibly hers, over a story that leads nowhere."

Ray's tone was anything but composed. "I hear ya trying to suggest it's all perfectly acceptable. I mean, what self-respecting, professional would willingly compromise his integrity for profit, huh?"

Humiliation dawned, then died quickly in the lawyer's eyes. "Okay, now you have all the facts, Chief, and I think we're done here. If your officer's back to give me a boost, I can still make it in time to shake Earl's hand and congratulate him on his freedom." He stood up and slid his chair back in place. "That's what a devoted lawyer does for his client."

With a curt nod, Ray rose to his feet. "Just one more question, Richard. When Sarah left your office, did she say where she was going?"

"No, but as I said, she was pretty upset. She did tell me, in no uncertain terms, that she wouldn't be going to Earl's party. That was a big relief for me, 'cause I was worried she might bring up that five-thousand-dollar offer again in front of Earl, which could get me into a whole new mess of trouble."

The men bundled up and headed outside to find that Dan had finished jump-starting the car. The lawyer offered a modest "thank you," as he quickly hopped inside and drove away. Dan tossed the cables into the back of his car and settled behind the wheel as Ray slipped into the passenger seat.

"See, Rookie, ya did your good deed for the day. And what did ya do with Mitch?"

"He's back at the hotel, callin' anyone in town we could think of who might've had some contact with Sarah. I left him your car phone number, but I told him not to depend on gettin' through on that damn ornery gadget. I said if he's got somethin' important to tell us, he should call the station."

"Okay, good. Speaking of the station, did you check in?"

"I didn't think to do that, Boss."

"Really?" With a heavy sigh, Ray glanced over at the rookie and asked, "Did ya at least think to check in on Wally, for Christ's sake?"

"Yeah, Boss, I did for sure, eh? I didn't want to worry Eleanor, so Wally and me spoke at the front door.

But everything was okay there. How did the talk go with the lawyer?"

"Well, let me think how to put this." He paused for a few seconds and stared intently out the window. "How did it go? Well, I would've liked to reverse the contacts on those jumper cables and blown the shit out of his car, that's how it went." He turned toward Dan, flashed a cynical grin, and continued. "But see, Dan, an experienced cop like me would never do somethin' like that. So let that be a lesson to you. Now, I wanna take a leak, get a hot cup o' joe, and check for messages. Drop me off at Tim's. You drive on up the street, and look in on Mitch at the hotel, I'll meet you there in about fifteen minutes."

* * *

Mitch was at the front desk on the phone when Ray bolted inside looking enraged. As Mitch glanced up from the phone, he felt his heart turn to ice. "Are you okay, Sir?" He timidly asked. Ray ignored the question and ordered one of his own.

"Where the hell is Dan?"

"Uh, he went into the john a minute ago. Officer Ray, can I do something?"

"Just keep making those calls, Son," Ray bellowed as he headed toward the men's room.

Mitch shouted back, "Okay, but do ya mind if I do it from home? Mr. Reynolds gets a little uptight about me hoggin' the phone."

Ray waved but didn't slow down. "Yeah, go ahead."

* * *

Ray's massive hand grabbed onto Dan's arm and pulled him out of the washroom.

"Jeez, Boss, ya could've at least let me dry my hands."

"Wipe 'em on your fuckin' coat," he sniped as they headed out the front door. "We gotta get to Brockville now, and I'm drivin'. Gimme the keys." Seeing the police chief's face red with fury, Dan quietly tossed him the keys, and hopped into the passenger seat. His door had barely closed before the car burned rubber.

"What's goin' on, Chief?" Dan timidly asked.

With eyes fixed on the road, jaw pulsing, Ray growled. "I just called in for messages, and there was one from Riggert, the undertaker. He mentioned our visit to his wife, and she remembered who worked for them that year. She took pity on the guy 'cause o' his family issues. She even got him connected to family services. That fuckin' little weasel." He pounded his fist on the steering wheel.

"Who ya talkin' about?"

"Doug Fergusson. That little turd lied right to my face."

When they arrived at Doug Fergusson's home, Ray bypassed all formalities and ploughed Doug's door open with a burst from his meaty shoulder.

Doug skittered into a corner. "What the hell?"

"Hell is where you're goin' if you don't tell me what you knew about Berger's fake death; and what you've been up to every fuckin' minute of this day. Ya got that?"

Doug's gaze volleyed frantically back and forth from one officer to the other, until finally, in a peculiar act of calm collection, he lifted a defiant chin and exclaimed, "Do you really think ya could bring me any more goddamn pain than I've already had?"

"Pain?" Ray moved in, towering over the cornered rat. "Ya think your swollen nuts or black eyes was pain, you little weasel? You can't imagine how bad I can mess you up and never leave a mark!"

The loud rumbling that followed was the merging sound of Doug's shaking bones and dry heaving.

Ray stepped back and watched Doug attempting to pull himself together. "You got exactly forty-eight seconds to start talking." He warned.

Doug held up his hand as if to shield himself from the officer. "Okay, okay...but don't come any closer. Please, don't."

"Nope, I'm stayin' right here, but officer Dan is gonna stay right up close in case ya decide to make some asshole move. Ya got that?"

Doug grimaced. "Yeah...got it."

"Good." Ray slid a chair across the floor with his foot. "Now, sit down."

Doug did as ordered.

"Now, let's start with why ya repeatedly lied to a cop. I mean, nobody should be that dumb."

"I'm not dumb..." Doug spotted the two officers' dubious expressions. "I'm not! I'm just scared to death. You don't know Berger. He's insane. He said, 'no way was he goin' to trial with the others.' He made me apply for that job at the funeral place. He said if I didn't do it, he'd murder me and my whole family. He told me he had nothin' to lose so he'd have no problem doin' it." Doug shifted in his seat, crossed his legs, and continued. "All he said I had to do was get a special paper from the undertaker's office, fill in what he told me to, and sign Riggert's name to it. Then I had to pay some stranger who looked good in a suit to deliver an urn to Aunt Gladys. That's all I knew. Except, if I ever told anybody, he'd hunt my family down, torture every one of 'em right in front o' my eyes, and kill 'em, and then me." He looked at the officers again, "And now, he's back, and he's slowly beatin' me up and tearin' me down, so I'm scared shitless every minute of every day that he's gonna go after my mom and sisters next. If it was your family that was bein' threatened, you'd do the same. Anybody would."

    The confession brought Ray's boiling hot anger to a slow simmer. "You're not a kid now, Dougie. Ya could've told me all this on any of our little visits and I woulda arranged police protection for your family..."

    "And for the Miller woman? And for that journalist lady? All the others? How big a force ya got? Look, Berger ordered me to send those dolls, 'cause he wanted to scare the journalist off. He said he didn't want her findin' out stuff he needed to keep hidden. When he kicked the shit outta me and put me in the hospital, he musta stolen that last doll and sent it hisself, 'cause I swear, I never slammed that one through the window. And I never put the one in the Miller woman's mailbox, neither. You saw, I only had one more of those damn dolls left. No, Sir, those last two were all Berger's doin'."

Ray dragged a chair closer to Doug and mounted it like a saddle. "All right, tell me this Dougie, did ya see the journalist today?"

He nodded. "Yeah, of course, when I picked her up."

Ray leaned in and stared quizzically at Doug, "What in hell do you mean, you picked her up?"

"Isn't that why ya busted in here?"

"Where was she?"

"Walkin' down the street, like Berger told me. He said she'd likely stop at the grocery store when she left the Miller place, around five o'clock, but I had to be there way ahead, in case she came by earlier...and it was good I was there too, 'cause she was really early. He said I should offer her a lift when she came outta the store."

Dan looked nonplussed, "And she just willingly got in your car?"

An unintended sneer raised Doug's upper lip. "Yeah, of course she did. Do ya think I'd force her? Well, I got news for ya, just 'cause my name's Fergusson, doesn't make me one o' them sick bastards. I wouldn't hurt nobody. I knew she felt kinda bad for me last time you were here, so, when she looked in the car and saw I was upset, she got right in. Berger said to tell her about you waitin' at my Aunt Bindy's for her. He said Bindy had important information that'd help you and me, and Mrs. Berman's news story too." He paused for a moment while a satisfied grin crept across his face. "Yeah, she was gonna get the real goods on Earl and the Miller woman and all. I gotta admit, I liked that. Berger said to tell her, she shouldn't talk to nobody 'bout it, or else she'd get nothin'. I figured she'd be safe for sure, with you and Aunt Bindy there. Berger swore he just wanted to talk to her so when she'd write about him in her book, bein' alive and stuff, she'd get it all straight."

The two officers were transfixed as he continued, "Anyway, she said she had an errand to take care o' first. So, I said I could drive her, but she didn't wanna be a bother, she wanted to get her own car and follow me instead. I said since you were gonna be at Aunt Bindy's, you probably wouldn't want her drivin' back alone on those dark, country roads, ya know, 'cause she might get lost or somethin'. For some reason, that idea made her smile, and she hopped in. I took her to do her errand, and then I drove her to Aunt Bindy's. So, Officer," he looked at Ray expectantly, "how come ya didn't see her? Berger told me you'd meet her at the top o' the driveway at six-thirty, but I was to drop her by the high hedges at 6:25 sharp and go right home. And I did just what he said. But I swear, I wanted to go back to give her the bag..."

"The bag?" Dan repeated looking perplexed.

"Isn't that what ya came for?"

Ray abruptly rose from his chair. "Show it to me!" He demanded.

"Wait, Officer...You think I swiped it, don'tcha?" He walked to a shelf, retrieved a handbag, and handed it to Ray. "Go ahead and ask Mrs. Berman, she'll tell ya. She left it in my car when she jumped out at Aunt Bindy's. I wanted to go back and give it to her, but I knew if I didn't follow Berger's orders exactly, I'd be in deep shit. I swear, I never once looked inside. I figured she'd be callin' me to get it to her...but I never thought she'd send the police to break down my door."

With a bewildered shake of his head, he shared another thought. "Ya know, Officer, if you woulda just rung the bell and asked, I woulda handed it over to ya."

* * *

All police services in the county were notified to speed to Bindy Fergusson's, with no lights or sirens. Dan's beat-up '73 Ford Torino was no match for the Chief's spiffy, new 1991 Chevy Caprice that they didn't have time to pick up; but Dan pressed the pedal to the floor and prayed she'd rise to the occasion.

As they drew near the Fergusson house, Ray couldn't resist a jab. "Christ, Rookie, this heap drives like an old golf cart. The thirty-minute drive felt like a two-hour bumper-car ride."

Dan chuckled as he pulled off to the side of the road by Bindy's property. "Look over there. Ya see Boss, the only vehicle there is the same, old rust bucket that was parked over there last time. So, it looks like Berger isn't here yet, unless he made somebody drive him out here so there'd be no strange car sittin' there lookin' suspicious?"

With raised eyebrows and a vigorous nod, Ray responded. "Ya know what, Dan? You're not as dumb as ya look. I think that's exactly what that son-of-a-bitch did...and I'll bet it was Doug doin' the driving. If that little weasel lied to me again, I'll have his..."

The rookie shook his head and made a stab at defending Doug. "Aw come on, Boss, cut him some slack. He was pretty shook up. We didn't ask, and maybe he didn't think about it while he was shittin' his pants."

Ray offered up a swift tap to the back of the rookie's head. "So, you're the teacher now, huh, Rookie?"

Dan playfully rubbed the spot and cleared his throat. "Uh, I meant no disrespect, Sir. I was only..."

"Relax, Dan. I'm pullin' your leg." A trace of a smile on the chief's face quickly disappeared, "How's your marksmanship?"

"Top o' my class."

"Good. You may need to prove it. Take your gun out o' your holster, but don't take the safety off, okay?"

It'd been years since Ray had drawn a gun on duty. The most handling it got was during target practice and cleaning...but today, it felt fitting to enter armed and ready.

Ray and Dan prepared to exit the car as several police vehicles and an ambulance quietly rolled up behind them, no lights, no sirens. The team of officers quietly vacated their vehicles and gathered behind the tall hedges in the pitch-black, waiting for orders. Ray explained the plan as best he could. The officers fanned out around the property, while Ray and Dan approached the front door. Ray gently twisted the knob and confirmed it was locked. As he took a step back to ready himself, Dan put his arm out to stop him. "Let me, Boss. I've always wanted to do this," He whispered.

"Stop talkin' and do it then," Ray muttered.

Dan kicked open the front door with all the force he could muster, then winced from the counterblow he received.

Ray couldn't help but smirk. "Thought it was easy, like on TV, huh, Rookie?"

Dan clenched his teeth as the pain torpedoed up his leg and through his groin. Ray shook his head, shrugged, then proceeded to enter with Dan following haltingly behind. Bindy stood at the end of the hall, frigid as an ice sculpture.

"Where's Berger?" The chief demanded.

She remained stock still and unresponsive. He repeated the question with more authority. "I asked you, where the hell is Berger?" She remained motionless and mute.

"For the love of God, if ya don't speak up, we're gonna tear apart every corner of your house."

"Earl's house," she croaked.

"I don't give a shit whose house it is. You're livin' here, so it's your world I'm gonna crush."

The ice began to melt, and Bindy Fergusson's words flooded the space. "Well, you're too damn late. My world was crushed the day I married into this family. I was a beautiful, young teenager that got turned into a used-up hag by an animal more than twice my age. Take a good look, Officer, this is who I am, just seventeen years later. There ain't nothin' ya can do that can be any worse than what's already been done ta me, by him. So go ahead, give it your best shot."

Caught by the shock and sadness of her candor, it took the chief a moment to respond. "Ma'am, I'm not trying to do something to you, I just wanna know, where's Berger?"

She jeered at him and hung her head in exasperation. "Jesus, you people don't listen or learn, do ya? I told you when ya came here last time: I ain't seen him. Yer so damn ungrateful. I risked everythin' to get ya those numbers so you could find 'im and put him away, and ya didn't. And now you're askin' for my help again? No, not askin'...you're orderin' me to do your dirty work, even when ya know it could cost me 'n my kids our lives. What I wanna know is, why in hell ya'd think he'd be here? I mean, do ya really imagine I'd be hidin' that stinkin' piece o' garbage anywhere near me?"

Ray paused and tried a different approach. "Mrs. Fergusson, I know this is tough on you; but can you just tell me this; have you been home all day?" He cautiously asked.

"No, Sir. I just got back from drivin' a load o' movin' boxes out to Gladys's. Since I got nowhere ta go, she's lettin' me move in with her 'til I can get my kids back from foster care. All's I care about is getting' my kids back." Her lips quivered and her hands shook.

Ray extended an empathetic nod and continued, "Mrs. Fergusson, we'll try and be as quick as we can; but right now, we're gonna need to have a look in your attic."

"Look anywhere ya like. Here, I'll even take ya." With determination, she led a march along the back corridor, but after a few yards, she halted abruptly and whimpered, "Oh Christ. Oh Jesus! The rug...The rug's crumpled."

Dan whispered to Ray, "This place is a dung heap, and she's worried about a messy rug?"

Ray scowled at Dan and sidled up to the terrified woman. He placed a comforting hand on her arm and softly inquired. "Does the crumpled rug mean something, Bindy?"

She shook herself out of her daze and replied, "Uh, sorry. Yeah, a sign. Well, it used ta be...but...but I was sure that bloody nightmare was over!"

Triggered by her mention of a nightmare and still holding onto Bindy's arm, Ray turned his eyes to Dan, "Go outside and get a couple o' officers to stand with you right here by this rug. And tell the others out there to stay alert."

Dan nodded then paused. "What about Mrs. Fergusson, Boss? Should I take her outta here?"

"Just do what I asked. I'll look after her." With a gentle tug of her arm, he led her into the living room.

"Okay, Mrs. Fergusson, please sit down."

Overwhelming fear engulfed her as she obeyed his instructions and sat on the edge of the worn sofa, dazed and terrified.

Ray crouched in front of her. "Now, please, tell me what's got you so agitated?"

She remained static. Ray waited, patiently.

"Bindy, I can't really help if you don't talk to me. Gettin' this bastard could maybe help get your kids back and rid you of those roaches who've been doin' their best to destroy you. Isn't gettin rid of them what you want? If it is, then talkin' to me is the only chance you've got to make it happen. I honestly want to help you, please let me."

"Enough." She rasped. After releasing an exhausted groan, she whispered. "Enough...I'll talk to ya."

Ray eased himself into a seat beside her. She looked at him as if seeing him for the first time. Her eyes welled up, and she acquiesced. "Maybe ya don't recall, 'cause ya weren't in charge back then; but when Zane and them others was arrested, police searched this house and the barn." She trembled like a willow in a storm. "I swear, Chief, I wanted to tell 'em, but I knew me and my kids mighta got killed for tellin'. Then, when all o' them bastards got sent to prison, I figured we was safe, so I didn't need to say nothin'. Now, you're gonna find out and we're all gonna be dead." She fell back in her seat, panting, spent.

Ray took a moment to contemplate the impact of her words before empathetically asking. "Bindy, do you remember the nice lady that came with me to see ya?"

She glanced up at him and nodded.

"That's good. Well, we think Berger took her and he means to harm her. You know better than me what he's capable of. So, please, if ya know somethin', ya gotta tell me. You're not in danger, I promise you."

Ray stood up. "In fact, you got the best police protection there is, with me and the three waitin' by the carpet and, a whole army waitin' outside. Now's your chance to do somethin' to help someone who really deserves it." Ray paused.

He watched as the broken twig of a woman, slowly rose, and wandered, mumbling to herself as seconds ticked by. Then, with renewed urgency, she approached Ray, grabbed his wrist, and pulled him back along the hallway.

She stopped at the crumpled rug. Ignoring the cops standing guard, she whispered to ray. "Under the rug, is a wood plank."

Ray sighed in frustration but bent over and folded the rug back. Seeing nothing unusual, he straightened up and looked to Bindy who was facing away from him. He grumbled, "All right, I removed the rug, I see lots of planks, now what?"

"If ya look close, there's a big black nail in one plank.

Dan and another officer stooped down for a closer look. Dan shrugged and muttered to Ray, "I don't see any black nail, Boss."

Bindy jerked her head around. "Oh, no...oh Jesus...Then it's gone?"

Appearing completely flummoxed, Dan peered closer. "There's a hole in one of the planks, if that means somethin'?"

Bindy shrieked. "It's gone, the nail...it's really gone!" The words escaped from Bindy's throat in guttural gasps. Then, in a trance-like recitation, she uttered, "Pull the nail...stamp twice...pop up...you wait...it goes down."

The cops stood by, mouths agape, waiting for any of it to make sense. Quietly and calmly, Ray asked, "What does it mean, Bindy? What pops up?"

"Uh, plank..." She groaned.

Ray shook his head vigorously. "Bindy, we don't understand. Please, tell us what you mean."

With terror filled eyes, she looked at Ray, and complied. "Stamp hard on the plank, twice,...It'll pop up." She paused to catch a breath. "You'll see a handle. A trap door. But, if the nail's gone, somebody's down there...in the secret cellar."

"Holy Christ, Boss, a secret cellar? This is like...we're in a horror movie." Dan choked out the words.

Ray looked up sharply, "Bindy, if someone is down there, can they hear us?"

She shook her head. "It's got a ceilin' and walls thicker than a bomb shelter. Ya can't hear nothin'."

"Are there steps, or a ladder?"

"Steps. Wobbly steps."

"How many, do ya figure?"

"Maybe, uh, twelve."

"Okay, men, listen up. This guy is dangerous as hell, but if he's down there, he likely doesn't know we're here...so, surprise is our best weapon. One o' you take Mrs. Fergusson out to the squad car and stay with her. Tell the rest of the guys to get in here, now! Tell them, when we open this up if we have to jump down, we jump. You'll all need to draw your guns, but don't point or discharge unless you get the go-ahead from me. No flashlights, until you get my three-tap signal. Understood?" A flurry of nodding and grunting followed.

One of the rookies headed out the front door with Bindy. Cops trooped in and stood by while Dan popped the plank. The stench of skunky beer oozed from below. Ray whispered through clenched teeth, "Open the trap and prepare to breach."

Ray raced down the stairs into blackness with Dan and the legion of cops following close behind. The chief called into the abyss, "Police! There's an army of us here, Berger, so I'm advisin' ya to step forward with your hands in the air."

The space beyond the stairway remained murky black except for the slow-moving glow of a smoldering cigarette in the distance.

Ray held his gun steady and tapped his flashlight against it. On the third tap, his men took aim and flooded the area with light. The rapid brightness was momentarily blinding; but soon, Sarah came into view. Her arms were extended, and she was tied by her wrists to the wall. She was motionless, her eyes were closed, and her head hung limply to one side, A disheveled madman stood beside her, pointing a hunting knife at her throat, and grunting like a wild boar. "Don't even think 'bout comin' near me, you pigs! Don't play hero. I've gutted many a hog in my life, an' I can slice this sow open before ya get even one shot off."

"Berger, you've got six guns pointed at your head, and a seventh is mine, and I get to shoot first. But I'd hate to waste a bullet shootin' somethin' with no value. I'd get no pleasure seein' your brains splattered, 'cause they're like cow shit to me. So, I'm aiming at the thing ya prize most. If ya don't want to spend the rest of your life without your balls and dick, ya better put down the knife and step away with your hands above your head."

Dark sweat bubbled like stew on Berger's mottled forehead as he tightened his grip on the knife. Ray stepped forward confidently with his gun still aimed at the assailant's crotch. Berger twitched and Ray shouted. "Drop the knife and put your hands up, now or so help me, I'll take the shot and blow your junk to hell!"

Berger grimaced, grunted, and pointed the knife toward Ray before letting it land with a thud on the dank floor. He sneered, spat on the ground, and raised his hands to the ceiling. Ray kept his eyes and his gun on the snake as he shouted to his men, "Fellas, get this piece of shit outta here before I..." He was interrupted by the shivering sound of glass being pulverized underfoot as the rush of officers advanced.

Ray rushed to Sarah's side, silently praying for signs of life, but not finding any.

Dan cuffed the beast, and two of the officers dragged him over a minefield of glass shards and up through the trap door.

Ray cut her bindings and she flopped into his arms like a ragdoll. In a frenzy, he carried her up the steps and out the front door, placing her on the waiting stretcher. As the medics rolled her into the ambulance, one called out to Ray, "Jesus, she smells like a brewery?"

Ray curbed his fury and gathered his wits. "All's I wanna know is whether she's alive."

"Her pulse is really weak, Chief. We gotta go." The ambulance doors closed, and the vehicle raced away with sirens blaring.

"What the fuck?" Ray muttered as he charged toward Sergeant Hanes, who was holding on to the grinning assailant. "Hanes, I need a minute." He dragged the repugnant Berger away by his cuffs and whispered in his ear. As the words penetrated, the beast dropped to his knees.

Ray called out to his rookie. "Dan, I'm gonna follow the ambulance in your car. Sergeant Hanes is gonna shove this bag o' shit into his cage car and take him back ta Brockville. I want you to go with him and watch this scumbag get locked up. But listen carefully, once he's processed, I don't want anyone talkin' to him or even getting near him. I'll interview him myself when I'm ready. When you're done, meet me at the hospital. The rest o' you guys stay here and tape off the area. It's a crime scene, so collect, but don't trample on the evidence. And take Bindy somewhere safe."

"Sure thing, Boss."

"Hanes, ya might wanna put a plastic sheet down in your back seat before ya throw that piece o' crap inside. I think our tough guy just pissed himself. Who knows what he might do next?"

CHAPTER TWENTY-NINE

A discordant cacophony of sound filled the emergency room, while in the waiting area, visitors paced, silently prayed, and watched intently as doctors, nurses and orderlies drifted in and out of the intensive care unit like alien predators.

Through it all, Sarah remained unresponsive. The doctors found abrasions and rope burns, but no acute injuries to her body, no evidence of violent assault, sexual or otherwise.

A brash young intern swaggered into the waiting area, "I'm Dr. Mike, and I have a question. Would any of you describe the patient as overly emotional?" Ray scowled at the baby-faced newbie and walked away. The junior was unbowed. "Hey Chief, how about you?"

Ray winced at the intrusion but turned back and offered a pointed response. "She has her moments like we all do, but no, I definitely don't see Sarah as overly emotional."

With unsolicited temerity the young resident stroked his beardless chin and prophesied; "Well, psychiatry is my field of interest, and I would say, she's suffered a psychological breakdown due to trauma, which makes recovery tenuous.

The unsolicited and unwelcome opinion from an egoistical dilettante was eating at Dan: "I don't mean to be disrespectful, Mike, oops, Dr. Mike...but how can ya possibly know what's goin' on in her brain right now when it's off in Neverland?"

Before the resident could add gas to the bonfire, Ray pounced like a wounded lion. "You think you can tell what the hell's goin' on inside her head just by looking at it from the outside? Jesus, don't you think ya should at least wait 'til the grown-up doctors have had a chance to weigh in and figure out what it's not, first?"

Ray's piercing glare set the jittery intern darting to the elevator.

"God, I hate shrinks," Dan muttered. "Especially wannabes."

Ray offered a faint smile and nodded.

* * *

Wally received a call from Dan who was back at the police station. "Listen Wally, Ray asked me to let you know what's happening here with Sarah. He says, you have ta tell Eleanor, but, he said...and I quote, '*tell Wally, he has ta break the news to her, real gently.*'"

Wally hung up and stared numbly at the phone while trying to conjure up the gentle words he was instructed to deliver. He sat and studied Eleanor, who was occupied with her sewing.

"Eleanor, Ray says uh, Sarah's got uh, some kind o' problem or something." Eleanor looked puzzled for a moment and offered a "Hmm." She smiled wanly and noted, "Good God, what's she up to now?" She remained seated, sewing a button on a shirt while awaiting his reply.

Wally rushed to the front closet pulled on his coat and retrieved her jacket. He returned to the spot, released an irritated moan, and barked. "Come on. We gotta go."

His tone unnerved her. The needle pierced her finger causing her to set down the shirt, grab a tissue and dab at a blood droplet. "Wally, I'm not moving until you tell me what's going on!"

He steadied himself and took a deep breath. "Okay, alright. I wasn't supposed ta tell ya this but, listen Eleanor, Sarah's in a coma and we gotta get to St. Gabriel's, now."

Eleanor's lips trembled; her hands shook, and she couldn't move, speak, or breathe.

Wally paced frantically, hoping to come up with a plan. "Eleanor, you've told me that Sarah stood by you when everyone else walked away, didn't you?"

Eleanor wasn't listening. She was locked in a time warp of haunting images of St. Gabriel's. Her mother's death, her vicious attack, and now her old friend in peril in that place? She remained motionless.

"Eleanor, like you told me, she stood by you. I know it's hard, but don't ya think ya oughta return the favour?" He pleaded then stomped away to put on his galoshes.

Eleanor sprung from her chair, bundled up, and stood by, waiting impatiently for Wally to zip up his boots.

* * *

Everything at St. Gabriel's seemed to be happening in slow motion. Doctors and nurses floated in and out of the room, but Sarah remained unchanged. Doctors took Ray aside and asked question after question. "Who's her emergency contact? Who's her next of kin? Do you know her blood type? Do you know her family doctor in Toronto? Who can we call?" The chief pounded his fist into his open hand and shrugged. He simply had no answers.

Ray returned to the waiting area to find that Eleanor, Wally, and Shiny had arrived. He managed to nod and smile discreetly to Eleanor, who attempted to return the same. Some in the group were pacing, some chattering mindlessly, and others, like Eleanor and Shiny, appeared to be on the verge of panic.

With a short, brusque "Hey," he got everyone's attention. "Listen up. Sarah's in good hands, and there's nothing we can do 'til the doctors figure it all out. I need one o' you to go ta her hotel and search through her things to find a number to contact her family. Let's hope it never comes to it, but someone may have to make a tough decision here today."

All present remained stock-still like Madame Tussaud's wax figures.

"Damn it. Look, her family has a right to know...and maybe it would help her, if they were by her side." He shook his head in despair.

Shiny thawed first. "I'll go," she croaked, "Reynolds'll let me in. I'll give him a call."

"I'm going with you," Eleanor insisted as she sidled up to Shiny.

"Okay, good," Ray acknowledged. "I have to go to the station. Wally, if there's any news, call me there or try my cell phone. It works there, some of the time."

* * *

It was well past midnight when Ray walked into the police station.

"He's in the interview room. We've got him cuffed and shackled," Dan proudly announced.

"Why?" Did ya really think that spineless maggot was gonna try and run?" Ray glowered like a red alert. "Get in there and take off the damn cuffs and shackles. I don't want him screaming police brutality."

"Sorry, Boss. I just felt better knowin' there was no chance he could get away this time. I mean, if he'd really been cremated, none o' this woulda happened."

Ray heaved a heavy sigh. "Yeah, I can't argue with that. By the way, Dan, it really did smell like a damn rancid brewery in that basement. Is he sober?"

Dan hunched his shoulders and clicked his tongue. "Jeez, Boss, I know this sounds nuts, but I don't think he's had a drop of alcohol. He reeks, but I think it all came from the broken bottles. It looked like a prohibition raid down there. When we walked off the last step, I think we were inches deep in broken glass and booze."

"Has the bastard said anything?"

"He hasn't said a word since ya whispered some sweet nothin' in his ear."

A faint grin surfaced on Ray's face as he patted Dan on the shoulder. "Good to know."

Dan loosened his tie and scratched his neck, "C'mon Boss, what'd ya say to him?"

An impulsive smirk spread across Ray's face as he whispered, "I told him I lied about wanting to shoot him in the nuts. I didn't want him going to prison without his manly parts, and I didn't want him dead either. I was aiming for his knees...'cause without them, he'd be a captive bitch for his prison buddies. Ya think that might've upset him?"

"Well, he did piss himself again on the way here. Glad he wasn't in my car." Dan gloated.

Ray smiled, gave a thumbs-up, and entered the interview room.

* * *

The droopy-eyed night clerk lazily pushed the room key toward Shiny with a warning: "Make sure I get it back. I'm not gettin' inta trouble over this. Reynolds may've said it's okay, but when somethin' goes wrong, it'll be my head that'll rolls."

* * *

"I feel like a peepin' Tom goin' in there," Shiny whispered.

Eleanor nodded. "I know, but Ray's right, we've gotta let someone know. Here, give me the key. We can do this."

Eleanor opened the door and stepped inside with Shiny close behind. She snapped on the light and scanned the room. She emitted a slight gasp. "Shiny, have you ever been in Sarah's room before?"

Shiny shook her head. "No, why?"

"Well, I have, and I can't imagine her leaving the place looking like this."

The bed linens were dumped on the sofa in a heap, her dresser drawers had been rifled, and her clothes tossed on the floor.

"We've gotta get outta here," Shiny insisted. "Someone has taken this place apart and I don't want us to be next."

As they rushed out the door, Eleanor stopped to grab an item from the nightstand. She held it up for Shiny to see. "It's Laurie Cowan's business card. She told me he's gonna work on getting her a divorce lawyer, so maybe he has contact information?"

Shiny nodded, looking around furtively, "Okay. Now can we get the hell out of here?"

* * *

When they returned to the lobby, they found the clerk asleep in his chair. Shiny banged on the counter with her fist and shouted, "Hey! Here's your key. I don't suppose anythin' gets by you, huh? But ya might wanna call the police and tell them there's been an illegal entry in Ms. Berman's room. Oh, and for the record, yes, we were in there, but no, it wasn't us. You gave us a key and your permission, remember?"

* * *

Rather than hang around the hotel lobby waiting for the Brockville police to arrive, they decided to head over to Eleanor's to phone the Toronto lawyer.

They had barely stepped inside when it became obvious that Eleanor's house had also been raided.

Eleanor wandered about the house in a daze. Shiny tugged on her elbow and whispered, "Eleanor, please, we've gotta go."

"No, I have to check everything. I have to check...the basement, my designs. I can't let..."

"Shh...Listen to me, Eleanor." She kept her voice barely above a whisper, "They could still be here, hiding, maybe even in the basement. We gotta go." Shiny pulled the dressmaker out the front door, and into her car.

* * *

Ray entered the interview room and locked the door. He dropped a pen and legal pad on the table. Berger didn't react, he simply set his gaze on the opposite wall and refused to notice.

"Pick up the pen, Berger."

He didn't respond.

"Pick up the damn pen and write down what I tell ya, or I'll jam this pencil through your empty skull."

Berger leaned back in the chair and smirked feebly. "You're fuckin' crazy. Do ya know I can sue ya fer assault!" he sputtered. "Ya think I don't know my rights? You think 'cause I was holdin' a knife, ya got me? Of course, I held a knife, to defend myself. Ya broke inta the place and scared the bejezus outta me. I didn't know if ya was gonna kill me or what. I just went down there to get a beer and I found her like that. I was about ta go for help when ya busted in like a bunch of savages. And I didn't do nothin'."

"You're gonna do something now. You're gonna write what I tell ya."

Ray pushed the pen into Berger's hand and directed it onto the paper. "I said, write."

Berger sneered. "If ya think yer gonna force me to confess to somethin' I didn't do, yer fuckin' nuts."

"No worries there, Berger...I'm not askin' for some ramblin' confession. You're just gonna write a few words, that's all. Now, I'm gonna stand over here, across the room, so I don't make ya nervous. Let's begin. Write the word *Interested*."

Berger tossed the pen aside.

Ray darted forward with clenched fists. "You'll write what I just told ya, or I'll break your fuc..."

Berger withered like a busted balloon. "Okay, okay, I'm writin'." He picked up the pen and cleared his throat. "I didn't hear the word, 'cause you was mumblin'. Say it again?"

"*Interested...*"

Berger scrunched his face in concentration. He scribbled, then tossed the pen on the table. "Okay, I done it."

"Now write *arranged...*"

"This is some stupid game, but okay, if that's how you cops get yer kicks, I'm playin.' *Arranged*. Done."

"Ooh, you're doin' good there, Berger. Now write *When...*"

Berger sneered, then wrote with newfound determination. Ray continued with his list: *"Friends... Who...Between...*Okay, that's it. Let's have a look."

Ray grabbed the yellow lined paper and marveled at the man's unusual penmanship and command of English. "*Intersted, arangd, wen, frends, hoo, beetwean...*"

"Hmm, fascinatin' Berger. Let's have a big finale here. Last one...*Eleanor*."

The Prescott Journals

"I don't know that word." Berger barked as he pushed himself away from the table.

"Sure ya do, Asshole. Ya wrote it on the message ya left in her mailbox. Ya spelled it E-L-N-E-R. Ya shoulda stayed in school, Berger."

"Why? So, I coulda learned ta be a dumb pig like you?" Berger spat on the floor.

A severed doll's head suddenly whipped through the air like a heat-seeking missile. The suspect winced as the projectile landed in his crotch.

"What the fuck...?" Berger threw the object on the table and jumped to his feet but was shoved back into the chair by the powerful hand of the furious police chief.

The chief picked up the item. "I'm only sorry it isn't attached to a big rock like the one ya smashed through Shiny Dumas's window."

"Are ya kiddin' me? I didn't break no window with that thing."

Ray hovered over him squeezing the doll head in his fist. "Do I look like I'm kidding, Berger? But you're right. Ya didn't do it with this thing. We've got another one just like it, except it has your prints all over it."

Berger, momentarily stunned, managed to rally his confidence. "Even if I broke the fuckin' window," he wiped an ooze of sweat from his chin, "and I'm not sayin' I did, but it woulda been a dumb prank. So, at my age, what's the charge for a prank, eh? Twenty-four hours in lock-up and a fifty-dollar fine? It might be worth it for a little harmless fun."

"Did ya have fun, Duh-Wayne?"

"Why? Is havin' fun a federal crime now?" He replied with an odious snort.

There was a brisk, hard knock on the interview room door. Ray stalked across the room and flung it open.

"This better be good, Dan, or it's gonna be your ass."

All five-feet-eight-inches of Dan quaked under the imposing chief's glare.

"Boss, ya gotta come out here." He pointed toward the waiting area. "It's real important."

Peering down the hallway, past the bustle of officers and staff, Ray caught a glimpse of Eleanor's back, and he could tell from her frantic pacing and laboured breathing that she was in distress.

"Dan, keep your eye on the perp. I'll be back."

He cautiously approached Eleanor and gently placed his hand on her shoulder. As she turned toward him, he was taken aback by her distraught look. "My God, Eleanor, what's goin' on?"

Barely a squeak was heard as she tried to summon the words. Ray glanced around and, in a voice louder than intended, he shouted, "Where the hell is Shiny?"

"Here. I'm here, Ray. Sorry, I was uh, in the john," Shiny stammered, as she stepped to Eleanor's side.

His explosive exhale of breath revealed his panic. "Okay, then, what's the story here, eh? Is it about Sarah?"

Shiny stitched her brow as she queried. "Sarah? No. I was just gonna ask you about Sarah. Have ya heard anythin'?"

"Nothin' yet. Now, tell me, what's this about?"

Shiny took a tentative step forward. "I'm gonna tell ya, but I may need to head for the john again 'cause this whole thing has given me the runs."

Leaned on the front desk and steadied himself as he stared at the two women, hoping for some insight. "Jesus, Shiny, just tell me!"

As Shiny described their experience, Eleanor anxiously fidgeted with her scarf. When Shiny finished, Eleanor offered an addendum. "Uh, Ray, earlier, I'd been soaking some sheets in a pail of Javex. I opened the back door to throw out the water and, uh, I'm worried that I may have left it unlocked.

"Just now, when we walked in on the mess, I felt a cold breeze on my legs which had to have come from the open back door."

Ray tried to conjure a comforting smile as he took Eleanor's hands in his. "It doesn't matter, Eleanor. Your home was invaded and that's all we need to know. I'm gonna send you girls over to the hospital with one of my men. You can tell Wally we need him back here. I know this is all pretty scary, but did ya happen to find Sarah's next o' kin?" He asked as he slowly released her hands.

Shiny interrupted "Uh-uh, not exactly, but we're workin' on it, and we'll let ya know." She shot Eleanor a subtle glance, interlaced their arms and they hurried away.

Ray turned toward Officer Dan, who was observing the action like a spectator at a hockey game. "Dan, snap out of it. I need you alert, and I'm gonna need more officers too, so ask your buddies to step up."

"What do ya want us ta do with Berger, Boss?" Dan naively asked.

Ray snorted. "He's not goin' anywhere. We'll let that useless side o' beef marinate in his piss and booze 'til we get back."

Two police cruisers and the Ford Torino headed to Prescott, two with lights and sirens blazing. They arrived at Eleanor's house first, and carefully searched but found no sign of violence or vandalism. However, it was obvious that someone was looking for something.

Deep in thought, Ray silently paced back and forth over the dizzying checkerboard tiles of Eleanor's kitchen floor. Suddenly, his eyes lit up and he reached for her phone. "I'm sorry, Ma'am, to be calling at this time of night, but it's important we speak to Mitch."

Ket Hall's raspy voice and empathetic words came as a relief, "It's no problem, Officer Ray. We understand. We've been very worried about Sarah. Is she okay?"

Ray swiped the back of his hand across his damp forehead. "Uh, I don't have any information I can share with you at this time, but we're all keepin' the faith. I hope ya understand."

"Of course, Officer. Okay, Mitch is right here."

"Hello Chief."

"Hey Mitch, can ya tell us who ya got in touch with tonight, and if anything stood out in any of your conversations?"

"There were a couple o' strange remarks, Sir. But I made notes on everyone I spoke to. Do ya want me to read them out to you?"

Ray quietly pumped an optimistic fist in the air, then snapped his fingers to get Dan's attention. "Uh, no, Mitch, it's okay. It'll be easier if we go over 'em with you. Dan and I'll come by right away."

* * *

The cops were ushered inside and quickly became aware of how busy Mitch had been. He'd called every town local on the list Dan constructed, and then added a few of his own. He peered up from the paper with a look on his face that one gets when they smell something putrid. "I, uh, think I had a pretty weird call with Earl White..." He mumbled.

Ray's face turned a particular shade of eggplant. "Wait a damn minute. Ya called Earl White. Why in hell would ya do that?"

Mitch tried his best to hide his trembling knees and quivering chin. "I uh, I did it, 'cause Mrs. Berman was writing a story about him, and I, um, figured since he once made a creepy visit to her room, he might be someone worth talkin' to."

Ray paused to consider Mitch's initiative, then momentarily rested an 'attaboy' hand on the boy's shoulder. "Okay, Mitch, I get why you talked to him. But what was weird about it, other than the obvious?"

"Well, Earl said, 'Good. With any luck, she's packed up and left for the city.'" Mitch paused a moment, and looked at Ray. His face had gone from purple to pale. He continued. "Now, I'm thinking, if Earl was pressuring her to write his life story, why would he want her to leave town? And another thing...you'd already been at his place, so he knew you were lookin' for her."

Ray listened as Mitch continued, "Oh, I also called Mr. McCall, and he said you'd just left his house." Mitch paused for a second., "But ya know what, Chief? Now that I think about it, he sounded kinda freaked out."

Dan shared a puzzled exchange with Ray before jumping in. "Ya say you spoke to Richard at his home, after we saw 'im? But Ray and me watched him drive off for Earl's place; and I'm bettin' he doesn't have a car phone."

"Well, I'm tellin' ya, I spoke to him, soon as I got home, which was just a few minutes after you guys left for Brockville."

* * *

Richard's bleary-eyed wife wasn't happy to see the two police officers at her front door. "It's well after midnight. What could you two possibly want from a real estate lawyer in the middle of the night?"

"We just have a few questions for him."

She turned up the collar of her housecoat against the cold. "Well, he's not here. He went to that Earl White's damn party." She considered the two men standing on her porch and arrived at a decision. "Ah hell, you guys look cold and exhausted. Come inside and I'll make you a hot cup of tea and a sandwich or something?"

Ray smiled and politely tapped the brim of his cap. "That's real nice of you, Ma'am, but we really need to talk to Richard, so maybe we'll just head out to Earl's and see if he's there."

She shrugged and pulled her collar tighter. "Suit yourselves. I'm cold and going back to bed. Goodnight, Officers. Oh, and tell Richard not to dare try and wake me up to make him breakfast, if he knows what's good for him," she declared with a cheeky wink as she closed the door.

* * *

Without the flood of festive lights, Earl White's castle took on a more baleful façade. The immense property was in complete darkness, except for a glow in one, small room at the back of the house. Ray rapped on the sliding glass door and shouted, "Police. We need to talk to Earl White." They heard a choir of yapping, howling dogs in the distance, but the house was silent.

"I'll stay here and watch for any movement." Ray whispered to Dan. "You go around the front and ring the doorbell."

At the ring, Ray watched as Earl, his wife, and Richard hurriedly tiptoed away from the dimly-lit room. Dan rang the bell again, but still no response. Ray arrived at the front door and pounded on it. "Open up now, Earl, or I'm gonna break it down."

As Ray paused to catch his breath, the door slowly opened.

The trio of Earl, Ruby and Richard huddled behind the door, as the two intimidating cops crossed the threshold.

Ray turned to his rookie. "Officer Dan, you take Earl and Ruby somewhere nice and cozy while Richard and I have a quiet little chat in the kitchen."

Dan sucked back a grin. "Sure Boss." He then turned toward the couple and asked, "Any preferences?"

Ruby replied, "I suggest the bar area?" With that they exited the foyer.

Ray followed Richard into the kitchen and pulled out a chair. "Have a seat." Ray sat down across from him. "Now, Richard, let's talk. We saw ya drive off earlier at quite a clip. We chose to ignore it, 'cause we knew ya were late for Earl's big party, and we didn't want to make it any more difficult for you. So, tell me, what brought ya back home just minutes after Dan and I gave your car a boost?"

Beads of sweat resurfaced on Richard's forehead. The chief raised an eyebrow and smirked. "Are ya worried about somethin' there, Richard?"

Richard shook his head to dislodge the drops of sweat that were now creeping down his face. "Nope, tired, that's all."

"Ya haven't asked about Sarah. Aren't ya interested in whether she got home safe and sound?"

"You didn't give me a chance. How is she?"

"She's lying in a hospital bed, looking close to death."

His eyes widened as the words penetrated. "Oh God. Oh my God, that's...awful."

Ray nodded. "Yup, it sure is."

Richard slid his trembling hands off the tabletop and placed them in his lap. "W-what happened to her?"

"You didn't hear anything about it, huh, Dick?"

"God, no..."

"Well, we don't know exactly what happened yet, but we're hopin' for the best." Ray tilted his head toward Richard, who was looking anywhere but at him. "Maybe your good friend, Earl, will know something? So, I'm asking you again, Dick, why did ya head back home?"

Richard replayed the previous ritual of stalling, groaning, and sweating until finally, he whispered, "Listen, the truth is, I hadn't planned to go to Earl's party at all tonight, but Earl called just before you came by my place. He said he was worried about something, and he wanted to see me right away. So, I got in the car to head out there. And that's when you pulled up.

"When you told me that Sarah might be missing, I started to panic. There's still this little voice inside me that doesn't completely trust Earl. So, even though I intended to go out to Earl's to see what the drama was...something told me to turn back and call Earl and find out about it from a safe distance. Then, just as I walked in, Mitch called and told me he was worried about Sarah, but he wouldn't say why. He just wanted to know if she'd been by to talk to me or Earl. That made me more worried than ever that Earl's panicky call had something to do with that...like maybe he found out she was writing some stuff about him he'd rather she wouldn't...and maybe he did something about it. So, I called him."

Ray's nostrils flared and his breathing laboured until his anger exploded. "No. I fucking don't get it. If Earl was so bloody anxious for Sarah to write his life story, then what in hell would you need to be worried about, eh?"

With a sudden show of backbone, Richard howled. "Why would I worry?! Why?! Because of Bindy, who called Earl tonight and told Ruby that..."

Suddenly, Earl screamed and tore into the room. "Yer a fuckin' idiot! Ya call yerself a lawyer? Even I know ya don't have to answer any questions 'til ya speak to a real lawyer. So shut yer goddamn mouth!"

Dan stood by, looking helpless. "Sorry, Boss. He heard that outburst from the other room and I..." Before he could finish the sentence, Ruby had joined the fray.

Earl puffed out his chest and strutted like he was King Tut. "Damn right I heard it and so did Ruby, right Babe?" She folded her arms and nodded perfunctorily as her husband continued. "And our guess is you was coercin' this wimp. He don't know nothin', but you still keep harrassin' him. Maybe ya need a good beatin' to teach ya who ya can and can't fuck with."

Ray pushed his chair back and rose to every inch of his towering height. "See what you've done, Earl? Now I have to take you in, 'cause ya interfered with a police investigation; and ya threatened the Chief of the Brockville Police. That's a big no-no, Earl." He nodded to Dan. "Put him in restraints and take him and Ruby to the farthest end of this tomb."

With a broad smirk on his face, Earl stretched his hands out in front of him. Dan grabbed them and cuffed him behind his back. "And Dan, if ya need to gag him, ya got my permission. Earl and I will have our little talk with or without a lawyer, after Richard and I are done with our chat." He shifted his gaze back at Richard. "Do you want a lawyer, Dick?"

Richard didn't hesitate. "Absolutely not."

"Good." The chief grinned as Dan led Earl and Ruby along the corridor.

A momentary ray of relief lit up the lawyer's face. Ray sat back down. "Now, where were we? Oh yeah...Bindy told Ruby what?"

"Bindy said she gave a bunch of old pictures and stuff to the journalist. She kept a few interesting photos for herself, but there might be some incriminating ones in among what the journalist took that would make life very difficult for Earl and Dwayne.

"Earl told me she was crazy, 'cause everyone knew Berger was as dead as dead gets. But Bindy said she had proof he was alive, and if Earl didn't do whatever it took to protect her, Gladys, and their kids, and make sure they had a decent place to live, then she'd make sure that the pictures and anything else she could find went directly to the police and the newspapers."

With a twinkle in his eye, Ray cynically asked, "So I take it Earl didn't agree with her proposal?"

"He drove right to my house. Thank God my wife was out." He sighed and crossed himself. "Earl told me to get behind the wheel of his car and drive around to the back of the O'Brien Hotel. He went in and came back out a couple of minutes later."

Ray stroked his chin in thought. "Hmm. Was he carrying anything?"

Richard shook his head. "Nothing. I don't have a clue what he was up to and why he needed me to drive. But then, he had me drive him over to Prince Street and wait. He came back with nothing again, but this time, he was freaking out and insisted I take him back out to his place. I figured someone from the party would drive me home later, but when we got here, there was no one else around. Ruby said the guests all ate and drank like boors, and then left. She was furious that they wouldn't wait for Earl to come back. It turns out, the only guests were his construction workers, who'd never been to his house or any house like it before. They likely came to have a look at how the rich live, and wolf down as much free booze and food as they could." An image raced through Richard's mind, and a grin appeared on his face. "I bet they were all incredibly relieved that Earl wasn't here."

The comment elicited a snicker from the chief, who replied, "That's a safe bet."

After an uncomfortable silence, Richard took a deep breath and offered up an unsolicited statement. "Ray, I'm being completely honest with you. I've told you absolutely everything I know."

CHAPTER THIRTY

It was just before 2:00 a.m. Police floodlamps blazed across Bindy's yard, lighting it up like a parade ground. With Dan now in the passenger seat of the new cop car, Ray pulled onto the site and into a flurry of activity.

"Holy shit, Boss," Dan shouted as he watched heaps of boxes, crates and furniture being dragged along and loaded onto a large flat-bed truck. Dan pictured his future being buried under a trash heap of evidence. "Jesus, Chief, I'm gonna have ta miss a whole season of hockey if I have ta weed through all that. I mean, how in hell are we gonna sift through all that crap?"

"That's what we've got new newbies for, Rookie."

Dan shook his head in exasperation. "Come on, it'd take the entire force from Brockville to Kingston and maybe Ottawa too, to pore over that mountain of trash, Sir."

Ray sunk a playful punch into Dan's arm. "Nope, my young pessimist, the best clue we need is usually staring right at us, and we'll know it when we see it." Ray turned his attention toward a young officer who was waving at him. He shouted to him. "Hey Bobby, whatcha got?"

The officer rushed over. "Ya won't believe it, Chief, but that cellar is loaded with hidden cubby holes.

We found 'em; and there's all kinds o' shit in 'em, includin' a bunch o' kiddie sex tapes that were way worse than the ones they showed at the first trial. We popped a couple of 'em in the VCR to have a look." He smirked, and pointed toward a cop who was sitting hunched over a wood pile. "After two minutes, Jimmy over there, upchucked into the lady's kitchen sink. Ya wouldn't believe how disgustin' those videos are. Do ya wanna see one?"

Ray scowled at the novice. "Just load up the damn crap and make sure it all gets checked in." He switched his focus to a box near Jimmy and hollered.

"Hey, Jimmy, what's in that cardboard box over there?"

"Uh, Sir, Sarge tells me they're, uh...sex toys...I'll never understand why they'd be called toys. Ya don't really wanna see one, do ya?"

Ray shot him a deadly look.

"I didn't think so. They look really effin' scary. Lord, when I think of those poor kids..."

"Don't think about them. Just do your damn job, bag, and tag 'em."

"Yes, Sir."

"Let's go Dan." The chief pointed to his car. As Jimmy picked up the box and slunk away, Ray and Dan got in and shut the doors to block out the noise, but in seconds, Sergeant Hanes was knocking at the driver's side window. Ray reluctantly lowered it. "What is it, Hanes?"

"Sorry Chief, but I thought you'd wanna know I found a kitchen funnel down there."

"And why in hell would I care? Ray sputtered.

"Well Sir, It's got a thick pad of white cotton glued inside and plasticine stuffed in the hole in the end."

Ray's scrunched up face was a sure sign he was still bewildered.

"I get it, Chief. It made no sense to me either; but Officer Kelly over there used to work at a vet clinic, and he says he could smell traces of chloroform on the cotton. He says they use the stuff to knock animals out cold when they have ta neuter them and stuff. So, I'm thinkin' maybe Berger used that shit on Sarah."

Ray slammed his fist on the steering wheel and let out a triumphant, "Yes! Hanes, if ya didn't smell like piss n' booze, I'd jump out and hug ya."

Hanes flashed a cautious grin and backed away.

Ray suddenly leaned out the window and called out to him,, "Hey, wait. Where in hell would he get the stuff? And how could he use it without knocking himself out?"

Sergeant Hanes shrugged and stepped closer. "Well, Kelly says it can be kept in a dark, glass bottle with a tight cap, ya know, like a good British stout beer. We didn't find a bottle like that yet; but trust me, we'll be searchin' every inch of this shithole for it."

Ray placed his hand on Dan's shoulder. "See kid, I told ya, the clue we'd need would be starin' at us. We just have to find it and then follow it. Now, jump out, run inside, call St. Gabriel's, and tell them that Sarah might've been knocked out with an elephant-sized dose of chloroform." As Dan darted away, Ray shouted after him, "And please, find out how she's doin'." He turned his attention back to the sergeant.

"Ya got any other eye-openers for me, Hanes?"

"Well, Sir," he continued, "There's a room near the back that's got decades of old racist shit glued to the wall. Wanna see?"

He shook his head. "No thanks, I'll pass on the scenic tour for tonight...but be sure to photograph all of it."

Dan emerged from the house and hopped back into the car. "No change in her, Boss, but they sounded eager to get the information."

Ray offered a curt nod. "Good. Close the door, Dan, and let's go." The chief turned to Hanes. "I'm headin' back to the station. You've still got plenty o' work ahead here, but I'll send you a relief crew in a couple o' hours."

* * *

Ray sniffed the air in the station and chuckled. "Ah, smells like home tonight...a Fergusson home: booze, urine, and flop-sweat."

The duty officer jumped to his feet. "Sir, we've got Berger in number one and we're holdin' Earl in four. We wanted to make sure they were far enough apart so they couldn't hear each other."

"Man, oh man, good for you. You guys are thinkin' with *Colombo's* brain tonight. I'll start with Berger...but before I go in, I've got a job for our lovely desk clerk." She looked up at him with no enthusiasm whatsoever. "Come on, Amy, be a sport and get me a sandwich, a bag o' chips and a Coke."

She stared at him quizzically then asked a question that was dripping in sarcasm.

"Oh sure, Chief, that would be my greatest honour. Any special kind of chips? Salt and vinegar. BBQ? Ketchup? Diet Coke? Regular? And what kind o' sandwich would you prefer, tuna, spam...ham?"

He sneered and shook his head. "I couldn't care less. It's for the slimy suspect in room one, so what kinda sandwich do ya think a snake would eat? Ya know what, Amy; on second thought, just get chips and a Coke. I don't want to be using good money to feed a maggot. Bring it right in to me when ya get it...and get the same order for room four. And Amy, bring along the Polaroid camera and take a shot of me and the suspect in room one when ya come in, okay?"

She smiled and offered a mocking salute and headed off to the vending machine.

* * *

"So, Berger, we've got a lot to talk about. Of course, we don't need to wade through your bullshit anymore now that we've got Earl in custody."

Berger scoffed, "You're a lyin' bastard, 'cause everybody knows Earl just got freed up."

"Yeah, you're right, he did; but that was on the kiddie sex charges. We're talkin' about some other big stuff here, the kind that, strung together, gets ya two or three life sentences. We got lucky though, 'cause when you get right down to it, loud-mouthed, tough guy Earl is just a pussy. He's ready to strike a deal, and that's definitely not good news for you, Duh-wayne. He's been telling us all about some real interesting 'dates' you guys had a few years back. I believe he mentioned Eleanor Miller was one of your favourites."

"That's fuckin' bullshit. And he wouldn't tell ya nothin', 'cause he knows I could bury him."

"Well, Berger, I suggest ya start diggin', 'cause he's wieldin' the shovel in the other room right now."

The motion of this low-life squirming in his seat, stirred up stench from his urine-stained pants. "Oh yeah? Sayin' what?" Berger anxiously asked.

Amy knocked and entered with the refreshments. She crinkled her nose at the odor as she placed the items on the table in front of the suspect.

"Thank you, Amy. This is real nice of you. We like to treat our guests, first class. I take it you delivered a food order to the other room, as well?"

"Yes, Sir, I sure did." She smiled amiably and asked. "Can I take your picture, Chief?"

"Sure...You don't mind do ya, Berger?"

"I couldn't give a shit." He growled as he popped open the Coke can.

"Good."

Ray held his breath and crouched beside the leering suspect while Amy snapped the picture.

"Thanks, Amy. And please let everyone know we don't want to be disturbed for a while, okay?" She tossed her auburn locks and scuttled out of the room.

As Dwayne tore open the chip bag and stuffed his mouth, Ray appeared to be steeped in thought. "You know what, Dwayne, on second thought, while you have your little snack, I'm gonna go and finish up my talk with Earl and see if he wants to make that deal he was askin' for." He rose from his seat and headed to the door.

"Wait a minute," Dwayne called out as he lowered the chip bag onto the table. "What if I talk first? Do I get the deal?"

"Well, that's a big question." Ray contended, with his hand still firmly on the doorknob. "I'd need to know what ya got for me." He released the knob and took a few steps toward the table. "If, by some miracle, I like it, then maybe, we can talk about it."

Dwayne picked up the Coke can and offered a mock toast. "Now, to start with, I'm tellin' ya, I'm not talkin' unless ya promise yer not gonna send me to prison on them kiddie porn charges. I mean, Zane and the boys'll be out in a few years, and I don't wanna be sittin' in there all on my own. Look at it this way, Officer; I was hidin' out for like, four years; so, actually, I been servin' my time just like them," He sniggered. "That's why I'm not sayin' nothin' 'til ya promise me no kiddie porn charges." He took a swig of Coke, set it on the table, folded his arms assertively, and sat back in his chair.

Through gritted teeth, Ray offered up the best tale he could muster. "If you talk, Dwayne, I've got your back." Ray proclaimed with no sincerity in his voice whatsoever. "However, it's up to the Crown Attorney to make that decision. But I'll do what I can for ya."

"Good...but I'm eatin' while I talk." He picked up the chip bag and returned to devouring it as if it was his last meal.

"Of course. You'll need your strength. I realize that." Ray condescendingly offered.

* * *

It was pre-dawn, and Berger was still going strong. He hadn't stopped talking about his youthful escapades; from graffitying buildings, to vandalizing the Fleischman's shop and robbing gas stations in Prescott, Stutstown, Brockville and beyond. As he confessed, his attitude seemed to progress from anxiety to arrogance. "Yeh, some people think Earl's got the brains in this family, and I let 'em think it; but I'm done with that shit. The truth is, people need ta know, it's me."

Ray had finally suffered enough of Dwayne's obnoxious bombast. "I appreciate your being honest with me, Berger." With that, he rose slowly, placed his fists on the table, and leaned toward the suspect. "But no more bullshit. I need to know, now!" With his teeth bared, he stared into the coward's terrified face. With surprising calm, he asked, "Why were ya holding Sarah Berman captive?"

Dwayne shrunk as reality sunk in that he was a fly caught in the police chief's web.

"It was 'cause that little weasel, Dougie, told me she was collectin' all kinds of shit that could hurt me. I didn't want anyone knowin' I was still alive, and I needed to know what she had." He ended with an attempt at an innocent shrug; but judging by the grim expression on the cop's face, he needed a new approach. "Okay, look, Chief, I admit, I tried to scare her back to the city with them doll threats, but she's either dumb or nuts, 'cause she didn't take the hint."

The cop remained silent and unmoved, while Berger continued. "Ya still don't get it. I had to get her alone to uh, you know...uh, persuade her. That's all I was tryin' to do when ya cops blew in like a bunch o' wild apes."

Ray raised an eyebrow. "So, she chained herself to the wall?"

The *fly* twisted himself deeper into the clutches of the cop's web. "Uh, no, nope. Uh, ya got it all wrong. She just...uh...passed out. Maybe, she was hungry or feelin' poorly. But, I figured, before that fuckin' Bindy came back nosin' around, I'd...uh...bring her downstairs where we could talk, private like. But then I slipped and fell over the side, and knocked over a crate of booze, and we both went crashin' down on it. Well, she was still out like a light...and I didn't want 'er layin' there on broken glass, so I, uh...stood her up and cuffed 'er to the wall...so she wouldn't get hurt."

Ray ran his fingers through his hair and took a restorative breath. "Berger, I suggest ya stop there for now, 'cause we gotta get on to some other important issues I need to hear about, okay?" Ray managed to conjure a trace of a smile in the hope it would lower the temperature.

He took the bait. "Sure, Officer. What do ya wanna hear?"

Ray folded his arms, settled back in his chair, and glibly responded. "Well Dwayne, I already heard one colourful version of what happened on the beach that night with Daisy Panasar, so it's only fair to hear yours."

The words *Daisy Panasar* appeared to set off frenzied alarm bells in Berger's head. His face became a ruddy swamp. "Holy crap, he told ya about that? Well then, that fuckin' bastard's already buried himself in shit up to his eyeballs. So yeah, why should I give a damn?" With a loutish grunt, he sat forward, interlaced his grubby hands on the table, and fixed his menacing eyes on the cop. "Yeah, fer sure, Earl was pissed when Zane sent that picture to McCall's mother. He blamed Zane as much as the Injun girl for McCall gettin' sent ta frog town. He liked havin' that little weasel, Dickie, around, 'cause it made him feel like a big man. Earl wanted payback so bad the crazy bastard was willin' ta do anythin'. Any damn thing at all.

"He told me he knew the Injun went down to the beach ta swim every night. Well, we got down there, an' sure as shit, there she was."

An odious cackle escaped from the confessor's bowels. "Sorry, Officer, it just tickles me to remember. Anyway, Earl grabbed her from behind and I covered her mouth, jist so she wouldn't howl like we was scalpin' her. It wasn't real dark out yet, so Earl said we gotta get some privacy..."

Ray gritted his teeth before doggedly interjecting. "And uh, what year was that?"

The creep scratched his head and generated a sleazy smile. "Uh, I don't exactly remember..."

Ray fortified his breathing and kept his cool as he waited for Berger to continue. "I think it was back in the fifties or sixties, there was some big swim race or somethin'. Anyway, we took her inta the change house and we had a go at her 'til it got dark. That was some good Injun pussy..." he smacked his lips and coughed.

Ray paused, seized a breath, and uttered, "Continue."

Berger hocked a loogie and spit it into the waste can beside him. "That's better. Yeah, okay. Anyways, Earl said he wasn't leavin' no witness behind, this time. So, he knocked her around like a punchin' bag 'til she was out cold. I hope yer hearin', I said Earl did it, huh?" Ray sat stock still as the wretch continued to spew his verbal bile. "Yeah, it was Earl beatin' on 'er, not me. I only helped him get her as far out in the river as we could go. Earl held her under the water 'til he was damn sure she weren't a witness no more...and then we left and went home. She washed up the next day, and nobody figured nothin'."

The reprobate relaxed, shook his head, and chuckled under his breath like a kid who'd overheard a slightly off-colour joke. And just like that...Berger had, by his standards, shared a *mundane, ordinary* event.

Ray's heart was racing after hearing the ruthless confession. But something else Berger said in passing had Ray's mind swirling. He gathered his mettle and calmly asked, "I'm curious, Dwayne, what did you mean about Earl not wanting to leave a witness behind, *this time*?"

"Well, ya said ya knew all about that Miller bitch; so ya know she coulda been a witness if she weren't scared shitless." Berger snorted.

Ray's cheeks flushed red-hot, and his heart pounded like a snare drum. He continued on in clipped sentences. "Yeah, Berger. He told me about her. So now I need to hear it from you. 'Cause the way Earl tells it...it was all you."

Seemingly unfazed by Ray's accusation, Berger was eager to parallel the confession that Zane Fergusson had previously offered, and with the same kind of macabre and remorseless indifference. The offender pushed his chair back, spread his legs, and waved his hands about dramatically as he took over the stage. All through the accused's chilling account of Eleanor's rape, the police chief exercised every measure of resolve to control his desire to use the narrator for target practice. Finally, unable to take it any longer, he stood abruptly, and dropped a lined yellow pad and a Bic pen on the table.

"Write down and sign the confession you just offered of your own free will. I'll be back, after I see what more Earl has to offer." Ray took several steps toward the door, then paused and pulled a Columbo move. He stepped back and leaned toward the confessor; "One more thing, Berger. I'm curious. What do ya think is gonna happen to you now?"

Berger confidently shrugged. "Happen ta me? Nothin'." He then effected a slow, self-assured smirk as he expounded. "Yeah, sure, I might have to spend a couple o' nights in jail for tryin' to talk some sense into that Klein bitch, but I don't give a crap. Any judge'll understand I needed to protect myself. Everyone around here knows journalists are nothin' but fuckin' vultures. They near ruined this town with all their moral bullshit about them kids. The judge who hears my story about how that nosy bitch was gonna mess this town up again, might be givin' me a medal for keepin' her from doin' it again. Or..." He paused and then hooted like a chimpanzee. "Ooh, ooh, Jeez, I was just thinkin', I might get a judge who diddled them kids hisself. I heard there were a few."

After the horrendous events Ray had seen and heard that day, he was determined not to let this beast's vile utterances push him over the deep end. He ignored Berger's attempts to unnerve him. He stood tall, smiled, and tapped his finger on the pad.

"Before I leave here, Berger, you gotta give me your word, you're gonna write down everything ya told me, otherwise, the prize goes to Earl. Let me hear ya say it."

"Yup, I'm gonna beat Earl again. I'm writin' everythin' I tole ya down, just like ya said ta do."

Satisfied he got Berger to engrave his confession in ink, he left the odious culprit with the pad and pen, and an officer to babysit him. After he shut the door, a sardonic grin spread across Ray's face as he headed to the next interview room. He opened the door quietly, nodded to Dan, then calmly entered with a pretense of contrition.

"Earl, jeez, sorry to keep ya waitin'. My visit down the hall took longer than I planned."

Earl's arrogant smirk was a clue that he believed he was still in control. "Yeah, well, I can't say I'm lettin' ya off the hook that easy. I mean, now I gotta get my lawyer involved, 'cause I been sittin' here wastin' my valuable time." He crumpled the empty chip bag and dropped it on the table, raised the Coke can in a toast to the cop before belting back the last drop.

"I hear ya, Earl. But trust me, it was well worth my time." Ray sat down and motioned for the detainee to lean in. "Earl, I could hardly believe it," He snickered. "Did you know, that Duh-wayne Berger can't spell for shit?" Earl appeared completely baffled before breaking into a high-pitched horselaugh. "Berger, eh? Fuck, that's actually hilarious."

Ray smirked as he continued to reel him in. "No, I'm serious. Honestly, he really can't spell. But boy, can that asshole ever talk."

Earl shook his head and leaned back, "Do ya think I don't know a setup when I see one? Even for a cop, this bullshit is about as desperate as it gets. You know and I know that Berger's dead as dead gets, eh?" He resumed his raucous laughter.

Ray offered a chuckle of his own before adding another tidbit of information. "Oh no-no-no, Earl, he's very much alive. We've got it on real good authority, don't we Dan?"

The rookie obliged with a firm nod. "Sure do, Boss."

"You're actually gonna believe that desperate retard, Bindy? I know, that's where this crap's comin' from. Believe me, if Berger was alive, he woulda been on my doorstep beggin' me for cash like the moochin' son-of-a-bitch he always was."

"Dan, what's the matter with you? Ya haven't reunited Earl here with his old buddy yet?" The chief cast a discreet wink toward the rookie.

Dan shook his head. "No, Chief. I thought you'd want the pleasure for yourself."

"Look, when you guys get done with yer *Three Stooges* act, ya can tell me where ta pay my fine." With that, he slid his chair away from the table.

Ray squinted at Earl. "Hold it. Is that what you think is gonna happen here, Earl? You're gonna pay a fine and walk out o' here?" He shared a cynical grin with Dan.

Earl stood up but made no effort to exit the room. "Yes, that's exactly what's gonna happen, unless you guys wanna show how powerful ya are and keep me locked up overnight. Oh, that's right, it's too late…it's already mornin'. So, let's move this bullshit wagon along."

"Sit down!" Ray bellowed.

As he watched and waited for Earl to resume his seat, the chief slid the Polaroid out of his pocket and waved the back side of it in Earl's face. "Mm-mm-mm. I just had a great snapshot taken about an hour ago during a fascinating and informative chat. Oh, look at that, would ya, Dan? It's even got the date stamped on it. These fancy Polaroid cameras are amazing, huh? You snap a picture, and in minutes, there it is…right in front of ya like a miracle. That's the nineties for ya, one miracle after another." He dropped the photo onto the table. "Recognize him, Earl? He's a clever bugger don'tcha think? Still don't believe he's alive?"

The shameless, self-assured brute, suddenly became a cowering milksop gasping and dripping snot.

Ray pulled a stick of gum from his pocket, slowly unwrapped it and rolled it into his mouth. "And man, that Berger can yatter. He has a great memory too doesn't he, Dan? You know, Earl, he goes way back to happier days when ya were kids, havin' a great old time knockin' off gas stations, scribblin' graffiti, and a load of other stuff."

"Scribblin', or pilferin' a till or two?" Earl pulled a hanky from his jacket pocket and blew into it. "That's what he's been telling ya?"

"Uh-huh. He sure has." Ray quietly replied.

Earl shoved the dank handkerchief back into his pocket. "Big fuckin' deal. So now yer tryin' ta add fines for a few dumb juvie crimes from years ago? Go right ahead if ya think it'll stick. I've got the cash."

Ray kept his eye on the weasel as he continued. "So, Earl, you're tellin' me he's not lying?"

He shook his head. "Nope. I'm not gonna deny it. Berger may be dumb as a doorknob, but he ain't no liar. He never coulda been a lawyer or a cop, 'cause he never could lie to your face without it bein' obvious, even to an idiot. So yeah, when we was kids, we did do that stuff. He's got it right. We was havin' a little fun is all."

"Sure, just a little fun, right, Dan?" Ray repeated as he tapped the rookie on the back.

Dan nodded and responded in kind. "Yup, it's important ta have a little fun now and then, eh Boss?"

Ray smiled and continued. "Right. And it's always good to know our witnesses are truthful. Now, how about burning down shops, all that fun stuff? Jewish owned shops o' course?"

A long, guttural belch was Earl's response. "Tsk, pardon my manners." He jeered. "Must o' been the stale Coke. But, yeah, Berger mighta done that. Maybe he had somethin' against them Jews. I don't remember, 'cause they wasn't important to me."

Ray pursed his lips. "Mm, hm, I understand you, Earl. Those people can really get under your skin, right?"

Earl slapped his knee and snickered. "See, you understand. Shit, yer smarter than I figured. Ya know you can't do nothin' about them goddamn Jews no more, huh? Hitler tried and blew it. Then, they all ended up comin' over here to ruin our country. Maybe ole Berger was just lettin' them know they wasn't welcome here. But did they listen? Nope, they never do. They just keep comin' an' takin' over. They already own our banks and movies and shops...a whole bunch o' shit like that. We was just doin' the town a favour...even McCall's mother agrees. I had long talks with her when Dickie boy started workin' for me, and she knew the score, even if her son didn't. I've kept my eye on him for her."

Ray continued to probe. "So, when ya tried to break up Richard and Daisy...that was just to protect him, right?"

Earl wiped a deluge of sweat from his forehead with his snot-wet hanky. "Christ, he told ya about that?"

Ray leaned forward and whispered conspiratorially. "Oh, yeah, he did. All about how ya caught them on the beach one night gettin' cozy and took a picture and sent it to Richard's mom."

A self-induced coughing spell gave Earl the brief pause he needed to invent a cover story. "Oh, that. Nope. No, that wasn't me. In fact, I was pissed they sent that picture and got Dick sent away."

Ray nodded in faux sympathy. "That must've been a bummer for you, losin' your buddy like that?"

"Yeah, but when he came back to town, like a grownup lawyer, I was gettin' up there in the business world and I needed one, an' there he was. See, it all worked out. Listen, Chief, I'm feelin' bad about them petty crimes we did when we was kids, so maybe I can make a donation to yer police charity or somethin'. What do ya think's a fair amount? Whatever it is, let me pay up and get the hell home."

Dan noticed Ray's clenched jaw was throbbing which was never a good thing. "Uh Boss, um what do you think of Earl's offer?" Dan waited on a razor's edge for a response. Suddenly Ray pushed his chair away from the table, stood tall, and began to pace. His long strides back and forth across the room were loud and deliberate, but he remained silent as seconds ticked by. Finally, he sat down, leaned across the table, and conjured a sardonic grin.

"Well, I think, that's noble of you, Earl, to want to own up and pay for your crimes."

Missing the point of Ray's retort, Earl offered a smug grin over his assumption he'd won.

Ray continued. "However, Earl, I'm afraid even you haven't got the funds to pay off this penalty. Nope, I think it'll take a couple o' life sentences to pay back what you owe."

Earl's watery eyes bulged as the words slowly sunk in. "What the fuck are ya talkin' about?"

The cop settled back in his chair and grinned at Dan's startled look. "It's odd, Earl, that you're the only one in the room who doesn't know what I'm talkin' about. Dan, you know what I'm talkin' about, right?"

Dan pulled himself up straighter than a steel beam. "You're damn right I do, Boss. I guess Mr. White isn't all that smart after all, huh? But go ahead. Don't let me hold you up. I'm sure he's anxious to hear all about it."

Ray cleared his throat. "I agree. Well Earl, what I'm talking about is the brutal rape and murder of Daisy Panasar, and the vicious rape and attempted murder of Eleanor Miller."

Earl sputtered and raved. "Are ya fuckin', crazy? What kind o' shit is that? Did Berger feed ya that bull? He's still nothin' but the lyin' bastard he's always been!"

"Earl, for heaven's sake," Ray quietly chided as he held out his palms in dramatic supplication. "Man, we've got it on tape that ya just vouched for his truthfulness." Ray's gaze sharpened, and a hard edge returned to his voice, "and you need to know, you depraved bastard, we've got a trainload of witnesses ready and willing to help put you away."

Earl screamed, "Ya think a jury's gonna believe a bunch o' pedophile convicts? It didn't work last time, did it? No one's gonna believe 'em...and ya ain't got one piece o' hard evidence this time, neither. So, gimme the paperwork and let me go home. Tell Berger, I look forward to seein' 'im alive and in person, real soon."

Ray smiled triumphantly, and all but skipped toward the exit. "You sit tight, Earl. I'll be sure to give your old pal the message."

* * *

The chief bounded through the door. "Have ya finished yet, Berger?" he asked in his most casual approach.

"Almost. I'm makin' sure it's all said just right."

Ray sat, patiently waiting for the final moment when the suspect signed and dated the document. Berger frowned at the pad, laid down the pen, and nodded. "Okay, now I'm done." He slid it across the table. Ray picked it up and looked it over, relieved to find that, although the spelling was indeed atrocious, the confession was actually legible.

Ray took the pen back and announced, "Yup, you're right, it's done." But his lack of enthusiasm indicated there was a dark, lingering doubt hanging over their encounter.

The chief glanced again at the confession and shook his head. "I'm curious, Berger. You don't seem too concerned about your future. Ya kept yourself hidden these past years 'cause you said you were afraid of getting sent to prison, and now, after all this time, you're confessing? Why is that, huh?"

Berger offered up a wry smirk. "Well yeah, sure, that's 'cause we made a deal that ya can't send me up on them kiddie porn charges."

Ray raised an eyebrow and looked up from the paper. "I never said that Berger. I said I'd do my best. But like I also said...it's not up to me, it's up to the Crown Attorney and others in the justice system. And I'd say that even if the law decides to let ya go on those charges, it won't matter a smidge, 'cause you're goin' down for two rapes and a murder."

A sardonic grin crept across the suspect's face, his eyes narrowed, and his voice dropped to a threatening whisper: "I ain't goin' nowhere, Chief. Ya need to learn a few lessons about the law. See, I make it my business to keep my ears wide open."

Ray offered an open hand. "Continue please, educate me, professor."

Berger leaned in. "Okay, smart guy. Yer first lesson is...ya can't do a damn thing about them old crimes 'cause there's a *statue* of limits that says ya can't do nothin' if the crime was done more than seven years ago."

Ray looked over at Dan who was covering his face with his hands to thwart a laugh. Suddenly, a chuckle escaped, leaving Ray unable to hold back his own. Berger sat stunned as the two cops engaged in a much-needed release of pent-up tension.

Berger was a *blowfly* that was undeniably trapped. But still oblivious, he continued to blather.

"You guys don't know shit. I know what I'm talkin' about. You'll see."

Ray wiped a joyous tear from his eye and continued. "Oh Berger, you shoulda gone to school instead of watchin' the boob tube."

Ray's comment bewildered Berger. "Oh yeah? Well, ya know what? You spend all yer time in the back woods and hick towns arrestin' shoplifters, drunks, and kiddy-diddlers, but ya don't know nothin' about any big-time law cases. Ya wanna know how I know all about the *statue*? It's on all them crime shows on TV fer us to learn about it. Maybe ya should watch a little more TV, Officer. You might learn somethin' about the law."

Ray nodded, schooling his features to look contrite. "Good advice, Berger. But if I do, I'll be sure to get my TV law degree from watchin' Canadian TV crime shows. In this country, we've got lots of *statues* of important heroes and the like, but we don't have any *statute* of limitations, asshole...so you're as guilty now, as ya were in...what was it...'57 or '58? We'll get it right, with Earl's help. Is the video tape still rollin' out there, guys?"

A voice boomed back over the intercom. "No problem, Sir. The only thing is, we kind o' broadcast some of it into interview room four by mistake, and Earl's pretty upset. He says it was Berger who was always the head honcho, the man with the plan, the ringleader..."

Berger puffed up like a helium balloon. "Did he really say that? Honestly?"

CHAPTER THIRTY-ONE

A platoon of masked and smocked medical professionals huddled around Sarah's bed, hooking her up to a crisscross of iridescent tubes, flashing lights, and multi-colored wires that resembled a homemade bomb; but still she remained unresponsive.

With their job efficiently completed, the medical team evacuated the room, passing by the visitors who had been peering through the window. Without waiting for official permission, Eleanor, Shiny, and Sister Catherine, crept inside to watch over the motionless patient. They held her hands, stroked her forehead, and waited for a hopeful sign, while the dissonant sounds of life-buoying machines marked time.

Sister Catherine suddenly gasped. "Did you see that?" The pair looked at the nun in bewilderment. "Seriously. It looked like her eyes opened a little bit."

Shiny leaned in almost nose to nose with Sarah then shook her head. "I don't see it. They look closed to me. Maybe it's a reflex." She straightened up and looked at Eleanor.

Eleanor squinted and focused on Sarah's eyes. "Hey kiddo, can you see me? We're all here with you." She sighed and stepped back. "Maybe. I'm not sure." She looked hopelessly at Sister Catherine who shook her finger at the two doubters and proclaimed, "I'm not taking any chances. I'm going to get the doctor."

"No. Please don't. Not yet, Sister," Shiny implored. "If they come back in, they'll make us leave. And if she's waking up, I want her to see us first, so she won't freak out."

All eyes remained fixed on the patient. "We're all waiting for you to wake up Sarah. Please..." The dry rasp in Eleanor's voice exposed her emotional exhaustion.

"Any change?" Ray asked as he entered the room.

The nun offered her appraisal. "Her eyes seemed to open a bit, but we don't know if it was just a reflex."

His shoulders slumped as he quietly asked, "What does the doctor say?"

"Nothing...and that's my fault," Shiny admitted. "The 'eye opening' question just came up a minute ago, and I've been hoping, with Sister Catherine on our team, we might see a miracle; so, I didn't want to her to call him in case he made us leave."

"Miracles be damned. I'm getting the doctor." Ray insisted as he headed out the door.

Eleanor took a reviving breath and chased after him. Her whispers softly echoed off the corridor walls. "Ray, I heard talk there'd been a couple of arrests..."

He stopped her abruptly "I can't talk about it, Eleanor. For now, let's just focus on Sarah."

His reply clearly didn't quell her anxiety or her disappointment. She turned sharply and returned to the patient's room.

As Ray strode purposefully along the corridor, he was interrupted by the ringing of his cell phone.

Where in hell ya been, Son? I called the station first thing, and they couldn't find ya. Then the sister gave me this other number, but I couldn't get a connection all day. What use are those damn cell phone gadgets if they don't work? How in hell am I supposed to call right away if I can't reach...

Ray scrubbed his hand over his face. "Christ Dad, it's working now, so could ya get to the point?"

Okay...the point is...I got ta thinkin' about that black and white snapshot ya showed me with that huge goddamn Nazi flag hangin' over the guy's head...and I remembered years ago, goin' to a house out there in the boonies, lookin' for stolen property...and there was this bedroom wall covered in all this Nazi shit. It really pissed me off, so I told the parents to get rid of it or else. But there really was no, 'or else'. The law said, we couldn't do nothin' about it and the kid laughed in our faces. But I'm bettin' that picture was taken at an old house that bastard, Earl White was livin' in. So, what do ya think o' your old man now, eh?

Ray smiled a genuine smile for the first time that day. "I think, you've still got it, old man."

Now, you listen to me, Son, ya gotta be smart here. Earl may be a lowlife sonofabitch, but he knows how to get around the law.

"I hear ya, Thanks, Dad. I gotta go."

* * *

Night had seamlessly blended into day. At the break of dawn, Wesley and Mitch had arrived at the hospital showered, rested, and anxious to help. However, it was impossible for them not to notice how completely exhausted Shiny and Eleanor appeared.

Wesley stepped up. "Hey, listen, you both look like wrecks. Mitch and I can take this watch while you two go home and get some rest."

Shiny grunted. "Home? Nah, I might look a wreck, but I'm doin' fine. And you haven't seen how Eleanor's *home* was trashed. It doesn't seem like a restful or safe place right now."

Eleanor offered a feeble nod and replied. "You're right about my place, Shiny, I'm definitely not going there for now. But you need to get home to your husband."

Shiny shrugged, and grimaced "Believe me, it won't do Ronnie any good to have me walkin' in at dawn lookin' like a ghost. He knows I'm here, and I'm safe, and he's okay with that. So, thanks, but it looks like neither of us are leavin'!" With that, the two women sat down, firmly indicating their minds were made up.

Wesley held up a finger and whispered, "Wait, just one minute." With that he headed to the nurse's station.

After a cordial nod, a nurse marched over and confronted the defiant women. She placed a hand on Eleanor's shoulder and stated. "You two, come with me." They dutifully followed as she led them into a room with two empty beds.

"You girls lie down here. If anything happens, I'll come and get you right away. I promise."

The women looked wistfully from the beds to the nurse. It didn't require two promises. The nurse gave an upward nod, smiled, turned off the lights, and closed the door as she left the room. The women had barely laid their heads on their pillows before they fell into a dead sleep.

* * *

Word reached young Officer Bobby, that Ray wanted the colour photos he had shot at the crime scene. He wanted to show them to his father. At warp speed, Bobby set out to meet his boss at the seniors' home.

After several minutes of studying the photos, Bill Connell pursed his lips, blew an exaggerated whistle, and raised his head. "Yup. These pictures are from the same damn place I told ya about. Well, Son, do ya think ya got enough now to get those rotten bastards?"

Ray cast a weary sigh and a doleful shrug. "To be honest, Dad, I doubt it's enough to stand up in court and guarantee a conviction. But I gotta find out for sure from someone more invested in the law than Crown Attorney Dunn."

When he returned to the station, he found Richard McCall seated on a bench in the hallway with his head bowed low. Ray, seething with distain, shouted; "You're gonna defend this piece o' shit again, huh, Dick?"

Tears blurred Richard's vision as he looked up at the enraged cop. "Ray, please, tell me Earl's just messing with us? Tell me all these years I wasn't providing legal services to a murdering son-of-a-bitch? Tell me, Ray!"

Ray looked away but said nothing.

"Holy Mother of God, please tell me it's not true," Richard shrieked as his ruddy face became a cold, grey mask. His body shuddered violently as if demons were raging inside. Still, Ray said nothing.

The police station ground to a halt as everyone stopped and looked on in shock. The venom that roiled inside of Richard McCall was about to explode in a torrent of vomit. On impulse, Amy slid a garbage pail in front of him, then rushed away, returning with a wet towel and a glass of water.

Ray looked on with indifference as the lawyer, coiled in pain, dropped to his knees, and began to retch.

Amy, taken aback by Ray's unusual detachment, knelt down beside Richard. "Mr. McCall, let me drive you to St. Gabriel's."

The chief gritted his teeth and weighed in. "No. You've got things to attend to, Amy." The chief growled, but as he well knew, Amy was not easily deterred. "Chief, please, he really needs to see a doctor."

Ignoring her plea, Ray removed his winter jacket and draped it over his shoulder. "Amy, I'm goin' in to talk to Earl," Then he turned to face Richard. "I need ta know if he's hired a criminal lawyer?"

Richard managed to signal with a shrug before dry heaving a couple of times.

"I take that to mean you don't know?" The chief coldly snapped.

"I swear I don't know, Chief." He croaked.

The chief squinted and nodded as a thought occurred to him. "What about the Toronto lawyer? Is he comin'?"

Richard lifted his face from the pail, wiped his mouth, and took a deep breath.

"Yeah...he'll be here." He flopped back in the chair, took a sip of water, and pressed the wet towel to his forehead.

Ray's tolerance was edging toward a breaking point. He gritted his teeth and spat out the question. "Are you effin' insane? I just asked you if Earl hired a lawyer and you straight up lied to me."

Richard held up his hands in a gesture of surrender. "No, I didn't lie, I swear."

Ray dropped his jacket on a chair and rushed toward the lawyer. "Jesus, Richard, what kinda weaselly prick are you? After what you found out about Earl, how could you call and ask that guy or anyone, to defend the bastard?"

Richard dolefully shook his head. "I didn't call him."

Ray's breath hissed through his teeth. "Jesus. You didn't call him? So, he's what? Telepathic?"

"No. I only know I didn't call Cowan. Someone else must've. After Dan came by my place and told me what happened with Sarah, I got ready to head over here. But just before I left, Cowan phoned from a highway rest stop...and asked to meet me. I said I'd be at the Brockville police station, and he said he'd meet me here; and then he hung up. That's all I know. When

I got here, I asked a cop if Earl made a call to Cowan. He told me, no; he only made one call and it was to me, but I didn't answer. After hearing that Earl was involved in this horror story, I might have considered killing the bastard before I'd consider helping to represent him." He paused to catch his breath while Ray sat down beside the terrified dupe and waited for a moment of calm.

Beginning to feel an undercurrent of nausea of his own, Ray took a deep breath, and looked the cowering wreck in the eye.

"Listen Richard, I know this has been a hell of a shock, but even feeling the way you do about Earl, I figure, that Cowan guy's still the only lawyer he knows."

The lawyer humbly added, "Criminal lawyer, you mean?"

"Yeah, sorry, I meant, criminal lawyer." Not accustomed to apologizing, Ray's voice amped up once again. "But, Richard, if you're not representing him, I can only hope you'll be able to impress on Cowan, why he'd be smart to stay clear of Earl's mess. Do ya understand?"

"I understand completely." Laurie Cowan's voice echoed along the police station corridor. "Just so you know my position, there isn't enough money in the federal mint that could tempt me to represent Earl White again." Laurie stopped in front of the two men, and took in the alarming sight of Richard, who was more green than white.

"Richard, you look like crap. I hope you're okay, but I'm only here because I got a call telling me that Sarah had been attacked, was in a coma, and her condition was critical. So, if this meet-up is a waste of time, then I'm gonna leave and head over to the hospital." He pivoted toward Ray, who seemed completely dumbfounded by his presence. Laurie stretched out his hand, and the chief obliged with a firm shake. "So, Chief, what can you tell me?"

"First, Mr. Cowan, can you tell me, are you a personal or professional acquaintance of Sarah's?" Ray asked with an involuntary grin.

"I am." Laurie slyly replied. "Now, before I head over there, can someone take a minute and please tell me what's going on?"

"We can do that," Ray agreed. "But it'll take more than a minute, and ya may have some trouble believin' what you hear. Have a seat. I'll getcha a coffee...and maybe a dose of horse tranquilizer on the side."

* * *

The nurse snapped on the light and called out; "Hey, you two, it's time to wake up."

Eleanor opened her eyes and tried to focus. "Oh, God! What happened?" she gasped as the nurse came into view.

Shiny raised her head and sputtered, "Everything's good, right?" She flung her feet over the side of the bed and sat stupefied. Eleanor lifted herself onto her elbows and stared at the nurse's face, as if hoping the answers would magically appear on her forehead. The nurse ignored the hysteria, reached under the bed, and handed Shiny her sneakers. "Here Barefoot Contessa, you're gonna need 'em. As Shiny laced them up, Eleanor threw back her covers and slid off the bed. It took a moment for the two of them to get their bearings. Finally, Eleanor pleaded; "Please tell us? Is she awake? Is she...okay?"

The nurse bobbled her head from side to side, in a *so-so* gesture. The women held their breath, waiting for more. "Well, she isn't exactly awake," the nurse began, "but we've removed all the bells and whistles ya saw attached to her a few hours ago. Now, we wait and see."

Shiny balked at the idea and shook her head vigorously. "No, no, no. What in hell does 'wait and see' mean? Wait and see, what?"

Eleanor placed her hand on Shiny's arm and softly suggested, "We have to do what she says, Shiny. We'll wait and see. But can we do that in her room, nurse?" She asked as she stepped into her shoes.

"Of course. Why do you think I woke you up?" The nurse smiled and motioned for them to follow.

They arrived in the room to find Sister Catherine sitting by the head of the bed, with Wes and Mitch standing by the foot. The two latecomers took their places on either side of the patient. There were no signs of consciousness, but all present waited in pensive silence for any sign that she was coming around.

* * *

A kaleidoscope of grey and white fragments ascended and descended in graceful, slow motion until the flushed face of an angel came into focus.

Suddenly, the most anticipated sound of the past twenty-four hours was heard. It was barely audible. It was soft and gravelly.

"Is...this...heaven?" Sarah haltingly whispered.

A rush of excitement filled the room. Wesley squeezed her hand. "It's not my idea of heaven," he chortled. "But I'm no expert, yet."

Sarah's eyes drifted from face to face, and her words were slurred, but she was there. She was alive. "I saw...an angel...like...on TV." She mumbled.

Shiny brushed away a strand of hair from Sarah's cheek. Through a curtain of tears, Eleanor managed to quip, "If she can remember TV, she's gonna be just fine."

Mitch noticed that Sarah's eyes were unfocused and wandering erratically.

"Hey, Mrs. Berman, listen, tryin' to follow the action in this room is makin' ya go cross-eyed; and I gotta say, it's not an attractive look." The attempt at humour appeared to initiate a trace of a smile from the patient.

"Is this a hospital bed?" She mumbled.

"It is." Wes bluntly replied.

"What am I doing here, Wes? What's the story?"

He took a deep breath and paused to consider how best to answer her question. "Yup, Sarah, there's a story for sure, and we'll tell you all about it, later, when you're out of here. I promise," Wesley vowed.

"It must be...a hell of a story...if you...had to call in...a nun. No offence...Sister...Cath..." Sarah's eyes fluttered shut as her voice drifted off. Never had snoring sounded so melodious. Wesley kissed her hand and exhaled a sigh of relief.

The nurse approached. "I think she needs her rest and so do all of you. Shoo now," She smiled and clicked her tongue like a farmer herding his sheep.

The visitors obeyed and headed into the waiting room to find Richard McCall frantically pacing.

"What the hell are you doin' here, Richard?" Wesley barked. "You don't see that this is insane, under the circumstances?" He seethed. "I mean, if Earl's somehow mixed up in this, then it seems to..."

Richard stamped his foot in protest. "Damn it! I know how it seems," he shouted.

Wesley's usual cool, even, temper had passed the simmering point. "No, you damn well don't. 'Cause if ya did, ya wouldn't be here." Wesley paused to calm himself. "I need some space." He growled as he slipped out of the waiting room.

Silence fell like a murky fog over the room as each visitor privately waded into their concerns over their friend's traumatic experience, and the unwelcome arrival of someone who might have had a hand in it.

Wes re-entered the room in a rage. "What in hell's going on, Richard? Why in hell is Laurie Cowan down the hall talking to Sarah's doctor. If he's defending any of those reprobates, he has no right to be talking to anyone connected to Sarah, especially her personal physician."

"Wes, you need to calm down!" Shiny chided.

Wes, offended by her tone, snapped back. "Are you kidding me? Have you completely lost your mind?" He snorted.

She grabbed onto his arm. "He's not here for Earl White, Wes. He's here for Sarah. I called him last night to see if he had any contact information on her family. I briefly explained the situation ...but all I expected to get was a phone number." Shiny shrugged. "But here he is, and if he's talking to her doctor, then he's more than a little worried." A puckish smile crept across her face, "I betcha those two have got somethin' goin' on."

Wes grinned and plopped into a chair. "Seriously, folks, how did I miss that? Hell, I'm the one who told her to put on somethin' sexy and go meet him." The entire group succumbed to the giggles like a pack of grade school kids.

As Laurie entered the waiting area, the group quieted down and pretended they had no idea who the stranger in their midst was. They looked everywhere and anywhere, except at Laurie, who was curious to know who everyone was. Once the introductions were over, the room ascended into a buzzing exchange of information, updates, and stories, both hopeful and humorous, about the person at the centre of their concern.

The tabloid cabal was interrupted by Sarah's nurse. "Uh, excuse me, your friend is asking for you."

"Which 'you' is that?" Shiny asked with a hint of frustration. "I mean there's a whole boatload o' nervous 'yous' here as ya can see."

The nurse smiled calmly at the stormy sea of anxious faces. "Well, she didn't actually say, but I'm pretty sure she meant all of you. Go on now. Don't keep her waitin'."

Wesley seemed hesitant. "Is she coherent now?"

The nurse tapped her chin and smiled. "Well, let's see, she's already tried to make a deal with the administrator and the doctor to release her this afternoon, and she's asking for something to write with."

A rush of excitement riffled through the crowd.

"Shame on you all for doubting that miracles can happen," Sister Catherine mused.

Shiny laughed quietly and offered the sister a friendly shoulder nudge. "Oh crap, will I go to hell for that, Sister?"

Sister Catherine laughed. "I think, under the circumstances, God will let you off the hook. Now, get in there before she thinks you've all abandoned her."

"Aren't you coming, Sister?" Shiny asked.

The nun shook her head. "I have to get back to the residence, I've already missed helping with the breakfast service. But give her a hug for me."

"What about you, Laurie?" Eleanor asked.

"You go on ahead. I'll be there in a while," Laurie replied, then added, "Would you guys do me a favour, and please don't tell her I'm here."

As they disappeared, Laurie took a seat across from Richard and eyed him with laser focus. "Now, Richard, you and I are gonna have a very frank conversation."

As the words echoed in Richard's ear, he shriveled in his seat.

* * *

Shiny led the procession along the corridor and into Sarah's room. There was a rushed crescendo of voices mumbling their oohs and aahs at finding her sitting up in bed.

"Oh my God, you're all here?" She began to weep softly as she studied their faces.

The group encircled the bed as if a seance was about to commence. They'd all been eager to see her awake and alert, but now no one seemed to know what to say.

She waited for someone to say something, but not even Shiny spoke up.

"Jeez, can someone please tell me what happened?"

The only sounds heard were the uncomfortable shuffling of feet and clearing of throats.

"Okay, let me tell you what's what. I asked the nurse why I was groggy. She said I was heavily sedated, but I looked, and there's no incision for appendix or gallbladder or anything like that. So, what happened? I have scratches all over me. Why are you all looking at me like I'm dead?"

Wesley smiled warmly and gave her arm a light pinch. She giggled. "See, you're definitely alive," he jibed, "and you're gonna be just fine. But can you please wait 'til you're feeling a hundred percent before you start investigating? For now, don't be a journalist, just be a compliant patient, okay?"

"I'm feeling, let's say, ninety percent, so can you at least tell me how I got here?" She asked with pleading eyes.

"Oh Sarah, Sarah, you're as stubborn today as you were as a kid." Wes's banter delivered a little tension relief to everyone. He continued. "Come on, Sarah, show a little restraint, and before you know it, all will be revealed. In the meantime, are ya hungry?"

"I'm starving." She eagerly replied. "Actually, you know what? I could really go for a burger and..."

"No Sarah, trust me. You definitely don't want a *Berger*." Shiny chuckled.

"Too greasy?" Sarah asked.

"Definitely too greasy," Mitch chortled. "Maybe you better start with something easier on the stomach, like toast."

* * *

With all his years of dealing with the accused and witnesses, it occurred to Laurie that he'd get a better result with a more hospitable approach. "Richard, why don't we head down to the cafeteria?"

Richard hastily agreed.

Over carrot muffins and coffee, they established a more civil interaction.

"What I don't understand, is why Earl broke into Eleanor and Sarah's places? What was he looking for?" Laurie innocuously asked. "I mean, it doesn't make sense, does it?"

Richard's nascent flop sweat, ruddy complexion, and shaky leg, all materialized in unison. "Christ, Laurie, you're asking me as if you think I know. Earl just told me to drive, and like the coward I've always been, I did it. When I took him over to the hotel, I had no idea he was going to Sarah's suite. And since I was parked a good distance away from Eleanor's house, I didn't have a clue he went in there either. I don't know what he was looking for, but I don't think he found whatever it was, because he seemed more pissed-off each time he got back in the car empty-handed. I suspect he was looking for photographs and other stuff that Bindy Fergusson told Earl could ruin him. She supposedly gave it all to Sarah."

Laurie sat and let the information sink in. "I'm guessing you told Ray about it?"

Richard looked everywhere but at Laurie, "Well, not in so many words. I mean, just finding out I had unknowingly chauffeured Earl to those break-ins, disgusted him, so, me trying to defend myself woulda put him right over the edge."

"I see." Laurie stood up, took a long deep breath, and declared, "I'm going to see Sarah now, but it would be best for everyone, if you don't."

Richard hung his head and contritely stated, "You're right, Laurie. But I hope you'll believe me when I say, I have no intention of interfering with Sarah, Eleanor, or anyone involved. However, I promise, I'll do whatever I can to help."

Laurie hesitated and looked down with a twinge of empathy for the broken little man before him. "Okay. Good."

CHAPTER THIRTY-TWO

The gurgle of a flushing toilet, in harmony with the swoosh from a water faucet, was *musicale grandioso* to Laurie's ears. It was a sign that Sarah was able to navigate to and from the washroom on her own. While he waited for her to appear, he remained by the window, staring out onto the snow-dusted street below.

The door opened and Sarah emerged. Although unaware that a visitor was standing nearby and watching, she still struggled to keep the flimsy hospital gown closed as she shuffled and weaved to the bed.

As a means of signaling his presence, Laurie theatrically cleared his throat. "Ahem."

"Holy Moses!" she gasped as she flopped onto the bed.

"Is that surprise, or a Jewish epiphany?" He gibed as he took stock of the scene.

She pulled the covers over and up to her chin, and grimaced as she tried to make sense of the situation. "Oh my God, Laurie. Why...what...are you doing here? When...How did you get here?"

Laurie chuckled as he straddled the arm of the leather chair beside her bed. "Okay, but first, you tell me, is the *why, what, when,* and *how*, the journalist, or the drugs talking?"

A schoolgirl blush spread from her collarbone to her cheeks. "Uh, no drugs. It's just me. I'm glad to see you. I was just thinking in the bathroom how grateful I was that there was no mirror in there. Now, I'm regretting it, 'cause, I must look like crap."

Laurie grinned and leaned forward. "Funny, because I'm thinking, all things considered, you look pretty good. And I never realized how sexy hospital gowns could be." He snickered.

She clasped the covers even tighter. "Oh, please tell me it wasn't open?"

Laurie laughed. "Are you kidding me? You were gripping the back of that thing, like it was a lifeline."

She giggled and breathed a sigh of relief. "Thank God for good impulses. So, now can you answer my questions?"

"Sure, I can: I drove in this morning." He paused for a beat, gathered his composure, and continued, "And I came because I was kinda worried about you." He awaited her response, but it wasn't what he expected.

She gaped at him as if he had suddenly morphed into an alien. "You were worried? It seems as if everyone was worried." She delivered a perplexed shrug. "Everyone looks at me as if I was just resurrected. No one's telling me anything, and I don't know how I ended up here. Do you? If you do, please tell me what's going on?" Tears streamed down her cheeks.

He moved over to the edge of her bed and calmly suggested; "I'll tell you what, Sarah. How about we start with what you remember, and by the time we get through that, maybe Ray will be here to fill in the rest."

Sarah frowned. "But that's a problem, 'cause I don't remember anything."

Undaunted, he asked. "Can we try? Can you free up one hand for me?" Her pinched brow indicated she was dubious, and yet she relented. He placed her hand between both of his. "That's better. Now, let's start with the early, morning-before, whatever it was happened, and try, try your best to remember, okay?"

Sarah sighed, acquiescing. "Okay. I had breakfast in my room and then I left for a meeting."

"That's it?"

"Uh-huh, sorry..." Sarah frowned, "No, wait, first, I got a bunch of phone hang-ups that kind of unnerved me. Oh yeah, because of that, I stopped at the desk on my way out, to pick up my extra room key. I didn't want it lying around. There was no one there, so I leaned over and took it."

"Did you go right to Eleanor's after your meeting with Richard?"

"Hold it," Sarah demanded. "I never said who I was meeting with, or that I went to Eleanor's."

Laurie held a hand up in supplication, "Right, well, let me put your mind at ease. It was Richard who told me about your meeting."

Sarah raised an eyebrow. "He did, huh? He told you about Earl and Daisy Panasar and his racist mother?"

Laurie nodded. "All of it, okay? And then Ray told me you'd been at Eleanor's in the afternoon." He let the information register for a moment before continuing, "What I want to hear from you though, is what happened after that."

She strained to fit the pieces together. Suddenly, her eyes widened. "Hold on, I remember that Richard's story upset me, and I wanted to verify the details. I called his mother and arranged to go over there to have another chat with her." She paused for a moment, as if her present thoughts were catching up with her past memories. "Oh yes, I stopped by the grocery store and picked up some flowers. They worked for Wesley when we visited her, 'cause she opened up like a book; so, I figured another bouquet might do the trick. And since I didn't want to walk back later in the bitter cold, I headed to the hotel to get my car. That's when Doug Fergusson drove up and asked me to get in, 'cause he had an urgent message for me."

"Fergusson? You've got to be kidding? A Fergusson pulls up to the curb and you just hop in? You don't recall the whole Fergusson pedophile thing that brought you here in the first place? Seriously?"

Her baffled stare and puckered brow were clear indications that Sarah was offended by Laurie's stance. "Well, that's pretty damn judgmental of you, Laurie. First of all, Doug Fergusson, in spite of his name, is not one of *them*; and, in any case, you might have noticed, I'm not a child and I'm not an idiot either."

Laurie withdrew his hand from hers and ran his fingers along the back of his neck. "I know that, but I don't get it. You're defending a Fergusson? What's happening here? Honestly, I'm in a fog." He rose and wandered back to the window.

Silence hung in the air, while outside, delicate snowflakes fluttered about. The balletic movement caught Sarah's eye, creating a moment of reflection for both of them.

After seconds of quiet contemplation, Sarah spoke. "I understand where you're coming from, Laurie. After wading through material related to Earl and his Fergusson family, I get it. But honestly, in spite of the name, this kid is not one of them. He's journeyed through hell to escape the legacy of that family. I'm telling you, he's different."

Looking a little less dubious, Laurie leaned against the windowsill, shoved his hands into his pockets, and signaled her with a nod. "Okay, I'm listening. Go ahead. Why do you think he's different?"

"Well, he survived a lifetime of mistreatment and took responsibility for his family when his abusive father went to prison. He worked his way up to a respectable job right here in this hospital. The kid even moved his mother and sisters in with him while he searched to find them safe accommodations. And now, he's going to night school to improve his prospects. He's scared and confused, but he's not a bad kid, I mean it."

Laurie pushed himself away from the window, strolled back to the leather chair and sat. "I'm not quite sold." He noted, as a cheeky grin emerged. "But I'm still a potential buyer. So, tell me, what was the message he was so anxious to deliver when he picked you up?"

The scene was changing. Both parties now seemed invested. Sarah lifted and fluffed her pillows and sat up. She paused for a moment to refocus.

"Well, he told me that Ray was out at Bindy Fergusson's place and wouldn't be able to reach me out there in the sticks, on his cell phone. I guess Bindy had got a hold of Doug, and asked him to find me, and give me the message. When I told him I was surprised he found me, he said it was easy. All he had to do was drive along the five blocks of Main Street and there I was, coming out of the grocery store."

"But I still don't get, what was so urgent?" Laurie prodded.

"Oh, I was supposed to meet with Richard's mother about the Earl White story I'm working on. But it seems that Bindy discovered a load of important new information she thought would help me, and maybe Ray too. So, Doug was sent to find me and drive me out there. Her place is way out along a dark country road and what he said to me about driving out there alone made perfect sense. I mean, what if I got lost, or my car broke down? It was a really good point, 'cause I can get lost a few blocks from home in Toronto, so there was a pretty good chance it could happen."

"Did you cancel your visit with Mrs. McCall?"

"No. I told Doug about it, and he offered to drive me to her house and wait for me." She glanced at Laurie then lowered her head as if hit with a dose of guilt or embarrassment.

Her reaction bewildered him. "Uh, okay. So why the red, hot face?" He teased.

She touched her face and found it was indeed hot. She groaned. "If you must know, I felt really bad about having him wait for me. It was bitter cold outside, which meant he would either have to freeze, or waste gas running the engine to keep warm; but he was adamant about waiting. So, why the red face? Because, I did have him wait, and I think I was taking advantage of him."

Laurie grinned and clicked his tongue. "Tsk, tsk, for shame, Sarah. But please, go on."

She hesitated and released a querulous sigh. "I'm gonna let that jab pass and get back to 'trying my best to remember,' like you asked. Okay?"

This time it was Laurie who wore the red face. "Sorry. Yes, please keep trying."

"Then here I go. When I got to Estelle's house, her weekly canasta game had just ended, and the ladies were leaving. Mrs. Perkins, that nice old lady I told you about who used to make those amazing cinnamon jawbreakers? Well, she was really happy to see me, so Estelle invited her to stay behind for another pot of tea." Sarah smiled as her mind drifted back to that scene. "Close to an hour and a couple of cups of tea later, I realized I wasn't going to get the chance to ask my questions in private, so I said my goodbyes and headed out to Doug's freezing car.

"I remember insisting that we stop at Tim Horton's before heading out to Bindy's. I had to get rid of all the tea I drank, and I wanted to treat Doug to a hot coffee and donut for his trouble. He waited once again, while I headed to the washroom to take care of business. I got back in the car, we ate our donuts, drank our coffee...and that's it. Uh, maybe I dozed off en route because...that's honestly, the last thing I remember." She paused and an impish grin lit up her face. "It was the last thing...until I saw a 3D image of Sister Catherine floating above my bed like an angel." She snickered. "Anyway, when the world finally came back into focus, I asked if I'd had some kind of surgery. A nurse said I hadn't. That didn't stop me from checking, but there was no incision. Then I was terrified that I'd been uh..." Sarah's breath caught in her throat, "been uh, se...you know. Thankfully, I was reassured that never happened. But then, I noticed there were scratches, cuts, and bruises all over me, and that's when I realized we'd been in an accident."

"An accident?" He repeated.

Sarah nodded. "A car accident. Then I was worried about Doug. But a few minutes ago, when Francis Murk, the hospital administrator dropped by, she assured me that Doug was fine and working his scheduled shift. So, now that I know we're both okay, I told her, all I want to do is get out of here."

Laurie gestured with both hands to stop. "Whoa up there, Kiddo. You may need a little more healing time before you get back in the race."

"No, if the doctor says I'm good, then there's no reason I can't go back to the hotel today. I can drop back here tomorrow for tests or results or whatever they need. But before I check out, I want to speak to Ray. I need to know what he found at Bindy's that was so important."

"I'll tell you what, Sarah: you rest up and I'll go find Ray for you." He promised as he held out his hand.

"Deal." She said, giving it a perfunctory shake.

He smiled coyly and judiciously asked, "Do I have permission to give you a hug before I go?"

She responded to the request with a warm smile and open arms. "I think it might even be compulsory."

They sealed the deal with a warm embrace.

* * *

The waiting room was still buzzing with well-wishers. Laurie signalled Shiny and Eleanor and asked them to step out for a private minute. "Listen, right now, Sarah's taking a nap. But she's insisting that she's gonna leave the hospital and go back to the hotel, today. Does that sound like a carefully thought-out plan?"

Shiny rolled her eyes and scoffed. "A carefully thought-out plan? I've learned this much about our friend, Sarah: that woman doesn't always carefully think out plans. She's more of a spur o' the second thinker and doer."

The truth of the quip broke the tension and all three chuckled.

"Laurie," Eleanor whispered. "Is Sarah aware that someone ransacked her hotel room?"

He shook his head. "She doesn't know about any of it. The last thing she remembers is drinking coffee, eating donuts, and taking a drive in the country. She's concluded she was in a car accident, and I didn't attempt to change her mind. I'll leave that to Ray. In the meantime, we need to try and convince her to stay here for a couple more days."

The two women exchanged a cynical glance that prompted Shiny to speak up. "Laurie, if Sarah's determined ta leave here, she's gonna be outta here like streak lightening. So, I think, Eleanor and I need to head to the O'Brien right now and try to put her place back together...in case she gets her way."

* * *

As the day wore on, the racket echoing from Sarah's hospital room sounded more like the howling of wild animals than a conversation among civilized humans. Ray bellowed like a pissed-off grizzly, Sarah yelped like an angry fox, while occasionally, Laurie could be heard baying like a lone wolf.

"Jeez Sarah, why can't ya listen to reason? It's a bloody bad idea." Ray shouted as he turned to the lawyer for support. "She's not listening to me Laurie, maybe you can make her see how *effing* insane this is."

Laurie shook his head. "To be honest, Ray. I don't see what the harm is."

"Okay, since I'm obviously not gonna win this, then here's the deal, Sarah: if you're up to it, I'll let ya."

"Perfect. That's all I wanted to hear," Sarah clapped her hands triumphantly.

Ray folded his arms over his chest and stood firm. "Hold on a minute, I wasn't finished. I'll let ya...I'll bring ya there myself, but not 'til tomorrow, and that's only if the doctor says it's okay for you to leave tomorrow, and if Francis agrees ta sign your release."

Sarah grimaced, "Come on, Ray, now that I know the whole epic story, surely you can see I'm tough enough to face it. So why do I have to wait 'til tomorrow? Do you have any idea how long tonight will be for me, if I have to stay here?"

Ray heaved a weighty sigh. "Long or not, the deal is for tomorrow! Besides, I'm gonna need a few hours sleep myself."

"Fine," she blurted.

In an attempt to lower the temperature, Ray appealed to one of Sarah's most basic pleasures. "I'll tell ya what, since you've agreed to stay here tonight; tomorrow I'll bring Eleanor over to your place uh, around seven...along with pizza, donuts, and any other junk food you want. What do ya say?"

She groaned but delivered a wavering thumbs up. "Junk food? Pizza? You win."

Ray rolled his eyes and looked over at Laurie, "You'll join us too, right?"

"Do you have to ask?" He grinned and affected a two-finger salute.

"All set, Sarah." Ray confirmed. "Once they check you out tomorrow, I'll pick you up, and Laurie, if you're staying nearby, I can drive you both back to Prescott."

"Thanks, Ray, but I've got my car, so I can drive Sarah back once she's released."

Sarah threw up her hands in jest. "Eeny-meeny, miney...Come on guys, I don't care how I get there, I just want to get out of here. Do I have to wait for the doctor to show up in the morning to sign my prisoner release papers like I'm leaving the Kingston Pen."

"See that, Laurie?" Ray's eyes twinkled, "It's only been three minutes since we made a deal and she's already wheedling to renege."

* * *

The old, town hall clock chimed three as Sarah slowly ascended the hotel stairs with Laurie close behind. As she turned the key in the lock, her trepidation was quickly abated at the sight of her suite; neat, clean, and adorned with fresh flowers, helium balloons, and a fancy fruit basket.

"Wow, look at all this, Laurie. It's amazing!"

"And you can thank Eleanor and Shiny for it."

"I sure will. Oh, look over there. Holy crap! I don't believe it. I swear to God, that's a brand-new TV! Now there's irony for you. Just when I'm about to leave town, Reynolds finally pays attention. I guess all I needed to do was get kidnapped."

Laurie chortled. "Yeah, that and the fact that some creep got into your room with a key from the front desk, which means the hotel could be held liable and sued up the wazoo. Now that's an attention grabber."

"Does the lawyer in you ever take a rest?" Sarah teased.

He grinned. "Yup, in fact, I'm gonna do that rest thing in a minute."

"A good idea," she purred, "and when you do, I'm gonna take a long hot shower and try to scrub some of the trauma away." She leaned in to smell the flowers and noticed a get-well card: *To our friend, hometown hero, and one-day-to-be, award winning journalist, we send our deepest wishes for a complete return to health, and to her pen and notepad.*

It was signed by all those who had stood by her bed wishing or praying for her recovery. Her eyes brimmed with tears, but she stoically held back the rush and continued to stroll around the room, admiring the decorations and examining the slick, new TV and the right out-of-the-box remote.

While Sarah was busy appreciating her favors, Laurie was discreetly checking the bathroom and looking under the bed. Confident that there were no monsters lurking, he announced, "Since you wisely suggested we both need a rest, I'm going to leave you to play with your new toys, or do your spa thing, or maybe take a nap. Are you going to be okay with that?"

"If you mean do I need a bodyguard, the answer's no. With Earl White and that Berger animal under lock and key, I feel pretty darn safe."

"That's great, but would you humour me and let me take your extra room key with me? I promise I won't use it unless you disappear with some Fergusson again."

She managed a giggle as she rummaged through her handbag to produce the key.

"Jeez, I didn't even thank Ray for rescuing my purse."

Laurie smirked, "I think your heartfelt *thanks for saving my life* speech at the hospital pretty much took care of that. Now, you may not admit that you need rest, but I confess, I do. So, I'm going to my room, and I'll see you in a while, okay?"

"God, Laurie. I haven't even considered how exhausting this has been for you! I mean, you drove all this way two days ago, and I can't imagine you've gotten much sleep. I don't know how I can ever thank you."

"Maybe we can discuss some ideas when you're back to normal."

A mischievous smile crept across Sarah's face as she mulled over his cheeky innuendo. "It's really sweet that you think I have a normal state to get back to. Even Shiny thinks I'm a bit odd," Sarah laughed, "and that's coming from someone who's the queen of odd."

* * *

Sarah stood transfixed under the steaming shower, silently reviewing Ray's vivid account of the past two days and trying to assimilate the freakishly traumatic events.

While she attempted to scrub away all traces, real or imagined, of her captivity; deconstructed visions dashed through her mind at warp speed. Each troubling image took its place in the slow formation of a completed puzzle; and all the pieces of the macabre mystery were connecting. The smells and sounds from her abduction echoed sluggishly through her brain, like an underwater scream. In that moment of clarity, Sarah realized how close she'd come to never leaving that cellar. Until then, she'd thought of Ray's official account, like a crime drama with a fictional victim in the lead role, who wasn't her.

Sequestered by the white noise of the blanketing waterfall, Sarah sank to her knees and sobbed.

Twenty minutes passed before a sudden drop in temperature shocked her back to reality. Propelled by vigorous shivers and withered digits, Sarah toweled off, donned her robe, and dissolved onto her bed.

Try as she might, she couldn't hold back the relentless flood of tears. She cried for her failed marriage, her estranged children, her floundering career, and her clumsy handling of Eleanor's private pain. What made her imagine she could ever be a journalist? How could she have made such reckless decisions? How could she have not been aware of the danger that was stalking her?

In spite of her earlier declarations to Ray and Laurie that she felt strong and secure, her startled response to the phone ringing told a different tale. She trembled and took a deep breath as she held the receiver to her ear. "Hi Sarah, I have a quick errand to run, but I should be at your door in about twenty minutes, okay?" Laurie cheerfully announced.

With a sigh of relief, she simply replied, "sure."

"Oh, and don't forget, Ray's coming by at seven with Eleanor, and dinner."

"Oh crap, I did forget." She moaned. "I gotta go and get ready."

She hung up and rushed to dry her hair and put on sweats, but there was no time for makeup, which meant that, once again, she'd be caught with a naked face. It was a quirky habit she'd adopted from her mother, who was never seen in public without a dash of rouge, a dab of mascara, and a glissade of lipstick.

Twenty minutes exactly...just like a lawyer, Sarah thought as she heard the knock.

Through the closed door, Laurie identified himself.

"Okay, I'm opening the door now." She turned the handle and stepped back. He stepped inside.

There was no mistaking her swollen eyes and somber mood. He cupped her chin, and studied her face, and in one fell swoop, he wrapped her in a comforting embrace and affably whispered. "I brought you something. I'm told it'll help you feel better." He withdrew a small bag from his coat pocket and placed it in Sarah's hand. The strong, sweet scent of cinnamon that hung in the air, instantly performed its healing magic.

"Oh my God, thank you so much! I can't believe you thought of this, and I'm amazed you got them, 'cause Mrs. Perkins said she only makes them on special days like Halloween or Valentine's Day."

"Then, I guess this is Sarah's Day. And you were right, I had one and they're just as wonderful as you said. So, does that mean I should believe everything you say from now on?" He winked.

She smiled, "If you're trying to cheer me up, it's working."

She'd inadvertently led him directly to the concern her friends were anxious to address. "Speaking of cheering up, Sarah? Some of us are kinda worried that it's been a bit too easy. What I mean is, you haven't seemed to really react to all the trauma you've been through, the way one would expect? I mean, watching you do cartwheels, trying to leave the hospital yesterday, especially after Ray telling you in graphic detail what happened to you in the last forty-eight hours or so. And you wouldn't agree to speak to the psychologist at the hospital. There were no tears, no outrage, no hysteria. Honestly, Sarah, it's worrying me and your friends." Sarah sat at the kitchen table and invited Laurie to join her. The two wisely respected a moment of silence.

Sarah cleared her throat. "Laurie, I'm gonna try and explain. I don't know if it'll make sense to anyone but me, but I'll try. You have to let me get through this saga without comment or interruption though, agreed?"

He nodded and knocked on the table.

"Okay, thank you for that." She steadied herself and began. "This is not easy but here goes: in Toronto, before all this began, I had declared myself an utter disaster, a failure. I'd had everything, and then in a blink, I lost everything. Well, everything in my life that mattered to me.

"On the urging of a friend who couldn't stand to see me wallowing, and knew I'd had an interest in writing as a kid, I was encouraged to take this ten-week course in journalism, and I really liked it. I ended up a freelancer at a local newspaper. But then, I saw that child abuse headline in the Toronto Sun Times, and it haunted me, and continued to haunt me, I stupidly thought I could write a blockbuster story and become a Toronto Sun Times journalist.

"I know, it was delusional, but that's how all this began. When I came here months ago, it was for all the wrong reasons. Though being reacquainted with my childhood mentor, Wesley, gave me the confidence and reassurance I once had but lost along the way, I discovered that I could actually learn on the job. I began to believe that maybe, eventually, I could work my way into the profession for real. But to do that, I needed to show patience, courage, and determination. So, I tried my best to adopt a veneer of bravado, and hope that no one saw through it...especially Eleanor and you."

She lowered her head and paused. "Laurie, here's the hard truth. If you'd shown up around a half-hour ago, you would have witnessed a meltdown the size of a Titanic iceberg! I withered to my knees in the shower, unable to move, speak or think. All the tears and trauma spiraled down the drain. You would've called the men in white coats. I'm not saying, 'all's well,' or, that it ended well, but Shakespeare aside, I learned from that experience that I'll probably need some real help dealing with it, and I won't hesitate to reach out to professionals when I get back home."

Laurie slumped back in his chair and exhaled. His eyes remained focused on Sarah. "Wow! I gotta say, thank God for meltdowns. I know this sounds insane, but, in my profession, I routinely see people fall to pieces from trauma. I was worried about you not falling apart, I mean, for a moment. I guess this means, we can all be more assured, that you're, uh, normal."

Reva Leah Stern

She playfully slapped his hand. "More assured? Huh! You mean you have doubts?"

"See, that's the *normal* I thought I knew, and maybe I'll get to know better."

CHAPTER THIRTY-THREE

"It's seven o'clock, pizza's here. Open up!" Ray shouted.

Sarah, still slightly woozy from the previous day's events, opened the door to an eagerly welcoming trio: Eleanor holding a large pizza with a bucket of fried chicken perched on top. Laurie, brandishing, a sixpack of Moosehead lager and a pack of Diet Pepsi; and behind them was Ray, weighed down with a tactical police bag over his shoulder and clutching Bindy's infamous wooden chest. A shudder ran up Sarah's spine as her eyes fixated on the dusty, rough-hewn crate. Laurie and Eleanor entered and set their supplies on the kitchenette counter. As Ray was about to step inside, Sarah held up her hand, "Please hold up, just for a second."

He did as asked, then watched as she rushed across the room and returned with a thick newspaper which she spread out on the floor. "Sorry about that, Ray. I just want a safety shield," She shrugged. Ray smiled, stepped inside, and carefully set the unsettling box on top of last week's edition of the Prescott Journal.

Mission completed, crate safely delivered, Ray offered a flippant salute and proclaimed. "This is it, folks. Tonight's the big unveiling."

"Yeah, I wouldn't get too excited, Ray." Laurie interjected. "Remember a few years ago, Geraldo Rivera hyping the big unveiling of Al Capone's secret vault? Well, we all know how that turned out." He quipped.

* * *

By eight o'clock, the pizza and chicken had been devoured, half of the beer and Pepsi cans were empty; but the crate was still sitting by the front door, unopened.

"Okay, enough." Ray insisted. "I've got a crowbar, let's do it," Ray declared as he removed the tool from his bag and raised it over his head.

"Laurie, I'm bettin' you've had to use video footage more than once in your line of work, huh?" The lawyer grinned and nodded.

"Good, then you'll be Spielberg tonight," Ray stated as he pulled a video camera from his bag. "We'll tape the procedure, starting with unsealing the crate. Can you handle it?"

"Sure." Laurie agreed as he accepted the camera.

"Listen, I'll leave it to you to use that on/off button at your discretion. Just make sure to film what comes outta that box and not the people or their comments from the sidelines." Ray looked around at the apprehensive faces. "Ya ready?"

Laurie murmured, "Uh-huh." He looked through the viewfinder and hit record. Ray shoved the flat end of the crowbar under the lid, and pressed down until a crunch and snap was heard.

Ray was about to peer inside the open crate when he was distracted by Sarah, who quickly shambled across the room. He held up his hand like a traffic cop and turned to Laurie. "Can you turn the camera off for a sec?" Laurie obliged.

"Sarah, ya can't see what's here, from over there. Ya gotta get closer." She pressed herself against the frosty window. "I'm good over here," She anxiously affirmed.

"Really, Sarah? After the hell you've been through in the last few days, looking inside this old crate is a bridge too far?" Ray gibed.

With an empathetic mien, Eleanor inched closer to Sarah. "He's got a good point there, Sarah, don't you think?"

"Maybe," she replied. She leaned away from the window, sniffed the air, then timorously smiled. "Yeah, I guess so. I don't smell any chloroform, and I don't hear any wild animals snarling in there; at least not from here." She grimaced.

"Good. Ooh, wait, before you make the big crossing, Sarah." Ray turned up his nose as if there really was something rotten in the air. "Sarah, we could use some more newspapers, 'cause as I remove whatever's in here, might end up on the table...and who knows what creatures have been livin' in there all this time, eh?" He teased.

Eleanor heaved an exasperated sigh. "That doesn't help, Ray. Sarah's not a fan of crawly creepies, or flying creepies, for that matter."

Sarah winced, but asserted, "Honestly, I'm fine." She pulled a few more newspapers from the night table and handed them to Ray. He laid them across the table, and sat down on the floor beside the crate. He snapped on a pair of latex gloves and withdrew several clear evidence bags from his rucksack.

"Okay, Laurie, as they say in Hollywood, *action*!"

The video camera rolled: Ray lifted a well-used book from the crate, held it up to the lens, slipped it into a zip-lock, sealed, and marked it.

"I wouldn't have expected any o' those guys to even know how to read." He scoffed. "Ah, now I see, they only needed to know how to turn pages," he snickered as he crammed a pile of tattered nudie magazines into another bag. From a long cardboard tube, he withdrew a stack of posters. He held each one up to the camera and provided a running commentary.

"Oh, here's a keeper: A group shot of a KKK gathering, complete with a two-story burning cross. Christ, these look like real Nazi propaganda posters. Shit, I think they're actual cartoons, from World War II. Just what you'd expect from that pack of animals. I'll hold them up, Laurie, and you can shoot the images. Feel free to read the captions to yourselves."

Each poster was as shocking as the one before it:

Hitler standing on a dais above throngs of Nazi-saluting supporters. Caption: **Make Germany Free...Kill a Jew Today.**

A grotesque caricature of a bearded Rabbi ordered onto his knees by a Gestapo officer while another Nazi urinates on his head. Caption: **A dirty Jew being given a refreshing shower**.

The camera dipped for a moment as Laurie paused to take a breath. "Sorry. I'm sorry, Ray. Keep going."

A baby with a splay of dollar bills in its tiny fist and an SS officer about to drop the infant from the roof of a synagogue. Caption: ***Jew...***

Sarah shrieked. "Stop! Please Ray...no more."

"My apologies, Sarah, I get it," Ray noted. "Believe me, I'm as disgusted as you are, and I understand completely."

She lowered her head into her hands and shook vigorously. "No, no, no, no! You can't understand completely. For God's sake, I'm a Jew, but neither can I. I'm not a Holocaust survivor, so how could I possibly claim to understand the horror of their experience? But as a Jew, growing up in a small town, I endured my share of terrifying threats and harassment at school, in the skating arena, on the street...Jew hatred burned and stabbed like shingles."

The room fell silent.

"Recently, Wes told me about an incident that happened many years ago, when a couple of kids covered the walls, of our makeshift second floor synagogue, with horrible Antisemitic graffiti. They ripped up our holy books...they vandalized the place. Most of the town was disgusted and wanted the kids sent to prison immediately. But my dad had a different take on the situation. He took the vandals under his wing, talked to them, enlightened them, and in the end, helped turn their lives around. One of them went on to become a high school teacher in Ottawa with a wife, kids, the whole package, and the other joined the RCMP. But just 'cause those kids seemed to be an anomaly, doesn't mean there weren't other actual neo-Nazis living near by back then." She wandered back to the window and stared into the frosty night, adding one last comment. "Sad to say, for many Jews, that was life in small towns."

Laurie lowered the camera. "You didn't have to live in a small town to experience Antisemitism, Sarah. I grew up in Toronto when Jews still weren't allowed to eat in certain restaurants, join fraternities or golf clubs, check into hotels, or even swim in public pools. In our parents' day, there were signs all over the city saying, 'No Dogs or Jews Allowed.'"

Sarah turned her attention to Laurie as he continued.

"And those were official signs, government-sponsored regulations, not protest placards by ignorant Antisemites who were only too ready to blame the Jews for any conspiracy fable they could invent to scapegoat our people. In the thirties, as war was looming in Europe and Jews were being rounded up, many tried to escape to the US and Canada by ship, but neither country would let them in. Even before the Holocaust, there were quotas that limited the number of Jews permitted in Canadian universities...especially for law and medicine. And after the massacre of 6 million Jews, change began way too slowly. Sad to say, but Antisemitism is a chronic disease that only seems to have disappeared. It hasn't, it simply went underground. Make no mistake, it continues to flourish down there, always ready to erupt into another infestation of hate and genocide."

"He's right," Sarah added. "It's true. Imagine, Holocaust survivors finally landing on these shores, after what they'd just endured, and having to trust that they weren't going to be hauled off to concentration camps again, just for being Jews."

Silence blanketed the room. As Sarah gazed from one to the other, guilt began to set in. "I'm sorry everyone, for initiating this conversation. I do get intense when it comes to discrimination, of any kind. I'm not just a one-cause kind of advocate either. I had a great mentor in my dad who was a human rights champion, and my hero. Anyway, please keep going, Ray."

"Are ya sure?"

"I am. But no more posters, okay?"

"Sure. Laurie, start rollin'." Ray called out as he leaned over and resumed sifting through the crate. Suddenly, he raised his head and cried out, "Wow! I think we just discovered the 'Hope Diamond of Fascism'. I only hope it comes with the legendary curse for Earl and his clan. Have a look at this." Ray withdrew a red crocheted Afghan with a black leather swastika stitched into the centre. "How's the workmanship, Eleanor?"

She shuddered and looked away without comment.

He returned his focus to the crate and sifted through an array of black and white snapshots. He sighed, leaned back against the wall, and dropped his arms to his sides. "That's it, Spielberg. You can turn off the camera. The treasure chest is empty, and I don't see any direct, damning, smoking gun evidence." He cynically declared. Disheartened and frustrated, He rose, popped open another can of beer and slumped into a chair. "So, Laurie, you were right. It was the dreaded Geraldo moment after all."

"That's it?" Sarah gasped. "I don't understand. Why keep old photos and despicable posters sealed and hidden away like this? We all know that Earl, Berger, and the rest of them are degenerates, so what could this junk reveal that would've made Earl frantic enough to break and enter?"

"I don't get it. But Bindy must o' thought there was somethin' incriminating in there, or why else would she have called Earl the other night threatening to give over 'evidence' she was sure would get him convicted. This damn crate had to be what he was searchin' for," Ray contended.

"But Bindy told us she had no idea what was in the crate," Sarah recalled.

"And what makes you think Bindy was telling the truth?" Laurie replied.

Ray scoffed. "Come on, you guys! The crate was sealed and painted shut. It's grungy, peeling, the nails are rusty; it clearly hadn't been opened in decades. And it doesn't matter anyway, because Berger knew, and I'll bet his wife knew too. So, Bindy, at the very least, figured Earl knew what was in there." Ray hissed and kicked at the crate. "But what in hell did he think was so damn incriminating? And if it was, why didn't

Berger use it as leverage?" Failing to come up with a logical answer, the room became subdued once again.

While the other three were debating, Eleanor had been silently staring straight ahead. Suddenly she jumped to her feet. "Sarah, can I have that ribbon from your fruit basket?"

Bewildered but curious, Sarah handed it over.

"Uh, do you have scissors?" She asked and again, Sarah obliged.

"Thank you." All eyes turned to Eleanor as she dangled the ribbon inside the crate. With determination, she snipped a piece off and set it aside. "You know, if there's one thing I'm good at, its gauging size." She then held the piece of ribbon to the outside. "I knew it. It falls short by about five inches." She contended. "I don't think you've hit the bottom, Ray."

"She's right," Sarah burbled.

Ray hoisted the crowbar and gestured to Laurie to turn on the video. With little effort, Ray dug in and lifted up a Masonite panel which revealed a false bottom. He removed a cigar box from the secret compartment and emptied it, one item at a time. The contents included two jackknives, one crucifix, a small pouch of marbles, and a yo-yo. He placed each object in a separate evidence bag.

As Laurie lowered the camera, a thought occurred to him. "In the '50s, it was pretty common for teenaged boys to keep a cigar or shoebox under their beds filled with inexplicable 'collector's' items. I did, and I'll bet you did too, Ray. Maybe we've just stumbled onto Berger's secret youthful, civilized past." He jeered.

All eyes looked askance at the suggestion. Ray scowled as he continued his search. Suddenly he flinched. "Holy shit, Holy shit! Get that camera goin' Laurie!"

Taping resumed as Ray lifted another item from the crate and began to read. "St. Lawrence Swim competition, entry medallion." He turned it over to find Daisy Panasar's name, and the date, engraved on the back. "This has gotta be her official pass for the big race that summer."

Eleanor pressed her hands together against her chest, as if in prayer. "Oh my God! Oh, sweet Jesus!"

Sarah's heart raced, "Ray, is this the evidence you need to prove that Earl killed Daisy?"

Laurie pressed the off button and set the camera on the table.

Eleanor interjected. "Wait. If this stuff belongs to Berger, how does that medallion implicate Earl?"

"It might, if it still has identifiable prints on it." Ray replied.

"Is that possible, after all these years, Ray?" Eleanor asked. "I mean, it dates all the way back to the year she died."

"I'll defer to the city lawyer." He replied. "Laurie can tell ya more about fingerprints and maybe about this new science that'll uncover information about a suspect or a victim that can boggle your mind. Am I right, Laurie?"

Laurie nodded enthusiastically. "Absolutely. It's called DNA testing. They take biological evidence from a crime scene, analyze it, and compare it to offender profiles they've collected in a DNA database. It's the most reliable means to identifying a perpetrator ever created."

Sarah and Eleanor glanced at each other in a state of complete bewilderment. Eleanor turned to Laurie and asked. "I don't understand what kind of evidence they'd need to do this testing, Laurie? I mean, there isn't always a smoking gun, as they say on those crime shows."

He smiled politely. "No, it's not a gun. What the crime lab will do is take tiny samples from hair roots, skin cells, fresh or dried body fluids; any evidence left on anything found and collected at a crime scene. It's called DNA evidence. Then they try to match it to the DNA of potential suspects. It's an amazing discovery that they're already using, admittedly in a limited way for now. But imagine what they'll be able to do in another year or two. Courts are beginning to see it as irrefutable proof, and I use it whenever I can."

"That's incredible," Eleanor murmured as she sat down, cross-legged, on the floor.

"Don't go countin' on that DNA thing though," Ray warned. "We're likely gonna need more than a medallion."

Eleanor moaned and bowed her head. "This is too much."

"I agree with you, Eleanor." Sarah commiserated as she slumped onto the floor beside her friend. "This is wrong. No, it's worse than wrong, it's hopeless."

A more optimistic version of Ray suddenly emerged. "Listen, I'm not sayin' it's hopeless. I mean, it's great that we've got what we've got. But I'm still worried it's not enough. I know Berger confessed an' all, but I also know how lawyers work; present company excepted. I mean, usually, if there's not enough hard evidence, and if a lawyer can get a confession thrown out, then the guy's gonna walk, right?" Ray looked pleadingly toward Laurie, hoping he might help to bail him out of this tipping canoe.

Laurie paced about the room. "Ray, what if all this crap here turned out to be evidence of other crimes you never knew about? I mean, Berger could be some kind of serial perp, and all these items could be his trophies."

Sarah rolled her eyes, "Come on, Laurie, in the big city, maybe. But out here, there just aren't the numbers o' missing or dead bodies to support the idea of a serial killer."

Laurie shook his head. "It doesn't have to be about serial killings. They could be souvenirs from rapes, beatings, robberies, any vile act that got their adrenalin going."

Ray weighed the theory for a moment. "Okay, how would these marbles or that book figure into your theory?"

"I'm not saying they all have to be connected to a crime. But I suggest you show this stuff to Berger. He seems anxious to talk. Watch his reaction, and hopefully, he'll tell you what they mean."

"That's exactly what I'll do." Ray enthused as he offered two thumbs up and turned his attention back to the crate. "Hmm, this paper bag is all that's left in here." He frowned as he peered inside. Without comment, he rushed to retrieve a snapshot from his coat pocket. He glanced at the photo and urgently motioned to Laurie to resume rolling.

"Jesus, Eleanor, you may not want to see..."

"Don't finish the sentence, Ray. Whatever it is, I do want to see it." She insisted.

With the camera rolling, Ray lifted the bag from the crate. He reached inside and as he withdrew his hand; a ragged piece of cloth fell to the floor. Reaching in again, he withdrew a long scarf and placed it on the table. Eleanor's eyes were fixed like lasers.

Sarah moved in for a closer look. As she reached for the scarf, Ray pushed her hands away. "Don't touch it!" Ray barked. He picked it up again with his gloved hands and carefully snaked it into a large evidence bag.

"Is, uh. Could that really be, uh, the scarf, Eleanor?" Sarah dazedly asked.

Eleanor managed a few clipped, breathless words, "mother...made...it..."

Rattled, but still on the job, Ray explained, "Sorry, but the chain of evidence must be beyond reproach. Nobody can touch it. Listen to me. In the picture, Berger's wearin' the scarf, but I'd bet my life that the picture was snapped in Earl's bedroom after the assault."

Laurie added. "If we can get DNA from it, we'll have them both."

Ray bent down beside Eleanor. "Kiddo, do you think you're up to answering some questions?" She sat stupefied, still staring at the floor.

Ray removed his gloves and knelt down beside her "...We don't have to do it tonight," he whispered.

Weary but struggling to find her voice, Eleanor gasped, "Oh God..."

Ray placed his hands firmly on her shoulders. "Eleanor, we'll stop right now, okay?"

"No! No, I can do this, Ray." She contended. She steadied her breathing and continued. "There, on the floor...Sarah...it's my uh...my...they cut off...it's, uh...it's proof...isn't it?"

Eleanor broke down, sobbing uncontrollably, and Sarah's lips trembled as her friend's jumbled words began to tell the tragic story. Drained of all hope, Eleanor leaned into Ray. He wrapped his arms around her and whispered: "I'll do everything possible to lock those bastards away forever, I promise you. Will you trust me?"

She took a swooping breath, looked into his eyes, and whispered "I want to."

* * *

The ghosts of Sarah's darkest memories haunted her dreams throughout the night. Recollections of Earl White's terrifying incursion into her suite, and the contents of the despicable crate tormented her. She awoke and tried in vain to open her eyes. She listened to the ticking clock as it measured her anxiety minute by minute. She heard a sudden noise, her heart thumped like a bass drum, and she frantically called out, "Who's there?"

"It's me, Sarah."

"Laurie? Oh God, I can't open my eyes. What's wrong with me?" She whimpered.

He calmly replied. "They're just swollen. I'll get a cold cloth." He hurried into the washroom.

"I've seen monsters on the ceiling and heard awful noises...I can't fall asleep no matter how hard I try." She shouted above the sound of rushing water.

"Here, I'm gonna place this cloth over your lids." He gently lay the wet towel over her eyes. "Just press lightly," he instructed, and she did as advised.

"Thanks, Laurie. How did you get in here?"

"I have your extra key, remember; in case of emergency?"

She let out a relieved sigh. "Oh, of course. But why did you think to check on me in the middle of the night? She sat up slowly, "Can I remove the cloth now?"

"Are you unstuck?"

"I think so." She removed the washcloth and slowly opened her eyes. "What the heck? It's light outside." She remarked with astonishment.

"I would suspect it would be, at 10:00 a.m." he chuckled.

Sarah squinted at the clock, "Oh hell no, that can't be! I was supposed to be dressed and ready to meet Ray downstairs at nine. He's going to be so pissed with me after I coerced him into letting me do this. I've got to be there. I've got to go."

Laurie sat on the edge of the bed and calmly explained. "Ray had to get back to Brockville, but he's not upset. In fact, he was relieved that you slept in. All of us sane people know you need more time to recuperate. I told Ray I would drive you in, so stop worrying. I'll leave you to get dressed and I'll go pick up coffee and muffins for us to eat on the way." He stood up to leave but a thought struck him. "Do me a favour and walk me to the door so I can be sure you're not gonna pass out when I leave."

She smiled, pulled on her robe, and walked steadily to the door.

CHAPTER THIRTY-FOUR

Words and movement hung in the air like a fading jet stream as Sarah hesitantly entered the police station with Laurie at her side.

"Hi there Mr. Cowan...and I take it you're Ms. Berman? I'm Amy. I'm happy to see you up an' about. Can I get either o' you a coffee, tea, or water? Or I can send out for somethin' to eat if ya want?"

Laurie shook his head. "I'm good, thanks."

"It's nice to meet you, Amy, but I'm fine. Will I be able to see the chief soon?"

"Oh, yeah, there's no problem, eh? He'll be out to getcha in a few minutes."

Sarah melted onto the bench while Laurie circumspectly paced the area.

* * *

"Is she here?" Ray hollered from down the hall.

"Yup, sure is." Amy shouted back, then turned to Sarah, "Sorry, Ms. Berman. Sometimes," she flippantly suggested, "he conveniently forgets he has an intercom. We think he does it on purpose to keep us on our toes. Anyway, he'll be here in a minute." She offered an amiable smile and returned to her paperwork.

* * *

Laurie sat down beside Sarah who was lost in thought. All morning, she'd been formulating questions she wanted to ask, but was now wondering if she'd have the courage to hear the answers.

Heavy footfalls reverberated along the corridor as Ray hurriedly approached. He nodded a hello to Laurie, then turned his attention to Sarah. "Hi, Sarah, first things first. Did ya get over to the hospital for those test results?" He asked with a sense of urgency.

She nodded, "I did, and everything's normal."

"Well, that's good then, eh? Now, I hate to be a pain in the ass, but I'm askin' you again: Are ya sure ya wanna do this?" Ray seemed more impatient than usual.

Sarah nodded again, "Uh-huh, I do."

Ray looked dubiously at Laurie. "Does that sound convincing to you, Laurie? Because it sure as hell doesn't to me."

With an edge of defiance in her tone, Sarah exclaimed. "If I tell you I'm ready, then I'm ready," she barked.

Laurie offered an innocent shrug. "You heard her, Ray." He turned toward Sarah and offered a comforting smile as he pledged, "I'm gonna be right here when you're done." She offered a grateful nod in reply.

"Okay then, Sarah," Ray declared, "Let's go and look in on the animals."

* * *

A rankling sound met her ear as Ray opened the door to the observation room.

Sarah winced and plugged her ears as the din reverberated once again.

"What's that horrible noise?" Sarah whispered.

"It's the asshole in the interview room snoring into the mic," Ray replied. "Here, have a look." He led her around a bend to a window, through which she could see the suspect slumped in a chair with his head plonked on the table.

"Damn useless tool. He slept in a comfortable cell, the taxpayers bought him breakfast, and all I wanted was for him to have a shower 'cause the bastard stinks like hell. If ya decide you wanna get up close and personal with him, don't inhale." He smirked.

She whispered to Ray, "Right here is as close as I plan to get. So, what happens now?"

"Now, you sit right here and watch and listen while I go in and have a little chat. Are you gonna be okay here? I can bring Dan in to stay with you if you want?"

"Thanks Ray, but I'm fine. I have a question for you though?"

"Sure, go ahead."

"Okay, this might sound a bit weird but, can he see me?" She nervously inquired.

"No, not at all. It's a one-way mirror." He assured her.

"I understand, but what if I want him to see me?" She pluckily asked.

Ray was mystified. "You'd want that?"

She shrugged and opined, "How do I face up to my attack, if I can't face my attacker?" The cop was speechless. "So, Chief, is there a way I can be seen?"

Ray took a deep, energizing breath and replied. "Sarah, if you really feel you're up for it, then you can flip this switch, and then yes, he can see you."

She slapped her thigh, and agreed, "Let's do it!"

"You're one ballsy lady, Sarah Klein," he smirked "Okay then. But there is one thing..."

She held her breath and waited for the letdown. "He'll see you, but he won't be able to hear you, okay?"

Relieved, she nodded her acknowledgment. He tapped her reassuringly on the shoulder and exited.

In a flash, he entered the interview room, strode forward, and pounded his mighty fist on the table. Berger recoiled and squealed like a pig. "What the fuck?"

"You've got company, Duh-wayne, so sit up and try to act human." He nodded toward the mirror.

On cue, Sarah flipped the switch. She lit up like Broadway and although her knees trembled and her stomach played leapfrog, she felt empowered and safe.

Through crusty eyes, Berger strained to see who was in the spotlight. As recognition set in, a look of amusement spread across his face. "So, she's alive, eh?"

Ray stiffened and sniffed back his urge to crush the soulless cockroach. He took a breath, slapped on a smile and calmly replied, "You seem surprised there, Berger. Were ya hoping ya killed her?"

Berger sniggered, shook his head and leaned back in his seat. "Nah, like I told ya, I was just gonna talk some sense inta her so she wouldn't make no trouble. I mean, with me bein' *dead* an' all, and her gettin' chummy with Doug, it was jist a matter o' time 'til that little asshole slipped up and told 'er I was alive. I had ta make sure Bindy didn't find out."

Ray settled a buttock on the table and leaned in. "Well, Duh-wayne, it seems that Bindy knows where all the skeletons are hidin', 'cause she says she's got some real good evidence stored in her attic."

"That's bullshit. She ain't got nothin'." He shifted in his seat and snarled. "An' ya know how I know she's got nothin'?"

Ray smirked. "No, Duh-wayne, I don't, but I'm interested. So do tell."

"Okay," he growled, "when Gladys heard I was dead, Dougie told me, she took all my stuff ta Bindy's. I told him to pick up the whole works and burn every last bit of it. And trust me, when I tell Dougie to do somethin', he does it. Like, I asked him to drive her out ta Bindy's fer a meetin'; and he did exactly what I told 'im, didn't he?" He cackled like the wicked witch of Oz while Sarah cringed.

"So, you didn't think that Bindy might've noticed you were breathing, and walkin' around in her house?" Ray scoffed.

Berger sputtered. "I ain't no idiot! I knew Bindy weren't gonna be there, 'cause I told Gladys ta get 'er outta the house and keep her busy, and she better not tell her nothin' about me...or else."

"Uh huh, so you thought that the farm, where all those crimes were committed, was the best spot for a meeting with the journalist, huh? And no one would ever think to look there?" Ray glanced up at Sarah, who gave him a reassuring nod.

Berger sneered and spluttered. "Yeah, that's right. For years, we was down there in the *love hole* runnin' our business and you dumb cops never had a clue we was even there." He shifted in his seat and scoffed. "You assholes couldn't find a shoplifter if he was stuffin' the stolen goods in *your* pockets. Ya searched the place, but ya never found the love hole, did ya? Nope, you thought all that shit was happenin' up there in the house and the barn. Too dumb to know what was right under yer feet. Oh, and this is a good one; the night o' the big arrest, two upstandin' city folk, from Cornwall, got stuck down there drinkin' and gettin' ready fer a bit o' fun an' them kids weren't even down there yet, 'cause we got the flashin' signal that you guys was up top goin' through every room. So, we jist waited down there a couple o' days 'til ya thought ya had everythin' and everybody, and ya left. We had plenty o' food and alcohol down there...like a bomb shelter. Except you was the bomb we needed shelterin' from.

"But this time, my dumb wife let that freak, Bindy, come home early, and let you cops in. I bet she even showed ya the cellar door, didn't she? Ya don't have ta tell me, but when I get outta here...Bindy and Gladys'll be sorry bitches, I can tell ya that."

Hissing with fury, Ray walked to the intercom and pressed the button. "Amy can ya bring in the cart?"

Without hesitation, Amy wheeled the trolley in with the crate on top.

"Ya can leave it, Amy. If I need to, I'll call ya to come and get it."

Berger's squinty eyes followed her out the door.

"Nice ass, eh? I mean for a broad past her teens."

As much as he wanted to, Ray couldn't ignore the crass insult. "Ya know, Berger, people have said a lot of nasty things about you, but I couldn't imagine, they'd all be true. I was completely wrong. You really are every bit as disgusting as you smell."

Strange as it seemed to Sarah, watching from a safe place, it was equally curious to Ray that he detected a twinge of humiliation from Berger, who abruptly changed the subject. "So, what's this here package? A gift?"

A fresh wave of tenacity and smugness washed over Ray as he initiated a game of cat-and-mouse. "Ya don't recognize it, Duh-wayne? You don't remember that box o' treasures ya asked Dougie to burn? Tsk, tsk, tsk. Well, this here is your ashes reincarnated."

Sarah held her breath and watched intently.

Berger looked away and snorted. "I ain't never seen that box in my life."

"Oh yeah, I know, it looks a little different now, 'cause Gladys thought to put a thick coat o' paint on it and use it for a coffee table," he casually explained. "But then, somehow, it ended up in Bindy's attic, where it was kept nice and safe, 'til I rescued it." Ray shook his head and wrinkled his nose. "I'll give ya, it's a nasty shade o' puke green, but it's definitely yours. Gladys and Bindy both swore to it, on paper, and they signed it, too."

Berger's face burned crimson. He tried to speak, but his words were muffled by a coughing spasm. Ray paid no attention. "Do you remember what ya kept in there, Berger?"

"How would I?" he croaked. "I ain't seen the inside o' that box in more than forty years."

"Uh huh, I'll take that as a 'no' then. So, that bein' the case, let me show you some of the gems we found inside this treasure chest."

Ray dramatically presented the bags of photos, a book, marbles, and a yo-yo. But the performance seemed to somehow empower Berger. "Ya think yer gonna arrest me and Earl for savin' a few pictures and toys from our good 'ole times together?" He guffawed like a donkey.

"So, this treasure isn't all yours. Is that what you're sayin'?"

"Yeah, not all of it...but I was the keeper." He paused to snigger. "Yeah, I was the man, all right. When we was kids, the cops'd bust inta Earl's house all the time, lookin' for stuff he stole. He was worried he'd get caught, so he said it'd be safer to keep all our stuff together at my house. When he gave me that big crate, it had a few magazines and posters an' crap like that in it, so I dumped my pictures and stuff in too and sealed it up. The cops always said I was too dumb to be trusted with anythin', so they never hassled me." He sat up straighter in the chair, sniffed the air, and resumed his bumptiously smug monologue. "An' it turns out, I'm the smart one. I was the one who kept our secrets. Earl may've had the plan, but I was the man. I had boxes o' chocolate bars, an' cartons o' cigarettes from gas station break-ins, I had money, jewelry...you name it, all stashed around our farm. We were the best, 'cause we never got caught. But when I heard, Gladys let Bindy give ya a shoebox o' my pictures 'n stuff, I knew she'd be dumb enough to mouth off about me fakin' my death. So, I had ta worry 'bout me; but I don't have nothin' ta do with Earl, and I don't give a flyin' fuck what happens ta him."

Ray held up the picture of Berger 'modelling' the scarf.

"Tell me about this memorable event," he said as he dropped the snapshot on the table.

As Berger glanced at the photo, colour drained from his face. He pushed the photo away and mumbled, "I don't remember."

"Oh, really? You don't? Look here, Duh-wayne, you're wearing the biggest trophy o' the night. Remember how you guys raped and beat Eleanor Miller? Ya told me all about it just yesterday. Would ya like to see the video playback? Remember how you were so sure you wouldn't get arrested?"

Berger became uniquely silent. Ray seized the moment. "Anyway, I'm about out of time here and I have another visitor waitin' on me, so unless Ms. Berman has any questions she'd like to ask?" He glanced up at the window.

Sarah nodded and rose from her chair, which took Ray by surprise.

"Come on in if ya want and ask away." Ray tipped a phantom hat toward her.

Dan opened the door, and Sarah appeared on the threshold.

A gap-toothed grin spread across Berger's face. "We had a good ole time, didn't we?" He taunted. She didn't flinch. She took a couple of steps inside and stared her assailant down. "I have a question: Why did you write *Sarah Klein* on the envelope you left at the hotel?"

"That's your name, ain't it?" He jeered.

She flatly replied, "It was, many years ago."

"Yeah, well Doug tole me Earl was plenty worried after he found out the truth about who was interviewin' him fer his story. Doug was too dumb ta know why Earl was all pissed about it, but I knew, it was 'cause o' your old man."

Her deep throated gasp revealed her shock. She could never have imagined her family's name becoming part of this ugly interaction.

"Aw, look at that. Not such a big shot, nosy journalist now, huh? Yeah, your 'ole man was a big pain in the ass. Always talkin' ta the cops 'bout us botherin' the Jews, the Chinks, the Pakis...all them foreigners who came here ta take over our country. Earl ain't scared o' the law, but I bet he was scared you'd find out and write about him huntin' them Jews. These days, it ain't good for his real-estate business. I get a good laugh outta that, 'cause as much as he hates it, he's gotta deal with a bunch o' them damn Jews now." His heinous laugh filled the room. "I love it. Look at you, lookin' all surprised. Did ya really think we wouldn't remember Sarah Klein? How many fuckin' little Jew girls were there back then? I'll tell ya..." he held up two fingers, "two...you an' that skank from the restaurant. We woulda had her that night if that stupid Miller bitch hadn't come along. Then Earl tried to grab ya behind the school, but that got messed up too. So much fer Earl's big plans."

Berger slid forward on his chair; but Sarah didn't wince. She folded her arms and stiffened her resolve. Berger's eyes settled on the book Ray pulled from the crate. Berger guffawed. "Ah, so yer gonna lock me up fer not returnin' a library book, huh? Well, news flash, Earl took it, not me. He kept it, 'cause it was the Jew girl's."

Sarah's complexion turned ashen, a reaction that didn't go unnoticed by Berger.

"Uh-huh, ya don't remember, do ya? Maybe Earl forgot, too, but I'd never forget. Ya know why?" he leaned back and pointed at the book. "Go ahead, have a look inside..."

Ray snapped on a pair of latex gloves and slipped the book out of the bag. Sarah leaned in to take a closer look. There was no flashy dust cover, just the dark green leather binding stamped with the faded title: "Of Mice and Men."

"Go on, open it. First page," he sniggered.

"I won't touch it," Sarah whispered to the chief. "But I want to see it. Can you do it, please?" Ray nodded and opened it to the first page.

Under the title, neatly written in cursive, it said: *This book belongs to Sarah Klein, Grade IX, Home teacher, Ms. Evanson.* A flood of memories congregated in her head, but she managed to show little on the surface. "Okay, it's my book. So what?"

Berger leered with hideous glee. "Now turn to the back page. Go ahead...show her." Ray flipped to the inside back cover where he saw a shoddily printed message:

Of Rats an Jews. The only good Jew is a ded Jew. Signed *Earl White.*

A riptide of loathing threatened to engulf Sarah. She steadied herself. "Well, Mr. Berger, as you can see, this Jew is very much alive, and living free in this great country, in spite of your pathetic attempt. But when all the facts come out in court, you, on the other hand, will die a miserable death locked up in a cage like the rabid beast you are."

Ray turned toward Sarah and nodded his approval. He then glowered at Berger. "You are one, fucked-up, slimy snake."

Berger sloughed off the insult like a serpent sheds its skin. "Maybe..." Berger shrugged, "but that's still better than bein' a Jew." He sneered at Sarah, "Let me tell you a good joke, Sarah Klein. It goes like this. *Jews are like cockroaches, no matter how many ya stomp on, ya just can't kill 'em all. But it shouldn't stop anyone from tryin'.* It didn't stop Hitler, now did it?" He laughed uproariously. Suddenly, he lowered his voice to a raspy whisper. "It don't matter none, though, Sarah Klein, 'cause when Christ comes, you Jews'll all be prayin' to him, or you'll all be dead."

Sarah abruptly turned to Ray. "Okay, I've heard enough."

She spun on her heel to go, but the chief grabbed her elbow. "Hold up a minute, Sarah. I think, as a journalist, you'll be interested in Berger's theory about the *statue*."

The puzzled look in Sarah's eyes convinced Ray she was curious enough to stay.

"What *statue* was that again, Berger? Please, tell Ms. Berman. I'm sure it would interest her." Berger looked completely baffled which delighted Ray.

"Shy, are ya, Du-Wayne? Then let me have a go at your theory. See, our genius here says the *Statute of Limitations,* well, that would be the *statue of limits*, as he refers to it, applies to him, which he thinks means he can't be indicted for crimes committed more than seven years ago. The trouble is, Berger here, watches way too much American TV." A spontaneous laugh burst from both Ray and Sarah.

The humiliation Berger now realized was galling enough, but to be humiliated by a Jew was his breaking point. Berger clenched his fists and exploded in a torrent of outrage. "Go ahead, you assholes, and laugh all ya want. It don't fuckin' matter, 'cause Earl was the big honcho, the kingpin of the whole kiddie porn thing, and he beat very one o' them charges; so why in hell do you think a stupid old picture o' me in some ugly scarf is gonna send me to prison? It's a fuckin' joke. Ya got shit all, is what ya got."

Ray waited patiently for a pause in the harangue before he continued. "Oh, that's not true, Duh-wayne. Here's some homework for ya. I want you to memorize three letters of the alphabet, if ya can: D-N-A, 'cause they're gonna help send ya to prison. Oh, and we're not counting on that old snapshot to do the job: no, we've got so many amazing pieces of evidence, including the scarf you and your buddies tied around Eleanor Miller's neck when you dragged, beat, and raped her...and we're gonna hang ya with it."

Berger's colour ranged from crimson to purple as Ray held up the evidence bag with the scarf inside.

"We'll leave ya to let this all fester in that genius head o' yours for a while."

Ray returned everything to the crate and steered the cart and Sarah out the door. Berger sat in stunned silence.

The minute the door closed, Ray placed his hands firmly on her shoulders, looked into her eyes, and said, "I'm tellin' ya, Sarah, you did great in there. That took a lot o' self-control. You're gonna be one hell of a great journalist." He gave her a playful shake and suggested, "Let's head to the front, 'cause I'm sure Laurie's gonna want to know what happened. Besides, we need a break. We'll hop next door to the diner for lunch before we jump back into that pile of pig shit."

An unexpected shudder rippled through her. "I feel like I need a Lysol shower, Ray. And to be honest, I have no appetite, so I don't need a lunch break."

"Well, I do...and I don't intend to argue 'bout it. We're all gonna go and have a bit of a breather."

* * *

Over the soul-pleasing comfort of a bowl of Irish stew, Ray filled Laurie in on the interview. Laurie watched with concern as Sarah fidgeted mindlessly with her napkin.

"All things considered, Laurie, Sarah held up like a pro. She never let that piece o' crap unravel her. We can all be really proud of this ballsy journalist."

Sarah remained detached from the conversation, staring mindlessly into space, her scrambled eggs and toast untouched.

Laurie's smoldering silence was an indication that he too was fixated on something else. "Hey, city lawyer," Ray teased. "I was tellin' you what a great job Sarah did in there, and you played possum. Come on, I'm sure you heard me, so what's buggin' you?"

The lawyer looked up and offered a conciliatory smile. "Yeah, sorry Ray, I heard you and I agree, we should all be proud of her. But I was thinking and hoping that you also held up well. I mean, hoping that you didn't unravel and cross a line in there with that lowlife. Because I'd worry that even a Crown Attorney, as incompetent as the one I encountered here, would try to use it to torpedo the case."

Hearing those words, sent panic sweeping over Sarah, but Ray calmly responded. "Listen, Laurie, it's true, we don't deal with the overwhelming number of crimes, or the viciousness of them, like you do in the big city. And if I'm being frank, sure, it worries me. So, before I head in to talk to Earl, since you know a lot about him, can you offer any advice or strategy?"

"Officially no, but hypothetically, I would uh, hint at what you might have on him. Show him some evidence; a few items you think would unhinge him. Let him hang himself. He has a big mouth, an enormous ego, and a delusion of power, let him use it all to talk himself into an arrest."

* * *

Earl was pacing in circles around the table when Ray entered the interview room. With bubbles of sweat popping out on his forehead and air whistling through his nose, he resembled a wild boar ready to attack. "Who the hell do ya think you are, keepin' me waitin' in here? I could make one phone call and get you drummed out o' here in a minute." Spittle dribbled down his chin as he spat out the words, "badge, gun, pension." He counted out each loss on his fingers, then with a wave of his hand he declared,., "All of it, gone. And I'm the guy with the power ta do it."

Ray smirked and shouted. "Sit down, Earl."

Earl crossed his arms and leaned against the wall. "I feel like standin'."

"It wasn't an invitation. It's an order. Sit down and shut up, 'til I tell ya to talk!"

Earl grudgingly slid onto the chair. A welcome silence filled the air for a few precious seconds, until Earl set his anger and bluster aside and tried a new approach.

"Chief, do ya know how many people are dependin' on me? Without me, all them poor, dedicated construction workers would be out on the street. Is that what ya want?"

The door opened and Amy entered, pushing the trolley with the crate on top. She parked it by the door and as she turned to exit, the chief called out. "Amy, can you send in our guest, please?"

"Of course, Chief. Right away." She puckishly smiled and saluted before making a quick exit.

Ray planted his 6'2" muscular self on the edge of the table and looked down at the flabby, withering little man who now seemed much less confident. Ray leaned in. "I should mention, I've invited a guest to join us, Earl; and I'm sure you'll be pleased."

The door opened, and Sarah stepped inside.

As Earl laid eyes on her, his limbs began to spasm like they were doing a hurly burly. His lips twitched and his red habanero fury accelerated. "What the fuck is she doin' here? I came back here today, willingly, ta sort out a shitload o' false accusations, so why's that two-bit journalist here?" In the midst of his tirade, Earl abruptly stopped, placed his palms gently on the table, exhaled an exaggerated sigh; then managed a ludicrous smile. "Chief, come on, you and me are here to straighten out the crap that little weasel, Berger's tryin' to sell you. He says all kinds o' stuff with no damn proof. He jist makes it up like one o' them fairy tales. If ya knew Berger, then you'd know anytime he's talkin', he's lyin', 'cause that's who he is."

Ray shook his head and clicked his tongue. "Tsk, tsk, tsk, Earl, I'm so disappointed in you, 'cause you swore to me that Berger never lies. But listen, setting Duh-wayne aside for now, you'd be amazed at what we can prove."

Earl rolled his eyes. "Yeah, sure, I know. You'll be draggin' that bunch o' pedophiles back inta court and I'll be struttin' right outta there again. All ya got is more ramblins' from a freakin' dirtbag this time. Who's gonna believe a guy who deserts his family, fakes his own death, and makes up a whole bunch o' insane crap to try and stay outta jail?"

Ray nodded at Sarah, who took another bold step into the room. "This journalist doesn't think they're insane stories." Ray proposed. "I mean, she's got so much information. In fact, she's been tellin' me, she might have ta turn her little news article into a thick, juicy tell-all book, instead."

"She can't write 'bout any o' this without my permission, and I'm not givin' it, so she can get the hell outta here, right now."

"Well Earl, that's not a very nice way to treat your biographer now, is it? See, I invited her here to watch and listen, because it might help shed light on your story, which you gave her your permission to write. She has a copy of the paperwork your lawyer, Richard McCall, drew up for you, that you signed and dated. So, it's all good and lawful." The chief stood up, placed his hands firmly on his gunbelt and declared, "Just to be very clear, Earl, you don't get to give orders here. I do. And Ms. Berman stays. Her work isn't complete yet. You wouldn't want her to write your life story without havin' all the facts now, would ya?" Ray grinned victoriously. "Come, you're welcome to join us over here, Ms. Berman. We're gonna have a little Show an' Tell for Earl." Ray taunted.

Sarah inched toward the table and stood close to Ray.

"Would you please, have a seat, Ms. Berman?" She did as he asked. "Now, Mr. White asked why you're here. So, if you like, Ms. Berman, please feel free to respond. He's all yours, so to speak." The thought was both comical and disturbing to Sarah, though it motivated her to move ahead.

"Thanks, Chief. Uh, Mr. White? I hear you're a collector," Sarah stated. "I also find it useful to keep souvenirs from the past, how about you, Ray?"

"I sure do. And you wouldn't believe the weird places people hide their trinkets; but when we do a thorough search, we find 'em." Ray slowly pulled on his latex gloves, giving them a determined snap at the wrist. "Are you okay, Earl? Because you're lookin' a little pale and sweaty." Ray snickered at Earl's flinching over the ominous snap of the gloves.

Ray stared intently at Earl as he rolled the crate over to the table. He watched for any sign of recognition, but there was none. "Earl, have you ever seen this box before?"

Earl stretched his neck to get a better look, then shrugged and sat back. "Nope, never seen it. Why? What is it?"

"Well, ya might not know about this, Earl, but here's the story. After Berger's pretend cremation, Doug was supposed to burn those boxes of all that nostalgic stuff you guys stored away at his place. But as you can see, he just couldn't bring himself to burn this lovely, painted treasure chest. You might not recognize it 'cause Gladys did a fancy paint job on it, so it looks a bit different on the outside, but it's still the same on the inside. I'm gonna show ya." He reached in and pulled out the bagged scarf and photo. "I guess ya remember this lovely, handmade scarf and the photo that ya took of Berger wearin' it, right after you brought this souvenir home, eh, Earl? I understand that there's also a matching photo of you wrapped up in that lovely scarf, too. And it's gonna be dropped off at the station any minute now. But even without the picture, after we get it tested and find your DNA all over the scarf, we'll know you wore it. Wait, I know you're thinkin', what in hell is DNA, right?" Earl sat corpse-like, looking utterly confused. Ray smirked. "Live and learn, I always say. And Earl, you're soon gonna learn, that DNA might be your worst enemy, 'cause DNA is as positive as proof can get."

    Sarah interrupted, and in a calm, measured tone, offered her judgment. "Earl, I know the system didn't get you for the horrific crimes against those innocent children, but I have a feeling that, for many years to come, you're gonna personally experience what those kids endured."

    "You're talkin' outta your ass like the rest o' your kind." He sputtered. "And you, Mr. Big Shot Police Chief, like I said, 'ya got no proof', DN...whatever, is just more bullshit made up ta try ta scare me. Does that fuckin' scarf have my name, signature, or a confession on it? No, it don't. So, ya got no proof I had anythin' to do with whatever's in that box."

"Could you please, Ray?" Sarah asked as she pointed to the book. Ray obliged and slipped the novel out of the evidence bag. He held it open to the back page for Earl to see while Sarah narrated. "*Of Rats and Jews,* huh? Mr. White, I believe that novel does have your name, signature, fingerprints, and DNA all over it, and it's definitely my property."

The caged beast began to snort and sweat like a raging bull while Ray continued, undeterred. "And, Earl, you may not have personally engaged in sexual relations with those kids, but we found a shitload of your accounting books for the kiddie porn ring ya organized and profited from."

The suspect's twitching and spasming accelerated as he fumbled for words. "Yer, uh, full o' shit. I uh...never...I never uh, left no books nowhere."

His unnerved response brought a triumphant grin to the faces of Sarah and the chief. As Ray gathered up the evidence to return it to the crate, he paused to share another thought.

"It's true, Earl, Berger did order Doug to incinerate a bunch o' boxes you'd been storing at his house over the years. Yup, Doug was ordered to burn it all. But first, he wanted to photocopy the entire shitload of your record books. I mean, why not? He had free access to the funeral home's copier for weeks. But he got cold feet and wisely decided to burn a pile of old newspapers outside in an oil drum instead. He gave those ashes to Berger and saved the original books. Then he had to figure out the ideal hiding spot for them. And do ya know what he did? He found a very secret subfloor in the very secret cellar..." Ray smirked and leaned back in his seat, "in the house owned lock, stock, and 'love hole' by you. Doug's not so dumb after all, huh?

"Oh yeah, I almost forgot, we also have Berger's signed testimony that you murdered Daisy Panasar, and we have the evidence to support his accusation. We have evidence on you, of rape, assault, murder, Antisemitic hate-crimes, and child sex-trafficking. And, I have a feelin' we're just skimming the surface." As Earl drooled and trembled like a weeping willow, Ray turned toward the door and smiled, "You got anything you wanna add, Ms. Berman?"

"Yes, actually I do. Mr. White, you have my word that I'll be in the courtroom as often as I can bear to listen to your voice...and I'll make a great witness. All those threats, past and present, are stored in my memory; and good journalists never forget." She stood up and graciously slid her chair back in place.

Earl tried to jump up but was pressed back into his seat by the chief's firm hands. Hate spewed from every cell in the criminal's body as he forced his parting message onto Sarah.

"You fuckin' bitch! I'm only sorry I didn't give ya whatcha deserve back when I had the chance. You fuckin' Jews are nothin' but slime on the bottom o' my shoe. You wait. Your reckoning will come when Jesus comes back and destroys all ya foreign pieces o' shit that don't belong here."

Ray placed a comforting hand on Sarah's arm and stepped in front of her. "Earl, what do you imagine Jesus would say to you in the next world?" The chief asked as he tauntingly stroked an imaginary beard. "Yeah, what a question, eh? Sure, I know, it's a dumb question, Earl, 'cause you'll be in Hell, wading nose-deep in shit. But no need to wait, 'cause while you're still here, you'll be nose-deep in shit, fending off those prison mates that can't wait to welcome you."

* * *

Eleanor's dining table was aglow in candlelight. Her crystal and bone china glistened, the scent of the exquisite centrepiece was intoxicating, and in the background, Tony Bennett dreamily crooned.

For the first time in Eleanor's life, she was experiencing the joy of friends gathered around her dinner table. From exotic appetizer to flaming dessert, Eleanor had wowed her six special guests with her culinary élan.

Ron offered the first toast: "Here's to Eleanor, for an amazing, gourmet meal you'd never get at the Best Service Diner."

Shiny snickered and added, "That's for sure. And here's to old neighbours and new friends."

The clinking of glasses was music to the hostess's ear.

As the evening progressed, the conversation turned to the topic of *tomorrows*. Wesley began by asking: "So, Sarah after this whole traumatic experience, is investigative journalism what ya really want to do with your life?"

"Why? Do you think I suck at it?" She playfully pouted.

Wes chuckled "Nah, you can drop the act, kiddo, You know full well what I think. We all know, you've proven to be pretty darn good at it."

Sarah arched her brow. "Wow, from you, that's high praise. And yes, Wes, it's definitely what I want to do."

"Then, would ya like me to arrange a meeting for you with the editor of the *Ottawa Post*?" He enthusiastically offered.

She felt a flush of excitement rush from her head to her heels. "You know him?"

Wes nodded amiably. "Yes; and I already talked to him, and he's looking forward to your call."

"Oh my God," she whispered as she bounced in her chair. "I don't know what to say! From day one, I was asking myself, why did I come here? Why at this time? What did I expect? And I didn't know the answer. But maybe now I do."

Wes shrugged. "You said it yourself, Sarah, it was fate, kismet...or uh, *Busheet* was it?"

Laurie glanced toward Sarah with a puzzled expression. "Do you mean, 'B'ashert'?" he enquired.

"That's it, *Bashirt*," Wes did his best to repeat.

Sarah smiled with delight. "Wes, you old fart," she teased, "it's been months since I inflicted that Hebrew word on you; so huge kudos to you for your sharp memory."

"Fate, or whatever it was, I'm just grateful you came." Eleanor uttered. "I never dreamed that justice was possible...but you did. I know you're gonna be back for the trials, but I hope after that, you'll want to come back just to visit."

Sarah leaned over, gave her friend a one-armed hug, then replied, "Of course I will, and Eleanor, remember, the train travels both ways you know," She playfully teased.

Laurie tapped his plate. "I don't mean to change the subject, but I'm changing the subject. Eleanor, I know someone who might be interested in your designs. I represented this woman a couple of years ago in a fraud case."

"So, what would she want with designer dresses in prison?" Ray quipped.

"Hmm, she was actually the unfortunate victim, Ray," Laurie deadpanned, "but she's also the producer of a television show that searches out new designers. I could give her a call if you like."

Eleanor managed a bashful half-smile. "I can't thank you enough, Laurie, but right now, the last thing I want is to spend any more time locked inside my house, sewing. I want to go to Ottawa to see the Parliament buildings, and Toronto, to visit my friend, see live theatre, and eat in a gourmet restaurant." With a faraway look in her eye, she scanned the faces around the table. "You know, my dad was a pilot and I've never been on a plane. I'd likely be scared out of my wits, but someday, I want to fly to Italy or some other exotic place."

"Make it Ireland, and you've got company," Ray teased as Eleanor's cheeks flushed a kaleidoscope of red.

"I'm so tempted to mock you two," Shiny giggled. "But Ron'll embarrass me all to hell if I dare, so I'm keepin' my mouth shut," She vowed.

"We'll see how long that lasts," Ron added with a snicker. "Anyone got a stopwatch?"

Shiny eyed him with faux daggers before she burst out laughing. "Yeah, okay, I just proved you're not wrong, Hon."

As the evening ticked by, talk and laughter threatened to fade into a vacuum of silence as Sarah glanced at her watch and broke the spell. "Oh jeez, I hate to say it, but it's really late and I've got a train to catch in the morning. This has been an amazing night, but...I better get going," she sadly declared.

As usually happens when one person gets up to leave the party, the rest soon follow. The guests rose and began their exchange of goodbyes, causing a bit of a logjam in the foyer as they tried to retrieve their winter gear from the front bench. Shiny was first in line searching through the pile for her coat.

As Sarah waited her turn, Laurie drew near and asked in a hushed voice, "Listen, Sarah, about that train ride. Do you want to cash in your ticket and drive back with me?"

"Hm," was all she said, as she weighed her options. "You know what, Laurie, I thank you for the offer...but um..." She stopped mid-sentence, distracted by Shiny, who was struggling to get her coat on. "I was...hold on a sec, Laurie."

"I can't believe you're trying to steal my coat," Sarah loudly but impishly alleged.

Shiny shouted back, "Oops. All these long, black winter coats look alike. I thought it was mine. Thank God it isn't, 'cause I was worried that Eleanor's dinner had already put twenty pounds on me. Sorry about that," She snickered as she passed the coat to Sarah.

"Thanks, but there was a scarf tucked into the sleeve. Do I need to have the chief frisk you?" Sarah teased as she pulled on her coat.

Shiny retrieved the scarf from under the bench and waved it like a flag of surrender.

Sarah squinted and gave a thumbs up to Shiny.

Laurie summed up his offer. "So, Sarah, train, or car, your choice." He inhaled deeply as he waited for the answer.

She paused and weighed her options. She tapped her finger on her chin, pursed her lips, and wrinkled her brow...all done in dramatic contemplation. Her face lit up as she replied. "Hmm, thank you for the offer, Laurie. Car it is."

"Good." He gave a perfunctory nod and slowly exhaled. As he moved away to retrieve his coat, Shiny caught sight of a warm beam that flickered across his face.

She sidled up to Sarah and whispered, "Come on, Sarah, admit it. You were hoping for that offer all night?" She chuckled.

A subtle hint of a *Mona Lisa* smile was Sarah's only response.

REVA LEAH STERN

My publisher asked that I tell you about myself, without the formality of the usual, lengthy bio.

So here goes: I grew up in Prescott, the very town, in which I dared to set this fictional thriller. The unspeakable crimes in the novel, "The Prescott Journals," never happened; but some of the ugly incidents actually did. Perhaps, the fictitious story was fiendishly inspired by real events.

I spent most of my professional career as a Stage and TV director/writer, but after almost 100 stage productions and over 40 TV series in the US and at home in Toronto, I found my passion was reignited by writing captivating novels in the quiet comfort of home.

I've had many articles and stories published in newspapers and anthologies, but my first published novel

Reva Leah Stern

was "The Water Buffalo That Shed Her Girdle" in 2008. It was followed by, "I Say My Name" in 2021, and now my third, "The Prescott Journals."

Next will be a collection of short stories, "The Strange Spectrum of Mysterious Mishaps aka The Book of Curious Colour." Stories not meant for the kiddies.

My publisher also wanted me to write something personal and quirky about myself and my writing. I found that to be an awkward task, so, I reached out to some writer colleagues for their input on my output, and these are a few random samples of what they had to offer.

"Reva's a kind of quirky intrepid writer who geeks out on digging into underlying baleful motives, plots, places, and personalities, like she's got some kind of unique X-Ray vision".

"She consistently lays out a rich buffet of colour, marrow, flavour, and characters for the reader to feed on."

"Breaking news: Reva drinks decaf coffee! Come on. What author can write a great and gripping mystery novel while not buzzed on caffeine? Well, she can. And she does. But, thankfully, she lets her deranged perpetrators and distraught victims quaff the real stuff."

So, their words are about as personal as I can get.
For more info, please visit my website:
www.revaleahstern.com

Printed in the USA
CPSIA information can be obtained
at www.ICGtesting.com
LVHW091749170124
769058LV00032B/161